I0619694

ADIRONDACK

A Novel by

A. DUDLEY JOHNSON, JR.

Copyright © 2017 by A. Dudley Johnson, Jr.

Cover Painting by my cousin, Ann Frederick Lewis

Thanks to Deni Doherty, Rick Hunt, Flo Selfman, and Barry Schwartz for help and thoughtfulness in editing and proofing this book.

For my husband, Barry, who gave me the love and support to write this book.

This book is based, very loosely, on my great-great-grandmother's diaries. For the most part, she described what the weather was like each day, who came to visit, and who she had lunch or tea with. There were a few good descriptions of how people traveled to Keene Valley in the 1890s and activities that occurred while they were up there, which I used to help make the book more authentic.

I have applied creative license in various places. So I apologize ahead of time to those who know the Adirondacks intimately, as not all places, trails, etc., are exactly where I have them appear in the book.

CHAPTER ONE

Fairfield, Connecticut   June 1897

It was chilly and dark out and only five in the morning, but the two boys were already awake in their beds. They had hardly slept a wink all night. Today was the day. They waited all winter for this day. The last month of school was torturous. Even more so than usual. It wasn't just summer vacation they were looking forward to. That had started a few weeks ago. Today they were leaving to spend the summer in the mountains. The boys were eight and ten years old and had been making this trip every year since they were babies, except for the year that Sam, the younger brother, was born. He was born in early June so they weren't able to make the trip. His older brother Paul, although only two at the time, still held it against his little brother. That was the year of the great bear fight between the census taker and a giant she-bear. It was Sam's fault that Paul missed it and he never let him forget it. Today, however, they were both so excited that nothing was going to ruin it. They waited in their beds as their mother had instructed. She told them they had a big day of travel ahead and they needed a good night's sleep. They obeyed because this was one day they didn't want to anger their mother. The concept of actually sleeping, though, was out of the question.

"Paul, do you think we can get up now?" asked Sam.

"Shhhh." In a whisper, Paul retorted, "Forget it. Don't even think about it. You made me miss one summer in Keene Valley. You're not going to make me miss another. Mother said if she heard one peep out of us before six o'clock, she'd make us stay here in Fairfield with Aunt Harriet and repulsive cousin Mildred."

"Ugh, she keeps trying to kiss me," said Sam. "Okay, I'll be quiet."

There was the noise of a door opening down the hall and the boys heard footsteps.

"They're awake!" Sam yelled as both he and Paul bounded out of bed, raced out of the room and ran right into their father, Will, still in his nightclothes.

"Father, good morning! Isn't this the best morning there ever was?" Sam said excitedly.

"We couldn't wait a minute longer, Father!" said Paul.

Their father looked around carefully and furtively whispered, "Neither could I. Come on."

He put his arms around the shoulders of each of the boys and led them to the end of the hall. Just as they reached the landing and turned toward the stairs, they saw their mother, Anna, standing there, arms crossed, with a wry smile on her face.

"Hmmm, five ten," she said, looking at a clock. The boys cowered and Will smiled at Anna. "I thought you three would never get out of bed. We've got a million things to do before we leave today and if you think Colleen, Millie, and I are going to do everything ourselves," she said as she started down the stairs, "well, think again." She stopped and looked back up at them. "So, what are you waiting for? Go get dressed. Colleen's got flapjack batter ready to griddle."

The boys yelled hooray and took off to their room. Will stepped uncomfortably down the stairs to Anna.

"Looking forward to the summer?" Will asked.

"I always do, Will, you know that. I can't wait to breathe that magical mountain air again. I love it so."

"It will be wonderful for you, I'm sure," said Will, without much conviction. Then, excitedly, "But you know me. I've got a lot of work back here that I'll need to get to soon."

"I know, Will," said Anna, sadly.

Will tentatively gave her a peck on the cheek. "I'll go get dressed, too." He headed up the stairs and down the hall. Anna tenderly brushed her cheek with the backs of her fingers and looked after him thoughtfully. After a moment, she turned and went down the stairs.

Anna and Will had known each since they were children. Both were raised in Philadelphia and their families were acquaintances. Both families were from old wealth. Anna and Will had met at several society functions and get-togethers and had always had an attraction for each other. It was easy to tell they liked one another because he used to pull her hair and she would sneak up behind him and put ice down his shirt. As they grew older, she would see him at young people's dances and whenever his name came up on her dance card, she would always remember to have a piece of ice ready to slip down his shirt as they started to dance. But then, instead of getting angry, he would joke that dancing with her always gave him a chill up and down his spine. Then he would unavoidably manage to get his fingers caught in her hair and pull it. How could Anna resist such charm?

When Will's family moved to Connecticut, Anna and her parents would visit occasionally and stay with the Tattersalls at Ambleside, their large Victorian home. It had very high ceilings and oversized windows and doors. There was a large veranda that circled the house where they would spend many romantic evenings swaying on the porch swing — at least, as romantic as it could be with every busybody in the house snooping on them to make sure everything was on the up and up. If they wanted to take walks together, it was a major logistical nightmare for everyone to coordinate so as not to intrude, but also to be properly close at hand to supervise. Anna and Will loved being mischievous and making it as difficult as possible for all the chaperones. They would lead them on merry chases along Fairfield Beach on the Long Island

Sound and out onto Penfield Reef. Sometimes they'd take picnics on Greenfield Hill, especially in the spring when the dogwoods were in bloom. This was particularly taxing for their escorts, as the flower-laden trees gave Anna and Will ample places to scurry in and around and drive everyone else to distraction, much to their delight.

One summer when Anna was still in her teens, the Tattersalls invited her and her family up to the Adirondack Mountains for few weeks holiday. Will's Great Aunt Lil had a summer lodge there in the town of Keene Valley in the upper New York State wilderness. Keene Valley was called "the home of the high peaks," as the forty tallest mountains in New York were within a day or two's hiking distance. It was becoming a popular retreat for the well-to-do's to summer at because of its untarnished beauty and pristine lakes and rivers. They hiked and picnicked on the tops of mountains, viewing spectacular vistas that made each and every one of them regard it all in awe. The wildlife was abundant and the fishing was incredible. In half an hour, one could catch enough trout to feed twenty people for breakfast.

Anna loved to take walks alone through the fields and foothills. She felt something instinctively drawing her along. She could walk for hours and always felt safe in what was around her. She loved the freedom and the wildness of the forests. There was a longing deep inside her to be part of that freedom. Free of the constraints of the society in which she was a part. Free to do whatever she wanted without anyone judging her. These walks only added to her fantasy.

One day, she chanced upon an abandoned, smoldering campfire and, worried that it might flare up, she filled her canteen from the nearby river and began dousing it. She suddenly heard a rustling in some bushes nearby. Out stepped a strapping young Indian boy. He was about Anna's age and dressed not unlike anyone else of the era, although he was dripping wet. They both stopped dead in their tracks at the sight of each other. He stared questioningly at her for a few moments.

"I'm sorry, is this your fire? I thought someone forgot to put it out," said Anna, wondering to herself if the Indian could even understand her.

"Someone did," replied the Indian in perfect English, which took Anna aback. "My brothers and I camped here last night and as we were getting ready to leave, we got to splashing each other in the river. The game took us downstream so I came back to check that everything was taken care of here. I see you've done that for me. Thank you."

"You're welcome," said Anna.

She had met Indians before, but none as gracious and well spoken as this one. Many Indians that she had seen around the valley were day workers or sold handicrafts, but she had yet to meet one who had such a command of the English language, with no trace of an accent. There had been an Indian man found drunk and asleep on Aunt Lil's front piazza one morning. Aunt Lil had her own way of dealing with such things. She had a large bell hanging out front that she used in case of emergencies. It happened to be hanging right near where the poor man had fallen asleep. When she saw him lying there, she was incensed at such an intrusion. She marched right over to the huge bell and began clanging it harder than she'd ever clanged it before. The unfortunate subject of her prank bolted upright in a state of inebriated shock, banging his head on the bell, making it clang all the more. Anna and all who were in the house came dashing out as the Indian teetered on the edge of the piazza, dumbfounded for a moment. He then looked at all the curious faces regarding him and, realizing his own embarrassment, took off stumbling down the street, to the delight of Aunt Lil and the befuddlement of the rest.

Anna said to the Indian boy, "You speak English very well."

"Thank you. I was born here in America," said the boy.

"I apologize. I didn't mean to sound rude," she said sincerely. "It's just that the few Indians I've met usually only speak their native tongue or broken English."

"I take no offense," the boy replied. "I've been to school in Massachusetts. My family summers here in the mountains."

5

"So does the family we are staying with," said Anna. "What's the name of your tribe?"

"I am an Adirondack Indian. My ancestors preferred to be called Algonquins because their opponent tribe, the Iroquois, used the term 'Adirondack' in a derogatory manner. It meant 'bark eaters' because our ancestors survived through the cold winters eating tree bark. I don't find it derogatory at all. I am proud to be an Adirondack."

"And well you should be," Anna declared. "To come from such a magnificent place. I only come from Philadelphia."

"Philadelphia is pretty magnificent in itself, as I remember," said the boy.

"I suppose," Anna halfheartedly agreed. "But it lacks the basic vibrancy of all this," as she swept her arms out around her indicating the beauty that surrounded them.

"If I may ask, what is your name?" inquired the boy.

"Anna Glover," she said a bit shyly.

"How do you do, Anna? My name is Ausable Hancock. I'm named for the river next to which we stand," indicating the Ausable River.

"Awe-say-bull. Ausable," repeated Anna wondrously. "What a marvelous name. How nice to have a face to put to this river," she said playfully.

"Thank you," said Ausable.

Just then they heard the shouting of boys from upriver calling for Ausable.

"Those are my brothers. I'd better be off. We have quite a hike in order to make it to the top of Giant Mountain by nightfall." He pointed up to the mountain, indicating its splendid summit. "It was nice to meet you, Anna."

"You as well, Ausable," replied Anna. "Have a good climb."

He started off, and then stopped. "Oh, I forgot something."

He went into the bushes behind the beach and pulled out three pieces of birch bark. There were paintings on all three of them.

"I like to paint," Ausable said, looking them over. "I did these along our hike."

"May I see them?" Anna asked.

"Of course," he said, as he held them out to her.

They were paintings of the mountains and trees that were around them. They were very impressionistic and done in oil paint. One looked like Giant Mountain as the sun was setting on it.

"These are wonderful, Ausable," said Anna.

"Thank you, Anna. I'm not that good, and I can only bring a few paint colors with me on hikes, but I enjoy painting. It allows me to capture my feelings in the moment and take them with me."

"Well, I really like them. Especially this one. Is it Giant?"

Ausable, somewhat taken aback, said, "Why, yes, it is. I'm pleased you can tell."

"Of course, I could tell," said Anna. "It looks just like it. Beautiful."

"Thank you very much." Then handing it to her, he said, "I'd like you to have it."

Anna smiled. "Oh no, I couldn't take this."

"Yes, please," said Ausable. "I'd be honored if you would. No one, except my parents, has liked my work. And they have to because they're my parents. Please take it."

"It would be my honor to accept it. Thank you," said Anna, taking the bark painting.

"Well, I had better be going. I have to catch up to my brothers. Have a wonderful summer, Anna Glover."

"I will. And thank you, again," Anna said, waving goodbye.

And he was off, disappearing as fast as he had appeared. She held out the bark to admire the painting. One more enchanting memory for Anna to have of that Keene Valley summer.

There was also a memory she had that was not so pleasant and which still beset her to this day. Anna went to a summer dance for young people at the Tahawus Hotel with Will. They danced beautifully together and were admired by all — except a girl from Boston named Margaret Bancroft. She had had eyes for Will for many summers in Keene Valley. But now he was here with Anna, and Margaret's green-eyed monster was emerging. She was outside with some other girls at the refreshment table when Anna came out for a cool drink.

"You are the one here with Will Tattersall," Margaret said to Anna.

"Yes, I am," Anna said, happily. "He's just the most wonderful boy I know."

"Isn't he, though?" said Margaret. "He and I have also had the most wonderful times up here together."

Anna was taken aback. What was this girl trying to say? Whatever it was, Anna wasn't going to take it lying down.

"Oh, well then, I suppose that's over for you," Anna declared. "Because Will is keeping company with me now."

"Don't be so sure," said Margaret, slyly. "He has a wandering eye. And he can wander my way anytime."

The other girls laughed and Anna turned away and went back inside to Will.

"Some awful girl out there implied that you courted her," Anna said.

"Who said that?" asked Will, as they looked to the door and saw Margaret blowing Will a kiss. "Oh, Margaret Bancroft. She's just a flirt. Don't believe anything she says."

"All right," said Anna. "I just hope I never see her again."

Anna and Will spent the rest of their time together discovering the new sensations they awoke in one another. And, as always, the end of their visits came much too soon. Will returned home and made every excuse possible to get their families together. He attended Yale Law School and when he graduated, he joined his father's law practice in Fairfield. Being the proper gentleman that he was, Will waited until he felt he was well enough established to ask Anna to marry him. She immediately said yes and she moved into Ambleside where the two were finally allowed to cuddle and coo unattended out on the veranda.

Two years after they married, their son Paul came along, named for Anna's father. Anna and Will couldn't have been happier and life was grand. Will's law practice was thriving and Paul was the apple of his eye. Anna spent her days taking care of Paul and joining in the myriad of social events that her mother-in-law, Kathleen, and she were involved with. They immersed themselves in charity affairs, teas, and cotillions. Every year at Christmastime, Kathleen and Will's father, Allen, threw a birthday ball in honor of the baby Jesus. Everyone attending brought presents which were later distributed to the less fortunate in the area. It was a grand gathering of Fairfield's finest, an event to which everyone always looked forward. Anna's family came up for Christmas and to spend time with their grandchild, who seemed to get more presents than all those that were brought for the party.

Although Anna's mother knew all the proper steps to be a member of polite society, Kathleen had a special way of doing things with extra flair, more than anyone Anna had ever known. She had a great imagination and was constantly coming up with new ideas and ways to implement them, all with the best of taste, of course. Anna couldn't learn enough and Kathleen, in turn, loved teaching them to the daughter she never had. Anna took quickly to life as a Tattersall and soon she and Kathleen were unstoppable as the expert party givers. It was also good for Anna, to help keep her busy, because Will was turning his father's small town practice into quite a thriving venture and it was keeping him away from home for longer and longer periods of time.

They summered with Aunt Lil in Keene Valley and, two years after their second son Sam was born, they bought their own house in the valley. They called it Idlenook. Unlike Aunt Lil's house which was right on the main road, Idlenook was set back down a long, curving drive. It was a comfortable cottage with a wonderful gazebo behind it, called a summerhouse, for entertaining outside. Down a long narrow path behind the house was a beach made mostly of well-rounded river-washed stones. The property sat on the banks of the Ausable River, a river Anna still associated with the Indian boy she had met when she was a girl on her first visit to Keene Valley. She had kept his painting and hung it on the wall of the screened porch, facing the river over which was a view of Giant Mountain. The house and the gazebo looked out over the crystal clear water meandering by. Their first summer there, Will built a playhouse for the boys near the path to the beach. He told them it was a playhouse, but it coincidentally served as a storage shed for the beach furniture in the winter.

One of the bedrooms was a sleeping porch with four beds that looked out over the river. On the warmest nights in summer, the whole family would sleep there and fall asleep to the sound of the river that once formed this valley, now languidly babbling its way past the beautiful mountains and meadows.

It was now six years later and they were readying for yet another summer in the Adirondacks. Anna felt the family needed this summer together more than ever before. Over the past few years, Will's father had slowly been stepping away from the business and the work now overwhelmed Will. The firm had become quite successful. Will had acquired clients from New York to Boston that kept him away from home for long periods of time. Anna did her best to keep herself busy, but she very much missed the playful Will she had grown up with. He was all business now and becoming more and more distant. She knew her husband was not the kind of man to see other women. He was just too good-hearted and loyal for that. To him, though, success was heady stuff. Work was something that Will thrived on and, although seeming obsessive, he was extremely happy. Unfortunately for Anna, she didn't feel that she fit into this world of his. Kathleen saw it, but the times being as they were, people didn't speak of such things. Will's father, Allen, tried to make him aware of it, but Will shrugged it off, saying it was what he had to do and that Anna understood. He said he had asked her and she said she was behind him. In fact, she had, for his sake, but she really didn't believe it deep inside.

For today, though, they were a family, getting ready for the great trek up to the Adirondacks where Will would spend a few weeks with them and then, later, get back up to see them when he could.

Anna headed down the stairs and called to Colleen in the kitchen, "They're awake. Get the griddle hot."

Millie was in the drawing room covering the last of the furniture with white sheets to protect it from the dust while they were gone. Will's parents had moved to the smaller guesthouse behind Ambleside when Allen started having trouble making it up and down the stairs. The guesthouse was one story and much more easily accessible. Will would be staying with them when he came back from the mountains, so that they didn't have to keep up the larger house without staff. Plus, he would be in New York City handling many cases much of the time.

The boys scrambled down the stairs and into the dining room only to find all the furniture in it covered up.

Paul called, "Mother, where are we eating?"

Anna came into the room. "We'll eat downstairs in the kitchen."

The kitchen was directly under the dining room and the food was usually sent up by way of a dumbwaiter. Paul and Sam ran around to the basement stairway and down. They could smell the hotcakes cooking already.

As they entered the kitchen, Colleen said, "Morning, boys. Fresh milk is on the table. Hotcakes will be ready in a minute."

They sat at the table.

"I love eating in the kitchen," said Sam. "It smells so good in here that you get all full just on the smells. Who needs to eat?"

"I do," said Paul. "Just give me his since he's so full."

"Oh no, it doesn't smell that good in here," said Sam quickly.

"You boys are up early this morning. Any particular reason?" teased Colleen.

"Didn't Mother tell you, Colleen? We're leaving for Keene Valley today," said Sam.

"Oh, and you're looking forward to this, are you?" she asked.

"Only since we came back from there last summer," said Paul.

Colleen O'Brien was a cheerful Irish woman whom Anna and Will hired soon after they moved into the house. Kathleen

11

and Allen had their own servants, so Anna and Will hired Colleen and Millie. While Colleen was fun and boisterous, Millie was a shy, quiet girl whom Anna had brought with her from Philadelphia. They hired Colleen when the Milletts, their neighbors down the street, discharged her for being too "cheeky" with her mistress. Anna had met Colleen before at the Milletts' home and enjoyed Colleen's exuberance. Kathleen always thought the Milletts were too stuffy and, therefore, encouraged Anna to go against public opinion and hire Colleen. Anna never regretted it. She got along very well with both of her servants and they all became quite close. Will was never too keen on Anna's friendship with the servants, but there was nothing he could do about it and it kept Anna happy, something he hadn't been able to do for a while. Aside from that, Colleen could cook like nobody's business. Whatever food was brought into the house, Colleen turned it into a culinary masterpiece of epic proportions.

The sun was beginning to brighten the eastern sky. It looked like it was going to be a beautiful day to begin their trek. Anna and Millie were going over a list of all the supplies that they would be bringing with them to the mountains for the summer. Things they couldn't necessarily get up there. Ten pounds of coffee, six boxes of yeast, vanilla, one pound of borax, twelve toilet soap bars, six toilet paper bundles, Domino sugar, one gallon of cooking oil ("Not enough," Anna noted), seven pounds of tea, six pounds of chocolate, laundry soap, shelf paper, ammonia, cooking sherry, fifty cakes of soap, and twenty-four boxes of safety matches. These were loaded on a carriage to be brought to the railroad station and shipped as freight ahead of them.

"That ought to do us for now," said Anna. "Will can bring things up as we need them when he visits."

Inside, Paul and Sam were soaking up the remaining maple syrup with the last of their hotcakes. Anna and Millie came into the kitchen.

"Do we have any more cooking oil, Colleen?" asked Anna.

Colleen went to the pantry and came back with a gallon tin of oil.

"This is about three quarters full," she said.

"Good," said Anna as she took the can. "We can take this with us. Since Will is staying with his parents, we won't be needing it here." Handing the can to Millie, she said, "Please pack this in the carriage with the other supplies."

"Yes, Ma'am," said Millie as she took the can and went out the back door.

"So, are you two all packed and ready to go?" Anna asked the boys.

"I am," said Paul. "But Sam isn't."

"I am, too," said Sam, annoyed. "I've been packed since last week."

"Oh, is that why you've been wearing the same underwear for days?" said Paul, giving Sam a hard time.

"I have not!" Sam protested.

"All right, boys, that's enough," said Anna. "Go upstairs and strip your beds and cover them up with the sheets I left up there. Then bring your valises out front and put them next to the carriage."

The boys started out.

"And no fighting or you're not going," Anna added.

"See what you did?" said Sam.

"*I* did?" objected Paul. "You're the one wearing day-old underwear."

"I am not!" Sam yelled as their voices disappeared upstairs. Anna smiled at Colleen and shook her head. Will entered.

"I brought your suitcases down, Anna," said Will. "I hope you were finished packing."

"I'm no different than Sam. I've been all packed for a week," replied Anna.

Will laughed. Then he said. "If the supplies are ready, I'll have the carriage sent to the station."

"All packed and ready to go," said Anna.

"You really are a wonder, Anna," said Will tenderly. "I'll send the driver on his way. Colleen, pour me a couple dozen of those flapjacks. Just thinking of that great mountain air gives me an appetite." And he was out the door.

"He's especially cheerful today," said Colleen.

"We all get excited about a summer in Keene Valley, don't we?" said Anna, happily.

By the time everyone was outside and ready to go, the sun was up and it was a glorious day, one of those sparkling New England days, cool, crisp and breezy, yet warming slowly by the rising sun. They would be taking the train to New York City. Once there, they would spend the day before boarding an overnight train to Westport in upstate New York that would arrive very early the next morning.

Will had a carriage and a wagon waiting. The wagon was loaded with their suitcases and Paul and Sam were already in the carriage, ready and raring to go. In the house, Anna and Millie were covering the last of the furniture as Colleen came up from the kitchen carrying a picnic basket.

"I brought along what leftovers we had in case we get hungry on the train," said Colleen. "And everything in the kitchen is all stowed away."

"Thanks, Colleen. You're a dear," said Anna. "I checked all the locks and windows. Everything seems secure. Shall we?"

They headed out the front door onto the veranda. Anna stopped to take a breath of the fresh, brisk morning air.

She called to Will. "Everything ready, Will?"

"We're ready to go."

The boys cheered. Anna locked up the front door of the house as Will helped Millie and Colleen into the carriage. Will's parents, Kathleen and Allen, appeared from around the back of the house just in time to wish them Godspeed. They all hugged and said their goodbyes. Even though he was feeling his rheumatism, Allen assured them they'd be up for a visit at some point during the summer. Anna told them she hoped they would and walked over to the carriage. Will turned to her and said, "Maybe this summer will offer something enchanting."

"Maybe it will," replied Anna, trying to sound optimistic. "Shall we go, Will?"

Will helped her into the carriage and indicated to the driver that they were ready to go. The driver snapped the horses to attention and off they headed, followed by the wagon full of valises, to the railway station. As they drove down the Boston Post Road, early rising neighbors waved goodbye to them, wished them a wonderful summer and looked forward to their return. As they passed the Milletts' house, Colleen turned and looked to the other side of the street to avoid the worrying memories of her tenure there. She, like the rest of them, was looking forward to a wonderful summer in the Adirondacks.

CHAPTER TWO

They arrived at the station well ahead of the train. Their provisions would go on before them as freight and be waiting when they arrived the next morning in Westport, New York. Unlike their supplies, they would get to spend the day in New York City before boarding a sleeper train that evening. There were a few other people awaiting the westbound train, most just taking it a stop or two to visit friends or do business in nearby towns. The women sat in the carriage as the boys raced around the station. Will chatted with the stationmaster, John, an old friend he'd known all his life. He saw him quite often of late, from his many trips to Boston and New York on legal business.

"Train should be right on time," John told Will. "Just heard from Bridgeport over the wire."

"Here it comes now," Will noticed. He called to the boys, "Train's here boys."

The boys ran to the edge of the tracks.

"Not so close, boys," Anna warned as she stepped down from the carriage.

The enormous, smoke-billowing locomotive blew its whistle and lumbered slowly into the station, metal wheels squealing amid blasts of steam and sparks. Millie covered her ears and hid from the monstrous engine as it screeched past and then finally stopped. Colleen comforted her. Millie wasn't one for "modern contraptions," as she called such things.

John rolled a set of steps up to a door of the train where the conductor was standing, greeting him. As a few people stepped off the car, Will and the drivers took the wagon to a freight car near the end of the train and started loading the supplies into it, aided by a railway worker who came out of the caboose.

As soon as the arriving passengers were off, Paul and Sam dashed up the steps and onto the train. Anna spoke to the conductor, showing him their tickets, and he helped the ladies up the steps. The conductor led them to a compartment with six seats, three on either side facing each other. The boys had disappeared somewhere down the corridor. Anna called out for them.

"I'll go find them," Colleen offered, and off she went.

Anna and Millie entered the compartment.

"I'm sure the boys will want the windows," Millie offered.

"I'm sure they will," said Anna, so they settled into the two center seats. Paul and Sam went dashing by and Anna called out to them. "Paul, Sam, we're in here."

The two boys' faces appeared in the doorway.

"We've seen the entire train already, Mother," said Sam excitedly. "It has sleeping cars and there are still people sleeping in them."

"Oh, I hope you didn't wake anyone," Anna said, chagrined.

"Don't worry, Mother, I made sure he kept quiet," said Paul.

Anna countered, "Yes, but who made sure you kept quiet?"

Paul smiled and shrugged.

"Where's Colleen?" asked Anna. "I sent her to look for you."

"I don't know," said Paul. "We didn't see her anywhere. Don't worry, we'll find her." And they were off.

Anna shook her head. A moment later, Colleen turned up in the doorway. "I can't find hide nor hair of those boys," she complained.

Anna and Millie looked at one another and laughed, as Colleen looked on bewildered.

"Come in and sit down, Colleen," said Anna. "They'll turn up."

Colleen came in and sat down next to Millie. The conductor led Will into the compartment. "Here we are, Mr. Tattersall." Will sat down next to Anna.

"Everything's all set on the freight car and our luggage is up front." he assured them.

The boys reentered the compartment.

"There's Colleen," said Sam. "I thought you were off looking for us."

"Sit down, boys," said Will. "Next stop, New York City."

The boys took their seats by the window, which was open on this beautiful day. A gust of steam blew past the window and the train lurched forward. Millie stifled a squeal as the train started drifting lazily out of the station. They spent the next three hours enjoying the beautiful vistas as the train moved through Connecticut along the Long Island Sound. The closer they got to New York, the more houses they started to see. The boys began spotting an automobile or two here and there. They couldn't wait to get to New York. Will had a surprise planned for them that he wouldn't reveal and the boys were bursting their britches to know what it was.

Paul begged for the hundredth time, "Come on, Father. Please tell us what the surprise is."

"You'll find out when we get there," Will said.

Sam put his head on his mother's shoulder and looked up adoringly at her. "You'll tell us, won't you, Mother?"

"You want to know what it is?" she asked.

The boys were on the edge of their seat. "Yes. What is it?"

She looked at Will devilishly, then back at the boys, whispering, "It's a surprise."

Paul and Sam collapsed with frustration.

Anna said, "The fact is, your father hasn't told me either. He wants us all to be surprised."

Will smiled to himself, pleased.

The train crossed a trestle bridge onto the island of Manhattan. Soon they were seeing tall buildings. Everyone leaned toward the window to get a better look. The boys were in awe. The train began to slow and the engineer announced they were approaching Grand Central Terminal. They were all exhilarated. A day in New York was an extremely special event.

It seemed to take forever until they finally arrived at the platform in Grand Central. The boys were sure it was even "grander" than the last time they were there. Will procured a porter to assist with the luggage.

Anna, being used to the boys' exuberance, had already enlisted Colleen and Millie's aid to restrain them from running off into the depths of Grand Central Terminal unattended. Millie's assistance left a bit to be desired, as her dread of big, bad New York City, and its grandeur, overwhelmed her. They headed up the ramp to the main part of the station. Will met them at the door. He had arranged for the luggage to be stored until they left that evening. Walking out the door and into Grand Central Station always gave them pause. It was magnificent, intimidating, and breathtaking all at the same time. The late morning sun streamed in through the massive windows towering overhead, making the marble-laden interior glisten so much that it almost hurt one's eyes. Millie nearly fainted.

"Are we going to take the elevated train, Father?" asked Sam.

"Not this time, Sam," said Will.

They crossed the huge terminal and exited on Forty Second Street, where the first of Will's surprises was waiting. New York had recently begun its first taxicab service and there at the curb was an electric hansom cab that was ready to whisk them off into the streets of Manhattan. The boys bounded into the motorcar, then Will helped the women in. With a little coaxing, Millie reluctantly entered the vehicle but sat rock solid still with her eyes squeezed shut. Anna and Colleen just looked at each other, shook their heads, and smiled. The driver closed the door, got in, and slowly eased the cab into the

19

traffic, consisting mostly of horse-drawn carriages interrupted by the occasional motor vehicle.

The ride was splendid, smooth as silk. Even Millie opened her eyes in disbelief. The sensation was enchanting. They rode along watching the beautiful edifices of New York glide by. In all the excitement, no one thought to ask where they were going. And no one seemed to care. As they drove along, the driver took them past the Brooklyn Bridge and they watched the elevated trains disappear from view over the bridge. From Battery Park, Will pointed out the Statue of Liberty that they had visited a few years earlier.

Along the way, they stopped for lunch at a restaurant Will frequented on his business trips into the city. It was the famous Delmonico's. Will explained that the columns by the entrance were said to have been imported from the ruins of Pompeii. The maitre d' greeted his friend, Will, who was very pleased to introduce his family. Will treated them to a delicious meal that included Lobster Newburg and ended with a flaming dessert prepared right at the table. Colleen liked the flaming touch at the end and said she would remember to use that in the future.

After lunch, they got back in the cab. They went through Central Park, finally pulling up in front of a large stone structure, the Metropolitan Museum of Art.

"Here's surprise number two," Will exclaimed.

"The museum?" asked Paul, a bit disappointed. "We've already seen all those old paintings, Father."

"Don't worry, Paul, we're not going to see paintings today."

"What is it?" asked Sam.

"You'll see," Will replied giddily. "Come along." He paid the driver and thanked him as they got out of their first cab ride. Even Millie had to admit the ride wasn't so bad.

She said, "It's the first time I've ridden that long and don't have a pain in my... my... well, you know what I mean." She blushed, unable to say the word. They all agreed they knew what she meant.

Led by Will, they marched up the steps into the museum, an entry nearly as imposing as Grand Central, yet even more beautiful.

Anna walked next to Will. "What are you up to, Will?"

"Magic, Anna. Modern magic. Wait here, everyone."

Will went to the ticket booth as the rest waited with bated breath. Anna didn't recognize this man. *This was the Will I used to know and love. The old Will had been gone for so long. What was going on? Did New York City make him come alive like this? Was this why he was so successful here? Well, I don't care. I like this man, always had. And I am going to enjoy every minute of it.*

Will came back to them. "Okay, all, we're just in time. Follow me, if you will."

He led them up the staircase and down a hallway. They came to a room with a sign posted at the door announcing in great big letters, "New York City - The First Moving Pictures!"

"Moving pictures?" Sam inquired. "Does that mean 'paintings' that move?"

"Not quite, Sam," said Will. "They'll explain it all to us inside."

Will handed an attendant their tickets and they entered a room set up like a theatre. Wooden chairs and benches were arranged facing a large white cloth against one wall. About half the seats were already taken up by other people. At the opposite end of the room was some sort of large apparatus. Millie was immediately suspect.

"I don't think I'm going to like this," she said.

"We're going to see some play," moaned Paul. "Big deal."

"Yeah, big deal," added Sam, trying to contain himself like his big brother was.

Will found an empty row and they filed into it.

"You're going to love this, Anna," said Will. "It is most extraordinary."

"I can't wait," Anna said, pleased but a bit confused at the moment.

A museum official dressed in a tailcoat came out from behind the white cloth and asked for everyone's attention.

21

"Ladies and gentlemen, welcome to what we at the Metropolitan Museum believe to be a historic event. You are about to witness the world coming alive by means of moving pictures. It's from the laboratory of Thomas A. Edison, his greatest marvel. We present to you a variety of scenes from our great city on an Edison Vitascope. Please don't be frightened, ladies and gentlemen, this is pure entertainment and I assure you, you will not be harmed by what you are about to see. And now, I present to you -- New York."

The lights were turned off and the room went black for a moment. Then the large contrivance at the back of the room began to come to life. It churned and lit up the white cloth across the room. All of a sudden there appeared on the cloth a scene of a New York City street. There were people walking and carriages passing. It was as if one were looking out a very large window, yet everything had a sort of yellowish hue. The audience took a breath in unison and held it, enraptured. The cloth went white again and now the New York Harbor came into view. Freighters were being loaded with goods off the docks. Again the cloth went white, but this time, when the pictures returned, not only were the images up on the screen moving, but now the spectators had the feeling they were moving. They were being taken across the Brooklyn Bridge as they watched the towers appear to move above and past them. Millie was beginning to feel dizzy. Sam and Paul sat with their mouths open. As they got to the end of the bridge, the cloth went white again and they were at the ocean. It was a peaceful scene, as people strolled a boardwalk and enjoyed the sea air. The scene suddenly shifted to the ocean itself and the people in the theatre recoiled in shock as a large wave came toward them, filling the screen and crashing on the shore in front of them. Anna grabbed Will's arm for a fearful moment. Drops of water appeared to remain on the cloth before it went white again. They now saw a tunnel with railroad tracks running into it. It was as if they were sitting on the tracks. All of a sudden, a train appeared out of the tunnel and came barreling at them. The audience screamed as the image of the train seemed to rush over their heads. Millie hid her eyes and screamed the loudest. A man in the front row was so startled he fell backwards in his chair and landed on the lap of a woman behind him. The cloth went white again and the lights came on. The stunned audience gathered themselves for a moment and then burst into cheers. It was a spectacular wonder. Everyone had chills and goose bumps. Not one of them had ever seen anything like this before. The boys were beside themselves with ecstasy. "Father, can we see it again?" they both cried out. "Will, darling, thank you for giving us such a marvelous experience," said Anna adoringly. Will smiled, happy that he could do this for his family.

They spent the rest of the afternoon shopping for last-minute items for the summer that they couldn't get in Connecticut. Their train left at six that evening and they would dine on the train. Sam kept begging to go on the elevated train, and much against Millie's protestations, they gave in and took the El to Grand Central.

This time, when they boarded their train to go up north, they were in a sleeper car, which would deposit them at the edge of the Adirondacks, the Westport station on Lake Champlain, at three in the morning. After this exhilarating day in New York, no one, not even Millie, worried that they wouldn't be able to sleep on the train that night.

After they settled in and the train left the station, they all gathered in the dining car for a fine meal as they watched the sun set over the rolling hills leading to the Catskill Mountains. It was a beautiful trip and they always regretted that it had to be taken at night. They missed the transition from one place to another. From the most vibrant, modern metropolis on earth to the unending wilderness of the pristine and untamed Adirondack Mountains, no two places could be more diametrically opposite and yet somehow exactly alike. Each in its own way, wild, alive, and powerful.

CHAPTER THREE

It was three o'clock in the morning when the conductor came by to wake up the family. They would be pulling into the Westport depot in about fifteen minutes. He had all of their bags at the door and ready to go. The boys were up in a flash, pulling open the curtains and ecstatically opening the windows, hanging out for a better look. The wonderful, familiar woodland smells came wafting into the compartment and brought a smile to Anna's face. All the warm memories of summers past came rushing back to her. She felt such a kinship with these mountains that was almost like an intimate relationship, one she could explain to no one else and barely allowed herself to understand.

The train whistle broke her reverie as it announced their arrival at Westport. They had all slept in their clothes. They would change and wash up later at the hotel next to the train station. The train braked and steam blew up into the boys' faces. They jumped backed and Sam landed in Millie's lap, scaring the daylights out of her.

They descended from the train and walked toward the darkened Westport Hotel. They would sit in the rockers on the porch overlooking magnificent Lake Champlain until the hotel opened at six o'clock. They didn't want to wake up anyone in the hotel. Their supplies had arrived earlier by freight train and were loaded into a wagon waiting for them. The conductor wished them well and the train trudged northward, headed for Montreal.

The boys began getting a bit noisy. "Shush, boys," said Will quickly. Colleen settled them down on a cushioned bench, covering them against the damp morning chill with a quilt from the wagon. Within no time they were sound asleep. Anna and Will sat in rockers next to each other, enjoying the view, and were soon asleep themselves.

It seemed no time that the birds began singing and the sun showing over the Green Mountains of Vermont across the lake woke them. Anna stepped around to the side of the hotel -- and there lay the great Adirondacks. Massive green and some craggy peaks towered above her, breathtaking in their splendor and glorious in their rugged beauty. So unspoiled yet by mankind and now, happily, protected by a legislative act, to be deemed "forever wild."

Mr. Durant, the hotel proprietor, soon appeared at the door and welcomed them warmly. He had been greeting them for years. He'd watched Paul and Sam grow up as he'd watched Will go from a young man to a husband and father. Even though he saw them only a couple of times a year, he felt he knew these people like his own family. He had arranged rooms for them in which to change and clean up and ushered them inside. When they were done, breakfast would be waiting for them in the dining room.

An hour later, they came down dressed and refreshed. Mrs. Durant had prepared a wonderful mountain breakfast including fresh eggs, lake trout, steak, and all sorts of muffins and breads. The Durants joined the Tattersalls for breakfast and caught up on all the doings over the winter. Mrs. Durant told them about the great ice storm they had had in April, which caught everybody by surprise and paralyzed the area for a week. It seemed an early spring had forced the spring flowers to come up. They were soon frozen solid under icy sheaths and looked like natural paperweights made of wondrous colors stuck to the earth. Mr. Durant saw none of the beauty in the freak ice storm and only talked of the devastation and loss of life it caused. He had to put a new roof on his barn, replacing the one that collapsed from the quick change in weather and sudden freezing temperatures. Unsuspecting boats were frozen into the lake and the people on them needed to be rescued, to the great danger of the rescuers. The whole town pitched in. One of the Durants' kitchen workers lost his life when he fell through the ice trying to save a couple of fisherman stuck out in the lake. His body still had not been found.

The boys were fascinated but Mrs. Durant realized this wasn't polite breakfast talk and quickly changed the subject to more pleasant topics. They discussed plans for the summer and hoped to get up to the valley at some point to pay the Tattersalls a visit. Anna said she'd like that. She really enjoyed the Durants. To her they were always the overture to her summer that she had long looked forward to.

They were all full from breakfast. The stagecoach had arrived and was ready to take them on the last leg of their trek to Keene Valley, a trip that would take them several hours over dirt roads. It was a large stagecoach and was designed to be as comfortable as possible riding on the rough roads. And though this one even had rubber tires, it was a far cry from the New York City cab they had taken the day before. The first half of the ride from Westport to Elizabethtown was rather flat and easygoing. It was the second half, a treacherous route over Spruce Hill, that took an experienced driver to maneuver safely.

The driver was named Brown. He had driven this stagecoach for years. He delivered the mail, supplies, and news, as well as transporting people in and out of the area. The sound of the stage coming into town and stopping at Bailey's Hotel in Keene Valley was always heralded as an event, something people relied on as a connection to the rest of the world. Everybody looked forward to Brown's arrival in hopes of receiving a letter or something they had ordered or an arriving guest.

Brown was a master at handling the rut-strewn road to Keene Valley from Elizabethtown. He was also quite a character and could spin a yarn, more to his own amusement than to his passengers'. The boys enjoyed listening to his tall tales of the exploits of all sorts of mountain folk.

The ride took them north along Lake Champlain and soon turned west and began to head up into the beautiful Adirondacks. The nearer they got to Keene Valley, the home of the High Peaks, the more dramatic the views. The stagecoach came perilously close to the drops into the chasms alongside the uneven road. Of course, Brown had stories of terrible close calls and near tumbles into the depths.

Brown said, "But in all the years of making the trip, I ain't never lost even the smallest piece of mail. Oh, maybe a passenger or two, but nothin' important as the mail." They all got a good chuckle out of this.

As the long ride went into its final hour, Brown had a new story to tell. It involved "Adirondack Murray" and his famous deer-hunting incident. Murray's stories of the Adirondacks were infamous and credited as one of the main causes of the influx of tourism in the area.

"It seems Murray and his guide, Steve, were out a-huntin' one night. They was doin' what's called 'Jack-shootin', where you wears a light on yer head to attract the deer. They bagged themselves a buck and dropped it. As they neared it, that damn buck ups and takes off and starts to escapin'. Murray lunges at him and grabs a hold of his antlers and that buck takes Murray for a merry ride, neither about to give up the fight. The deer finally manages to throw off Murray into a thicket, but Steve is there just in time to grab onto the beast's tail. Now, you know, the tail of a deer is about as big as a tufted titmouse, and just as fluttery. But that Steve was able to hang on and to mostly keep hisself away from those kickin' hooves, looking like a dancin' marionette without no strings. The buck tried to escape by heading into a river, but Steve was able to jump on his head and he drowned the creature."

Sam and Paul were enraptured by the story. "More, more," they begged, and Brown was always happy to oblige. Millie and Colleen napped while Anna took in the familiar sights and smells of the forest. She watched as chipmunks and squirrels darted across the road. Some sat and watched the carriage,

27

almost as if with contempt, as this weird horse- drawn coach disturbed their harmonious existence.

As they crested Spruce Hill, the valley magically revealed itself to them through small glimpses between trees or evergreens and blindingly white birch. All of a sudden they reached a clearing and there was the vista of the high peaks. And nestled below them was Keene Valley, dotted with small houses and farms amongst meadows and fields. They could see Noonmark Mountain's pyramid shape standing alone as a beacon at the far end of the valley. Next to it the range of Dix, Saddleback, Wolfjaws, and the tallest of them all, Mount Marcy. Brown stopped the stage for them to take in the awe-inspiring panorama. They all were silent in reverence for God's handiwork.

They headed off and were now coming down into the valley itself, arriving at an intersection in the road. The north led to Lake Placid, the south to Keene Valley, just a few more miles or so. At last. They'd be at Bailey's in no time. Aunt Lil would be there with her buckboard ready to take them to Idlenook. And if Aunt Lil was there, she'd have the whole town there and whipped into a frenzy over their arrival. Not to mention the usual excitement over the stage's appearance.

As they drove the road, they passed the Bradley Farm and waved to old Mrs. Bradley out tending to the early summer crops. She bade them welcome back. They could see she had corn, tomatoes, and bean stalks growing already. They passed many houses and were greeted warmly by old friends sitting on their front porches enjoying an after-lunch respite. It was a very small close-knit community and everybody knew everyone else. And their goings on. Gossip was deemed very impolite but was one of the main recreations of valley denizens.

They crossed the Ausable River and rounded a bend. They passed the town library and the Keene Valley Country Club with its new tennis courts. And ahead, they saw the crowd gathered in front of Bailey's to greet them and the stage. And, as predicted, there was Aunt Lil's buckboard ready and waiting with stout Aunt Lil atop it. The stage pulled to a stop next to Lil's carriage.

Lil examined her watch and said to Brown, "Twelve minutes late, Brown. It's not nice to keep an old lady waiting for her family this long."

Brown tipped his hat. "Mrs. Tattersall, my sincerest apologies. It will never happen again." He made no excuses, knowing they would get him nowhere. Besides, he was right on time.

Everyone waved hello and greeted the Tattersalls. Those expecting mail and parcels met excitedly with Brown as to what he had for them. The family disembarked, greeted a few people, and went straight to Aunt Lil's carriage.

"Sorry to keep you waiting, Aunt Lil," Will said. "We stopped to look at the view from the top of Spruce Hill."

"You're not really late," Aunt Lil said. "I just like to keep Brown on his toes so he knows his place. He can get very cheeky if you let him."

Anna and Will stifled smiles and each gave Aunt Lil a hug. The boys were reluctant to. Their experiences with Aunt Lil almost always resulted in their being embarrassed by her in some way. And this was no exception. As they stood back, hesitant to kiss Aunt Lil, she called them over to her, rather loudly. They just stayed back and shuffled their feet.

"Say hello to your great-aunt, boys," Will demanded.

They hesitated again one moment too long and Aunt Lil was outraged. "What kind of boys are these?" she bellowed, gaining everybody's attention. "My own great-nephews won't give me a kiss hello. I am in shock." She was getting very dramatic. And she was very good at getting things her way and knew how to do it.

"What could two boys such as these have against such a lady as myself?" she went on, now acting hurt. "What have I done to offend you? What have I done to deserve such public humiliation from my own family?"

The boys realized there was only one way to stop this. They looked at each other and jumped into the wagon and hugged Aunt Lil like there was no tomorrow. They kissed her and even acted as if they were fighting over her.

Aunt Lil put an immediate stop to all this. "All right, that's enough, you two. A simple kiss on the cheek would have sufficed." Paul and Sam just shrugged and jumped down from the buckboard.

After loading their things into Aunt Lil's horse-drawn carriage, she ordered her driver to proceed and they headed off. Millie and Colleen had to ride in the wagon with the supplies, as Aunt Lil was from the old school and didn't allow help in the carriage with her. Aunt Lil offered for the Tattersalls to stay the night at her house, but Anna wanted to get Idlenook opened up and get things ready. They had plenty of time before bedtime to do all that and she was anxious to get there. Aunt Lil still insisted they at least come to dinner, as she had a lavish welcoming banquet all prepared. Martin, one of her hands, had shot a deer that morning just for the occasion. How could they turn down such an offer? Of course they'd be there.

They passed the Congregational Church and stopped a moment to say hello to Pastor Thomas Baker. Anna and the pastor were particularly good friends and organized many charitable events together over the summers past. She was extremely pleased to see him. It was more than a friendship that Anna had with Tom. He had become one the best friends she'd ever had and someone she could say anything to. They would talk for hours and he was always there to offer counseling and comfort, especially over the last few years as she and Will had grown more and more distant. She was eager to fill Tom in on the change in Will over the past two days.

They soon passed Aunt Lil's house, newly painted a lovely shade of deep green with a woodsy, tan trim and looking stunning. She was extremely proud of it. She had been there for a month already but still had a lot of plans to spruce the place up. Most of the prominent summer homes were up drives and hidden from view off the main road, to be more private and exclusive. Not Aunt Lil's home, though. She was right on the main road, watching everyone going by, and letting all who rode by see her and her admirable home. She ruled her roost from there. She wasn't going to hide up on a knoll, behind trees. That was not how Aunt Lil conducted things.

It was only half a mile further when they arrived at the turnoff to Idlenook. Just past their road was a tavern called Mills. The tavern was only allowed to serve a beer called "two-percent" as it was only two percent alcohol, but everyone in town knew they had stills in the mountains and stronger potables could be obtained. Aunt Lil strongly disproved of Mills and his tavern and didn't know why Will had bought a house so near to such a place.

They turned into the drive to Idlenook. "How high the field grass has become," Will commented. "I'll have to get to that directly." The small dirt road wound through a meadow, soon emerged through a thicket, and there stood Idlenook. Hidden from view from the road, it was a small, cottage-like mountain house cozily snuggled amongst maidenhair ferns and lilies, and caressed by the sounds of the Ausable River, trickling in its banks, right next to the house. It was here that Anna felt truly at home.

CHAPTER FOUR

Aunt Lil had already had her servants open up Idlenook for the Tattersalls. Everything was uncovered and dusted, the window shutters opened and the porch furniture placed out front ready for them. She had stocked the pantry with food. Will thanked Lil for her kindness and Anna said how much she appreciated all the help. Millie and Colleen were particularly appreciative but said so only to each other. The boys ran off to check out the beach that changed shape after each spring's snowmelt. Sometimes it left a deep pool perfect for diving. They always hoped for that.

Anna entered the house and took her first breath of that wonderful balsam aroma that the house had held for all its years. It smelled like no place else she had known and gave her a soothing, pacifying sensation. Any unpleasant or disagreeable feelings she had melted away. The totality of the effect was like no other she had ever held.

Will took the wagon to unload the supplies and Aunt Lil came in to show off all that she had done for them. Anna was very grateful. Aunt Lil understood Anna's love of this place and the valley and knew she wanted some time alone with her memories. "Get yourselves settled, Anna dear," she said. "We can talk later at dinner about all the goings on in the valley. I'll expect you at six sharp. That's when night draws on Giant," Aunt Lil announced.

"I wouldn't miss it, Lil," said Anna.

And Aunt Lil left to get things prepared. Anna stood on the porch and watched as her carriage crossed the field and disappeared past the thicket toward the main road. Beyond the drive she could see Baxter and the Twins, mountains that made up the spectacular view from the front porch of Idlenook. Off the dining porch in the back of the house, overlooking the river, you could see Giant Mountain, with its bald granite crest, rising majestically above the valley. Giant was probably Anna's favorite mountain, not only because of its beauty, but because it was the first of the high peaks that she conquered as a child when she visited. And upon reaching the top, there was the incredible view of the entire Adirondacks, and back across Lake Champlain to Vermont. It seemed to stand above all, silently dominating, as if commanding the other mountains to bow down before it. Anna couldn't wait to climb into Giant's embracing arms, to get to the top and hear nothing but the breeze as it wafted across from miles away. She always tried to see Idlenook from up there but could never quite pick it out, nestled in the trees and fields as it was. She could see the village from up there. She could also see Lil's house, imposing along the main road, as if defying Giant to bow down to it.

Sam and Paul came dashing in with the news that the beach was much larger this year. The river had pushed out much further right where it doglegged to the west. And the river was much narrower. Maybe deeper. They couldn't wait to jump in and try it out.

Anna asked, "You mean you didn't try to go in already?"

To which Paul replied, "Well, I wanted to, but Sam said the water was too cold."

"I did not," Sam retorted.

"You put your foot in the water for only a second and when you pulled it out, you were shivering like a leaf."

Anna said, "Well, it is very early in the season. The snow runoff is still melting so I'm sure it's very cold. There will be plenty of time for swimming later. Any sign of trout?"

Paul said, "We forgot to look. Come on, Sam, race you back to the beach."

And they were off again. Anna thought what a perfect place this was for her boys. And what a perfect place it also was for her.

Will came in, speaking as he entered. "All the supplies are stored and the horses are stabled," he said. "Lil did a great job, don't you think, Anna?"

"I couldn't thank her enough. She wants us at her house at six this evening."

"Sounds good." He paused, showing his usual uneasiness with her. "So, uh... glad to be here?"

"I couldn't be happier anywhere else," she replied as she looked up at Giant.

"I know," he said, a bit forlornly.

They both gazed out toward the mountain, but he stood uncomfortably a foot or so away from her. The man she saw yesterday in New York City was retreating back inside this resigned facade. *Perhaps he was becoming entranced with the modern age and all of its toys and less captivated by the simple things as I am*, Anna thought. He did spend a lot of time in Boston and New York lately and his exuberance yesterday gave a glimpse of the old Will she knew and loved. He was still in there; she just hoped she could find a way to get him out before he got too far away. She had a couple of weeks with him before he returned to work and she vowed she'd do all that she could to get him back.

But first to the tasks at hand. There was still a lot of work to do to get the house in order. Aunt Lil's heart was in the right place, but she loved to rearrange things her way. Anna would have to discover where various items were put away and put them back in their places. She reached over and squeezed Will's hand.

"I've got a million things to do to get this place in order. Why don't you sit on the porch and I'll bring you something cool to drink?" said Anna.

"Thank you, no. I think I'll go to Bailey's and see what's going on in the village. Can I pick up anything while I'm there?"

"I can't imagine there's anything we forgot. I need to go through everything. If there is something we need, we'll get it tomorrow."

"Okay. I'll be back soon."

"Have a good time. Say 'hello' to everyone for me."

And he was off. She knew the boy in him just couldn't wait to tell the other men about their day in New York, the taxi cab ride, the moving pictures. She would love to have seen the look on his face as he told the story. She would get to see it tonight at Aunt Lil's when he recounted it for her. Of course, if wouldn't be as much fun. Aunt Lil would pooh-pooh this as just so much folderol. The boys wouldn't even attempt to get Aunt Lil excited about their day, they were so afraid of her. When they were younger, whenever they knew Aunt Lil was coming over, they would hide under the house until she left. They had a great time trying to keep from laughing, as they would hear her commenting above how she never sees the boys when she visits. After she left, they would emerge all dirty and satisfied with themselves and run down to the river to frolic themselves clean.

As they got older, they learned to sneak past Aunt Lil's house on the way to the village when she was holding court on her front veranda. They would walk close to the thick brush on the same side of the street as Aunt Lil's house and as they neared it, they would slow to a creep to see if she was out front. If she wasn't there, they would make a mad dash past the house. If she was out there, that's when it really got tricky. They had made a small pass-through in the underbrush. And through a long, circuitous route behind boulders and bushes, they would make their way up a ledge. Once on top of the ledge, they could run down a grade on the other side to a small pond with a path that had been worn around it. It was a place many young lovers would come to stroll on a warm evening. The path led to a road that came out behind Bailey's. It took a while, but the boys loved that they had once again fooled Aunt Lil. They also actually liked going that way but would never admit it.

As Anna was arranging things in the linen cupboard, Paul and Sam came back with the news that they had spotted "literally hundreds" of trout up the river where the water was forming rapids as it ran over the rocks. They wanted to know where the key to the playhouse was so they could get their fishing poles out and go fishing right away.

"Not today, boys. We're due at Aunt Lil's for dinner in a little while. You can fish tomorrow."

Sam said, "But if we wait until tomorrow, they might be gone."

"Don't worry, Sam," Anna reassured him. "If I know trout, they will still be there. And just to be sure, we'll all get up bright and early and you can take us to where you found them and we'll fish for our breakfast. How would that be?"

"That would be great, Mother. You won't believe how many trout we'll catch. We'll stuff ourselves for sure."

"Anything you say, Sam. Now, I want you two to go upstairs and start getting ready to go to Aunt Lil's. Millie will draw you a bath. And don't forget to dress proper. We're talking about Aunt Lil, you know."

"I'll make sure he does, Mother," said Paul.

"And I'll make sure Paul does," Sam chimed in.

"I don't care who makes sure who does what, just as long as there's no fighting and you both are ready on time."

"I'll make sure Sam is," said Paul.

"Oh yeah, and I'll...."

Anna cut him off, "That's enough out of both of you. I don't want to hear another word. Now, skedaddle."

They started to talk. Anna held a single finger up and gave them a stern look. They saw that and took off upstairs to undress. The cottage had a bathtub in a room behind the icehouse. Millie had been boiling water and filling it for them to use.

Anna looked over the curtains in the parlor. She decided that she needed new ones and she would go to Lake Placid one day soon to pick up some fabric to make them. She hoped they had as good a selection as she had seen recently back home. They were coming out with so many wonderful new designs lately and Idlenook could use some sprucing up. Also, she would need things to keep her busy once Will went back home. There were always the inevitable teas and card games. The Keene Valley Country Club was planning many social activities and she and Aunt Lil were going to run a crafts fair to raise money for the church in town. There was always the big dance at Eggerfield's, a local hotel, which was the last bash of the summer. It was quite the affair and only the crème de la crème were invited. Will didn't go in much for dances and Anna didn't even know if he would be back up for the party. She could very well go with Aunt Lil, but she dreaded being a lone woman at gatherings like this. She also preferred the simplicity of the mountains, and this kind of party was like bringing a piece of home with its social complexities that she had left behind for a few months. She came here to get away and feel the independence that the Adirondacks offered her. There would be time for that, too, she assured herself.

• • •

Dinner at Aunt Lil's was always a wondrous experience. Like her cousin, Will's mother, Kathleen, she had the greatest imagination and would come up with new and extraordinary ideas to decorate the table and the house for a gathering, and Anna really appreciated them. Aunt Lil never failed to amaze. As the Tattersalls arrived in their carriage with Will driving the horses, it was still light out. Even so, the house was shimmering with candlelight. Aunt Lil had the veranda festooned with fir branches and pine cones. She had carved out the center of the pinecones and inserted a candle through each of them and then placed them in her candleholders. There must have been twenty candles burning across the front of the house to welcome them. Through the window, one could see many more flickering inside. The warm candle glow showed off Aunt Lil's finest china, which traveled with her from Philadelphia every year. She had woven braids of forsythia with its bright yellow flowers into wreaths that surrounded the china hors d'oeuvres plates of local crudités. Aunt Lil had fashioned a four-foot spray of forsythia in a large vase that was on the serving table. There was also one on the sideboard in the dining room. The entire effect was overwhelming. Anna studied each and every ornamentation and made mental notes of how it was done for future reference. Aunt Lil knew how much Anna appreciated her decorating prowess so she always went the extra mile when Anna would be there.

They all took their usual places on the porch, Anna in a rocker to the right of Aunt Lil's rocker, Will and the boys on the other side of the front door to her left. They rocked and watched as night drew on Giant. Aunt Lil had a spectacular view from here. She could look from Noonmark to the south up past Giant to Spread Eagle to the north. As the sun set behind them, it seemed as if a magic shade were being drawn up on Giant. Slowly, the shadow would creep up from the valley floor. Giant was composed of several ridges; the three largest they called the Baby, the Mother, and, at the apex, the father, Giant. The ever-rising shadow would change to different muted colors, from pale pinks to bright oranges, deep purples and misty blue-grays. It would first envelop the Baby, slowly caressing it with its soothing pastel shades. Gradually it would slide up the much larger Mother, turning her green pine-covered shoulders ever darker. When she was totally engulfed, it left Giant himself alone in the last of the sunlight. A beacon for the whole range to admire. It was all part of the enchantment of the Adirondacks.

Aunt Lil rarely missed the striking event and most of her plans revolved around it. Nothing made Anna appreciate Aunt Lil more. Even the boys sat in silence as the wizardry took place. When Giant was finally in darkness, all waited for Will's inevitable, slightly naughty joke. He would look up at the mountain and say, "Once again, we can see the "night drawers" on Giant." Aunt Lil would roll her eyes and remind Will for the hundredth time to be careful and not mention bedclothes if there were guests other than family there. Will always promised he would, but even if friends were there, he would always make his silly little joke. Everyone looked forward to it, even Aunt Lil.

Once the show was over, they went inside for a delicious meal of venison, roasted potatoes, and corn fresh off the cob, picked today at Pru Martin's farm. They told Aunt Lil of their day in New York City and, as expected, she wasn't one to appreciate all of the new and wonderful things they had seen. The boys tried to get her to understand how exciting the moving pictures were, but when she compared it to the natural phenomenon on Giant they had just witnessed, there was no convincing her.

Aunt Lil brought them up to date on the goings on about the valley, who was there, who was coming. One of the artists who frequented the valley asked to do a painting of Aunt Lil on her veranda. He claimed it was to preserve a memory that many had of Keene Valley. She flatly refused, as she knew he was only in it for commercial gain and it had nothing to do with preserving memories. Artists were a big part of Keene Valley summers and were quite responsible for attracting the wealthy to the area. They would spend summers painting in the Adirondacks and then go back to the cities to sell the artwork. When their buyers saw how beautiful the Adirondacks were, they began visiting the area and many ended up buying summer homes there. As the people who had money to buy art and visit galleries were the well-to-do, these were the people attracted to the wilderness getaway. Anna had known many of the painters who came every summer and she often let them sit on her porch to paint the view from Idlenook. On a visit to Boston, she passed an art gallery on Newbury Street and she was amused to see, sitting in the window, a painting with her view looking back at her. People paid exorbitant amounts for something she saw every summer day.

They discussed the upcoming crafts fair and Aunt Lil was already at work on various items to donate. Everyone made such beautiful things, so they would make a lot of money for the church, Anna was sure. There was to be a play put on at the Country Club as part of their Summer Performance Show and Aunt Lil expected Paul and Sam to try out for it. The boys balked at the suggestion, but they knew, if Aunt Lil wished it, it was so. She also disclosed to the boys a rumor she had heard that a traveling gypsy circus would be in the area that summer and if they were very good, she would treat them to it. Now the boys were excited.

The night was turning cool as they finished dinner so they had coffee and dessert in the parlor. Aunt Lil asked one of her servants named Holmes to play the piano, as they ate crème caramel and petit fours. Holmes often played at St. Huberts Hotel on special occasions and he was well known for playing the latest tunes with unbounded enthusiasm. But at Aunt Lil's he was only allowed to play classical music and religious hymns. The only time he could practice was when Aunt Lil was out, and the other help danced their way through cleaning the house when he played. The way he played, even the hymns were exciting to listen to. Aunt Lil seemed to take it all in stride, although everybody knew she was very proud of Holmes deep inside.

It had been a long day for the Tattersalls so they took their leave and headed home to Idlenook for a good night's sleep. The cool mountain air was the best kind for sleeping. And with promises to Sam that they would be up early to go fishing, they all went to bed, Anna to her room, Will to his. Anna snuggled under the quilts and breathed in the sweet balsam air. She felt safe and alive.

CHAPTER FIVE

The Tattersalls were up with the first sound of the whippoorwills singing to the dawn. Of course Sam was already up and ready to go. He was dressed in his fishing boots and had fishing gear hanging all over him. He wore a basket backpack loaded with more gear. He was out in the back meadow practicing fly-fishing, snagging leaves and clumps of grass. As Anna looked out from her bedroom window while she dressed, Sam gave the rod a massive swing and the hook end of the line ended up high in a large pine. She remembered when she first visited Keene Valley and Will did the same thing. His father said he was out fishing for pine cones. As Sam struggled to free his fishing line, Anna went downstairs and Colleen helped her gather the cooking implements she would need for a campfire trout breakfast in the woods.

The family trooped through the woods to the spot the boys had found. As they had said, the area was teaming with trout. It seemed that you could almost catch them in your hands. In no time, the boys had caught more than enough good-sized trout for a hearty breakfast. Will had cut some wood and had a nice fire going. The river rippled past as the fire crackled. Anna scaled and deboned the fish and soon the delicious aroma of sizzling trout, pan fried potatoes, bacon and eggs mixed with the smell of the fresh morning dew and the forest bed of pine needles unique to the Adirondacks alone.

"Breakfast is ready," Anna called to deaf ears. The boys were so wrapped up in fishing that they didn't care about eating. Will finally had to wade out into the water and scoop them both up under his arms and haul them to shore, which wasn't as easy as it used to be. He was amazed how much his boys had grown in so short a time.

Together the family enjoyed a marvelous mountain breakfast in the slowly warming air.

"Remember when I was little," said Sam, "and we found a fishing hole just like this? I was just a little kid then." Will and Anna exchanged a bemused look. It was probably all of two years ago. "I remember it was a day just like this, the cold air was getting warm and food smelled so good and we all just lay back and watched the clouds make shadows on the mountains, just like those." He pointed to the shapes the clouds made on high peaks.

"I remember one of them looked just like our dog, Dingey," said Anna.

"Yeah," remembered Sam, happily.

"Well, I remember Sam thought he saw a cloud shadow on the mountains that looked like the devil and he couldn't sleep for a week," said Paul.

"I did not."

"You were so scared, you said you'd never go fishing again or ever look at cloud shadows again."

Sam paused, thinking for a moment. "Hmmm. You know, I think I'm ready to go now."

Will grabbed Sam and hugged him. "Come here, my man. That was when you were just a little boy. Now you're actually a big boy and things like that don't bother you anymore."

Realizing. "Oh. Yeah, that's right. They don't." Looking at the mountains. "Hey, look, Paul. There's a shadow that looks like a pig. It looks just like you." He laughed hysterically.

"Very funny," said Paul.

The rest of the family enjoyed Sam's joke at Paul's expense. Anna wished this could go on forever, but she knew Will's family reverie wouldn't last for long. His exuberance at showing the family around New York City came jolting back to her. She hadn't seen him so happy in a long time and she knew she could never truly connect with him in that world. It all moved too quickly and frantically. She had to admit she found it fascinating and exciting, but only as a diversion, like an amusement park, not as a life. She knew this happy family camaraderie wouldn't last much longer. Aside from the fact that Will needed to return to his work, he would need to return to his world. But for now, she would enjoy their time together. And she hoped Will would, too.

After their bellies were full and the morning turned toward noon, they gathered their things and headed back home. Along the way, they spotted a family of deer munching in a distant field. They saw raccoons and the ubiquitous chipmunks, which Anna adored and fed near the house, much to Aunt Lil's consternation. They found a strawberry patch and picked a basketful. Anna and Colleen could put up some preserves and make a pie for dinner that evening.

As they returned to Idlenook, a wagon was just pulling away, having deposited large blocks of ice in the small, thick-walled room behind the kitchen. Colleen and Millie were shivering in there, trying to keep warm by busily cleaning the wooden shelves before storing the perishables in the icehouse. Anna gave Colleen the strawberries and remaining trout and headed off to change into her new visiting clothes. She hadn't seen any of the valley folks since they had arrived and she wanted to show off her new dress as she took a stroll through the town.

Will took Sam and Paul around back of the barn to help him chop some wood for the fireplace, much to the dismay and disappointment of the boys, who wanted to go off and visit their friends too. Will assured them they'd have all summer to do that.

Anna and Millie took the buggy into town, as they needed to pick up some fresh vegetables and milk that they weren't able to bring with them from Connecticut. They passed Aunt Lil's house but she wasn't in her usual spot on the front veranda. They approached the main part of town and started to come upon their summer friends.

Most of the people in Keene Valley in the summer were from wealthy families in the areas surrounding New York City. There were several families who lived in Keene Valley all year round. Martin Bailey, the owner of the hotel, a grumpy old mountain man who put up with the tourists in his hotel out of necessity. Mrs. Bradley, whose famous vegetable and flower gardens kept the valley well stocked with food and beauty. Her son Ronnie, who wasn't well in the head and didn't talk much. He took on the job of sweeping the main roads in town. The roads may have been all dirt but that didn't deter him from his self-appointed task. They were pinecone-free roads. The town also boasted its very own hermit who lived up at the top of Johns Brook in a one-room cabin. His name was Bill Patrick but everyone called him Uncle Bull-Bull. He came into town only rarely, to pick up some supplies he couldn't get in the woods, like cigarette tobacco and chewing gum. He loved to regale the townspeople with grand stories of his lone adventures in the wilderness. He had a booming voice so you always knew when Uncle Bull-Bull was around. The children adored him like a Pied Piper and dreamt of living the hermit life, free from the constraints of school and parents.

Occasionally celebrities would visit the area, usually staying at St. Huberts Inn or renting a camp on one of the Ausable Lakes. Last summer they all had a grand surprise when President McKinley passed though town on a tour of the "Forever Wild" Adirondack Park. He stopped to speak for a short time and all were very impressed. He seemed to be the embodiment of a statue in the Capitol rotunda come to life, tall and impressive with a soothing voice, who made one feel proud to be an American. The cynics thought his speech was all fluff and no substance, but the aura he gave off made up for any shortcomings.

Anna had Millie drop her off at the church so she could spend some time with her good friend, Pastor Tom. The day had warmed to a cool but pleasant degree and the air was crisp and clear. As she stepped up the front walk to the church, she turned back to look at Spread Eagle Mountain. Its shape looked like a giant eagle with his wings extended out caressing the

44

mountaintop, with his massive head resting on his right wing. Even if no one else had named this mountain Spread Eagle, the image it evoked was unmistakable. As she gazed at God's superb creation, the dark green of the pines against the cerulean sky, her reverie was broken by a familiar voice from behind.

"He still lies there guarding our little hamlet." She turned to see her Tom, Pastor of the Keene Valley Congregational Church, smiling warmly at her.

Anna said, "If he ever does try to take flight, you better grab him by his talons and pull him back. The valley wouldn't be the same without him."

"The same could be said for you, my dear." He gave her a warm hug. "Come in. I've made some improvements since last summer."

They went up the steps and into the white clapboard church. The sun was streaming though the southern windows and showing off the brand new pews that had been added since Anna was there last. Tom was beaming brighter than the sunshine.

"Tom, it's beautiful!" exclaimed Anna. "How did you do it?"

"From the generous donations of the summer people, we were actually able to order these mahogany pews from Rochester, machine-made and sanded. The gloss and comfort is unbelievable. The only problem is, if my sermon isn't exactly exhilarating one Sunday, these seats are so comfortable, I find people falling asleep."

"That never happens to you."

"The good side is, they also don't squirm as much in their seats," he chuckled.

"They're wonderful. The whole place looks brand new because of them."

"Here, try it out." He took her hand and escorted her to a pew and offered her a seat. Anna settled into it, wiggling a little into place.

"Mmmm. Delicious. You should be very proud."

"And what about you, Anna. How are things going? I've missed you."

"I've missed you, too. Especially our talks."

"How are the boys?"

"Sam is growing like a weed. Paul is torturing him as usual, like any older brother would. We had a great fishing breakfast this morning. The trout were practically jumping onto their hooks."

He hesitated. "And how are things with you and Will?"

"The same," she said, a bit sadly. "We spent the day in New York before heading up here. You should have seen him, Tom. He was like the old Will. Happy and exuberant. He had the greatest thrill showing us all the new and exciting things in the city. He's still the same Will underneath, but more and more he's growing away from me. The simple things in life aren't enough for him anymore. He's in love with electric this and motor that. I haven't lost him yet, but he is definitely drifting away to a newfangled world. I can only hope he doesn't drift too far before we can't pull each other back in."

"Boys and their toys, huh? Are you sure that's all it is?"

"Do you mean am I worried that he's found someone else? No. Not at all. Will is a very loyal husband and father. That's the farthest thing from my mind."

"I agree with you. He's never struck me like that."

Trying to lighten herself up, she said, "But we'll have a good couple of weeks while he's here. We have a lot of activities planned with the boys. They are the lights of his life. He was so proud showing them around his city. His eyes lit up every time their mouths dropped open."

"I'm glad to hear that. So, are you going into the village right now?"

"Yes. I've got to stop at the store and pick up a few things."

"And of course show off that incredible new dress to make all the other ladies jealous."

"Why Pastor Tom, you know I'm not like that."

"Oh, sure. Come on, I'll walk with you. They've always gossiped about us behind our backs. If we walk though town together, with you in that dress, their eyes will be popping out of their heads."

"Sounds like fun to me. Let's go."

He offered her his arm. "Madame."

Taking it. "Merci, Monsieur." And they headed out of the church.

It wasn't far to the center of Keene Valley where people were bustling about shopping, trading, and, of course, gossiping. Anna spotted her buggy in front of Alexander's Market, where Millie was most likely picking up the things they needed. She and Tom greeted passersby as all said how great it was to see each other back in the valley, how beautiful Anna looked, exchanging pleasantries and stories of the winter months apart. Anna knew her closest friends would be at the Keene Valley Country Club so she and Tom headed across the street.

The green main building contained one large room and several smaller ones where many social functions were held in the valley. A large open piazza that overlooked the green lawns and tennis courts surrounded it. From the lawn, as they approached, they could see people gathered on the piazza watching a match in progress.

"Oh good, the Dunhams have gotten here," said Anna, scanning the assemblage. "And there's Sally Merrick. I got the announcement about her new baby being born back in April." She continued looking, as they got closer.

"Oh boy, time for fireworks," cautioned Tom.

"What do you mean? Who's there?" Anna suddenly stopped in her tracks. Before her stood her archrival since they were young, Margaret Bancroft. Throughout the years in Keene Valley, she and Anna had clashed many times. But this meeting would really make everyone stand up and take notice — Margaret was wearing exactly the same dress that Anna had just bought down in Connecticut and was herself wearing, right now. "Oh, fine. Now what do I do?"

"We could just turn around and leave."

"But they've all seen me."

"Just wave and walk away and later you can explain that you suddenly remembered something you had to do."

"Sure. Those vultures would believe that. I've got to just face the music and march on up there as if nothing is amiss."

"That's my girl. I had a feeling you wouldn't back down."

"Besides — Margaret looks obese in her dress." Putting on her best plastered-on smile, she said, "Into the lion's den we go." And off they headed to the clubhouse.

As they neared, there were many *hellos* and *welcome backs*. Anna complimented Sally on how well she looked, only a couple of months after having had a baby. Edie and Paul Dunham greeted her. So did the Browns, whose son Peter was playing the tennis match they all were observing.

As she knew would happen sooner or later, the moment of truth was about to arrive. Having tried to avoid it as long as possible, Anna turned around and was immediately standing face to face with Margaret Bancroft. Twins from the neck down, although Anna had been right — Margaret's dress didn't fit quite as well as Anna's did. The rest of the throng tried to be polite and nervously kept talking, all with one ear to the impending conversation. Tom stood back, leaning on the porch railing, smiling with his arms crossed, just waiting for the fun to begin. There was an overlong, stony silence between the two women as each eyed the other up and down. Anna could feel the heat rising between them. But before Margaret could let loose with one of her condescending barbs, Anna broke the ice.

All smiles, she greeted her rival. "Well, Margaret, how was your winter? The cold weather doesn't seem to have cracked anything. And I must say, you have such wonderful taste in clothes."

"There was never any question of that, was there?" said Margaret. "And how is that captivating husband of yours?"

"Wonderful as ever, Margaret. He delighted us all with a magical tour of New York City just before coming up here. And we got to see moving pictures! It was breathtaking!"

"Sounds like the old Will I used to know so very well," said Margaret. "He was breathtaking."

"He still is," Anna said, smiling cunningly. "And he's still mine."

"Anna, I'm almost starting to find you interesting."

48

At that, Anna started away. "Good to see you, Margaret." She walked over to Tom. "Come on, let's go." He took her arm and they headed down the stairs and across the lawn, leaving the snickering assemblages of Keene Valley's best, having thoroughly enjoyed themselves, forgetting totally about the tennis match in progress.

As Anna and Tom crossed the lawn, Tom said, "And we thought you and I would be the talk of the afternoon."

"Let the games begin," said Anna. "And don't worry, they'll need something new to talk about in no time, and we'll soon be it."

They reached the road and crossed to Bailey's to have a cool drink and see what mischief they could stir up there. They ordered two lemonades and as the beverages arrived, Millie pulled up in the buggy.

"I've emptied out the coffers at Alexander's, Ma'am. Now I'll head up to Bradley farm and get some vegetables for dinner."

"Thank you, Millie. See if you can get some summer squash for Will. That's his favorite. Please pick me up here on your way back."

"Yes, Ma'am." She snapped the reins and was off.

"Maybe my summer squash recipe will make Will happy," Anna said to Tom. "It's such a terrible feeling. We were so close. Inseparable. But he's losing interest in the life we have. As the millennium approaches, it seems that all the changes it is bringing and promising are the only things that are exciting him. That and his work, which keeps him very busy. I mean, he's a great provider and he's wonderful with the boys. But what we had is gone."

"I'm sorry, Anna. I know how hard this is for you."

"It is. He's growing in a different direction, and I'm not. It's very hurtful."

"Have you tried to talk to him about it?"

"He and I don't communicate like you and I do. He's a very closed person and it takes a lot to get him to open up. We've been having quite a good time since we got up here, but I can feel him getting anxious. It doesn't show yet, but I know him well. Little things; small, impatient responses to the simplest requests. He'll be heading back soon, I'm sure."

"Well, we'll have to make the best of it, won't we?" said Tom. "Don't worry, we've got a lot of activities planned to keep us all busy up here this summer. The Wardwells' ball is this weekend."

"I just hope Will's still here to escort me." She took a sip of her lemonade and stared off at Giant Mountain, rising above the valley in its majestic beauty.

CHAPTER SIX

Dinner that night was an Anna masterpiece, created from the finest ingredients the fertile valley had to offer. She cooked luscious trout almondine from the fresh fish caught that morning, a baked summer squash oozing with brown sugar and maple syrup, and potatoes au gratin made with Old Farmer Mory's goat cheese. And to top it all off, a strawberry and rhubarb pie with fresh whipped cream. Anna did it all and let Millie and Colleen watch and marvel. She knew it was delicious and Will and the boys savored every mouthful. The boys told of meeting up with old friends from last summer and making new ones with boys in the valley for the first time. Surprisingly, Paul even talked about a new girl named Virginia visiting for the summer from Philadelphia that he struck up a friendship with. Anna and Will exchanged knowing looks as Paul tried to coolly impart his meeting with her, not wanting to admit a boy's natural attraction. Will more than enjoyed the meal, but was uneasily quiet. Anna realized she was right. The scarcity of excitement that Keene Valley offered him of late was again catching up with him.

Anna suggested a game of Parcheesi after dinner, which the boys eagerly agreed to. Will instead opted to head off to Mills to meet with the other men. He was the one who taught Anna the finer points of winning the game. Anna and the boys played two games out on the back porch, she winning the first and Sam winning the second, until it was too dark to see the dice anymore and the air was taking on a chill. She put the boys to bed and warmed herself by the fire Millie had lit in the parlor, lost in thought, waiting for Will to come home.

He had walked so she didn't hear him coming up the drive and was startled by his entrance into the room. She jumped and let out a small exclamation of surprise.

"I didn't hear you come in," Anna uttered, collecting herself.

"I didn't mean to alarm you," Will apologized. "The fire feels good," he said, warming himself in front of it. "Dinner was especially wonderful tonight, dear."

"Thank you. I'm glad you enjoyed it. How was Mills?"

"Oh, as expected. Same as always. Well, a few new faces, but mostly the usual crowd. The Beechers arrived today. Ray and Joan took the train up to Burlington to visit her cousin there and then the ferry across Lake Champlain. They've got a new ferry this year that gets across twice as fast as before. He said it ran quiet as a kitten purring. I'd love to check it out sometime."

Men and their toys, thought Anna. Will sat in the rocker facing the fire and they both watched the flames play with the birch logs for a few moments.

"I think I'll go back home this Friday," Will announced.

Anna was taken aback. "That soon?"

"Yes, I've got two litigations pending that need attending to."

"You know the Wardwells are having their Summer Welcome Ball this Saturday."

"Yes, we talked about that tonight at Mills."

"Couldn't you wait until Sunday to leave?"

"Well, you know everybody there. You don't need me."

"I'd like to go with you. We had quite a nice time of it last year. Remember? You taught everyone that new dance they're doing in New York. The Charleston. You were the life of the party."

"I have to admit, I did have a good time." He thought for a moment, then reluctantly. "Well, I suppose I can reschedule my appointments and take the Sunday train instead." Then playfully, "Madam, may I escort you to the Wardwell Ball?"

"I'd be honored, kind sir. And thank you. I appreciate it, dear."

"You're welcome. We'll have a good time." He sounded like he was trying to convince himself.

They sat and looked at the fire, Anna knowing he was just doing this for her, which was sweet of him, but which ultimately wasn't going to help their situation.

They spent the next few days together as a family, hiking, picnicking, and visiting with friends. There was a lightness about Will that could only mean the weight of being trapped in the wilderness was off his shoulders and in a few days he would be heading back to the mechanized world he thrived in. It was small consolation but one that Anna could only enjoy to the fullest. Until Sunday morning, she had the old Will with her again.

Most of Saturday afternoon found the main streets of Keene Valley deserted of women who were home slavishly preparing for the Wardwell Summer Ball that evening. Several maids were sent on last-minute errands to the general store for thread or buttons or to Pru Martin's farm for corsage flowers or decorative hair bouquets. Anna and Millie used pink and purple wildflowers the family found on one of their hikes the day before and entwined them into Anna's long hair, which she had put up on top of her head in a loose kind of wrap. The flowers perfectly matched her lavender gown and its pink shawl. She couldn't have planned it better. When Will passed by her bedroom door he glanced in and caught her looking at herself in her full-length mirror. He gasped silently and held his breath momentarily as he gazed at his lovely wife. She was the most beautiful person he had ever known. He loved her so, but he knew he was pushing away from her and no matter how he tried, he couldn't fight the pull from the other side. He didn't understand it himself. For years they were inseparable. Before the boys were born, they took an ocean voyage to Europe, where they bicycled through Italy and hoteled at a chateau in France. They went out west to California where they rode the cable cars in San Francisco and tasted an avocado for the first time. When Paul and Sam were born, they devoted every waking, and sleeping, minute to them. Will did as much of his work at home as possible to enjoy being with his family.

But as time wore on, his business grew and its demands took him away more and more. First to Bridgeport, then Boston, then New York City where he was becoming quite an up-and-coming attorney. He began enjoying the attention and privileges his new position afforded him. He met the powerful men who influenced the times and was exposed to the latest and greatest the world had to offer. It was overwhelming and excited him. Although his family's wealth afforded him luxuries beyond the scope of the small town he grew up in, he had spent most of his life tied there with his immediate family. He adored them, but was thrilled by all the newness inundating him. The draw was too great and, even though he knew he was hurting Anna, he couldn't help himself. He understood he was justifying it to himself that it was for his family's good in the long run, that he would make more money and meet a lot of influential people. He also could see he was fooling himself and that it wasn't really going to do his family any good at all. They were missing him and he knew it, but he couldn't tear himself away. And he was sure Anna felt it too, so there was no need to discuss it with her. It would eventually work itself out someday. He hoped.

He slipped away from Anna's door before she could see him. But Anna had already seen him reflected in the mirror and hoped he would come in. But he hadn't. She felt she had wasted her time. Why had she worked so hard to make herself look so good? Who was she fooling? She had lost his heart and feeble attempts like this weren't going to change that. But she was still a woman of pride and she wanted to make her husband look good, so she would hold her head high and enter the ball on his arm, ready to wow her fellow valleyites.

Anna gave herself some finishing touches of makeup and removed an out-of-place sprig of baby's breath from her hair. She gathered her small beaded evening bag and a shawl, took a deep breath and headed out to find Will. They met in the hall as

Will exited his room looking dashing in a navy blue pinstripe three-piece suit. Anna had a flower for his lapel that matched the ones in her hair. Without words, she took his lapel and placed the flower there. Will glanced down at it for a moment and smiled.

"Thank you," he said quietly. Then uncomfortably, "You look beautiful, Anna. Your new dress is lovely."

Anna just smiled, and then said, "Shall we go?"

"After you." And they headed off down the stairs.

Millie and Colleen were waiting in the parlor and made a fuss over how wonderful the two of them looked together. The matching flowers were a splendid touch. Will had the Kodak set up and asked Colleen to take a photograph of the two of them. Anna and Will thanked them and headed out to a waiting buggy.

The boys were playing in the meadow and came running over when their parents came out. They were covered with a day's worth of boys out playing and when Sam started to hug his mother goodbye, Will stopped him just in time.

"Hold it there, partner. Did you happen to notice that you're a filthy mess?"

Sam looked down at himself. "Oh, sorry, Mother. I almost ruined your beautiful dress."

"No harm done, Sam. You can give me that hug when we get home from the ball − after you've had a bath."

"Aw, I don't want a bath."

Paul chimed in, "Boy, do you need one. You heard Father. You're a mess."

Anna said, "Take a look at yourself, Paul. Both of you get baths tonight."

"But I'm not as much as a mess as Sam is," said Paul.

Will jumped in. "You heard your mother. Millie, make sure you scrub them both down a few layers."

Millie, joking evilly, looked them over. "I think I'll get out the lye soap for these two ragamuffins."

Will said, "I think that's a capital idea, Millie." Both boys gulped and looked very unhappy. Anna and Will smiled secretly at Millie.

"Shall we?" Will offered as he gestured Anna into the buggy. He helped her up and then jumped in himself. Will snapped the reins and off they started, leaving two sad-looking little boys being led into the house by Colleen and Millie.

It was a resplendent evening. As they reached the main road, they could see the sun had just dipped below the crest of Saddleback Mountain, its rays streaming upward as if to glorify heaven itself. Will stopped the buggy and gazed skyward.

"Nothing like it, is there?" he said wistfully, almost as if he knew he was going to miss this glorious haven in the world.

Anna didn't answer. She knew there was nothing to say. Nothing was going to keep him here. Or with her. Instead, she decided on just small talk and told him the story of her run-in with Margaret Bancroft at the Club. Will couldn't believe that Anna and Margaret were still going at each other after all these years. But he did compliment Anna on her handling of the whole affair.

"Let's hope she has the sense to wear something different than I am this evening."

"It wouldn't matter, dear. You'll outshine everyone at the party anyway."

She reported on the other goings-on at the club and it filled the time as their buggy slowly climbed the hill and they reached the Wardwell Lodge.

Twilight was just settling in and the house was ablaze with candlelight and gas lamps. The orchestra could be heard louder and louder as they approached. The field in front of the lodge was a mass of carriages, buggies, and horses, attended by a team of hands hired for the occasion. They waited in line to drop off their buggy at the front and have it taken by one of the men.

Philip and Elizabeth Wardwell never spared any expense. This was always the first and best party of the season. As Anna and Will waited, they waved to and greeted other arriving guests. Through the windows, they could see people dancing to the lovely music. The veranda of the Wardwell Lodge was wide and stretched along the entire front of the building. Adirondack chairs and rockers were filled with guests enjoying undeniably one of the best views the valley had to offer. The road to the house was a bit of a climb for the horse or on foot, but the view was worth it. They looked north from the southern end of the valley and the whole valley with the town nestled in its embrace was laid out before them. Giant Mountain through to the Elizabethtown Road was visible on the right and Porter towering over Keene Valley on the left. One could see the small lights of houses dotted throughout the valley and flickering lamps moving along the road on passing carriages. It was a spectacular evening, the air crisp and clear. As the sky darkened, the stars formed a dome of brilliance over the party as if the Wardwells had put in a special order to God for them.

Anna and Will greeted their many summertime friends as they slowly made their way into the house. Just inside, they found Elizabeth and Philip greeting their guests. They were thirty years Anna and Will's senior. On the outside they appeared to be the two most proper, aristocratic people imaginable. The confidence of old money and a long colonial lineage added to their luster. But when you got to know them, they were two of the most down to earth, fun-loving people to know. That's why their parties were always such a hit. And they adored Anna and Will. They'd known Will most of his life and took Anna to their hearts as soon as they met her. Their exterior belied the warmth underneath.

"Anna, Will," exuded Elizabeth as she reached for Anna and gave her a warm embrace.

"Oh, Elizabeth, it's so wonderful to see you. You look terrific as always."

"Isn't she sweet. And such a wonderful liar."

"Not at all, Elizabeth," said Will. "You get younger every year. What's your secret?"

Phillip chimed in, "She lies about her age so much, she's actually starting to believe it herself – and it shows."

"Mind over matter, I say," said Elizabeth.

They all laughed.

"Well, I'm not lying. You are a sight for sore eyes. And everything looks so beautiful. Summer has officially begun," Anna said.

"What plans do you two have for the summer?" asked Phillip.

"Unfortunately, I have to head back home tomorrow," said Will. "I only stayed this extra day to come to your party."

"He wouldn't miss it for the world," said Anna, giving Will a slightly sad look.

"Well, I hope you'll be back soon, my dear," said Elizabeth. "We have such plans this year — excursions to the lakes, climbs to uncharted peaks. Phillip here is even thinking of trying to find the bottom of Chapel Pond. In diving gear."

"Diving gear? Where did you get diving gear?" asked Will.

"An old friend at the Oceanographic Institute in Rhode Island lent it to me. It's quite a contraption. I know how you love such things. I could use your help figuring out how it all works."

"He could use your help in carrying the damn thing, it's so heavy. That's what he could use," said Elizabeth.

"Why, my dear, I never thought of that," Phillip said coyly.

Anna smiled, enjoying them. "You two are a caution," she said.

"I'd be happy to join you when I get back this summer," offered Will.

"Well, we'll discuss all of this later. Now, go off. Enjoy yourselves. The refreshments are set up over there," Elizabeth said, pointing in the direction of the parlor. "And the food's laid out in the dining room. Have a wonderful time."

"I'm sure we will," said Will, taking Anna by the arm.

"Thanks again," Anna said to them as they headed off to mingle amongst the ever-growing crowd.

The party was already in full swing. People were eating, dancing and thoroughly enjoying themselves. Anna spotted Tom across the room and waved. Tom crossed over to them.

"Hello, Anna. Don't you look beautiful tonight." Shaking Will's hand, he said, "Will, how's the world been treating you?"

"Just fine Tom, and you?"

"Not bad. We had a rough winter up here this year. Ice storm made the snow so wet and heavy it collapsed part of the church's roof."

"You didn't tell me that, Tom," said Anna.

"Yes, it happened back in February. I was working in the rectory and it was very peaceful and quiet. You know how it gets when the world is covered in a blanket of thick snow. Every sound is muffled. Well, I started to hear the strangest sounds. Slowly at first. A kind of low, deliberate creaking. I sat there for a moment, not imagining what this eerie sound could be. But it kept on so I got up and went into the church. The whole left front corner of the roof was sagging in about a foot. I just stood there dumbfounded."

"I can imagine," said Anna.

"Then it started to dawn on me that I probably should get out of there because the whole roof could give way.

"Good thought," said Will.

"You've got that right. I ran back to the rectory and grabbed everything I could that I thought was irreplaceable, and hightailed it out of there. I slogged through the snow and ice and put everything I could in the barn and ran back out front to watch what I assumed was about to be a catastrophe."

"The roof was still slowly creaking. I stood there impotent to do anything about it. No one was about on the streets as it was late and there had been all this ice. So I watched alone as part of the roof slowly sank into the church. But I wasn't alone for long."

"What do you mean?" asked Anna.

"Well, the part that collapsed was just to the left of the bell tower, and as soon as it finally let loose, the whole place shook and rattled and the church bells rang out across the snow-laden valley. People came rushing over immediately. It was a wonderful sight as I watched the small flicker of lanterns get closer and closer to the church, the light reflecting off the snow-covered trees, neighbors racing up to the church to see what was happening. As they arrived and discovered the reason for the pealing of the bells, they stood in bedclothes and boots in the moonlight and gazed up at the roof with me, all a bit stunned and not quite sure where to start and what to do. It was actually a most religious experience. I decided a prayer was appropriate, so I led the gathered in a prayer that we could repair the church before any more snow fell. And they all pledged that they'd pitch in the next morning and get it done. And we did. We got a makeshift roof up in two days that kept the weather out, and when the snow melted, the entire congregation helped rebuild the roof back to its original, but hopefully more solid, state."

"Well, I must say, you have had quite a winter, Pastor," said Will.

"That's a marvelous story, Tom. I'm sure it was the inspiration for many sermons," said Anna.

"Absolutely. And many more to come as well," he chuckled. "But enough of our travails. May I be so bold as to ask your lovely wife for a dance, Will?"

"Anna?" Will politely asked.

"I'd love to, Tom."

"I'll be over at the refreshment table," said Will.

"Shall we?" offered Tom to Anna.

She took his arm and he led her out to the dance floor. The orchestra was playing a slow piece so it gave Anna and Tom a chance to talk.

"How are things going with the two of you?" asked Tom.

"Will is leaving tomorrow," Anna said sadly. "He has to get back to work."

"That's pretty fast. I'm sorry," said Tom.

"Thank you," said Anna.

"I'm always here if you need to talk," Tom said.

Anna sighed. "I know." She looked about the room. "Everyone is having a good time. They all look so happy."

Tom gave her a little hug. "I'm sure you'll be happy, too. One day."

"One day," Anna said. Then, still regarding the room, "Look at Margaret over there whispering at the food table with the other women. That's exactly what she was doing the first time I met her up here."

"Some people don't change," Tom said.

"I actually think I feel sorry for her," Anna said, thoughtfully.

"Why Anna, do I hear correctly?" Tom asked, overly dramatically. "Are you perhaps saying something nice about Margaret?"

"Not to worry," Anna said. "It's a momentary lapse in judgment. We'll never stop sniping at each other."

"I certainly hope not," Tom said, laughing. "Talk about not having a good time."

They both laughed.

"Come on, let's get you back to your waiting husband. It's your last night together. You should spend as much time as you can together."

"Good idea. I also don't want to give Margaret a chance to steal him away," Anna said lightheartedly.

They headed over to the refreshment table where Will was chatting with some other fellows. He was recounting the family's trip to New York City.

"You should have seen the boys' faces. The moving pictures knocked their socks off."

Anna and Tom came up to them.

Will said, "Anna, I was just describing our extraordinary trip to New York."

"It was quite a fun day," said Anna.

"Of course the most marvelous thing was our maid Millie's reaction to riding in a motor car. Wasn't she a stitch, Anna? The noise, the smells; she was petrified the whole afternoon."

He laughed briskly out loud.

"Now Will," Anna mildly scolded him. "Poor Millie is very old-fashioned. She hasn't been to the city since she was a little girl and she was quite overwhelmed. We all were."

"It is pretty spectacular." Will beamed as if New York was his own private playground full of the latest toys. "I'm heading back there tomorrow," Will said gleefully. "I've got a case starting in a couple weeks. Big merger and extremely complicated."

Eric Montgomery, one of the gentlemen listening to Will, asked, "How long will you be gone, Will?"

"Hard to tell. If both parties are agreeable, it should be less than a month. But so far, they haven't been the friendliest of associates."

"Well, I hope they won't hold you up too long, Will. We have great plans for the summer."

"I know, Eric, and I trust my labors won't make me miss too much."

Jim Stoddard spoke up. "Times sure are changing, aren't they, Will? I have the same problems in my business. Everybody wants things now. There's no patience anymore. No finesse. Its just business for business's sake. The love of doing what you are doing is slowly slipping away for love of the almighty dollar."

"Yes, everyone wants a piece of the ever-shrinking pie," said Eric.

Will said, "The pie's not shrinking. It's just that there are a lot more people who want a taste of that delicious filling. We've had it good for a long time and now we have to fight a lot harder to keep what we've got."

Tom said as an aside to Anna, "Interesting theory."

Anna shushed him. "Maybe it's not just the toys."

Will turned to his wife.

"I haven't danced with the most beautiful woman in the room yet."

Anna looked around the room and pointed to someone. Playfully, "You'll have to wait, dear. Margaret has her mouth full at the moment."

He chuckled and offered her his hand. She took it and he led her out to the dance floor. They made an extremely lovely couple and moved elegantly together. Anyone would be hard-pressed to see anything wrong with their marriage. Even Anna was amazed at the good show they were putting on.

"As much as I hate to leave," Will said to Anna, "I really can't wait to get back into the thick of things."

"I know that, Will. Don't worry about us. We'll be fine. We have Aunt Lil and all our friends to keep us company. And I've got a lot of activities planned for the boys." She stopped dancing and looked at him ruefully. "I miss you already, Will."

He just smiled sadly, seeming to understand where they were in their relationship, and took her to him and started dancing again, saying nothing.

They danced until the song ended and, as the gathered applauded the orchestra, suddenly they all heard explosions coming from outside. Everyone hurried to the windows and out the doors onto the veranda and the lawns to see what was going on. Another explosion came and they all came to realize the Wardwells were setting off pre-Fourth of July fireworks. There were red, white and blue bursts and combination blasts that lit up the St. Huberts golf course in a patriotic array of color. The show was spectacular and probably would outshine the town's own fireworks show planned for Independence Day. But nothing the Wardwells did was ever on a small scale. "Philip probably made a trek to China and picked out the fireworks personally just for this occasion," several partygoers could be heard joking.

The show ended in a breathtaking finale that seemed to go on forever. The guests were thrilled and showed it with their raucous ovation - whistling and whooping like cowboys. It was a night to remember. Once again, the Wardwells had set the standard for the rest of the stuffy society types in the valley.

CHAPTER SEVEN

Will was up bright and early and ready to take the first stage out of town. He wanted to catch the noon train to New York if he could so that he would be home in Fairfield by morning. That way he could get settled and only miss one day of work on Monday. Colleen, of course, was up before Will and had a hearty breakfast of farm-fresh eggs and bacon and homemade just-baked bread hot from the wood stove ready for him. He graciously gobbled it all down as fast as he could, eager to head out.

The boys were still sleeping so he crept into their room and tenderly kissed each goodbye. Anna watched from the doorway, loving him and resenting him at the same time. She hated being so understanding. Will came to the doorway and put his arm around her shoulders.

"You know I have to go, don't you?" he asked Anna.

"I do, Will. As I said, we'll be fine."

"I know you will."

He kissed her obligingly on the cheek and headed down the stairs. Anna didn't want to follow him, but she had to make a good impression for Colleen and Millie. She descended the stairs and got to the drive just as Will jumped onto the buckboard and snapped the reins. Colleen or Millie would pick up the rig at Bailey's later in the day. With a jaunty tip of his hat to the ladies gathered on the porch, Will was on his way. As Anna watched him disappear down the drive, dwarfed by Porter Mountain ahead of him, a sinking feeling came over her. She wasn't so sure everything was going to be fine. What would she do without him? She had a foreboding feeling like never before that changes were in the air and she had no idea what to expect. She just knew that things were going to change. For good or bad, she didn't know, but something was in the offing.

Colleen and Millie offered to make her breakfast, but Anna said she wasn't hungry. She wandered down the path to the beach by the river and sat on the rocks. The day was clear and crisp, yet warming fast. The sun caressed her and soon her long nightclothes were becoming too warm to wear. She looked around, knowing the boys wouldn't be up for a bit and then slipped out of her robe and sat only in her nightgown.

She remembered back to days early in their marriage. The two of them would sneak out to the beach when they knew no one would be around and make love on the rocky riverbank. She was sure Sam was conceived on this very spot, with Giant Mountain peering down at them as they luxuriated in the pleasure of each other. They had such fun back then, and such adventures. Will was incorrigible in the chances he liked to take at finding new places to make love. Anna loved his verve and imagination and his daring nature. She supposed that he was still the same, but he had a new love and it was technology. Now it was the excitement of the city and all its pleasures that stimulated him. Suddenly embarrassed as she thought of this while lying on the rocks in her nightclothes, she quickly wrapped herself up in her robe and headed back to the house. All that was over.

Millie was rousting the boys when Anna got to the top of the stairs. Anna went into their room and motioned for Millie to leave. She told them Will had left early and had come in and kissed them goodbye but didn't want to wake them. Sam was angry but Paul was grateful.

Paul said, "Thank goodness. We always get up so early back home when we have to go to school. It's nice to be able sleep late when we're here."

"But aren't you going to miss Father?" asked Sam.

"Well, yes, but he'll be back. Mother, can you please ask Millie not to wake us up? It's not like there's anything we have to do right away, is there?"

"No, dear, sleep all you want. You're only young once. Go ahead, go back to sleep."

She headed for the door and stopped, a thought coming into her head. "Oh, by the way, I heard last night about the show this year. They're having auditions this morning at the Club. It's 'Scenes From Romeo and Juliet.'"

Paul snarled, "I did Shakespeare last year. I don't want to do it again."

"I understand." She started heading out again and stopped again. "I guess they'll have to find someone else to be Romeo to Clara Robinson's Juliet."

Paul cocked open a curious eye. "Clara Robinson's going to be in it?"

"Well, she has to audition like everyone else, but since she's so good, I'm sure she'll get the part. But you go back to sleep, Paul."

From across the room she could almost hear the wheels turning in Paul's head. She left the room and stepped just down the hall and stopped, listening. Anna could hear Paul bound out of bed and the rustle of his nightclothes as he quickly dressed for the day. It seemed no time that he came careening out the door and ran head-on into Anna, scaring the daylights out of himself.

"Golly, Mother! What are you doing here?!"

"Waiting for you, darling," she chuckled. "I thought you were going to stay in bed."

"Uh, yes, well, I changed my mind… you know, what with it being such a nice day and all. Bye." And he dashed off, springing down the stairs.

Sam sleepily came to the door, looking out. "What's all the noise, Mother?"

"Just your brother being… Paul."

"Oh, brother," Sam said, as he turned and headed back to bed.

Anna went into her room and, out the window, saw Paul barreling down the drive on his bicycle. She smiled happily knowing Paul was going to have a good summer this year. She just wished she were going to have the same fortune available to her. But Will was gone and she was going to have to make the best of things.

Anna spent the next few weeks getting involved in all the valley activities she could to keep her mind off her troubles. She had the women over for afternoon tea and went to their houses for tea, each trying to outdo the other. Aunt Lil always had projects going on at her house, so she was a good distraction. Anna played whist once a week on Wednesday afternoons and found a worthwhile partner in Martina Sturges. They had similar playing styles and were gaining a reputation as a formidable pair. Paul got the part of Romeo and was busy wooing his Juliet, Clara. Sam fished and played pirates with the other boys his age and generally came home each afternoon covered in some sort of muck from whatever part of the valley Blackbeard was stalking that day. All was going along as it usually did every summer, which normally made Anna safe and secure. But this year was different. Will's absence made her feel off-kilter and not totally comfortable in her own skin. A big part of her was missing and none of her activities could fill that hole. She wrote him letters, at least two a week, to let him know the goings on with the boys and in the valley. Will occasionally wrote back. But their letters were always just newsy and nothing more.

The only solace she derived was the time spent with Tom. He was a great friend and kept her laughing. He also was a great listener and glad to be there whenever she needed him. "After all, it is the job the Boss gave me," he would say, pointing skyward. But it was more than that. Tom genuinely liked Anna and she him. They had a special friendship that only they could understand. And that was obvious as tongues wagged all over the valley whenever they spent any time together alone, what with Will back home for such an extended time.

This also wasn't missed by the eagle eye of Aunt Lil. She wasn't sure what was going on and was too much of a lady to ask, but she had her suspicions that all was not well with Anna and Will and that Tom wasn't helping. She was also a very strong-willed woman and when things weren't going the way she deemed acceptable, she had the wiles and means to change the course of events to her design. She loved Anna, but was not going to let her embarrass the family with any kind of scandal. The matron of Keene Valley was no one to cross swords with.

Anna knew most of the town looked askance at her and Tom, thinking the worst; hoping for the worst being the gossips they were, but Anna didn't care. She was just a lost soul at the moment looking for comfort and needed it no matter what anyone thought. But she hadn't counted on the cunning of Aunt Lil to step in and squelch any inference at impropriety and to help make Anna's life just a bit lonelier.

Aunt Lil was never subtle. Anna was setting up to have the women over for tea in the summerhouse one afternoon. She and Millie had been to Bradley's farm and gotten some summer squash and had fashioned the most intricate sweet squash tortes, decorated to look like birds' nests. They then used cookie cutters to shape chickadees out of pound cake and placed them in the nests. Anna realized something was missing and added the final touch. She colored almonds with blueberry juice and added them to the nest as eggs. Not only did they look great, they were delectable. The presentation was splendid and even the most inflexible of her guests couldn't help to be impressed.

Anna had everything displayed on the table in the summerhouse next to the babbling Ausable River. She used evergreen boughs and nestled the bird's nests amongst the pine needles on the table. Everything looked enviably flawless. She was just setting out her finest china and adding some finishing touches when she heard a buckboard approaching up the drive. She checked her pendant watch. *Who could be here this early,* she wondered? As the buckboard passed behind a grove of shrubs, Anna could see the distinctive green umbrella that Aunt Lil had fashioned as a permanent sun parasol to her carriage. As it cleared the trees, she could make out Aunt Lil, alone at the reins, as she liked to do, heading toward her.

Aunt Lil reined in the horse and dismounted the buckboard as Anna approached her.

"What a lovely surprise, Lil. No one else is due for at least half an hour," said Anna.

"That's why I came early," said Aunt Lil, a bit sternly.

"I haven't spent much time alone with you this summer with all that's been going on. This will give us a chance to catch up," said Anna.

"That's exactly what I thought," said Aunt Lil, an uncomfortable edge in her voice. She ascended the steps into the summerhouse and surveyed the table. "Well, I must say, this is beautiful. You are most inspired, my dear," she said, softening a little. Then back to her more severe self. "I'm glad to see you've had time to do other things besides conducting surreptitious assignations."

Anna paused at this. It was only a matter of time before Aunt Lil wielded her iron fist about her and Tom. She had decided on a frontal flank approach.

Anna began, calmly, "There is nothing surreptitious about it. Tom and I are being quite open about our relationship and don't feel the need to hide it from anyone."

Aunt Lil was aghast. "You mean you admit that there is something going on between you and the Pastor?!"

Now Anna was starting to enjoy this. "Has been for years. You mean you haven't noticed?"

"I knew you too were very close, but I didn't realize you were… Well, I can't even bring myself to say it. No wonder Will left so hastily."

"What do you mean, Lil? You didn't realize Tom and I were friends?"

"Of course I knew you were friends."

Then frankly, "And that's all we are, Lil. We're friends. He's my pastor and he's a good listener and he's helping me through a rough time right now."

"You mean between you and Will?"

"Yes," said Anna, downheartedly.

"It's rather obvious something is amiss between the two of you, what with his not being here for such a great length of time this summer. Have you not been fulfilling your wifely duties?"

Anna bristled. "Why is it assumed that it's my fault?" She took a deep breath. "Lil, it's neither of our faults. We've drifted apart. He's found the thrill of his work and a love of the excitement of the city and I'm more for the simpler things in life. Home, family, summers in this glorious place. He's getting anxious for more. I tried to keep up and join him in his newfound world. He's a different man when he's in it. And he's not the man I fell in love with and married. I can only hope in time that we'll find a middle ground and come back together. Until then, we have an unspoken understanding. We still love each other but at the moment, we need to take care of ourselves in our own distinct ways."

"Well, I'm certainly sorry to hear about your marital difficulties. But in my opinion, it's the wife's duty to make her husband happy."

"Lil, I know you feel that way. But I've tried. Believe me, we both have. Our love has been fading for some time. Will's work is consuming him. And since the boys have grown they need me more and… it just happened. We saw it coming and were powerless to do anything about it. We both feel the distance and just hope that we'll work our way back to each other."

"Well, I hope so. If not for your sakes, at least for the boys."

"Especially for the boys," agreed Anna.

Soon the ladies arrived for tea and were duly impressed. They gushed and "oohed" and "aahed" over Anna's imaginative and delicious presentation. Aunt Lil's tune had changed considerably and she was drinking in the compliments heaped on Anna as if she had taught her everything she knew, much of which she actually had inspired. But Anna brought her own special flair and creativity to whatever she did and Lil still couldn't help but be impressed.

The day was a complete success and Anna was now the envy of the women at tea who had a new pinnacle to overtake to compete with Anna's spectacle. She had accomplished her goal. As good as she felt today, unfortunately, it wouldn't last. Anna was soon back in a lonely depression.

CHAPTER EIGHT

As the days wore on, Anna did her best to keep up appearances. She still went to teas and spent time with Tom. She helped Paul learn his lines for "Romeo and Juliet" and struggled to make Sam take baths in the evenings after a day's worth of hard play. He was no longer playing pirates. That was for kids. He was now practicing to be a cowboy and ride the range, much to the consternation of the horses in the barn. Anna spent much of her days doing needlework in the summerhouse, reading books all day, and idly listening to the river rush past. She often took long walks up into the mountainsides, alone. Having come here since she was a child, she knew the trails quite well and was never ill at ease wherever she ventured.

Colleen and Millie noticed a change in her. They knew she was depressed and missing Will. She had gone through periods like this before. But this time, it was different. Nothing anyone could do seemed to help. The only time she put up a good front was with the boys. She never allowed her mood to interfere with their happiness. In fact she went overboard, and they loved every minute of it. However, as soon as they were off on their own, she retreated into herself and spent the days going about her daily routines as if by rote.

Tom also was worried about her. They hadn't spent much time together lately and he thought that wasn't a good sign. He tried to talk to her about it, but she just said everything would be fine, she was just having a setback and she was sure it would soon pass.

But Anna knew differently. She was lost. Will had been there beside her for much of her adult life, and now she felt abandoned and was unsure what to do about it. She did her best to keep busy. The only time she felt even a bit of contentment was when she was alone on her walks on the Adirondack trails.

Her favorite climb was to Giant's Washbowl, a large erosion out of solid rock that filled with water from the mountain high above. The crystal clear water overflowed in cascading falls down a sheer cliff into the Ausable River somewhere far below. The western rim of the washbowl offered an excellent view of the valley below and the range of high peaks above. She often brought a picnic lunch in her wicker packbasket and went up there just to be alone with her thoughts. She was sure this wasn't the best thing to be doing. She should be spending time with people and keeping busy, but still, something kept drawing her to the mountains. An irresistible urge she didn't understand, but didn't mind either. She was comfortable there and she needed this respite from the predictable life she led down below in the valley. Or perhaps it wasn't that at all, she thought. Something was calling her to the mountains. And was setting her at peace. She came back refreshed and able to take on the day-to-day routine she had once cherished, and probably still did. She just yearned for something more. Perhaps it was the same way that Will felt. That desire for something else which he found in his work and the city. Maybe they weren't all that different from each other. Just searching for something more and when they found it, who knows what would happen. Perhaps they were each going through a phase and they'd come out the other end right back where they were meant to be. Whatever was happening, she didn't want to fight it. She would follow the path, wherever it led, and take the consequences of whatever was presented.

She sat along the edge of Giant's Washbowl, taking in the vista surrounding her. Frogs were singing among the water lilies that dotted the washbowl. She could see the carriages moving along the main road through town and occasionally, if

73

the wind was right, hear the church bells ringing, calling the townspeople to a meeting or such. Some of the mountains had meadows covered in summer blooms that burst into color alongside the rich, dark green forests that shrouded most of the mountainsides. She loved looking at the huge cliff that made up the face of Porter Mountain on the other side of the valley. It magically glistened in the sun, rising from the valley floor, pushed up by some cataclysmic event millions of years ago and still on view for the world to marvel at.

On hot days, Anna brought her bathing attire and took dips in the cool, pristine water of the washbowl. The water was usually quite cold and took her breath away, but that sensation made it all the more invigorating. When she was really feeling daring, she made sure she was totally alone and boldly went skinny-dipping in the water. The freedom she felt was exhilarating. It was about the only sensation she was allowing herself to feel of late.

She spent the hours up there reminiscing of earlier days with Will. She remembered when they were young and falling in love and the magic that the Adirondacks afforded them both. She recalled though that she and Will had never come up on this particular climb together. They had conquered many of the mountains and had picnics and made love in many secluded glens or lean-tos built by guides and explorers of the past. But Giant's Washbowl was hers and hers alone. She could get away there without any inner recollections to muddy the clarity of her thoughts. This was probably what was drawing her to this spot, yet still she felt there was some more important reason to come. She didn't tell anyone where she was going for fear they would come and disturb her reverie. At the same time, many hikers used these trails and she often hid to avoid being found whenever passers-by came through. She knew she was being ridiculous, but it was fun to be so completely undetected as well as somehow necessary for her well-being.

It also offered her a chance to catch up on the latest gossip. When other hikers came by, she would hide in the bushes. She never knew there was such a voyeuristic side to her. Most often people just passed through up the climb to the top of Giant. But, occasionally, picnickers would stop to eat lunch and enjoy the view as Anna did. Then she was in for some fun.

She heard bits and pieces here and there of juicy tidbits of the sort of everyday gossip one heard in the valley, but nothing big and newsworthy. Until one particular day.

It was an especially gloomy day. It seemed a storm was brewing in the distance. Anna hadn't been up to the washbowl in a week or so, having all sorts of valley activities and commitments at home. She was feeling a great need to climb and contemplate. She figured this would be a perfect day to be alone up there since the threat of inclement weather would keep other hikers away. The climb usually took her only an hour and by eleven o'clock she was up at the washbowl. She had packed some special raingear just in case, but scanning the sky, she thought she'd have plenty of time to descend before the rain hit.

She was just unpacking her lunch when she heard voices coming up the trail. Who, besides her, she thought, would be crazy enough to climb on a day like this? Tourists, she surmised. She quickly threw her things in the pack basket and found her usual hiding place. The voices came closer, but she couldn't quite make out what they were saying. Then they came into view. Anna was in shock, yet slowly a sly smile crossed her face. This was going to be good. Walking hand in hand like high school sweethearts were none other than the infamous Margaret Bancroft and the Browns' tennis-playing son, Peter. This was shocking. No one would believe Anna. But the scandal was so good, how could they not.

Margaret and Peter spread out their blanket and settled down next to the water. They were just out of earshot from Anna so she chanced getting a better look. Anna moved stealthily through the bushes, slowly toward them. She stepped on a fallen branch that broke with a loud crack and stopped frozen, dead in her tracks. She didn't want to ruin this opportunity. Luckily, Margaret and Peter were so involved with each other that they didn't even flinch. Anna decided to play it safe and stay right where she was. She wasn't going to miss whatever was about to transpire. And did things ever.

In no time, the lovers were locked in a passionate, heated embrace. Hungry with desire, they devoured each other like two mountain animals. They ripped and tore at one another, amorously kissing and playfully biting. Peter undid Margaret's tightly coiled hair and let it drape in long, flowing tresses. She undid the front of his shirt and pulled it down his back, locking his arms at his sides. Anna gaped at Margaret's bestial behavior. This was the prim, hard-nosed woman who tormented Anna and everyone in the valley. Anna chuckled cunningly to herself as she watched Margaret push Peter to the ground and, using her teeth, erotically pull at his chest hair and gnaw at his nipples. Peter moaned in ecstasy.

Anna was surprised at herself that she couldn't turn away. She felt this was obviously not something she should be watching, but she couldn't avert her eyes. She was riveted. And thoroughly enjoying herself. What a show they were putting on. Above her in the sky, the clouds were thickening and threatening to shower. She noticed this briefly but couldn't be torn away from the free peep show.

Margaret was now unbuttoning Peter's trousers to get to the rather impressive protuberance that had grown in his pants. She unbuttoned his fly slowly and teasingly, letting her fingers lightly ripple over the bulge down below, titillating and erotically torturing him as each button came loose. Peter suddenly could stand it no more and ripped his arms from the shirt that was binding them. He grabbed Margaret by the shoulders and strongly, but tenderly, lifted her off him and gently laid her down on the blanket. He kissed her passionately with the vigor of youth. Anna watched in astonishment as the young man skillfully made love like she had only imagined.

Peter unbuttoned the front of Margaret's dress, a bit impetuously, but oh so sensuously, Anna thought. Normally women wore quite a lot of undergarments but obviously Margaret had planned ahead and wore as little as was appropriately possible. All the easier for Peter to perform his magic. He reached carefully and sensitively down under her loosened bodice, caressing her breasts, and aroused Margaret to breathy laments of rapture. Peter then slowly peeled off her corset revealing her ample bosom. Anna silently giggled at how evil she felt and reveled in every minute of it. The clouds above darkened and threw an eerie blue-gray tone upon them.

Peter suckled on Margaret's right breast as he caressed the nipple of her left breast with his fingers, twisting and tickling it. With his mouth still on Margaret's breast, Peter pushed off his trousers and lay stark naked on top of her. Seeing this beautiful hard body totally nude gave Anna a wonderful shudder throughout her body. Peter reached down and pushed aside Margaret's bloomers. Using his fingers skillfully, he massaged and entered her, causing Margaret to arch her back in total rhapsody. She then reached down and held his penis in her hand and slowly started stroking it. Anna wasn't sure how much more of this she could take. It had been so long since she had had sexual relations with Will and the sight of Peter's masculine young body was stirring her. The clouds above billowed and darkened, looking more and more menacing.

Margaret quickly helped Peter slide a rubber onto his penis and she guided Peter into her. As if in sync with the coming storm, he began an undulating rhythm, slowly at first, moving his hips up and down and from side to side. Anna was starting to perspire with the excitement of the moment. Margaret and Peter began a quicker pace and Margaret was soon screaming with delight. As excited as Anna was becoming, she couldn't help but giggle at seeing Margaret Bancroft in such a state.

Their tempo quickened and the thrill heightened as Peter continued thrashing away on top of Margaret. It now began to drizzle but the two took no notice. Peter was young and had stamina. Anna was impressed with his holding prowess. Would he ever climax? Finally, Peter began to let out unearthly animal sounds that built to a fever pitch as he finally let go with a bellow that sent a flock of mourning doves swooping out of the brush. Peter shivered in rapture and slowly withdrew and rolled off a happily exhausted Margaret. The two cuddled together for a while as the light rain cooled them off.

Anna was also exhausted from the experience. She shook her head, trying to retain her composure. As she sat protected from the rain under a large pine tree, she realized she would have to concoct a way to spread the gossip of this unbelievable encounter without giving herself away.

But first she would have to get out of there. The rain was worsening and Margaret and Peter were between her and the trail. Surely they would leave soon. She would have to wait them out. She studied the sky and predicted a small summer shower. She realized it might aid in her escape. It might distract Margaret and Peter enough to allow her to sneak by. Luckily for her, they came out of their reverie and reacted to the ever-increasing rain.

They dressed quickly but paused long enough for a last, fiery kiss. Peter grabbed the blanket just as a clap of thunder rumbled overhead. The rain was falling harder now. The sky was blackening to evil shades. Anna watched Margaret and Peter take off down the trail. She could now make her escape. The rain was coming down harder now. She wondered whether it might be smarter to wait it out where she was. This was no summer shower. If she tried to go down the mountain, she could get caught in a muddy mess on the trail. Staying protected in her hiding place might be the best thing to do, she decided.

The rain was terribly strong now. The wind started howling and the clouds were black as pitch. The tree she was under offered little protection and she was getting soaked. Well, she joked with herself, at least this would cool her off from the scene she just witnessed. She hoped Margaret and Peter were making it down okay. It wouldn't do well for them to be discovered together, huddled on a mountainside. She now started feeling guilty about planning to gossip about them.

A bolt of lightning struck somewhere up on the mountain and was immediately followed by a blast of thunder that seemed to shake the entire mountain. It was getting close. This was a big storm, Anna thought. Where did this come from so fast? Anna had two options. She could try to make it down as quickly as possible or she could find a safe place out of the increasing downpour and ride out the storm. Rain was now coming down in sheets. Small rivers of mud started to overtake the trail. She realized there was no option. She was going to have to stay right where she was until this passed. The thought was a bit terrifying. This storm was building. It was no ordinary storm. It had an intensity and swiftness Anna had never witnessed. She had better find a good place to hide. And fast.

Since she traveled it so frequently, she knew there was nothing on the trail back down. She remembered that at the back of Giant's Washbowl there was some sort of cave where the boys used to like to play. If she could just find it, it might be her only salvation in the ever-increasing, raging torrent. The wind was blowing wildly, bending the trees at incredible angles and whipping the rain into her face. It stung like hundreds of bees attacking her skin. She had to shield her eyes and even then the pelting rain was so thick, she could only see a foot or so in front of her. As best she could, she pulled herself along, grabbing onto branches and small trees, heading for where she thought the cave was.

This was a violent cloudburst, the likes of which she had never seen. The inundation of driving rain was inconceivable. As it worsened, even the small trees Anna was using to pull herself along were giving way as the ground underneath her began to wash down the mountain. She was now terrified. If she didn't find some shelter, she was sure she would be swept away.

As the rain continued to worsen, she frantically made her way toward the cliffs above the washbowl, hoping to find the cave. As she did, the lighting flashed and the thunder crashed. She was in the middle of a tempest of immense proportions. As she struggled along, she wondered what was going on down below and trusted that Colleen and Millie were taking care of the boys. She then thought of Idlenook, lying right by the river. She was sure the river would rise with all this rain. Luckily the house was built on stilts to allow the Ausable River to overflow and run under the house. But a deluge like this could flood so swiftly, she was afraid the underpinnings of the house might not stand the force. Unfortunately, there was nothing she could do about that now. She had to save herself first.

She was now almost to the edge of the cliffs and, off to the right, she could see what appeared to be a dark spot, perhaps an opening. The cave she was looking for. Her heart eased a bit as she made a fervent attempt to reach it. She was only ten yards away when she heard a rumbling from above that she took to be another roll of thunder. But somehow it was different. She protected her eyes and attempted to look up the cliff. The driving rain kept her from focusing for a moment, but for an instant, she saw something that horrified her. The blinding white rain started turning blacker, as if the sky itself was cut open and hemorrhaging. Anna realized she was about to be engulfed by much of what made up Giant Mountain. She quickly tried to flatten herself against the rock face, but to little avail. The flow of mud and debris was overwhelming. It came rumbling down in a massive tide of muck, rocks, and trees. No matter how hard she tried to hold onto anything she could, everything gave way, washing away down the mountainside. As the torrents washed Anna with them, she was banged into trees and sometimes submerged under the mud. She couldn't see and couldn't breathe. She struggled and was afraid she was losing the battle for her life.

The mudslide just wouldn't desist as the rain continued to pour down. Anna became a small component of this tremendous surge. She felt like a cell flowing in the blood of the earth. As she bumped and washed her way along, she couldn't believe the unreality of it all and that she was having these kinds of thoughts. She felt so defeated that she stopped fighting and, dreamlike, allowed herself to be swept away. She thought of her boys and Will and was positive she would never see them again. Anna remembered a specific incident when she was twelve. She had found a puppy that had wandered into the yard. It was small and white and fluffy. She fashioned a leash out of a leather rein from the stable and walked the puppy all over town looking for its owner. No one claimed the dog. No one even recognized the dog. Since she couldn't find the owners, her parents let her keep the puppy. She called it

Fortune because she felt it was her good fortune to find such a wonderful animal. She and Fortune played and romped around the yard. Fortune slept at the end of Anna's bed. They became inseparable.

Unfortunately, fortune didn't shine on Anna and Fortune. The dog's original owners who had been visiting relatives in town heard weeks later that Anna had found a dog and came looking for her. Anna was playing in the front yard when Fortune's owners came by. Fortune went bounding across the lawn to them, leaving Anna confused and alone. They told her the dog's name was Snowball and their little boy was heartsick at having lost her. She must have jumped out of the carriage when they were passing by and they'd been searching for the puppy ever since. They thanked Anna for taking such good care of Snowball and started to put the dog into the carriage. The dog stopped, looking back at Anna as if to say, "Aren't you coming?" Anna sadly waved goodbye as the carriage carrying her best friend moved off down the lane. She stood watching, crying, long after she could no longer see them.

Anna surfaced out of the rolling mud and wondered why she had that recollection. She was still being flung every which way by the wash she was caught in. She felt all was lost. She was losing consciousness. She screamed to try to keep herself awake and alive, but she hadn't the strength to endure anymore. As she slipped beneath the mud one more time, she was suddenly yanked out as if something grabbed her by the arm. In all the turmoil, she couldn't see what was happening. She just felt that she was somehow being lifted out of the rushing deluge and away from it. The rain was still driving, making seeing nearly impossible and, in her state, she was barely conscious. All she knew was she was free of the whipping mud and on solid ground. Through her blurred state of mind and the teeming rain, she tried in vain to see. In her fogged vision, a face appeared. It was a strong, kind face with square features covered in mud. She tried to smile and whispered, "Thank you." Then all went black.

CHAPTER NINE

Anna awoke. She felt as if she were drugged. She was stiff and her body ached all over. At first she had trouble focusing on anything. She was lying on her back and thought she could make out that she was in a kind of lean-to. She was on some blankets with a pillow under her head. It was night and the sky became clearer. It was brilliant with stars visible through the towering pines. Somehow the inside of the lean-to was lighted. As she turned her head, she saw a fire burning in front of the structure. She lay still taking this all in. Where was she? What had happened? The last thing she remembered was washing down the mountain in a torrent of mud. How did she get here?

Obviously somebody had found her and taken care of her. As she was now starting to realize, she was pretty well cleaned up. There wasn't any mud anywhere on her or her clothes. Although she was happy to be clean, she was a bit disturbed to think that someone had washed her while she was unconscious. How long had she been there? And where was her savior?

Her head hurt terribly and she could see that she was bruised all over. She tried sitting up and a searing pain shot through her. She quickly grabbed her chest where the pain came from. She must have broken some ribs. She slowly lay back down, trying to ease her distress. It felt better lying down. What was she going to do? She hurt too badly to move. She wondered if the person who had saved her would come back. Whoever it was couldn't have been gone too long. The fire was blazing and looked newly stoked. She only hoped that whoever it was would return soon. She wanted to know what had happened and was impatient for answers.

She figured whoever had found her wasn't someone she knew or they would have alerted others who would have been here by now. Now? When was now? How long had she been here? A day? Two? More? Her boys must be so worried about her. And what about them? The storm had been incredible. She had never seen a cloudburst like that. At about the time it had hit, the boys could have been anywhere in the valley. And what about the house? Had the river overflowed its banks and washed away Idlenook? She was making herself frantic. She had to calm down. There was nothing she could do about it now. It was very frustrating.

She tried moving both of her arms and her legs. They amazingly seemed okay. At least she hadn't broken them. They were pretty sore and probably bruised, but she figured she could walk if she could get over the pain in her rib cage. She decided to try again, this time more carefully. She slowly inched herself over to the edge of the lean-to and gingerly turned her body so her legs were over the side. She was able to lower her feet to the ground by bending her legs at the knees, still lying flat on her back so her ribs didn't hurt too badly. She figured if she could scoot herself to the edge of the lean-to, she could use some leverage to help herself stand. If it didn't work, she wouldn't be in any worse shape than she was in already.

Anna tried very cautiously to sit up. The grimace on her face showed the pain she was feeling, but she didn't make a sound. It was just too painful so she lay back down. She now moved herself forward until her bottom was just hanging over the edge of the lean-to and, using the strength in her bruised and aching legs, slowly lowered herself to the ground, about a foot below. At least she was now sitting up. Resting against the front of the lean-to kept her ribs from hurting too badly. Now that her body was in an upright position, perhaps she could reach behind herself and use the lean-to to help her stand. She lifted her arms as high as she could behind her. The pain was excruciating. But she needed to stand and try to get down the mountain and to her boys. Whoever had rescued her appeared to have been very kind, but she didn't want to take any chances.

She struggled silently again, straining against the agony in her ribs. She was bound and determined to get up. Pushing with both her arms and her legs, Anna was able to lift herself almost to a standing position, but the pain was searing. She was unable to take it anymore, and she felt herself slipping out of consciousness. She battled to stay aware, but it was too much. Her eyes rolled up into her head and she fainted, collapsing on the ground in front of the lean-to.

● ● ● ● ●

When Anna awoke, she was back in the lean-to lying on her back. It was daylight. A warm sunny day and from the look of the shadows from the tall pines, it was late afternoon. She seemed to ache worse than she remembered the last time she awoke. Her little stunt probably hadn't been such a good idea after all. Anna lay there staring at the sky, her body suffering, and she felt defeated and lost. So many questions were in her head. Where was she? How long had she been here? Who helped her? And where was he? Or she?

Anna screamed out in frustration, "Where are you?!"

Quietly, a voice, from not too far away said, "I'm right here."

It was a pleasant, reassuring voice. Deep and resonant. Anna was at first startled, but as the tone of the voice sank in, she felt a great sense of relief and solace. She slowly turned her head to see who had spoken.

Sitting on the ground by the now extinguished fire was the man who came with the voice. She stared for a few moments. She had seen this face before. But where? she wondered. Then it came to her. Just before she blacked out after being washed down the mountain, this face appeared before her. He must have been there just as she fell and rescued her.

"Thank you," Anna said.

The man just smiled slightly and bowed his head. He was a broad-shouldered man with a dark complexion. Anna thought he was probably an Indian. He had very black, long hair, and strong, almost regal, features. He wore expensive hiking clothes and boots and had a pack basket next to him not unlike the type the very wealthy valley tourists used. She had never seen anyone like him. Most of the Indians she had seen were either beggars or drunkards. Maybe he wasn't Indian at all. Perhaps he was European.

The man took a canteen and a metal cup out of his pack basket and poured some water into the cup. He stood up and walked over to Anna with the cup. She noticed how tall and well-built he was.

In perfect American English he said, "I'm sure you'd like some water," as he offered her the cup.

Anna said, "Thank you," as she took the cup and drank. She handed the cup back to the man.

"How are you feeling?" he asked.

"Quite sore," replied Anna. "My head hurts and I'm afraid I might have broken my ribs."

"Yes, you did," he said. "I bandaged them for you."

Anna felt her ribs and realized they were wrapped in bandages. "I didn't even realize. I can't thank you enough. You saved my life."

He didn't reply. He just took the cup from her and returned to where he was sitting.

"I must have been a muddy mess when you found me. My clothes seem to be all clean now." Hesitantly, "Did you do that?"

"Yes, I did," he said matter-of-factly.

Anna realized this had been necessary, but she still felt uncomfortable. "Well, I certainly appreciate that. It just makes me feel a bit, well…"

He responded, sincerely. "I apologize if that makes you feel at all uncomfortable. I was only doing what I felt was essential at the time. I realize you don't know me at all, but I assure you I acted with the utmost propriety."

"Oh, I didn't mean to imply that you didn't. It's just that, well, please forgive my even questioning you. After all, look at all that you've done for me."

"Madam, there is nothing to forgive. Your concerns are perfectly reasonable."

"I appreciate that," said Anna. "I tried standing before and I guess I fainted. The pain is quite bad."

"I had wondered why I found you on the ground."

"How long have I been here?"

"The storm was three days ago. Today is Friday."

"Oh, no. My family must be frantic wondering what happened to me." She was about to tell him that she hadn't told anyone where she was going, but thought better of it, not knowing his intentions yet. Deep inside, though, she felt quite safe with this man. There was something strangely familiar about him that she couldn't put her finger on. But mostly it was his kind voice and soothing manner that comforted her. He had saved her life and cared for her for three days. He must be a good man.

"Where is your family," he asked.

"In Keene Valley. I hope they're all okay after that terrible storm. They are all I was thinking about as I was being washed down the mountain."

"I could go and try to find them, but I'm afraid to leave you for that long. Plus, the trail has washed away. And I don't think I should move you very much, as your broken ribs are close to your heart and lungs. I think it's best that we wait a few more days and hope that someone comes by looking for you."

"A few days. Oh my. I suppose you're right but I'm sick with worry about my boys."

"Boys?"

"My sons, Paul and Sam."

"Are they alone down there?"

"No, the housekeepers are there, and I have other family in the valley. I'm sure they're being looked after." She said this, but she was really trying to convince herself.

"I'm sure they're fine, other than being worried about you. But right now we have to concentrate on making you better so we can get you back home. If you don't mind, I'd like to check your bandages after your fall last night."

"That's probably a good idea."

He sat down next to her. "Shall I unbutton your blouse or would you feel more comfortable doing it?"

"I think I'd prefer to do it, if I'm able."

It was a bit painful, but Anna had little trouble unbuttoning her blouse. As she did, she saw how well wrapped up she was and that he had wrapped her over her undergarments. This gave her a great sense of relief. He must be a gentleman, she thought.

"I'm going to have to lift you up so that I can undo the bandages. Is that all right?"

"Yes, replied Anna.

He reached under her shoulders and, very carefully, elevated her up. Anna winced at the pain, but didn't make a sound.

"This won't take long,' he said.

Anna realized how strong his arms were as he held her up with one and carefully unwrapped her with the other. When he had the bandage removed, he laid her back down and sensitively felt her broken ribs. He methodically moved his hand along each rib to ensure that they were positioned correctly. Anna cringed a few times when he passed over a sensitive spot, at which point he would sympathetically pause, then continue when her flinching subsided. She loved the feel of his large hands on her pained body. They almost had a healing effect themselves. As he moved his hands slowly around her, even though she was in such pain, she couldn't help but feel somewhat aroused. But it wasn't really erotic. It was more the truest feeling of care and loving that she was feeling from him.

"Everything seems to be in place and should be healing correctly," he reassured her. I'm going to replace the dressing now."

"Okay."

As he slowly lifted her again and began rewrapping her, Anna watched this gentle man's face and felt truly grateful that God sent such an angel to her. How lucky she had been! At the moment of crisis, he appeared out of nowhere and hadn't left her since. How could she be so fortunate? She only hoped her family and friends were all okay as well.

"That will do for now, I think," he said as he gently laid her back down.

"I can't thank you enough."

"You're welcome. I think you should eat something. You've been unconscious for several days and need some strength." He went to his pack basket and retrieved some provisions. "Here is some bread for now. I'll get the fire going and make some soup."

Taking the bread, Anna thanked him.

"Don't eat too fast. You have to work back up to it slowly. And take small bites. It'll be easier going down."

"Okay," agreed Anna as she started to eat the bread. "Mmm, sweet. What kind of bread is this?"

"It's called monkey bread, although for the life of me, I don't know why. My mother learned to make it back in Boston."

"Boston? Is that where you're from?"

He started trying to light the already prepared fire. "That's where I lived most of my life. But originally my family came from here in the Adirondacks. We came up here for visits often as I grew up."

"So did my husband's family. Perhaps you know them. The Tattersalls."

He smiled sweetly at her naïveté. "I'm not sure that we run in the same circles."

Anna realized her faux pas. Of course families like the Tattersalls wouldn't associate with Indians. "Oh, I'm so sorry. I wasn't thinking."

"Please don't worry about it. I may have gone to the right schools and lived in the proper neighborhoods, but American Indians are still outcasts amongst most of society. People have pictures in their minds of us from books of savages roaming the country, looking to scalp every white man we see. Even being at the top of my class at Harvard didn't make any difference. On graduation day, some jokers pulled the tassel out of my mortarboard and stuck in a feather. It was humiliating, but I got them back."

Intrigued, Anna inquired, "What did you do?"

"I went to a wig shop and bought a toupee. I placed it in a hatbox and spread a little tomato sauce on it. I sent it to the worst of the offenders. The one I surmised put the feather in my cap. In the box I enclosed a note reading, 'An eye for an eye, and a feather for your father's scalp.'"

Anna giggled. She was enjoying this. "What did he do?"

"I hid across the street from the fraternity this man lived in. Immediately after the box was delivered, he took off, running down the street, headed for home to check on his father, the box clutched under his arm. I can only imagine the scene when he got home. I had a good laugh out of it. But I probably set back the plight of the Indians in the process. Aw, well, it was worth it." And he laughed to himself, shaking his head.

"You're quite a practical joker, aren't you?"

"Not normally, but he had it coming."

The fire was now going. He pulled a pan out of his basket, and a glass jar. He opened the jar and poured the contents, which looked like vegetables, into the pan along with some water and placed it on the fire. "Vegetable soup. This ought to help you heal."

"It's very kind of you."

Anna lay back in the lean-to and relaxed. The smell of the soup wafted over to her. "I don't mean to sound offensive, but I have to ask. How did you get into Harvard? I mean, they are quite strict on their admission policies."

"They certainly are. But as they say, money can buy anything. And my family is quite wealthy. Let's just say, they wouldn't turn down my father's offer, no matter who I was."

"Where did your family's wealth come from, if I may ask?"

"Of course. As I said, we originally came from the Adirondacks. In fact, my family, or tribe, managed to hold onto quite a substantial part of it after the French and Indian War. We held major land and logging rights for years. We also had acquired holdings in large corporations and had many other investments. When the Forever Wild campaign began and people started to appreciate the Adirondacks for their beauty and wanted to preserve the wonderful wilderness here, we donated our land back to the state of New York as a gesture of goodwill. That also helped clinch my getting into Harvard. Along with the fact that many members of my family sit on the boards of some of the top corporations in this country."

"Well, I must say, that's quite impressive. And what do you do now?"

"I've continued on in the family businesses. I studied business in university so I could handle our affairs when my father and grandfather no longer could. It requires a lot of my time, but I always manage to spend summers in the Adirondacks. It will always be in my blood."

"I feel the same way. There's something magical about these mountains, unlike anywhere else. Since my first visit as a child I've been undeniably drawn here. Summers that I had to spend back in Philadelphia with relatives were unbearable. I don't deny that I had a good time, but there is always a special comfort the Adirondacks and Keene Valley give me."

He ladled some soup for her into a canteen cap. "I understand. I, of course, was born here and spent my life here until I was six. The mountains will always be with me. In me. Part of me. And ever since we left, we still come up here every summer, as your family does." He handed her the soup.

"Thank you. Where is your house?"

"We have a large camp at the Upper Lake."

"We've been up to the lakes many times for picnics and overnights. It's beautiful there. Thank you for the soup. It's perfect. How did you happen to be at Giant's Washbowl during the storm?"

"The same as you, I suppose. I was out for a climb. I had spent the night here and was nearing the top of Giant when the skies started to turn. I didn't realize what was coming. I don't think anybody did. I immediately started heading down the trail. I could see it was getting worse and worse very quickly. I had reached the washbowl just as the clouds let go. I was trying to find a place to hide when the mountain seemed to detach itself and terrifyingly came washing down. I was running, looking for a place to hide when you landed at my feet. You passed out and were about to be washed further away but I was just able to grab hold of you."

"I'm sure I would be dead if you hadn't been there. How did you keep from washing down the mountainside yourself?"

"I held onto you with one hand and a strong tree with the other. And as luck would have it, just on the other side of the waterfall of mud, there was an indent in the cliff. I was able to swing us through the mud and behind the waterfall. There was an area about six feet deep into the rocks where we remained in safety until the deluge subsided."

"That's the cave I was trying to find."

"Actually, if you hadn't fallen at my feet, I never would have had a reason to find that cave. I probably would have kept running and who knows what could have happened. So in effect, you helped save both our lives."

"I believe we were both in the hands of God at that moment."

"There was definitely some greater force at work that day. Why were you up on the mountain all alone, if I may ask?"

"I just needed time to get away and to think. I always come back renewed from my walks in the woods."

"Do you come up here often?"

"The washbowl is one of my favorite spots."

"So if you come here frequently, wouldn't someone know where to look for you?"

"No. It's my secret escape and I, foolishly now, realize, I never told anyone where I go. I did see some people from down in the valley up here. They left just as the storm was hitting. I hope they made it down."

"Wouldn't they tell someone you are up here?" he asked.

"No. I hid from them," Anna said. "As I said, I like to keep this place my little secret. What about your family? Won't they be worried about you missing all this time?"

"I'm up here alone this trip so no one even knows I'm missing. I wish I could get down the mountain to tell your family that you're all right. But the trail has been totally obliterated. It's covered with mud and rocks and broken trees and limbs. This was quite a powerful storm. I think it would be too dangerous to try to navigate at this point, especially in your condition." And then he added, jokingly, "I know as an Indian I'm supposed to be able to track through uncharted woods, but I guess being in the city so long has made me lose my instincts."

Anna thought he was chiding her, but wasn't sure. "You are joking, aren't you?"

He just gave her a look.

"All right. I get it. You're quite charming, you know."

"Thank you. Now I think you should get some sleep. One thing my instincts do tell me is that sleep is the best healer for someone in your condition."

"I really wish I could get down to my boys," Anna said. "I'm so worried about them. But my ribs hurt a lot. I'm not sure I could move yet."

"You also have a large bump on your head," he said.

"I know," she said, feeling it. "I hope I don't have a concussion."

"We should be careful, but we'll go as soon as you feel you're ready," he said. "Now get some sleep."

"I am feeling rather tired. And thank you for the soup. I can already feel its healing powers working wonders on me."

"I'm glad. Would you need a blanket?"

"No thank you. It's such a lovely day, I'm plenty warm enough." Anna closed her eyes and smiled, reflecting on the luck that had befallen her – or whose arms she had fallen into. As she lay there thinking of his amazing story, she suddenly realized they hadn't even exchanged names. She opened her eyes and looked around. He was nowhere to be found. She hadn't even heard him leave. Obviously some of his

Adirondack ways were still with him. She smiled, closed her eyes again and was soon asleep.

CHAPTER TEN

Anna opened her eyes and it was night. She lay there for a moment, terribly stiff from the pain of her fall. A wonderful smell of venison wafted past her. She turned her head and saw the Indian cooking over the fire.

"Mmm," cooed Anna. "That sure smells delicious."

"Hungry?"

"Actually, I'm famished."

"This ought to be ready soon. I figured you could use some real sustenance."

"I think you're right."

The Indian leaned back on a rock and watched the fire.

Anna said, "You know, we haven't been properly introduced."

"My goodness, you're right. After all we've been through, we know each other better than most people, but excuse my manners." He stood up and walked over to Anna, extending his hand in greeting.

Anna took his hand. "How do you do. My name is Anna Tattersall."

"Anna Tattersall, it's so good to formally meet you. And my name is Ausable Hancock."

Anna was taken aback. She froze, still holding his hand.

"Is something the matter, Mrs. Tattersall?

"Did you say Ausable Hancock?"

"Yes." Then thinking, "Oh, well, Hancock isn't my birth name. We changed it to that to make it easier for people to accept us."

"That's not what gives me pause," said Anna. She smiled. "It's your first name. Ausable."

"Oh, yes. Well, as I said, I am an Adirondack Indian and was born here. My parents named all of us after rivers and mountains up here."

Anna just stared in disbelief. Ausable looked back at her, confused.

"Ausable," said Anna.

"Yes," he answered.

"I knew there was something familiar about you. It's been in the back of my mind since we met. I thought it was because I saw your face before I blacked out, but now I realize that there's more."

"What do you mean?"

"Ausable. I know this may sound crazy, but I think we've met before."

"We have? I'm sure I would remember meeting you, Mrs. Tattersall."

"I think we've been through enough. Please call me Anna."

"Anna. Where did we meet?"

"It was right here in Keene Valley."

"Are you sure? I don't mix in much with people in the valley."

"It was quite a while ago. I was just a girl and it was one of my first visits up here. I was alone down by the river near Will's – my husband's – family's house. I found a campfire smoldering and, thinking it was abandoned, I doused it with water. As I was doing that, a young Indian boy came out of the woods. He spoke wonderful English and his family was from Massachusetts. And his name was Ausable, after the river on which we stood. Are you a painter?"

Ausable studied Anna.

Anna continued. "You gave me a painting of this very mountain. I have it hanging in our house here in Keene Valley. I still carry the memory of our meeting. It made the Adirondacks an even more special place." Anna paused, and then said, "Well, I'm sure you don't remember. My running into an Indian boy was rather more unusual for me than you running into a girl from…"

Ausable cut her off. "Philadelphia. Yes. Anna Glover of Philadelphia."

Anna was stunned. She put her hands up to her face and slowly shook her head. "It really is you."

Ausable said, "I must admit, I've thought of you over the years when I came up here. I wondered if I'd ever run into you again."

"I wished I'd run into you, too. Although I never thought it would be quite such a dramatic reunion."

"I agree. But I must say, I'm glad it happened. You've grown into a beautiful woman, Anna."

Anna blushed. "Bruises and all?"

"Bruises and all."

"In fact, Anna. I painted you while you were sleeping." Ausable went to the other side of the lean-to and pulled out a piece of birch bark. "I hope you don't mind." He turned it to show to Anna. Anna was overjoyed.

"Oh my, Ausable. It's me!"

He handed it to her.

"I was lucky my paints stayed in my backpack with the canteen and other things as I slid down the mountain.

"It's wonderful. You really are a brilliant painter."

"Oh no. It's just something I enjoy and it keeps me busy."

"It's splendid. And so are you," exclaimed Anna.

"Thank you," Ausable said, smiling at her.

She lay on the floor of the lean-to, looking at his painting of her. She then looked up at him. This vision from the past, seated next to her. Anna smiled. "This is like a dream come true."

"I feel the same myself. And you still have the painting I gave you years ago?"

"I do. I treasure it," Anna said.

"Please, take this one, too."

A longing gaze passed between them. Neither knew quite what to make of it. But they both understood that the other felt the same way. The moment in time that they shared so many years ago still meandered around somewhere deep within each of them. Somehow enchanted, somehow magical, somehow unforgettable. Things like this don't happen in real life. People don't actually run into a moment frozen in time, a moment etched in their brains, decades later, do they? Anna thought maybe the fall was playing tricks on her. Was this real? Was Ausable really there? She reached up and touched her hand gently on his cheek. He nuzzled her hand slightly. He was there. She could feel him.

Anna withdrew her hand and shook her head as if trying to shake off a daydream. She looked back up at him, still there, still smiling sweetly down at her. Heat welled up inside her. She was scared. She was anxious. She was excited. The sounds of the breeze through the woods played music in her head. Anna's skin was tingling. She felt more a part of the Adirondacks than she had ever felt before. And staring down at her was one of the main reasons she adored the mountains. Remembrances come to life.

Anna reached up again and stroked Ausable's cheek. He took her hand in his and closed his eyes. He slowly turned his head and lightly kissed her hand. Anna lost her breath and gave a tiny shiver. She reached up behind his neck and pulled him willingly toward her. They both paused, just inches from each other. This was wrong. This was right. Yes, this felt so right.

They stared into each other's eyes for what seemed like a lifetime, yet it was only a moment. Anna raised her head to meet his and they kissed. Softly and deliciously, they kissed. Anna felt his strong muscular body enfolding her very gently. She felt warm and safe. She felt at home, for the first time in a very long time. They kissed more and more passionately. It was all so natural as if they had known each other forever. They were soul mates, meant to be together. And a strange sort of fate had arranged it for them.

Anna's mind raced and yet she was ultimately consumed by a feeling she wasn't sure she had ever felt before. True comfort, true excitement, true passion. There was nothing else at this moment in the world but the mountains and the two of them. Any pain she felt from the fall had drifted away. She was floating on a cloud of ecstasy.

Ausable began kissing the side of her neck. A wave of rapture coursed though Anna as he caressed her neck, moving slowly up to her earlobe. He was so gentle and loving, yet powerful and strong at the same time.

Anna's mind was racing. She had never made love to anyone but Will. And Will was nothing like this. He was reserved. Loving and gentle, but detached. This was more powerful than any emotion Anna had ever felt in her life. She turned her head to meet Ausable's lips, which were lightly brushing her ear. They kissed each other, softly at first, with tender little pecks. Then at the same moment, their lips pushed hard against each other's. They kissed passionately and with abandon, holding each other as tightly as possible. This was wonderful. They were lost in each other. They were the only two people in the world.

Then almost suddenly, Ausable stopped and picked his head up, as if he heard something. Anna was startled and came slowly out of her reverie. She watched Ausable sniff the air. What was he doing? He turned and looked toward the fire, then smiled.

"I hope you weren't too hungry."

Anna turned her head toward the fire and saw what he was looking at. The venison was on fire.

"Let me see if I can do something about that."

He got up and walked over to the burning meat as Anna watched, an amused smile on her face. Ausable lifted the meat from the fire by the stick it was cooking on and was able to extinguish the flames.

"I'm sure there's something edible in here that we can salvage."

Anna said, "Somehow at the moment, I forgot all about eating, Ausable."

Ausable smiled at her. "But you do need to eat something. You've been through a terrible fall and you need some nourishment. I'll cut deep inside and see what I can find."

Anna just lay back and heaved a warm, ecstatic sigh, still tingling from their encounter.

Ausable was able to find quite a lot of delicious venison, which he served to Anna on a large piece of washed birch bark. He sat behind her and carefully rested her back on his thigh so that she could sit up enough to eat. Anna winced a bit at the pain but she really was hungry and quickly ate the appetizing meat.

She set the bark down. "Oh my, that was good. I really did need this." She paused a moment, then laid her head back in his lap, looking up at him, he down at her.

Anna said, "Isn't it odd what life deals out to us? Who would have thought that such an astonishing thing as meeting you again could ever have happened? And how it happened. Could anything be more dramatic? My goodness, when I think of what might have occurred if you weren't there to rescue me. And then on top of it all, that it was you after all these years. You fascinated me years ago and you still do. What wonderful providence."

Ausable didn't say anything. He just smiled back at this beautiful woman, leant down and kissed her. She reached her arms up around his neck and they embraced, just as passionately, if not more so, as before.

They spent most of the night in each other's arms, talking about what had gone on in the years since they met at the river so long ago. But the more Anna spoke of Will and the boys, the more uncomfortable she became. She again told Ausable she was worried about her family. Because of the cloudburst, they probably thought the rushing water had washed her away. They may be dragging the river looking for her body. And she also was concerned about what might have happened down in the valley from all the rain. Their house was right on the river. It may have sustained some damage if it was still there at all.

Ausable was reassuring but had to remind her, there wasn't a lot they could do. He could go for help, but she was injured and he was afraid to leave her alone. Perhaps when it was light out, he could try to wrap her up more so that her ribs wouldn't hurt so badly and try to carry her down the mountain. He didn't really want to chance it in the dark. He did have the instincts of an Adirondack, but they were a little rusty. And even so, he didn't think it would be a smart thing to do. All that rain had washed away the trails and there could be trees down. He promised her they would try at daybreak.

But there was a bigger issue to discuss that went unsaid. What about the two of them? Neither would bring it up. There really was nothing to discuss. They had been through an incredible adventure, both physically and sensually. But both knew it couldn't go on. They were both quiet, both thinking the same thing, neither wanting to discuss what would happen in the harsh reality of dawn. They just lay down together, holding each other, and drifted off to sleep.

CHAPTER ELEVEN

Morning broke as Anna awoke. Once again, she was lying there alone. She didn't see Ausable.

Anna called out, "Ausable?"

His answer came from a little way down the mountain. "You're awake."

Ausable came out of the brush toward the west. "I was trying to see what damage has been done to our trail. There are a lot of downed trees, but I think I found a way we can get through. Of course, I don't know what we'll come upon further down. We'll just have to take our chances."

He sat down next to her. "How are you feeling today?"

She tried to stretch, then winced. "About the same, I guess," she said.

She took his hand and held it to her cheek. She kissed the palm of his hand. He bent down and they kissed. A long, soft kiss.

"I'll never forget you, Anna Tattersall," Ausable said bravely.

"I don't think I can say goodbye, Ausable."

"I feel the same. But we must. It's time to get you back to your family."

Ausable got up and retrieved his jacket. "I'll use this to wrap you in. Hopefully it will help bind the broken bones and keep them in place on the trip down."

Ausable skillfully wrapped the large jacket around Anna's upper body, just under her arms.

As he pulled it tighter, he said, "Let me know when it's too tight." He knotted the sleeves and pulled it slowly tighter until Anna squeaked.

"Tight enough?" he asked.

"Yes, I think that's about all I can take," replied Anna.

He tied off the jacket sleeves and looked her over. "Not very flattering, but I think it might work," he said.

Anna giggled. "I can't thank you enough."

"Sorry. But now I have to lift you. Are you ready?" asked Ausable.

"I'm ready," Anna said as she prepared for some pain.

"I think I am going to have to carry you on my back." Ausable squatted down in front of the lean-to, "Now let me hold your legs and you put your arms around my neck."

"Mmm. I actually might like this," said Anna as she sat on the edge of the lean-to. She let him hold her legs, then put her arms over his generous shoulders. Ausable stood up slowly and Anna moaned a bit.

"Everything okay, Anna?" asked Ausable.

She let out a heavy breath and girded her loins. "Yes, I have to do this. I'll be fine. Thank you."

"Okay. Let's take you home." He grabbed his backpack and put it over his arms in front of him. And slowly he started walking out of the campsite and down the mountain.

The cloudburst had washed a lot of the earth off the rock formations on Giant. There were new slides all over the area. Some weren't at too much of an angle, so Ausable could navigate down them. Others had huge, fallen trees that he used as ledges to make their way down. Ausable was very strong and skillful and they were making progress. Slow progress. But they were gradually getting down the mountain.

Anna said, "You are astounding. I can't believe you are finding a way down through all this mess and debris."

"I'm pretty impressed myself," Ausable said proudly. "Are you doing all right?"

"I'm doing fine," Anna answered. "Do you need to stop and rest? We've been going for over an hour."

"No, let's keep going."

They zigzagged through the forest, finding a new route to the valley floor, over, under, and on fallen trees, rocks, and piles of pine branches, leaves, and twigs.

Anna said, "You are wonderful to do this. I can't thank you enough for everything," as she squeezed his neck a bit tighter.

"You're welcome, dear Anna," he said tilting his head and nuzzling his cheek on her arm.

They kept moving and now in the distance they started to hear water rushing. Ausable stopped.

"I think we're getting close. I can hear the Bradley Brook."

Anna listened. "That doesn't sound like a brook anymore. It sounds like a torrent."

"There was a tremendous amount of rain. It must still be washing down the mountain," Ausable surmised.

"I hope we can cross it when we get there. I wonder if bridges have been washed out," said Anna.

"I don't recognize anything here. It's all changed," said Ausable. "Let's head to the river and see if we can tell where we are."

They maneuvered through more wreckage, trees thrown around and blocking their way. Finally they came to the edge of the river. It was rushing by, filled with fragments of the forest.

"Let me set you down on this rock, Anna," said Ausable.

He carefully squatted and let Anna slip herself off onto a large boulder. Anna moaned a little, trying to keep it to herself.

"I know it still hurts. I'm sorry. We'll get you help soon," Ausable said.

Anna reached out and squeezed his hand.

They looked across the river, trying to recognize something.

Anna said, "I think we might be near Chapel Pond."

"I think you're right. At least we're close to where we should be," Ausable said. "The road is washed away. But it does look much easier to traverse than this side of the river."

"There should be a bridge not too far from here. If it's still there," Anna said. "But it's in the wrong direction."

"It might be better to go north," said Ausable. "Hopefully we'll come upon some sort of road. And perhaps people."

"Things are in such a state here. I'm even more worried about my boys. And I can't imagine what my house looks like. I hope everyone is alright," Anna said, anxiously.

"Let's not waste a moment more," Ausable said encouragingly. "Hop on and let's go."

He squatted down and helped Anna onto his back. The walk was slightly easier since they were on flat ground. But there were still a lot of trees and rocks to circumnavigate.

As they moved along the rushing brook, they got to where it crossed under the road. There was no sign of the bridge that used to be there. Not even pieces of it lying nearby.

"This doesn't bode well," Anna worried.

"The cloudburst seemed very localized. We can only hope for the best," encouraged Ausable.

They were able to make their way along the Chapel Pond road toward Keene Valley. It seemed that logs and rubble had been moved in some spots. So work had begun repairing the road. But it would be a long time before wagons made their way along this road again.

Suddenly Ausable said, "I hear horses. Someone might be up ahead."

They soon came upon three lone horses grazing in a meadow amongst the broken trees. They weren't tied up or wearing riding gear.

"They probably got away during the storm," Anna presumed.

"Well, they are a blessing. You can ride one instead of riding me to get home," Ausable said as he lowered Anna to the ground.

"I've actually enjoyed the ride," Anna said smiling coyly.

Ausable chuckled. "I liked it too." He kissed her on the forehead.

"Let's see if we can get these horses to help us," Anna said. "It's a meadow here. I think I can make it to the horses."

Ausable helped her stand. Anna winced and tried to take a step, leaning on him.

They walked, Ausable helping Anna, to where the horses were grazing. These were obviously tame horses. They were not afraid of the two people approaching. Anna and Ausable patted the horses to assure them.

"I think we'll be able to ride them easily," said Ausable. "Might be a little difficult without saddles, but they'll help us. Which one do you like?"

"This gray one seems amiable," Anna said.

"Okay. Let's see if we can get you up there."

He helped her walk to the side of the horse.

"I'll try to boost you up there," Ausable said. "This is going to hurt."

"I'm ready," Anna stated.

Ausable put his arms around Anna's legs, not wanting to squeeze her ribs, and slowly lifted her up the side of the horse.

"Here you go," said Ausable.

And just as Anna was about to grab onto the horses back, the horse moved away from them, leaving Anna hanging in the air for a moment. Ausable stumbled and they fell backward. Ausable, in trying to keep Anna from getting hurt further, let her fall on top of him. They just missed a downed tree and fell onto the soft meadow.

"Oh dear," said a startled Anna. "Ouch, that hurt. Are you okay?"

They were lying there, Anna on top of Ausable, in his arms.

"I couldn't be better," Ausable said, squeezing her gently. "What about you?"

Anna felt her ribs. "I didn't hit my ribs, thanks to you. I think everything is where it should be," said Anna. Then coquettishly, "Especially me."

Ausable helped her down to his side, onto the soft meadow.

"I think we ought to rest a bit before we try that again." Ausable said.

"I think you're right," Anna said, gazing into his eyes.

They looked at each other, both feeling there was nothing else in the world. Warmth and exhilaration flooded through both of them. At this moment, nothing hurt. Nothing else mattered. Just them. Still, they both knew this was probably the last time they would see each other.

CHAPTER TWELVE

Anna and Ausable were on two of the horses and had made a rope of debris from the storm to lead the third one with them. They had to be very careful guiding the horses through what the storm had caused. They were getting closer to Anna's home.

"We're almost there, Ausable," Anna said. "I'm so worried about my boys. I hope they are all right."

"We'll see soon, Anna," Ausable said.

Anna, looking at the mess around her, said, "And I hope my home is still standing. The chaos this storm produced is scaring me."

They were nearing Keene Valley and things began to look more cleared out. They finally saw someone.

"Hello!" Anna yelled.

The man turned and she could see it was Mills, who owned the tavern.

"Who's that?" asked Mills.

"Mills, it's Anna Tattersall," she answered.

"Mrs. Tattersall! My God, it's you. Everyone has been so worried about you," Mills told her.

They came up to each other.

"I was up at Giant's Washbowl when the storm hit. I broke some ribs. And this nice Indian gentleman helped me," Anna said.

Ausable said, "How do you do? I'm Ausable Hancock."

Mills, a bit taken aback, said, "Nice to meet you. They call me Mills."

Anna said, frantically, "Mills, how are my boys? Do you know?"

Mills quickly answered, "They are fine. Colleen and Millie took them to Lil Tattersall's house as soon as the water started to rise."

"Oh, thank goodness! I'm so relieved."

"Mrs. Tattersall's house made it through, since she's away from the river."

"Do you know how Idlenook is?" Anna asked.

"Still standing. Flooded some inside. I hear it's a soggy mess. But she's still there," Mills answered.

"Oh, that's wonderful news," Anna said gratefully. "We've got to get to Lil's and see the boys. They must be frantically worried. Thank you, Mills."

"You're welcome, Mrs. Tattersall. I hear they were able to wire your husband. He's on his way up. Might be here by now."

Anna silently gasped. "Really?" she asked cautiously and looked over at Ausable as they exchanged knowing looks. Then, not wholeheartedly, "That's good to know, Mills." Changing the subject, "Oh, how did your tavern fare?"

"Made it through. Can't say the same for my stills. They were up in the foothills. Could be in Lake Champlain by now, for all I know," Mills confided.

"I'm sorry, Mills," she said.

"Say, are those Old Farmer Mory's horses? Look just like them," Mills said.

"We don't know. Luckily we found them wandering in a meadow upriver," Anna told him. "I'd be glad to know whose they are."

"I think they're Mory's. Mrs. Tattersall's man, Holmes, might know," said Mills.

"Thank you. And thank you for my good news. I've got to get to Lil's, "she said.

"Safe riding. Road's pretty clear from here to town," Mills told them. Nodding to Ausable, "How do."

Ausable nodded back, "Sir."

Anna and Ausable headed down the road toward Aunt Lil's.

"Oh Ausable, I'm so thankful to hear that the boys are okay. But we've got to hurry. They must be so worried."

"Yes. I think we can hurry up the pace since the road is clear," Ausable agreed. Then, "Anna, are you sure you want me to come with you? You shouldn't have any trouble getting there on your own now."

Anna stopped the horse. Ausable did as well. "Oh, Ausable, I really don't know," she said desperately. "You saved my life. I want the people I love to meet you."

Ausable asked thoughtfully, "Are you sure that's a good idea?"

Anna put her head in her hands and closed her eyes. "I hadn't thought ahead about all this. I just wanted to get home. And you're right. I can get there now on my own. Oh, maybe it's best if I do. But I don't want to. Oh, Ausable, I've never met anyone like you." She lifted her head and said, "I love you!" She looked over. She saw his horse. It was riderless. Ausable was gone.

Anna began to cry uncontrollably. The sobs hurt her ribs but she couldn't stop. Thoughts ran through her head. She had found what she had been looking for all her life. The peace and understanding of a wonderful man who enjoyed everything she enjoyed. He was caring and affectionate, yet strong and confident. And now he was gone. And she would never see him again. She kept crying.

CHAPTER THIRTEEN

After Anna pulled herself together, she got her horse moving. Luckily, the other two horses followed.

She passed the sign to Idlenook, which was pushed to an angle from the rushing water, she surmised. She looked across the meadow at the drive. It was covered in silt from the overflowing river. Someone had been down the drive. There were several marks from carriages, and footprints. She thought perhaps she should go see the house. Maybe everyone was there working to clean it up. No, she'd better not. Aunt Lil's was a safer bet.

Anna kept going toward town. She passed some men working to clear the road and drives to people's houses. All were glad to see she was safe. Yes, the boys were at Aunt Lil's house.

Anna approached Aunt Lil's on horseback and called out, "Paul, Sam. It's Mother! I'm here."

The screen door slammed open and out ran two joyously happy boys!!

Paul yelled, "Oh, Mother, you're safe!"

Sam, overjoyed, said, "I'm so glad to see you. Where were you?"

Paul asked, "What happened? We were so worried about you!" as they both jumped up and down, trying to get to her on the horse.

Anna cautioned, trying to calm them down, "Boys, boys, you've got to be careful. I've broken several ribs."

Paul asked, "You broke your ribs? Oh no. How?"

Sam chimed in, "How did you get on the horse?"

Anna answered, "It's a long story."

Aunt Lil called from within the house, "Boys, what's all that caterwauling out there?" She came out onto the veranda and saw Anna. "Oh, my dear. Anna! We were beside ourselves with worry. You're here! That's wonderful!" She ran down the steps to Anna's side.

"I'm so glad to see you all!" Anna said.

"Boys, back to caterwauling," Aunt Lil said ecstatically. "If ever there was a time to caterwaul, this is it!"

The boys jumped up and down yelling, "Yay" and "Hooray! Mother's home!"

Tears came into Aunt Lil's eyes. She asked, "Anna, what happened? Where have you been?"

"I took a hike up to Giant's Washbowl and got caught up there in the storm. It came so fast. There's so much to tell," Anna told them.

"Well, let's get you down off that horse," Lil suggested.

"That's easier said than done. I broke several ribs and it hurts a lot to move," Anna said.

"Let me get Holmes to help you." She called inside. "Holmes. Come here, please."

Holmes appeared in the doorway and was amazed to see Anna. "Oh, Mrs. Tattersall, we were all so worried. I'm so happy to see you."

"Thank you, Holmes," Anna said.

Aunt Lil ordered, "Anna has broken ribs so I need you to gently help her off the horse, Holmes."

"Yes, Ma'am," nodded Holmes.

He led the horse to the edge of the veranda and, standing on it, was able to painlessly help Anna off the horse.

"Oh, thank you, Holmes. I've been on that horse for quite a while. My ribs hurt, but so does my derriere now," Anna said.

Aunt Lil started, "Oh Anna. Such talk." Then, looking her over, "Where did that strange jacket come from that's wrapped around you?"

"Oh, Lil, I'll tell you all about it later. Right now I need to eat and rest. And I should see a doctor," Anna told her.

Aunt Lil, realizing, "Yes, yes, of course. Let's go inside and get you comfortable. Holmes, run and get Dr. Beecher, please. Tell him it's urgent."

"On my way, Ma'am," said Holmes and he ran off down the road.

Anna turned and looked up at Giant Mountain. A large swath of rock was showing that hadn't been there before. The cloudburst was so strong it had caused a considerable rockslide.

"Oh, my," Anna exclaimed, pointing to Giant.

"Amazing, isn't it?" Aunt Lil asked. "The cloudburst changed the look of Giant forever."

Anna gasped, "I think I was under all that washed down." Anna shuddered.

"We're so relieved you're with us now, dear," Aunt Lil offered.

Aunt Lil and the boys helped Anna into the house and settled her carefully down on a divan in the parlor.

"Shall we get that jacket untied from around you?" Lil asked.

"I think it's best we leave it on until the doctor looks at me. It might be holding me all together," Anna told her.

"Cook was just making lunch. I'll have her bring it out right away. Would you like some tea, too?" asked Aunt Lil.

"Water, please. I'm quite thirsty. And food would be wonderful. I'm famished," Anna said.

"Right away," and Aunt Lil was off to the kitchen.

Anna lifted one of the sleeves and rubbed it lovingly on her cheek and smelled it.

Paul piped up, "Oh, Mother, we're so glad to see you. We were so worried."

"Yes, we thought you were dead!" Sam added. His lower lip then started to tremble. "I'm so glad you're here." And Sam burst into tears.

Anna pulled him into her, and hugged him. She winced as she did it, but she didn't care. Her little boy needed her. "Oh

112

Sam, there, there. I'm so glad to be home, too. I was worried about all of you. Come here, Paul."

Paul came up to her other side and she held him as well. Lil was looking at them through the door and smiled warmly, tears in her eyes.

Sam started to contain himself. Through his muffled sobs he said, "Father is supposed to be here, too. But we don't know where he is."

Paul jumped in, "Aunt Lil wired him to come up here because we didn't know where you were. He was supposed to be here yesterday."

Aunt Lil interrupted, walking in with a tumbler of cold water and handed it to Anna. "Here you go dear."

"Thank you, Lil."

Aunt Lil continued, "The road is rough. Brown hasn't made it through from Elizabethtown since the cloudburst. So we don't know when Will can get here."

Anna said, "I'm sure he'll find a way. Your father's very resourceful."

Aunt Lil settled in her chair. "Now tell us what happened, dear."

"Yes, Mother, tell us all about it," Sam said excitedly.

Anna began, "I felt like taking a walk and a picnic by myself, so I went up to Giant's Washbowl."

"But no one knew where you were. Didn't you tell anyone?" asked Aunt Lil accusingly.

"The boys were off playing. Colleen and Millie were in town. I had no one to tell. I've been going on hikes every summer up here. I thought I was just going to be gone for an hour or so. I saw the clouds appearing as I was up there, but I thought it would be a little summer shower. When it started to come down in sheets of rain, I knew I was in trouble. It was the most terrifying experience of my life. The rain was demonic. It kept getting stronger and stronger. Soon the ground under me was giving way and trees were washing down the mountain. I tried holding onto things but they would let go of the earth holding them. I was trying to get to the cave that's behind the washbowl."

Sam jumped in, "Good idea, Mother. I love to hide in that cave."

"I know. That's how I knew about it. Well, I tried to reach the cave. But the downpour was too strong. I really thought it was all over. When out of nowhere someone grabbed me and pulled me to safety. Just in time, too, because I blacked out."

"Oh, dear," said Aunt Lil.

'When I woke up, I was lying in a lean-to. There was a fire going and my ribs were all wrapped up."

Paul asked, "Who helped you, Mother?"

Anna continued, "It turns out there was an Indian man up there as well. And he knew about the cave, too, and we were in the same spot at the same time, trying to get to the cave. But he had a better grip than I did. And he saved my life."

Sam said excitedly, "Wow, an Indian saved Mother's life! That's a better story than any that Mr. Brown has in the stagecoach!"

Aunt Lil then asked, "Were you able to communicate with this Indian? Did he understand English?"

"Actually, yes. He graduated Harvard and speaks perfect English. He was born up here in the Adirondacks, but moved to Boston when he was six. I owe my life to that man."

Aunt Lil interjected, "But dear, he's... an Indian." She shuddered. "Weren't you frightened?"

Anna stated firmly, "Lil, he cared for me, fed me. He's a wonderful man. Not to mention, he and his family have as much money as you do, if not more."

Aunt Lil reacted.

"They sit on the boards of corporations, for goodness' sake. No I wasn't frightened."

"Well, Anna," Aunt Lil said, being condescending, "That's what he said. You know these people are known liars."

"Oh, Lil. All I can say is, he was a perfect gentleman. He carried me down the mountain through unbelievable conditions. There is no trail anymore. He had to go around broken trees and fallen rocks. He saved my life."

"Well, I'm just happy you're safe. And you'll have a wonderful story to tell about the cloudburst that will top all the others' sad tales," Aunt Lil concluded.

Anna just rolled her eyes. "So tell me about Idlenook. I saw Mills on the way here and he said it survived."

Paul jumped in, "Oh, it's a mess, Mother. The river washed through the house."

"Yes, some of the furniture from the back porch was pushed up against the ice box," said Sam, excitedly. "And it's all filthy with mud!"

"Oh, dear," Anna said.

Aunt Lil joined in, "It is quite dreadful, Anna. But at least the house is still standing. The water rose and rushed under and through the house, only just above floor level. It's lucky the house is up above ground level. The river didn't stay too long at its height. I could see the water just across the road from here. It was very terrifying. Colleen and Millie are over there now cleaning it up."

"I wish I could go and help them," Anna said.

"Now, now, the doctor will be here presently. Then we'll see what you can do."

Rose, Lil's cook, entered with a tray of food for Anna. She placed it on the table next to her.

"Oh thank you, Rose. I'm very hungry," Anna said.

"I'm happy to see you well, Mrs. Tattersall. I thought the boys would like to eat with you. There's lunch for you two here as well, boys." Rose told them, and then hurried back into the kitchen.

"You all eat up," Aunt Lil said. "I'll have my lunch at the dining table."

As they started to eat, Sam said, "I'm really hungry all of a sudden."

Paul said, "Yes, he was so upset about you being missing, he couldn't eat a thing."

"I could too. I ate a lot, Mother," Sam countered. "I mean, I missed you. But I still ate."

Paul said, "You're telling a fib. You said you weren't hungry and Aunt Lil made you eat."

115

"Well, I ate then, didn't I?" Sam said.

Anna smiled. She was home and her boys were just fine.

"Okay, you two. We're all here now and there's lovely food. Let's enjoy being together again," Anna said.

They all ate their lunch, happy to be together.

CHAPTER FOURTEEN

It was that evening. The doctor had come and gone. He had given Anna some pain medication and wrapped up her broken ribs. He said the Indian had done a good job binding her ribs. He was amazed at all she'd been through that she was in as good condition as she was. He didn't see any jagged edges protruding. There were clean breaks. It would just take time to heal so she should take it slowly and he would check in on her.

They had a lovely dinner and Anna was able to sit at the dining table for a short time to enjoy it. She had to recount her escapades for Sam and Paul so they could get every detail of it right. Sam said he'd be playing Indian savior tomorrow with his friends.

Colleen and Millie had heard the good news and came racing over to see Anna. They were overjoyed and relieved. Millie had brought along some of Anna's clothes. They told Anna what they were doing to clean up the house. Some valley men were helping them move the heavy things. There was mud everywhere. But it would be good as new in no time. Anna said she would be by in the morning to see what was going on.

Aunt Lil had fixed up a daybed in the library for Anna to sleep in so she wouldn't need to go upstairs. The boys would still stay there too, until Idlenook was back in shape.

There was a knock at the door. It was Pastor Tom.

"Well, aren't you a sight for sore eyes," Tom said excitedly through the screen door.

Anna was now seated in an armchair in the parlor.

"Oh, Tom, come in. How nice of you to come by," Anna said.

He walked over to her and knelt next to her.

"Oh, Anna, I was so worried about you. I prayed every day that you were all right."

"Thank you, dear Tom. It was quite a harrowing experience, I must say," Anna told him.

"You are the talk of the valley, my dear. The way I hear it, you not only had to fight off the storm, but you had to fight off a wild Indian!" Tom said, half jokingly.

"Oh, no, is that what they're saying?" Anna asked. Then, quietly, "Wait until I tell you the real story of my time up there, Tom. Oh my. You won't believe it."

Tom excitedly whispered, "Tell me now."

Anna looked around. "I can't now. When we're alone I'll tell you the whole, sensational story."

"When? When?" Tom asked eagerly.

"I'll see if I can get away tomorrow. I'll have Holmes take me to you in the carriage," Anna told him. "Did the church make it through the storm?"

"Yes. Lots of heavy rain here, but the new roof held just fine," Tom told her.

Another voice from outside the screen door spoke.

"Hello, Anna," said Will as he opened the door.

"Oh, Will. How did you get here?" Anna asked. "I heard the road was out.,"

Tom got up on his feet, shaking Will's hand. "Good to see you, Will. Welcome back."

"You too, Tom." Then to Anna, "I decided to hike over from Elizabethtown. Took me a couple of days since the trails were nonexistent. But I made it."

"Good for you, Will," said Tom. "I will leave you two alone. You've got a lot to talk about. I'm so glad you are well, Anna."

"Thank you, Tom. And thanks so much for stopping by. I'll try to see you tomorrow," Anna told him.

"Fine. Good night, all," said Tom and he left.

Will turned to Anna. "Lil's wire said you were missing. I was so worried. What happened?"

"I *was* missing. I got caught in the cloudburst and… " Anna was interrupted as Paul and Sam appeared at the top of the stairs.

"Father!" "You're here!" they yelled as they dashed down the stairs.

As Will hugged the boys, "Great to see you boys!"

Paul asked, "Did the road get fixed?"

"No, actually, it didn't," Will continued proudly. "I hiked here."

"All the way from Fairfield?" Sam asked, amazed.

"No, Sam. I took the train up. I only hiked from Elizabethtown."

"Oh. Well, if you had to, I bet you could hike all the way from Fairfield," Sam said.

Will said, "For you, I'd hike all the way around the world if I had to," and he hugged the boys again.

Sam beamed.

"Did Mother tell you about the Indian saving her, Father?" Paul asked.

Will reacted.

"I haven't had time, dear. Your father just got here," Anna told them.

Sam jumped in, impatiently, "Yes, and she has broken ribs and the Indian wrapped her up and carried her down the mountain! Didn't he, Mother?"

"What's all this, Anna?" Will asked.

Aunt Lil heard the commotion and entered the parlor.

"Will, you made it," she exclaimed happily as she went to him and gave him a hug. "I'm so glad to see you."

"You too, Aunt Lil." Holding up his hand, "And before you ask, I hiked here from Elizabethtown. But it seems Anna has a much more interesting story to tell," Will said, looking at Anna quizzically.

Anna shrugged her shoulders and said, "Yes, I was saved from falling off Giant by an Indian. The cloudburst hit and I was washing away down the mountain and just as I blacked out, this wonderful Indian man grabbed me and brought me to safety. He tended my broken ribs, he fed me, and then, when he thought it was safe, he carried me down the mountain, put me on a horse, and here I am."

"My goodness," Will said. "I sure would like to thank him. Where is he?"

"I don't know. Once I was safe, he disappeared as fast as he appeared. Maybe he wasn't even real. Who knows? Might all just be an illusion."

"Oh no, Mother," Sam demanded. "It can't be an illusion. He has to be real!"

Anna chuckled. "He is real, Sam. Maybe we'll see him again one day."

"When were you able to get down the mountain, Anna?" Will asked.

"Just this morning."

"You were up there for four days?"

"Yes. I was in terrible pain."

"So you broke your ribs?" he inquired.

"Yes. I can't believe that's all I broke. I was really getting thrown around by that storm," she told him.

"I had Dr. Beecher look at her earlier," Aunt Lil added. "He said she'd be fine in no time."

"I'm very glad to hear that," as Will kissed her on the forehead. "Oh, how's Idlenook?"

Aunt Lil spoke up, "I've seen it. Still standing. The river rose and washed mud through the house. But Idlenook's strong. She isn't going anywhere."

"Colleen and Millie came by. They have been over there since the storm, cleaning it up. I haven't seen it yet. Perhaps we can go over in the morning," Anna said.

"Absolutely," Will said. "Now I think we all need some rest. I know I'm exhausted. But first, I need a hot bath."

"I'll have one drawn for you right away, Will," said Aunt Lil as she went into the kitchen.

"Off to bed, you two," Will said as he hugged and kissed the boys.

"Okay,. Goodnight, Father," Paul said.

120

Sam, yelling back to them, as they ran up the stairs, "I'm so glad you're both back."

"Us, too. Goodnight," said Anna.

Will pulled a chair up facing Anna, taking her hands. "I was very worried about you. I'm so relieved you're safe, Anna."

"I am, Will. And I'm very pleased you are here."

Will hesitated, then said, "So, this Indian man. He was good to you?"

"Oh, yes. He's not like any of the Indians we know around here. Although he was born up here, his family is quite wealthy. And he went to Harvard. He is a very kind man," Anna stated.

"And you were alone with him for four days," Will said, implying something happened.

"Oh, Will. It wasn't by choice. I'm sure you saw the state of things on your hike here. The trails were gone. Plus, I couldn't move."

"Well, it just doesn't look good now, does it, Anna?"

Anna nodded her head. "No, it doesn't. I'm sorry if I embarrassed you, Will."

"Well, we'll play it down in town. I'm sure everyone has a lot of cloudburst stories to tell," Will said hopefully.

"I'm sure they do," Anna half-heartedly agreed. "Will you help me to bed, please? Lil has set up a bed for me in the library so I don't have to climb the stairs."

"Of course, Anna," Will said, helping her up.

He led her across the room and into the library. He helped her onto the bed and gently kissed her. Anna gave him a smile. Will went to get Mary, Lil's maid, to help Anna undress while he took his bath. On the table in the library was Ausable's leather jacket that he had used to wrap Anna in. Anna picked up the jacket and reached into an inside pocket. She pulled out the rolled-up bark with the painting Ausable had done of her sleeping. She gazed longingly at it and tears appeared in her eyes. She would never see this wonderful man again.

Mary entered and saw Anna had tears on her face. "Are you crying, Miss Anna?"

Anna, wiping the tears, "Oh no, Mary. I'm not crying. Just bearing the pain, that's all."

"I'll be gentle."

"Thank you, Mary."

CHAPTER FIFTEEN

It was early the next morning. Anna was dressed and finishing breakfast with Will and the boys. She and Will were ready to go and see what shape Idlenook was in. Sam told them that the beach was totally different after the storm. He said they wouldn't recognize it. He just didn't know how deep the water was now, though. It was rushing by so fast, they were afraid to go in and get washed away. But the path to the beach was still passable. Anna and Will both said they couldn't wait to see it.

Aunt Lil told them some men in the valley had cleared the drive so they would be able to get to the house easily. She had Holmes prepare her buckboard to take them. He was out front when they were ready. They finished the last of their breakfast and thanked Rose for a delicious meal. Aunt Lil rolled her eyes at this. It was Rose's job to cook, Aunt Lil thought. She didn't need to be thanked for doing what she was required to do.

The boys were going off on their daily adventures, but said they would be back at Aunt Lil's in time for lunch. Anna and Will headed out to the buckboard and Will and Holmes helped Anna into it. She was actually feeling better than she thought she would. She supposed the pain medication Dr. Beecher had given her was helping. They rode off toward Idlenook.

Will said, "I was amazed coming through town last night how much rain had fallen. And the damage it did. Wagons and barrels washed up against houses. Part of the front piazza of Bailey's collapsed."

"Oh, my," said Anna. "I can imagine."

As they bumped along the damaged road, "And look at the road. It will need a lot of work to get it back into rideable shape," Will indicated.

"You should have seen the storm, Will. I've never experienced anything like it. It was relentless. And so strong. I was afraid for my life."

"It must have been a terrible fright, my dear. I'm very glad you made it through," Will said. He started to put his arm around her. "Oh, I better not. Don't want to hurt your ribs."

"It will be all right, Will," Anna told him.

"I'll be gentle," and he put his arm around Anna, carefully.

Anna leaned her head against Will and closed her eyes. Well, it was something, she thought.

Holmes announced, "Here we are."

Someone had fixed the sign out front. It was now standing upright. Will looked ahead down the drive.

"The drive is in pretty good shape. But all that mud in the meadow here. I suppose the grasses will regrow eventually," Will presumed.

They continued down the drive and passed the thicket. Idlenook came into view. It was still standing. Silt spread across the front lawn. And they could see traces of mud on the front porch where someone had tried to sweep it off.

"I'm amazed it's still standing," Anna said.

They continued down the drive and pulled up to the side of the house. Colleen and Millie heard the horses and came to the door.

Colleen exclaimed, "Oh, it's so good to have you both home."

"Thanks, Colleen," Will said.

Will and Holmes helped Anna out of the buckboard and up the few steps into the screened-in porch. They could see traces of mud all over the porch, and the screens on the river side were mangled.

"I'm not sure if it's best to wash this out or wait until it dries and sweep it," Will speculated.

"I think we'll have to do both," Anna stated.

124

Colleen took them on a tour of the house, showing them all the work they had tried to do. They said it looked a lot better than a few days ago. They had washed out the rugs and they were laid out in the meadow behind the house to dry. Some of the furniture on the screened porch was broken, but inside, things were not too bad. The mud had come in the outer doors and washed into the house, but it seemed Colleen and Millie had done a good job of getting that cleaned out.

Outside, the horse barn was a wreck and would need to be rebuilt. The boys' playhouse near the beach path was over on its side, but seemed to be in good shape. The summerhouse was pushed to a severe angle. Anna wouldn't be having any teas out there anytime soon.

Will opened the lattice under the house to inspect that area. There was dirt almost up to the floorboards. The boys wouldn't be hiding from Aunt Lil under there anymore. He noticed that the lattice facing the river had been destroyed and would need to be replaced. Colleen said she knew some men who were looking for work who could help with the repairs. She had used them to repair the drive and move heavy things. They seemed very reliable. Will was grateful and asked her to contact them. She said she could go into town right away to engage them before someone else hired them. Holmes offered to take her and he would come back to pick Will and Anna up. Will thanked them.

Millie was cleaning up inside the house as Anna and Will stood outside taking it all in.

"Well, this is quite a terrible mess," Will stated.

"It is. And I feel so helpless. There's so much I'd like to do," Anna fretted.

"Not to worry, Anna. You can supervise and keep everyone to their tasks. That will be a lot of work as it is," Will told her. "I'm going to get a pad and make a list of all that needs to be done."

"I'm feeling a bit overwhelmed. I'll go inside and rest a bit," Anna said.

She walked through the house to the screened porch and looked up on the wall. It was still there. The original painting

Ausable had done for her was up on the wall, safe and sound. Anna looked at it as if for the first time. She pictured the boy Ausable was, sitting along the river, doing a painting of Giant. And tried to imagine how he was the same man who sat and painted her while she slept a few days ago. Oh, how she wanted to see him again. How could she find him? He said he was up here alone at his camp at the Upper Lake. How could she get there in the state she was in? And was he even still there? As she started to recount that day in her head, she thought of Margaret Bancroft and Peter Brown. In all the confusion of what happened to her, she had forgotten all about them. Anna wondered if they made it down the mountain. And if they did, how did they explain their being there? This would be interesting. But first, she wanted to be sure they were all right. If anyone would know, it would be Tom.

When Holmes returned, she told Will she wanted to go into town for a few things. He was out pulling pieces of wood from under the house and around the grounds.

Anna said, "I'll check on Colleen and see if she's gotten the men to help you."

"Great, thanks, Anna," he said breathlessly as he hurled a large branch away.

Holmes helped Anna into the buckboard and they went off down the drive.

As they neared town, Anna said, "Oh Holmes, I need to speak with Pastor Tom. You can just drop me at the church."

"Yes, Mrs. Tattersall," Holmes said. "I can wait for you if you like."

"No, thank you, Holmes," Anna said. "I can have Tom take me into town for what I need."

"Very well."

They stopped in front of the church and Holmes helped Anna down.

"You seem to be a bit better, Missus," Holmes noticed.

"Yes, I think I am. Thank you, Holmes." Anna went up the walk to the church.

She found Tom inside the rectory working on his sermon. He looked up from his work.

"Anna, you're up and about," he exclaimed.

"Yes, I think I'm healing quite well," she told him. "Still a bit of pain and stiffness, but at least I can get around now."

"Wonderful. Have a seat," Tom offered.

"Thank you," she said, as she carefully sat. He pulled his chair up facing her.

"All right, let's hear it. I want the whole astounding story. And don't leave a word out," Tom pleaded.

"Where do I start? There's so much to tell," Anna said excitedly.

"Then start at the very beginning," Tom panted.

"Well, I went up to Giant's Washbowl to get away by myself. I brought a little picnic to eat."

"You were by yourself? This isn't very spicy," Tom lamented.

"Just wait." And Anna recounted the whole astonishing story. Along the way Tom said incredulous things like: "Margaret and Peter Brown? He's just a child!" and "You had met this Indian before?" and "You did what with him!?" and as she finished her story, Tom said forlornly, "That's the saddest story I've ever heard."

Anna wondered, "I don't know what I'll do if I ever see him again. Nothing can ever come of it. But, Tom, I never felt so alive in my whole life. I'm afraid I'm going to be more miserable than I was before all this."

Tom reached out and held Anna's hands. "Look, Anna. You know I can't condone what happened. But I am able to understand it. Now, don't worry. Things will work out the way they should. Will is here now and maybe you two will make things work."

"I suppose. Anything is possible," Anna said unconvincingly. Then changing the subject. "By the way, do you know if Margaret and Peter are all right?"

"Yes, I saw Margaret in town after the storm. I had no idea she was up on the mountain. She never mentioned it. And neither did anyone else. Looks like she made it down unscathed," Tom told her. "Haven't heard anything of Peter.

You were the talk of the town. Everyone worried about where you were."

"And I thought Margaret would be the great piece of gossip to chat about. After what happened to me with Ausable, I can almost understand why she did what she did," Anna said thoughtfully. Then, "Tom, I need to go into town and find Colleen. Is your wagon usable after the storm?"

"It is," Tom offered. "I'll go out and bring it around. Meet me out front."

Tom took Anna into town. There were signs of devastation all around, just like Will had said. And in the middle of it all, Ronnie Bradley was out with his broom, sweeping away the pieces of debris from the road. His personal calling was finally paying off.

They found Colleen at Alexander's General Store talking with the men she recommended they hire. Anna discussed the situation and came to a fair deal. They would start right away. She told them to speak to Will at the house. They said they would take Colleen back to Idlenook with them.

Anna and Tom continued to the Country Club. It was along the river, but higher up than Idlenook, so it fared better, with more rain damage than flooding. Anna spoke with the tennis pro, Glen McCann.

"Mrs. Tattersall! I heard you were all safe. I'm very happy to see you."

"Thank you, Glen, it was a harrowing time. Broke a few ribs, but I'm mending," Anna responded.

"I'm glad to hear that," Glen said.

Tom and Glen exchanged pleasantries.

"The club doesn't appear to have suffered," Anna said.

"The courts are full of pine branches and needles. And most of the nets are ruined. But we'll have things up and running soon," Glen told them.

"That's great to hear," said Anna. "I haven't seen the Browns yet. Are they all okay?" Anna asked.

"Haven't seen the Mr. and Mrs. But Peter came by yesterday to check out the courts," Glen told her.

"I'm glad to hear that," Anna said, relieved.

"Since the club is closed, people are gathering over at Bailey's," Tom told Anna.

"All right, Tom, we'll head over there to see everyone. Good luck cleaning up, Glen," said Anna.

"Thanks, Mrs. Tattersall. See you for our grand reopening."

"We'll be here," Anna replied.

Anna and Tom got into the church wagon and went down the drive to the main road.

"Glen is easy to read. If he knew anything about Peter and Margaret, he would have reacted when I asked about the Browns," said Anna. "He didn't."

"Then they must have gotten down the mountain and back without anyone knowing," said Tom. "Everything was so wild with the wind and rain, it would be easy to hide what happened."

"My ribs are hurting a little. But let's go over to Bailey's," Anna said. "If I know Margaret, she's not home cleaning her house." Then feigning toil, imitating Margaret, "It would be much too much, after all I've been through." Then, Anna stated, "As if the storm only happened to her."

Tom laughed and they headed over to Bailey's Hotel. Along the way, people said how glad they were to see Anna was safe and sound. She felt like a queen in a parade as they rolled along the bumpy road.

When they reached Bailey's, Tom helped Anna down. The front piazza, which had been damaged by the storm, was cleared away and temporary steps were in place. Anna and Tom went inside. Bailey's was a bit rustic but well-appointed, though not as nice as Graves Hotel in Keene, which had been around for decades and had the largest elm in the Adirondacks in front of it. Bailey's had a great big fireplace with a giant deer head mounted over it. There were paintings of Adirondack vistas for sale on the walls around the main room. Local artists mostly did these but a few were by painters who summered in the mountains. Off the back of the room was a kitchen where they cooked a small variety of meals served at a few tables along the rear of the room. And there sat Margaret Bancroft, holding court with several other ladies usually ensconced at the Country Club.

Anna whispered to Tom, "I wonder if Margaret has heard I was also up at Giant's Washbowl."

"I can't wait to find out," Tom whispered back.

The two strolled over to the ladies, who looked up as they approached.

Several women got up and dashed to Anna and also exchanged hellos with the pastor.

"Oh, Anna, I can't tell you how glad I am to see you safe," said Martina Sturges, giving Anna a hug.

"Not too tight, Martina. I broke a few ribs in the storm," Anna cautioned her.

Martina immediately let go. "Oh, I'm so sorry. I'm just so glad to see you."

"Me, too, Martina. Thank you, dear," Anna said.

Joan Montgomery came up to Anna, taking her hand, "You look wonderful, Anna. We were all so worried about you. Tell us all about it."

"Yes," said Martina, "especially the part about your lifesaving Indian friend."

Margaret chimed up, "Yes, we can't wait to hear about it. Four days all alone with an Indian man," she said, accusingly. "What must have happened during all that time? Alone."

Anna ignored her, and couldn't wait to tell the story. "It was all really quite traumatic," Anna began.

"Here, Anna. Take my chair," offered Martina.

"Thank you, dear," Anna said, as Tom helped her sit down. She was in a perfect spot, opposite Margaret. Tom went and got a chair and pulled it up right behind Anna.

"Dr. Beecher gave me some medication for the pain, but it still hurts quite a bit," Anna stated.

"We're all so sorry, dear Anna," Margaret said, trying to care.

Joan said excitedly, "So please, tell us all about your exciting adventure."

"All right. Well, it all began when I decided to take a picnic lunch by myself. I needed a little hike to clear my head and take in the scenery. I saw there were a few clouds in the sky but I never dreamed that I was about to be inundated by such a massive cloudburst."

Martina jumped in, "They say it was worse up on Giant. Were you near there, Anna?"

"Yes, I was, actually," said Anna. Then, waiting for it to sink in, "I just wanted a short climb, so I had my lunch up at Giant's Washbowl."

Both Anna and Tom watched as Margaret Bancroft's expression turned from bored to horrified and she looked down at her hands as the revelation began to sink in. She went pale. Then slowly looked up and straight at Anna.

Anna stared at Margaret, continuing. "I had seen a few other people hiking up there, too. I hope they got down safely." Anna turned and looked at the other women, "Anyway, as I was finishing my lunch, it started to drizzle. I thought it was just a passing summer shower, so I filled up my pack basket and stood under a tree, waiting for it to end."

Anna glanced at Margaret. Her eyes were darting about and Anna knew what she was thinking. Margaret knew Anna had seen her and Peter.

Anna continued, "But this was no summer shower. Suddenly, it was a downpour. I was never so scared in my life. Every branch and tree I grabbed onto gave way. The rain was so strong it was washing everything around me down the mountain. And me with it."

"Oh, my! That's terrifying," Martina said.

"I remembered there was a cave behind the washbowl and I was using every bit of strength I had to get to that cave. I thought it would be my only hope. But as I was just about to reach it, everything went out from under me. And just as the last grasp I had gave way, I felt my arm grabbed by something. With all the rain and mud in my face, I could hardly make anything out. But I thought I saw a face. And then I blacked out."

"Oh, Anna!" said Joan. "I can't believe you made it through that."

"I almost didn't. Except for that wonderful man who grabbed me."

"Oh. The Indian," Joan said breathlessly.

Anna smiled. "Yes, the Indian. His name is Ausable. And he is from the Adirondack tribe."

"Really?" said Martina.

"I didn't think there were any still living up here," said Joan.

"He was born up here, but moved to Massachusetts when he was young. Not only did he save my life, but, while I was knocked out, he managed to bandage up my ribs. Dr. Beecher said he had done a superb job," Anna told them.

"You are so lucky, dear," said Martina.

Joan noticed Margaret didn't seem to be paying attention. "Margaret? Isn't it wonderful about Anna and the Indian?"

Margaret was startled and looked up. "What? Oh yes. Wonderful. Listen, I must go. I need to oversee the workers at my house." She stood up, and then worriedly looking at Anna, "I'm glad you're well, Anna." And Margaret left.

"She certainly left in a hurry," Joan said.

"Very odd," said Martina.

"Well, you know Margaret. She doesn't always have the best of manners," Anna said, giving Tom a little smile.

"Anyway, tell us more about your Indian," Martina said. And Anna continued to tell her friends the public version of her story.

CHAPTER SIXTEEN

A few days after Anna returned, they were able to move back into Idlenook. But there was still a lot to do, and all were working, cleaning, and repairing the house when they heard a booming voice from outside. "HELLLOO THERE!" Everyone looked up and smiled. The boys ran outside, followed by Anna and Will, and Colleen and Millie, to find Uncle Bull-Bull standing in the middle of their mud-covered meadow, bellowing toward the house. "Where is everybody? Don't let a little storm scare you away!"

The boys yelled back, "Uncle Bull-Bull!" and ran to him. Uncle Bull-Bull was actually Bill Patrick. He wasn't a real uncle. Everyone just called him Uncle. The Bull parts were for obvious reasons. He was a wonderful bear of a man, with a twinkle in his eye. In his seventies and partially deaf, which explained why he talked so loudly. But still he had an educated elegance and a habit of calling everything "perfectly lovely." And everyone loved him for it. He was also a hermit who lived alone in a one-room cabin up in the mountains near John's Brook and rarely came down off the mountain. He had known Will since he was a baby and Anna had met him several times on her early visits to the valley.

"I came by to see how your house made out, Will, my boy," he boomed, shaking Will's hand powerfully. "You're so close to the river, I was worried. Looks like you fared fairly well."

133

"We did, Uncle Bull-Bull. We were lucky. The floodwaters didn't wash away Idlenook. Anna on the other hand has quite a story to tell," Will said.

"Really? Do tell, my dear," Uncle Bull-Bull said, interested.

"Oh, it's a very long story. Let me just say, I was up on Giant when the cloudburst hit."

Uncle Bull-Bull interrupted very loudly, "Giant?! You were up there? I went up to see the damage. I don't know how you survived!"

"I nearly didn't. I was almost washed off the mountain and broke several ribs. But I was saved by the most wonderful Indian man."

"An Indian man? I know a fair number of Indian men around here. What is his name?" asked Uncle Bull-Bull.

"Ausable Hancock," Anna replied.

Uncle Bull-Bull bellowed, "Ausable?!" which made Millie tremble from his loud roar. "I know Ausable. Perfectly lovely man. We've spent many a hike in the mountains together. He's a Harvard man, though. I'm a Yale man, myself."

"Yes, I know," said Anna.

Will said, "We'd love to thank him. Have you seen him lately?"

"No, I haven't since the storm. Has a camp at the Upper Lake. He usually comes by when he's in the area and sometimes brings me little gifts or paintings he's done. He's a perfectly lovely painter, you know."

"Yes. He told me," Anna said, biting her tongue.

"Well, isn't this a wonderful turn of things. I'd really enjoy hearing more about your adventure on Giant."

"Then you should stay to dinner, Uncle Bull-Bull. You'd like that, wouldn't you, boys?" said Anna.

"Yes, we would," said Paul

"Oh, please stay, Uncle Bull-Bull," pleaded Sam.

Uncle Bull-Bull laughed loudly. "Well of course I'll stay. How perfectly lovely of you, Anna. But I wouldn't want to put you out. I'm sure you have a lot to do here at the house."

"We do, but it's always a pleasure to see you. And it doesn't happen enough. The stove and the kitchen are cleaned and in working order, so it's no trouble. Colleen, please set another place for dinner tonight," Anna requested.

"Yes, ma'am. We've got plenty of food, Mr. Patrick. I know your appetite," said Colleen.

"And I know your cooking, Colleen. Always a special treat," offered Uncle Bull-Bull.

Colleen smiled and she and Millie went inside.

"I'm not one for a free meal, you know," Uncle Bull-Bull said. "So, Will, take me about and show me what needs fixing around here. I want to lend a hand."

"I know you won't take no for an answer," said Will. "So come around to the barn where I'm working on replacing some of the siding."

"Show me the way," Uncle Bull-Bull bellowed and the two of them turned and walked.

"I'll call you when dinner's almost ready," Anna said. She smiled and watched them walk down the drive. Anna was a bit excited. Uncle Bull-Bull knew Ausable. If he saw him, he would tell him we would like to see him. But would Ausable come? He probably wouldn't. Then again, it was Will who said he wanted to thank Ausable. Maybe he might use that as an excuse. Oh, she was being silly. But, if he had the same feelings for her that she did for him, and she was sure he did, he might not be able to stay away. She'd try to get Uncle Bull-Bull alone later and see if she could talk to him privately, which was never easy with Uncle Bull-Bull. Perhaps a walk down to the beach to show him how the river had shifted would work. They'd be away from everyone.

At dinner, after Anna had elaborated on her story, Uncle Bull-Bull told them his story about the cloudburst.

"Luckily, my cabin is on the west side of the valley. The storm was most severe on the east side, as you know, Anna. John's Brook was raging from all the rain, but my cabin is up on a small ridge and far enough away from the river. I did have several tree branches slam up against the side of the cabin, but no real damage," Uncle Bull-Bull told them.

"Very glad to hear it, Uncle Bull-Bull," said Will. "Boys, what would you think of a hike up to Uncle Bull-Bull's cabin one day?"

The boys were excited. "We've never been up there," said Sam.

"I'd love to go hike up there," said Paul.

"It would be perfectly lovely to see you!" Uncle Bull-Bull bellowed.

"When I get the house done, I'll take the boys on a hike," Will said.

Anna spoke up, "Uncle Bull-Bull? Before it gets too dark, I'd like to take you down to the beach and show you how the river has reshaped it."

"I would like that, Anna," said Uncle Bull-Bull. "I could use a stroll after this perfectly lovely meal." He yelled into the kitchen, "Impeccable dinner, Colleen!"

Colleen yelled back, "Thank you, sir!" then laughed.

Anna and Uncle Bull-Bull headed out of the house and toward the path to the beach.

"I see your summerhouse was hit quite severely," Uncle Bull-Bull noted.

"Yes. But the repairs are under way. It should be better than ever in no time," Anna told him.

When they emerged from the woods and onto the beach, Uncle Bull-Bull let out a gasp. "My goodness, what force there was to have caused this. I don't think I've ever seen sand on this beach before."

"Amazing, isn't it?" said Anna. "We're actually grateful that the flood washed away so much of the river rock. The boys have already been wiggling their toes in the sand."

She pointed to a large tree that was lodged in the bend of the river. "That tree is giving the boys a lot of fun, jumping off it into the deep pool it caused."

"Perfectly lovely fun to be a boy and discover such wonders," said Uncle Bull-Bull.

A small wooden bench had been brought down to the beach since the storm. Anna and Uncle Bull-Bull sat on it, looking up at Giant.

"So exquisite here, Anna," he said.

"It really is," she said. She paused, then, "Uncle Bull-Bull, I'd really like to find Mr. Hancock. He left so abruptly. Do you have any idea how that could be done?"

"Well, let me think," said Uncle Bull-Bull. "The trails to the Upper Lake are impassible. And I don't know if I've ever seen him in town. But then again, I'm not down here a lot."

"True. Do you know anyone else who might know him?" Anna asked.

"Oh, I think that man Brown, who drives the stage, probably knows him," Uncle Bull-Bull offered. "I'm sure he's driven him to and fro often."

"Oh yes, Brown. That makes sense. Oh, but the road from Elizabethtown hasn't been fully cleared yet. Brown hasn't been coming. They hired a group of hikers to bring in mail and other deliveries. I suppose I'll have to wait until the road gets cleared."

"Well, you never know. He may drop by for a visit with me. If he does, I'll tell him where to find you," Uncle Bull-Bull said.

"That would be very kind of you, Uncle Bull-Bull," and Anna gave him a little hug.

They sat there and looked up at Giant, watching the night pull its shade down.

For the next couple of weeks, all extracurricular matters were put aside and the tasks of cleaning and rebuilding took precedence. The men working on Idlenook with Tom did a splendid job adding new supports under the house, replacing the old latticework, and re-staining the outside of the house. They rebuilt the summerhouse better than before and were clever enough to add decorative fleur de lis curlicues around the top. Anna was thrilled.

Will was working every day on making the house perfect for them. Once again, it was like the old Will was back. He and Anna worked together on some of their projects and it felt nicely familiar. Both were happy and having fun together again. She was sure this wouldn't last. As soon as the house was finished, Will would be off to New York and she'd lose him again. As pleasant as it was to be together with Will for now, Anna had never felt the way she had in Ausable's arms. Anna was now more confused than ever.

CHAPTER SEVENTEEN

The staff of the new library in Keene Valley that opened the year before, thanks to a gift from Miss Sarah R. Dunham, had dried out all the books that got wet when one of the leaded glass windows was smashed in by a pine branch. They were having a fund-raising tea in the afternoon to raise money to replace what was broken. All the women in the valley had agreed to be there. And they were all going to bring any spare books they had to help restock some of the shelves, at least for now. Professor Thomas Davidson, famously known as "the wandering scholar," and who was the founder of the Glenmore Summer School in Keene Heights, would be speaking today as an incentive to donate.

Everyone was most excited to have an event to attend, as hardly anything had been happening because of the storm. All the ladies would be wearing their finest afternoon dresses. Some of them were still congregating at Bailey's, as the Country Club remained closed. But it was opening in a few days, so they were excited to get back to playing tennis and whist. Anna and her whist partner, Martina, had been practicing and were ready to take on the other players. Anna hadn't seen Margaret since they met at Bailey's. She wondered how it would go seeing her today.

Anna took their carriage for the afternoon so Will could keep working on the house. She had a small pile of books tied with twine. She stopped and picked up Martina so they could go together. Martina had a pile of books to donate as well. It was a rather dreary, hot and humid day and, even though they were perspiring, the two women were happy to have an event to attend and get back to life as usual.

As they rode along the newly smoothed-out road, Martina said, "I'm quite happy to have a day off from cleaning. I really am very tired of dirt and mud. But, of course, you have it worse at Idlenook, Anna."

"Yes. I completely agree. I've never felt so constantly dusty in my life," Anna concurred.

Anna hadn't told anyone except Tom about seeing Margaret and Peter before the storm, so she couldn't discuss the upcoming meeting with Martina. Anna wasn't quite sure how to approach this. She loved having something to hold over Margaret, but at the same time, she now understood Margaret's circumstances. Margaret and her husband John weren't close. He was up in the Adirondacks with her all summer, but rarely went on outings. He would gather with the other men at Bailey's or Mills. John would begrudgingly go to parties with Margaret, but he wouldn't dance or get involved in the festivities. It was no wonder Margaret was so mean.

Anna wanted to start some sort of conversation about Margaret. "Martina, have you seen Margaret lately?"

"No. The last time was at Bailey's when she ran out of there like she had seen a ghost. I don't know what's happened to her. And since her house is up alone on Cheney Plateau, it's not like you can stop by saying you were in the neighborhood."

"Will said John's had a lot of work to do shoring up the plateau," said Anna. "They almost lost their stone wall across the property from the storm."

"I'm sure John likes the excuse of doing all that work so he doesn't have to go about and see anyone else," Martina said teasingly.

"True. But I can't imagine Margaret is helping," Anna added.

"We'll see when we get to the library," said Martina.

Aunt Lil was helping with the proceedings at the library, so she would be there already.

There were many carriages along the road as they rode up near the library. Men were there to take the carriages for the ladies who drove themselves. Anna recognized one of them, George, who sometimes took over for Brown driving people from Elizabethtown.

"Hello, George," Anna called.

"Hello, Mrs. Tattersall," George said. "Let me take the carriage for you."

"Thank you, George. Will you take in the books that we brought?" asked Anna as he helped the women out of the carriage.

"Yes, of course," George said.

"George," asked Anna, "how is the road to Elizabethtown?"

"Almost passable," George answered. "We should see Brown here tomorrow, I think."

"Oh, that's wonderful news, George," Anna said. "He must have a lot of mail and packages to carry."

"Indeed he does, Missus," said George and he led the horses and carriage away.

"Things are really getting back to normal, aren't they?" said Martina.

"Yes. Very good," said Anna.

The two women adjusted their dresses and walked to the library. Aunt Lil was at the door greeting everyone.

"Oh, Anna, such a beautiful dress, dear," Aunt Lil gushed.

"Oh, thank you, Lil. I brought up several new ones and haven't been able to wear anything nice for a while," Anna said.

"Martina, so good to see you," said Aunt Lil, shaking her hand. "And don't you look lovely as well."

"So kind of you, Mrs. Tattersall," Martina said.

"We brought some books. George is bringing them in," Anna told Aunt Lil.

"Wonderful. Please, go inside first and see what needs to be done there. And literally piles of donated books are inside. The party will be out back, toward the Country Club," said Aunt Lil. "Have fun, ladies. And donate, donate."

"We will," said Anna.

They went inside and saw where one of the handsome leaded glass windows had been. There were many precious books laid wide to dry, yet still probably ruined, on the reading tables around the library. The library wasn't fancy. It was rather rustic on the inside, in keeping with the character of Keene Valley. But it housed a great number of books.

"It's so wonderful for our little hamlet to have such a wonderful library," said Martina.

"We are lucky, indeed," agreed Anna.

They went to a table where the donated books were piled up.

"My goodness, there are a lot of books," Martina said.

Anna picked up one of the books lying on the very top of the piles.

"Oh, my," said Anna, as she saw its cover. 'The Scarlet Letter.' It gave Anna pause. Had someone left this book out on top for a reason? Could it have been Aunt Lil? Did she suspect something? It couldn't have been Margaret. She was in the same predicament as Anna.

"Is something the matter, Anna?" Martina asked.

"Oh, nothing," Anna said as she replaced the book and shook her head. "Let's go outside and see who's here."

They went around to the back. There were tables set with beautiful linen tablecloths and napkins, done in brown and white to match the exterior of the library. Anna saw Aunt Lil's hand in that. One table held an urn for tea and two others were covered in little sandwiches and sweets. They could see past the tables to the Country Club and things did look well in order there.

About two-dozen women were already in attendance. Anna chatted with Elizabeth Wardwell and Edie Dunham, whom she hadn't seen since her incident. Both were very happy to see her well. Joan Beecher, the wife of Dr. Beecher, was there and would let her husband know how well she was doing.

Anna and Martina got some tea and sandwiches and found seats with friends Patricia Stoddard and Sally Merrick. There had been no sign of Margaret Bancroft. Aunt Lil joined them and Anna remarked on the color scheme of the table linens matching the library. Aunt Lil was very pleased to see that Anna noticed.

There was a podium set up near the library that the tables faced. A rather rotund gentleman stepped out of the library and Aunt Lil went up to the podium.

"May I have everyone's attention, please," Aunt Lil announced. "Today we are honored to be in the presence of the renowned Professor Thomas Davidson, who you all know is the founder of the exclusive Glenmore Summer School for the Culture Sciences on East Hill. Professor Davidson has travelled the world seeking answers to philosophical and ethical questions. And he's here today to offer a few of his ideas to us. I am proud to present Professor Thomas Davidson."

The ladies all applauded and Professor Davidson stepped up to the podium.

"Thank you, Mrs. Tattersall, for your kindness in inviting me here today on this marvelous occasion to help this magnificent library. I come here often to see if you have books I need for my studies and lectures."

Professor Davidson had a personal magnetism that made every woman there sit up and take notice. There was something about his demeanor and his kind, round face that drew everyone to him.

"It is one of my philosophies in life to associate with the noblest people I can find. Thus, that is why I am here with you noble people. It is most important to read the best books, which I have found here in your library, and to live with the mighty because of what they can do and what you can learn from them. But, also, one should learn to be happy alone, because, to rely upon one's own energies, you will not wait for or depend on other people. In this you will find simplicity, kindness, and thoughtfulness for all."

The speech continued for quite a while and the women were enthralled the entire time. When Professor Davidson finished, they all stood and applauded. After this captivating talk, a lot of donations were collected for the library.

Aunt Lil came back and sat with Anna and Martina.

"He was wonderful, Lil! How stimulating and stirring a man he is," Anna said excitedly.

"Isn't he, though?" said Aunt Lil. "We collected more than enough to repair and replace at the library. Just wonderful."

"Really brilliant, Mrs. Tattersall," said Martina.

"Thank you both," said Aunt Lil "Oh, people are leaving. I better go say my goodbyes."

Aunt Lil went to where the ladies were gathering to leave.

Anna said to Martina, "You know, I noticed Margaret didn't attend today. What do you think that means?"

"I can't imagine," said Martina. "As much as I dislike her, I do hope there's nothing wrong."

"Hmm. I do, too," Anna agreed.

Anna knew what she had to do. She had to go to see Margaret alone and talk to her. She wasn't sure what her approach would be, but she had to do something. Taking inspiration from Professor Davidson, she had to be a noble person.

CHAPTER EIGHTEEN

The next morning, things were looking wonderful at Idlenook. It was free of mud and restored inside and out. Will was very proud of all the work that had been completed. With everything done, Will was going to take the boys up to visit Uncle Bull-Bull today. Colleen was putting necessary items in the pack baskets. The boys were out at the pump filling their canteens with water. Anna was sitting on the dining porch just finishing breakfast when Will came down all dressed for hiking. He was wearing a soft felt hat and Balmoral hiking boots that he was very proud of. They were originally designed for Prince Albert as a walking boot that he could wear on the Scottish grouse moors of Balmoral Castle. Will's were all black and very stylish. Although they were now being called Oxfords in the States, Will still kept to calling them his Balmoral boots.

The boys came running in with the canteens.

"We've got all the water, Father," said Sam excitedly.

Colleen came onto the porch with the pack baskets.

"I've got your pack baskets here," said Colleen as she handed the two smaller ones to Paul and Sam and the larger one to Will, who thanked her.

"I've put lunch in there for you all. And I hope you don't mind, I've added a couple extra meals for you to leave with Mr. Patrick. I know he loves my cooking."

Anna walked up to them. "That's very thoughtful of you, Colleen."

"Well, let's get started, boys," Will said.

Anna kissed both of the boys. "Have a good hike. And send Uncle Bull-Bull my best."

"We shall," said Will. "We should be back by mid-afternoon."

"Have fun," Anna called, as Will and the boys bounded out of the screen door and down the drive.

Anna and Colleen watched them go, Will with his arms around the shoulders of his two boys.

"It's great to see them together having such a good time," Colleen said.

"It sure is," said Anna, smiling. But she knew, with the work at the house being finished, Will soon would be on his way back home.

"What have you got planned for today, Missus?" asked Colleen.

"I'm going to make a visit to Margaret Bancroft this morning," Anna said.

"Mrs. Bancroft?" Colleen was taken aback a bit.

"I know, I know. She and I don't get along very well. But it's time we fixed that. And that's just what I'm going to do," Anna told Colleen, trying to convince herself that this was the right thing.

Anna wore a rather plain dress. She wanted to make this meeting as neutral as she could. She still wasn't exactly sure how she was going to approach this. All she was sure about was that Margaret knew Anna had seen her and Peter. But as to what her demeanor would be, Anna would have to play it by ear when she got there.

Anna took the carriage alone and headed into town. As she neared Aunt Lil's house, Aunt Lil came out onto the veranda. She told Lil that Will and the boys were hiking up to Uncle Bull-Bull's cabin on John's Brook. Aunt Lil expressed how wonderful she thought it was for Will and the boys to be doing things like this together. Anna agreed. She told Aunt Lil she was just going into town for a few things and asked if she

146

needed anything. Aunt Lil thanked her but said no. They said their goodbyes and Anna headed for town.

As she passed the church, Tom was working in the garden out front. She stopped and called to him. He looked up and came to the carriage.

"So, this is the day," said Tom.

"I'm afraid it is. I have to nip this in the bud. I can't be the cause of Margaret hiding up at her house, afraid to come into town," said Anna.

"I think that's very brave and honorable of you, Anna. You're doing the right thing."

"Yes, I am," Anna said, still trying to convince herself.

"I'm just sorry you have to," Tom said with a little smile. "It was such fun watching you two go at it."

"Oh you," Anna said, blushing. "But you're right. It sure was fun. Okay, here I go."

"Good luck, Anna."

"Thanks, I'll need it," Anna said as she giddy-uped the horses.

Anna reached Bailey's and saw Brown's wagon in front. She stopped her carriage and went inside Bailey's to find Brown. The ladies had left Bailey's and were ensconced back at the Country Club. Anna was glad not to deal with them today. She had enough to work out.

She found Brown at a table eating a late morning meal.

"Hello, Brown," Anna said. "I'm glad to see you are able to make it through again."

"Hello, Mrs. Tattersall. Yes, the road is better than it was before. It was getting pretty ragged. I'm glad to be delivering people and mail again. In fact, there was a package for you from Fairfield. I sent it over to your Aunt Lil's for you with Holmes."

"Oh, thank you, Brown. That's good to know," said Anna. "Brown, I'm wondering if you know an Indian man by the name of Ausable Hancock?"

"Oh, yes, indeed. I know Mr. Hancock. He's ridden with me many times. Usually rides up top with me instead of inside with the other passengers. You know, they don't always feel comfortable cooped up with an Indian. I don't know why. He's a delightful man."

"Yes, I know. I've met him. In fact, I was up on Giant when the cloudburst hit and Mr. Hancock is the one who saved my life."

"You don't say. A hero too! That's wonderful," Brown said.

"He disappeared soon after he saved me and Will and I are trying to find him to thank him properly. I'm wondering if you have any idea where he might be," Anna said, hopefully.

"I'm sorry, Missus. I haven't seen him lately. But I know other people along the route who are acquainted with him. I'll put the word out that you're looking for him."

"Oh, that would be very nice, Brown. We really appreciate it."

"Glad to oblige, Mrs. Tattersall."

"Thank you, Brown. I'll leave you to your meal," Anna said and went outside and got back into her carriage, filled with hope that someone would let Ausable know she was looking for him.

It didn't take long to get up to the Bancrofts' house, which was up a small road on one of the plateaus, just high enough to have a spectacular view of the mighty Adirondack range. They called their house Boulder Lodge for the giant boulder, just behind which the house was built. The boulder was covered with lichen and maidenhair fern. It was a great old mountain house, stained red with green trim. To hold up the roof of the front veranda, smoothed-off pine trees with stubs of the branches sticking out were used. Adirondack chairs and rockers were spread across the front to take in the view. It was a very welcoming and comfortable house. Anna had trouble understanding how Margaret could be like she was, yet she bought a wonderful house like this. It just didn't seem to fit her personality.

Their drive went across the front of the meadow and then around to the side of their house. Margaret heard the horse's hooves and came out the front door. Anna saw her and waved. Margaret heaved an annoyed sigh and waved back. They both knew what was coming. Anna pulled the carriage up along the side of the house and stopped there. Margaret came around to meet her.

"Anna," said Margaret, nodding her head to her in a cold sort of greeting. "What brings you here?"

Anna knew she had to just dive in. "Margaret, I know we don't get along very well and haven't for years. But I think it's time we talked, woman to woman."

Margaret's face was getting red. Anna didn't know if she was angry or embarrassed. "All right. Anna, John's inside. We can't talk here. Let's take a walk out on the plateau."

"As long as you don't push me off the edge," Anna said, half jokingly.

"Don't think I haven't thought about it," Margaret said with a little laugh in her voice.

Anna got out of the carriage and they started toward the plateau.

"Don't you want to tell John where you're going?" Anna asked.

"No need. He won't notice I'm gone," Margaret replied.

The two walked silently along a path to where the plateau opened up to the entire valley. The view was impressive. The Bancrofts had set up several Adirondack chairs and ottomans out there. Anna and Margaret seated themselves.

Margaret started, "So, what do you want to tell me?"

"Margaret, this is hard to say and I'm not sure how to approach this…"

Margaret interrupted, "Does this have to do with being up at Giant's Washbowl before the storm?"

"Yes, it does," Anna confessed.

"I see. And I'm sure you relished what you saw and have told every woman in the valley about it…"

"No, stop. I promise. I haven't told any of the ladies," said Anna, telling the truth. "I wouldn't do that to you."

"Why not?" Margaret asked, straightforward. "We've hated each other forever. We're the perfect rivals. And we both revel in all our snide comments and the games we play. It's a lot of fun. All the other girls love to watch us spar."

"Well, I must admit, I do enjoy our competitiveness. It is a fun challenge. But back to why I'm here. To be honest, I did see you and Peter up on the mountain."

"Oh dear. I'm so embarrassed," Margaret said dissolving into a slump.

"Margaret, please. Don't be embarrassed. It is nothing to be ashamed of. I'm the first person to understand your need for that kind of liaison. I hate admitting this to you, of all people, but Will and I are becoming distant. He is happier in New York with all his work. He has less and less time for me. And frankly, I've tried, but I don't enjoy that urban way of life. I prefer the simplicity of being up here and at home in Fairfield."

"I'm very sorry to hear about you and Will," said Margaret. "I never would have known otherwise. It doesn't show."

"We keep up a good front," said Anna. "And I guess you and John aren't exactly, how can I say it…?"

Margaret interrupted, "We aren't in love anymore. In fact, we don't even like each other. It's a very sad state of affairs. So yes, I went looking for something to fill that lonely void. I know it is a mistake but, frankly, I really don't care. It is wonderful. And Peter knows exactly what I like."

"I'll say," Anna blurted out, mistakenly. "Oh, Margaret, I'm sorry. I didn't mean to imply…"

"Oh, come now, I'm sure you saw what happened."

Anna nodded and smiled. "I couldn't leave. You were blocking the trail and I didn't want to disturb you."

Margaret chuckled and shook her head, then continued, "To be clear, you haven't told anyone yet, and you're not going to, are you?"

"Margaret, my lips are sealed. I promise."

"All right, good. I don't want to break off this relationship, Anna, and it feels wonderful to let this out. You saw how breathtaking Peter is. He is almost feral in his passion, but gentle at the same time. I've never felt the way I do with him."

"Well, since we're being honest," Anna said, "I was very impressed. My goodness. How did such a young man learn to do what he does?"

150

"He has a very good teacher," Margaret said, smiling satisfied. "That wasn't our first time."

"How long has this been going on?"

"It started late last summer, at one of the parties at Eggerfield's."

"You're joking," Anna said, amazed.

"When he got back up here this summer, we picked up right where we left off. Oh, Anna, it's been so amazing. I know it's wrong, but I really needed this. To feel another human being next to me again. It can't last. I know that. Peter's not in love with me. He's in love with the sex. And that's fine with me. I'm not going to stop. I'm just going to be more careful about where we rendezvous."

"Speaking of that, how did you make it down in that cloudburst?" Anna asked.

"We left just in time. Peter was a wonder. He made sure I got safely down that mountain. We made it almost to the bottom of the trail when things really went wild. Of course, we couldn't tell anyone of our adventure. But everyone was having their own problems with the storm so we made it back unseen."

"Unfortunately for me, I waited until you left. I was hit so hard up there, so I was worried about you."

"That's sweet that you were worried about us. Actually, I'm dumbfounded," Margaret admitted.

"Well, Margaret, we may have not been friends, but I didn't wish you harm." Anna thought for a bit. "You know, the more I think about it, the more I'm realizing we are very much alike. Otherwise, why would we act like we hate each other so much?"

"You might be right," said Margaret.

And the two women had a good, long laugh about this.

"Won't this be fun at the Country Club? If we walk in arm in arm," Margaret said happily.

"Yes, what a shock it would be to everyone. Let's do it."

They shook hands on it.

"Margaret, I have to ask. Was it because of me that you weren't at the library yesterday?

"I'm afraid I was too embarrassed to show my face. I was sure you had told everyone. I'm so relieved and grateful that you hadn't."

Anna took a deep breath. "Now that we can be friends, I should tell you... I did tell one person." Then quickly, "But it is Pastor Tom. And, don't worry, he won't tell anyone. I promise."

"He'd better not. He's a pastor. He's supposed to keep secrets. But I should have known you told him. You two are thick as thieves."

"Yes, we are. I'm lucky to have him as a friend. We can tell each other anything. He knows I was coming here today. He encouraged it."

"Well, I'm glad he did. But I'm going to feel a bit awkward at services from now on."

"Oh, Margaret, he probably knows so much about everyone in town, his head would explode. But I can never get anything out of him."

"Well, that's reassuring," Margaret said. "This is fun, isn't it?"

"Finally," Anna said. And they laughed happily.

"So, now that we're telling secrets," Margaret said. "Tell me about that handsome Indian that rescued you."

"Oh, my," Anna revealed. "Yes, he is very handsome. How lucky we both were to have handsome men assisting us during that storm. He is a wonderful man. I wish I could find him again."

"Really?" Margaret asked, trying to lead her.

"Well, he did save my life. I'd like to thank him properly."

"Is that all?" Margaret prodded. "You two were alone up there for several days."

For years, Anna hadn't liked or trusted Margaret Bancroft. But now they were realizing how alike they and their situations were. And she had something much worse to hold over Margaret's head than what happened to her. This was probably the one person she could tell who surely wouldn't tell anyone. And Anna really wanted a woman's perspective on what had happened. It could be a mistake, but one she was willing to take. So Anna told Margaret the whole wonderful story.

When they were finished, Margaret said, "And you still have the painting he gave you? That's so romantic. Much more than my tryst with Peter."

"He really was so loving. I've never felt like that. And I don't know if I'll ever see him again."

"Well, we have to work together and find him."

"Really, you want to do that?" Anna asked.

"Of course," Margaret told her. "We disheartened women have to work together and find whatever little slice of happiness we can in this world."

"Well, Margaret. Since the world has turned topsy-turvy – I mean you and I are becoming friends. And we are both... I don't know how to say it, doing what we're doing...,"

"Yes, dear?"

"Let's tempt fate and see what happens."

"That's my girl," Margaret encouraged.

They both stood up and hugged each other.

Margaret said, "But first, we need a good plan to shock the ladies at the club. The whist club meets tomorrow. I know you're playing with Martina. I was supposed to play with Sally but I have been claiming to be ill."

"It's time for a miraculous recovery, Margaret. I'll tell Martina to meet me there and I'll pick you up on the way so we can make our grand entrance together."

"All right. I'll send my maid Jennie to tell Sally I will be playing with her tomorrow. Oh, what fun!" said Margaret, sounding the happiest Anna had ever seen her.

"Now, let's make a plan," said Anna.

CHAPTER NINETEEN

The next morning at breakfast, the boys were still chattering excitedly about their hike up to Uncle Bull-Bull's cabin.

"Mother, did you know Uncle Bull-Bull lives in only one room?" asked Sam.

"Yes, I've seen it, Sam," Anna answered.

"It smelled kind of funny," Sam said, scrunching up his face.

Anna and Will chuckled. "Yes, well, he's not as lucky as we are to have Colleen and Millie to help us keep our house smelling nice," Anna said.

"I don't know how he lives in there," Paul said. "Why doesn't he open a window?"

"We all have our own priorities, Paul," Will said.

"But the whole camp was really amazing. I'd love to live like that," Sam said as he leaned back in his chair, putting his hands behind his head. "Yep, free and easy. All alone. You could do whatever you want up there."

"You'd really like that, Sam?" asked Will.

"Oh, it would be splendid," Sam replied. "I could eat whatever I want, whenever I want. Climb trees, and hike everywhere."

"And where would you get the food, Sam?" Anna asked.

"I'd hunt and fish for it. There are so many fish in John's Brook up there."

"That would mean you'd have to fish and cook every day. That takes a lot of time." Will said.

"And don't forget, you'd have to clean up the camp, too. You wouldn't want it smelling like Uncle Bull-Bull's does, would you?" Anna said.

"Oh, no. I sure wouldn't want that. Yuck," Sam said emphatically.

Anna and Will and Paul were enjoying this.

"And, with all that hunting and fishing and cooking and cleaning, I don't know how much time you'd have for climbing trees and hiking," Anna said.

"Not to mention, you'd be all alone up there in the dark at night, hearing all those sounds in the woods," Paul added.

"Hmm, maybe I better think more about this," Sam said.

"Yes, I think that's a good idea, Sam," Anna said.

"It was still a great hike, though, wasn't it, Sam?" Will asked.

"It was, Father. When can we go on the next one?" Sam asked, excitedly.

"That will have to wait until I get back up here," Will told them. "I've really been neglecting my business. And now that the house is fixed up, it's time for me to get back."

"Oh no, not so soon, Father," said Paul.

"There is so much more to do here," Sam said, hopefully.

"I'm sorry, boys. I promise, I'll come back up here as soon as I can," Will told them.

"All right," said Sam dejectedly.

"Come on, Sam," said Paul. "Let's go down and jump off the log into the river."

Sam cheered up. "Let's go." And off they went, out the door.

Will looked at Anna. "You know I have to leave."

"I know," said Anna, smiling weakly. "When will you go?"

"Tomorrow."

"I'll see if Aunt Lil can come to dinner tonight. I'm sure she'd like to spend the evening with you," Anna said.

"That would be nice, Anna," Will said.

155

"I'll see her at whist club today and ask," said Anna. "It's our first day back at the Country Club. It's going to be quite fun." In more ways that one, Anna thought, smiling to herself. Anna made an excuse and had told Martina she'd have to meet her there. Anna and Margaret had decided to make sure they were the last to arrive, so everyone would see them.

Millie helped Anna into one of her prettiest afternoon dresses. Anna was giddy with excitement.

"You certainly are happy today, Mrs. Tattersall," Millie commented.

"Oh yes, Millie. The club is open again and we can finally get back to normal around here," Anna said. But she was thinking this was going to be a far from normal afternoon. And she couldn't wait. Anna left in the carriage alone.

The ladies were assembled in the main room of the Country Club, all commenting on how lovely everything looked and how nice it was to be back there. Aunt Lil was there with her whist partner, Edie Dunham. They had played together for years and were the ones to beat. The ladies were finding their seats at the playing tables. Martina went up to Aunt Lil.

"Mrs. Tattersall, have you seen Anna? She told me she had to stop and see a sick friend on the way, so she'd meet me here. I haven't seen hide nor hair of her," Martina said.

"No, I haven't, Martina," Aunt Lil said. "I know she was excited about today. I wonder who's sick."

Martina looked around the room. She saw Sally Merrick seated at her table, with no partner across from her. Martina went over to her.

"Hello, Sally," Martina said. "With whom are you playing?"

"Margaret is my partner," Sally said. "She's been ill, so I hope she can play today. Otherwise I won't have a partner."

"I'm waiting for Anna, as well," Martina said. "She's late, too."

"Well, if neither shows up, I suppose we can play together," Sally offered.

"All right," said Martina. "Odd though. Anna said she would meet me here because she needed to stop and see a sick friend. And Margaret has been ill."

"Really?" said Sally. "And neither is here. That is odd."

Just then, the doors at either end of the room opened with a bang, startling the ladies. And in from opposite sides of the room strode Margaret and Anna, each dressed to the nines and walking purposely toward each other. Aunt Lil stood up from her chair. The gathered women whispered eagerly to each other.

"Oh my," said Sally, nervously excited.

"This is going to be good," said Martina.

Anna and Margaret met, face to face, in the middle of the room, staring sternly at each other. The other ladies were anxiously silent. Aunt Lil was still standing, ready to break up a scuffle.

The two women looked each other up and down then stared back into one another's eyes. One could hear a pin drop.

Then both women broke into big smiles.

"Anna, what a lovely dress," exclaimed Margaret.

"Not as lovely as yours, Margaret," said Anna.

And to the astonishment of the gathered ladies, the two women kissed each other on both cheeks and then hugged, and started laughing happily.

The room was stunned for a moment, and then the other women joined in, laughing along with them. Aunt Lil breathed a sigh of relief and went over to Anna and Margaret.

"Very good, ladies," said Aunt Lil. "I applaud you. I was prepared to break up a brawl."

Anna and Margaret laughed.

"Believe it or not, Aunt Lil, Margaret and I made up," Anna told her.

"That's right," said Margaret. "We discovered we have a lot more in common than hating each other."

Other women came up and gathered around them.

"My heart has just now started beating again," said Sally.

"How did this reconciliation happen, Anna?" asked Martina.

Anna and Margaret had concocted a story of why they were now friends involving Anna taking a walk and finding Margaret with her foot stuck between two roots and saving her. Her ankle was still sore, which they figured would explain Margaret's recent absence. They got talking as Anna helped Margaret home, one thing led to another, and, now they find they are friends.

Everyone bought the story, but some were disappointed that the great rivalry was over. It was always fun to watch them top each other. Anna and Margaret agreed and said they would miss their skirmishes, too. But, all in all, friendship would be better.

The women found their places and had a wonderful afternoon back at the Country Club, playing whist. Aunt Lil and Edie won again, but, Anna and Martina's practicing had paid off. They came in second.

CHAPTER TWENTY

Will had left and Anna was busying herself with the annual crafts fair. Its focus had changed since the cloudburst. Not only would crafts be made and sold to raise money for the church, but clothes and household items would be donated and given to those who had suffered most from the storm, mainly year-round valley people. Everything was being collected at the church and Tom was busy organizing and cataloging it all. Anna and the other club ladies were there, lending helping hands.

Anna and Tom were working together, sorting clothing into like piles.

"Have you heard from Will? Did he make it back home safely?" Tom asked.

"He just left yesterday. He'll write as soon as he can, I'm sure," Anna told him as she put a shirt into a basket with other clothing. "If you find any that are torn, put them in here," said Anna, pointing to a basket. "I'll take them home and mend them. Margaret is coming by to help me sew these tonight."

"I may never forgive you for not letting me in on your stunt with Margaret," Tom said softly so no one else would hear him. "I'd love to have seen the look on those ladies' faces when you stood nose to nose. Especially Aunt Lil's!"

"Oh, she was ready to jump in and pull us apart," Anna said. "It was quite a masterful performance we put on, I must say."

"I'm not so sure telling her about you and Mr. Hancock was such a good idea," Tom said quietly. "I hope you can trust her."

"Because of what we know about each other, neither is going to say anything," Anna said firmly. "I think she's going to become a very good friend."

"That's amazing. Who would ever have believed it?" Tom said.

"I'd be the last one, believe me," Anna said. "Well, this looks like enough for now. I'll get these into the carriage."

"Let me help you," Tom said, picking up the basket.

They walked to Anna's carriage and Tom put the basket into it.

"I'll be back in the morning to help," Anna said, getting into the carriage.

"Thanks, Anna," Tom said. "And don't forget, if you get lonely, I'm always here."

"Dear sweet Tom. Thank you," Anna said, and rode off. She thought of what a good friend Tom was and how nice it will be to have a good female friend in Keene Valley as well. She needed close friends right now.

Anna turned the carriage into Idlenook's drive. Suddenly the horse started and the carriage jerked back. Anna was startled and almost tumbled out.

"I'm sorry," said a familiar voice. And out from behind the thicket stepped Ausable. "I didn't mean to frighten your horse."

Anna was stunned. "Are you all right?" he asked.

"Oh, Ausable." Anna jumped down from the carriage, not caring if her ribs hurt or not.

He caught her and held her as they stared into each other's eyes.

"I thought I'd never see you again," she said.

"I couldn't stay away," said Ausable as he pulled her into the thicket where they were more hidden and then kissed her passionately. They pressed against each other and kissed and kissed, starved for one another.

They stopped and Anna asked, "How did you find me?"

160

"The stagecoach driver, Mr. Brown, told me you and your husband were looking for me, to thank me for saving you."

"We were. Will wanted to thank you," Anna said.

"I waited until he left. I didn't want to see you when your husband was here," Ausable said. "It would have been too hard to maintain good manners."

They kissed again, moving their hands up and down, feeling every familiar spot that each missed of the other.

"Your ribs seem to be healing," he said, feeling that area.

"They are. The doctor said you were masterful in wrapping me up," she told him.

"I'm glad," he said, and they kissed again.

"Oh, Ausable, what are we going to do?" Anna asked.

"I'm not sure how, Anna," he said, "but we are going to figure this out. I have set up camp not too far from here where we can be secluded and safe. For now."

"For now," Anna repeated. "That doesn't sound very permanent."

"I'm not sure it can be," Ausable said. "But I know, right now, I can't live without you. We are taking a great risk here."

"I know it. And I curse it," Anna exclaimed. "But I'm willing to take that risk. Take me to the camp. Let's go now."

"We'll have to hike a bit. Are you up to that?"

"Yes. Let me stable the horse and tell my housekeeper I have plans for the afternoon. Where shall we meet?"

"On the beach behind your house. We can cross the river there."

"All right. I'll be along presently," said Anna, as she reached up and pulled his face toward hers. They kissed.

Anna stepped out of the thicket, straightened herself, and got into the carriage. Ausable disappeared further into the brush. Anna rode down the drive to the house, meeting Colleen coming out.

"I thought I heard you, Missus," Colleen said.

"Colleen, I've got a basketful of clothes that I'm going to mend tonight," said Anna.

"I'd be glad to help, Missus."

"Thanks, Colleen. And Mrs. Bancroft is coming to help as well."

"Mrs. Bancroft? Really? My, you two have become fast friends," Colleen said, amazed.

"Yes, we have," said Anna. "I'll stable the horse. Then I'm feeling like a little walk. It will be good for my healing. Not too far. I'll be back by dinner, Colleen."

"All right, Missus. I'll take the clothes in," Colleen said and she took the basket and went into the house.

Anna took the carriage to the stable and was on the beach in no time, with butterflies in her heart.

As he was wont to do, Ausable again seemed to appear out of nowhere, sneaking up behind her and grabbing her tenderly. He lifted her in his arms and carried her across the river. They disappeared into some brush, leaving no trace that anyone had ever been through there.

The walk up to his camp wasn't difficult. It took perhaps twenty minutes. Along the way they tickled and teased each other, playfully loving one another. Anna was lost in elation. They had yet to make love, but both knew the time was right.

When they reached Ausable's camp, she said he was right. This was very private. It was located far from any trail, so he was sure no one would stumble upon them.

The camp was set up with a large tent and a very comfortable old log to be used as a bench for sitting. But they had no inclination to sit right now. Anna pulled Ausable by his shirtfront into the tent. They knelt facing each other, and she quickly unbuttoned his shirt and began nuzzling the middle of his chest. He pulled off his shirt exposing his beautiful red-skinned, muscular body. There was already a large bulge in his trousers. Anna thought, all right, this is it, as she reached down and caressed the bulge, slowly fondling him.

As things became more and more heated, Anna quickly tore at her dress and popped a few buttons as she undid it. She didn't care. She had to have him. She undid her bodice and when her breasts were exposed, he carefully held them in his large smooth hands, tickling her nipples with his thumbs. She almost squealed and arched her back in pleasure.

162

Her dress dropped off her and he moved his hands slowly down her body and pushed her bloomers down and pulled them off her legs. Anna undid the buttons on the front of Ausable's trousers. She moved her hand lower and pushed his trousers down further and felt his large, muscular thighs. She then reached around behind and caressed his firm buttocks.

Ausable lifted Anna up and laid her on the soft blankets in his tent. He removed his trousers and they were both now fully naked. They slowly began a throbbing ride together, building a rhythm, rotating their hips together, faster and faster, together as one, until one final thrust, Anna rising to meet him, then both collapsing in a shuddering pinnacle of pure elation and love.

"I love you, Anna."

"I love you, Ausable."

Yes, love. It couldn't be denied. Anna and Ausable were in love.

They lay in each other's arms, still covered in sweet perspiration. Still trembling. Lost in the blissful world of the new unknown. Anna and Ausable cuddled happily in each other's arms.

Ausable closed his eyes. Anna looked at his beautiful face lying next to her. She had never felt so happy and so distraught at the same time. This was so right and so wrong, she thought. But she wasn't going to worry about that now. She was going to enjoy this ecstasy and take whatever consequences would come.

Feeling suddenly naked, Anna pulled a blanket up over her and stirred Ausable.

"Hello," he said, kissing her.

"Hello," she responded.

He pulled the blanket over himself as well and they made love once again.

CHAPTER TWENTY-ONE

Anna was finishing dressing, anxious to get home before anyone got worried.

"Oh dear, some of my buttons are missing," she said. "I'll just say my dress got caught on a branch. There are enough to hold me together for now."

"Here, I've found two of them," Ausable said, handing her the buttons. She put them in her pocket.

"Oh, Ausable, I hate to leave," she said.

"You have to. I know," he said.

Bracing herself, Anna said, "We should be going."

"I'll lead the way," he said, and they headed out of camp and into the woods.

"I'm not sure I can find my way up here again alone. How am I going to let you know when I can see you again?" she asked.

"You could send up a smoke signal," he said wryly.

"Ha ha," she said.

"Sorry. Bad Indian joke," he said, chuckling.

Anna started thinking. "Tonight, I'm sewing clothes for the crafts fair. And tomorrow I'm readying things at the church in the morning, then making crafts at Aunt Lil's in the afternoon. Can I see you tomorrow night?" she asked.

"Tell me when and I'll meet you on the beach," he said.

"It will have to be after dinner. I'll need to fabricate a story about where I'm going that late," she said. "Don't worry, I'll think of something."

"I'm not worried," he said, grabbing her and kissing her. "But I'll be counting the hours tomorrow until dark."

"I will as well. I'm just glad I have all these activities to keep me busy until then." And they kissed some more.

They continued down through the woods and came out right across from Idlenook's beach.

"Here we are," he said.

"Nothing in those woods looked familiar," she said. "You are a good tracker."

He pulled her out of sight of the beach and they kissed like they might never see each other again. It was sizzling and aching. Ausable pulled away, smiling sadly. "You better go."

Anna didn't say anything. She just turned toward the river, and then stopped. "Oh, I think I need a carry-over," she said laughing.

"Madam," said Ausable as he swept her up in his arms, carried her across the river, and deposited her gently on the beach.

"Tomorrow night," he said.

"Tomorrow night," she replied.

Anna turned and crossed the beach and went onto the path back to Idlenook. She picked a bunch of wildflowers along the way and held the bouquet as she entered the house.

"I'm back. Colleen? Millie?" Anna called.

"Hello, Missus," said Colleen from the kitchen as Anna entered with the flowers.

Millie came into the kitchen.

"Oh, those are lovely, ma'am. I'll put them on the table for dinner," said Millie. Millie went into the parlor and quickly returned with a vase.

As she took the flowers, Millie remarked, "Ma'am, your dress is missing some buttons."

"Oh, I know," Anna said. "I got caught on a branch on my walk. I went off the trail a bit to pick these flowers. I found two of the buttons. They are in my pocket."

"Don't worry, ma'am, I'll have that fixed for you," said Millie.

"Thank you, Millie," Anna said. "I'll go change before dinner." She started out, then, "Is Paul back from the play rehearsal yet?"

"Yes, he and Sam are both upstairs in their room," Colleen said. "Sam is helping Paul remember his lines. It's really adorable."

"Oh, good. I'll sneak up and have a listen," Anna said.

She went as quietly as she could up the creaky wooden stairs and stood in the hall listening.

Sam, as Juliet, reading:

What man art thou that, thus bescreened in night, so stumblest on my counsel?

Paul, as Romeo:

By a name
I know not how to tell thee who I am:
My name, dear saint, is hateful to myself,
Because it is an enemy to thee.
Had I it written, I would tear the word.

"That's right!" said Sam, astonished.

"Keep going, Sam," Paul said.

"Oh, right," Sam said. Then,

Sam, as Juliet, reading:

My ears have yet not drunk a hundred words
Of thy tongue's uttering, yet I know the sound.
Art thou not Romeo, and a Mon... Mon-tag-YOU?

"Montague, Sam," Paul said, annoyed.

Sam, sounding it out, "Mon-ta-gue. Montague. Okay, I've got it."

Anna chuckled quietly to herself in the hallway.

Sam, as Juliet, reading:

Art thou not Romeo, and a Montague?

Paul, as Romeo:

Neither, ... Um, Neither...

"Oh, Sam, now you made me forget. What is it?" Paul said, exasperated.

166

Sam, as Romeo, really acting it out:

Neither, fair saint, if either thee dislike.

"Right. Right," Paul said.

Paul, as Romeo:

Neither, fair saint, if either thee dislike.

"Very good, Paul," Sam said, applauding.

"Thank you, kind sir," Paul said, doing an exaggerated bow.

Anna came into the room, applauding along with Sam.

"I heard some of that from the hall. You're doing very well, Paul," Anna said enthusiastically.

"Thank you, Mother," Paul said, still bowing.

"He couldn't do it without my expert coaching," Sam said proudly.

"Oh, of course, Sam," Anna said, clapping for Sam. "I need to change my clothes. You boys keep rehearsing."

"Let's keep going from where we left off, Sam," Paul said.

Sam looked at the book.

Sam, as Juliet, reading:

How cam'st thou hither, tell me, and wherefore?

The orchard walls are high and hard to climb...

Anna smiled and closed the door. What wonderful boys Will and I have, she thought. How could she even think of being with Ausable? This is going to ruin everything. She needed to think long and hard about what she was doing and figure it out. She is really going to need Pastor Tom's counseling now. And she was looking forward to seeing her new friend Margaret tonight and soliciting her advice. Margaret had been in a similar situation far longer. Anna wanted to know more about how she was handling all this. Anna went into her room to change.

CHAPTER TWENTY-TWO

Margaret arrived just as the family was finishing dinner. She knocked on the screen door.

"Hello, all," Margaret called, seeing them through the screen at the dinner table on the dining porch.

Anna rose. "Hello, Margaret. Do come in."

"I don't want to interrupt your dinner," she said.

"Not to worry. We are just finished. Perfect timing," Anna said.

Margaret came in and Anna went to her and hugged her.

"Boys," Anna called, "you know Mrs. Bancroft."

The boys got up from the table and went to Margaret.

"Hello, Mrs. Bancroft," Sam said.

"Yes, hello," Paul said.

"Nice to see you boys," said Margaret. "Paul, I hear you're doing very well as Romeo."

"Thank you, Mrs. Bancroft," Paul said. "I'm actually enjoying it."

"That's wonderful," she said. "We all can't wait to see you in it."

"Boys, Margaret and I are going to work here on things for the fair," Anna said. "Why don't you go to your room?"

"Let's go rehearse some more," Paul said to Sam.

"You got it," Sam said. Then, teasing, "O Romeo, Romeo! Wherefore art thou, Romeo?" They ran up the stairs.

"They're a lot of fun, Anna," Margaret said.

Anna, smiling, said, "Yes, they are. I'm very lucky."

"I wasn't able to have children, I'm sad to say," Margaret told Anna. "Well, the way things are with John, we're probably better off."

"I didn't know that, Margaret. I'm so very sorry," Anna said.

"Thank you. We both have a lot to learn about each other," Margaret said.

"I'm looking forward to that, Margaret," Anna said. "Let's sit here at the table."

Anna summoned Colleen from the kitchen and introduced her to Margaret and asked her to bring them some coffee.

"I'll bring the coffee presently," Colleen said. "Let me clear off the table." Colleen removed the remaining dinner plates and went into the kitchen as the ladies sat at the table.

"The clothes that need mending are in this basket," Anna said, indicating a basket near the table. She lifted up her sewing kit and opened it, taking out needles and thread. Anna whispered to Margaret, "Ausable is back."

Margaret was shocked. "Really?" she said softly.

"I'll tell you everything once we've got our coffee and will be alone," Anna told her quietly.

"I'm on the edge of my seat, Anna," Margaret said.

Colleen came in with a tray with cups of coffee and cream and sugar. "Here we go," Colleen said. "Nice and hot." She put the tray on the table. Handing cups and saucers to Margaret and Anna.

"Let me take some of those clothes to mend. I'd love to help out," Colleen offered.

"Help yourself," Anna said. "I really appreciate it."

"Glad to do it," Colleen said as she took several items from the basket. "I'll be in my room if you need anything."

"Thank you again, Colleen," Anna said and Colleen left the room. Anna listened until she couldn't hear Colleen anymore.

"Margaret, we finally made love," Anna said, excitedly.

"What? Tell me what happened. I'm dying to know," Margaret said.

"Ausable met me at the entrance to our drive this afternoon." Anna said. "He said he had heard from Brown that Will and I were hoping to see him to thank him. But he waited for Will to leave the valley before he visited."

"Really," Margaret said.

"He wasn't sure he wouldn't be able to keep his hands off me and couldn't take a chance seeing me with Will here," Anna told her.

"My goodness," Margaret said. "That's so romantic!"

"It really is," said Anna dreamily.

"So, what happened?" Margaret probed.

"So… like he said, he couldn't keep his hands off me," Anna giggled. "And I couldn't keep mine off him."

"Oh, this is wonderful," said Margaret. "Tell me more."

"Well, he has set up a camp hidden in the woods. Only he can find it. And we went up there."

"And, and?" Margaret asked emphatically.

"And… Oh Margaret, we made love in his tent," she said joyfully remembering. "It was breathtaking!"

"Oh, Anna, I'm so happy for you," Margaret said.

"I am too. But I'm not so sure," Anna said seriously. "I mean, this isn't right. I have Will and those two wonderful boys upstairs to consider. This can't be happening."

"But it is, Anna. It is," Margaret said. "You can't deny how you feel."

"No, I can't," Anna agreed. "He's so astonishing." Then whispering, "And we said 'I love you' to each other," she told Margaret.

"Oh, my!" Margaret said, astonished. "That changes everything."

"I know!" Anna exclaimed. "I've never felt this way. Ever! Will never made me feel the way Ausable does. It's incredible." She dropped her head. "Am I being silly?"

"No, I think it's a lot more than that, my dear," Margaret said. "This is real. This is brilliant. This is life-changing."

"Oh no, don't say that," Anna said protested. "My family must come first."

"I know how you feel," Margaret said. "If it makes you feel so wonderful, follow your heart. You'll be a much happier person for it."

"Does Peter make you feel that way?" Anna asked.

"In a way, he does," Margaret said. "I'm a much happier person. He's changed my disposition. And, if it weren't for him, you and I likely would never have become friends. The point is, we both have someone who is giving us a new outlook, and making us happier women. We can't give that up, can we?"

"Well, I don't want to give it up," Anna said thoughtfully. "I'm just so conflicted."

"Come on, Anna. Have some fun. You know you deserve it."

"I do, don't I?" Anna said.

"Good girl," Margaret said.

"I'm so glad we're friends now, Margaret. I talk to Tom, but I needed a woman's point of view on this. Especially one who understands what I'm going through. Thank you."

Margaret grabbed Anna's hand and squeezed it.

"I'm here for you, friend," Margaret said. "Hm, sounds nice. I'm glad to have a friend, too."

"Well, let's get to the mending. I'd like to get all these sewn tonight if we can," Anna said, feeling better about things.

"Hand me a needle and a spool of thread," Margaret said.

They spent the evening sewing and talking and learning more and more about each other and were amazed at how much alike they turned out to be.

CHAPTER TWENTY-THREE

The next morning, Anna headed to the church to bring the mended clothes and help again with the crafts fair. As she rode, she thought happily about her talk last night with Margaret. They were both brought up in families of wealth and similar circumstances, Anna in Philadelphia, Margaret in Boston. They both had attended private girls' schools and neither felt a need to go on to college. Although Margaret had thought it might be fun to go to one of the Seven Sisters colleges in the Northeast, she decided she had had enough of schools for women only. They both had known their husbands since they were girls, even though Margaret married John more out of social convenience than love. She was expected to marry by a certain age, so with her family's strong endorsement, Margaret selected John, the best candidate to keep everyone at bay. They were happy for a while. Then, as the newness of married life wore off, they became content to lead their own lives and put on a good front. But Margaret knew she wasn't fooling anyone. At least now she had someone to commiserate with and Anna did, too.

Anna arrived at the church and tied her horse to the rail. She went inside and found Tom sorting through more clothing.

"Good morning, Tom," Anna said.

"Good morning, Anna," Tom said. "Look at all these clothes. People have been more than generous. This is going to be a wonderful fair this year."

"How nice," Anna said, looking things over. "And so many nice things. I might buy some myself."

"You seem pretty chipper this morning," Tom assumed.

"Actually, I am," Anna said. "I shouldn't be, and when you hear why, you will understand. But I can't help myself."

"So tell me," Tom said. "What secrets are you hiding?"

"I can't have anyone else hear, Tom," Anna said.

"This must be serious. Let's go into the rectory. We can talk there," Tom said.

They left the main church and went into Tom's office in the rectory. Tom closed the door and they sat together on the couch.

"All right, now," Tom said. "What is it?"

Anna paused, not sure she should tell him. It would make it too real. And Tom might talk her out of it. She should be talked out of it, but she didn't want to be. Not now. Not so soon. But Tom was her closest friend. She had to confide in him. He was always on her side.

"Ausable is back," Anna said.

"Really? That's wonderful," Tom said. "I'd like to meet him."

"Tom, you don't understand. Ausable is back only to see me."

"What do you mean, Anna?"

"He met me as I turned into our drive yesterday. And it was like the world went away. I was so elated to see him. To be with him. Tom, we made love."

Tom was silent for a bit. "Oh, well. That's quite a pill to swallow."

"I know," Anna said. "Tom, it was staggeringly remarkable. I've never felt this way. This isn't just lust talking. There is so much more there. As if we've known each other all our lives. This feels like it is meant to be. Tom, we told each other we loved one another!"

"Oh, Anna," said Tom, astonished. "This is very serious now."

"I know, Tom. It's all so wonderful, yet so terrible at the same time."

173

Anna started to cry. She needed to cry. She had to let it out. And Tom knew this and put his arm around her and held her and she sobbed onto his shoulder.

"That's good, Anna. This is what you need," Tom said, as he comforted her and gave her his handkerchief.

Her crying slowed and she wiped her eyes.

"Tom, you are such a dear friend," Anna said.

"You are too, Anna," said Tom.

"Oh, Tom. I really needed to let this out. It's all been building up inside of me."

"I can imagine," Tom agreed. "And don't worry. You don't need to figure this out now. Give it time. We can talk a lot about this. You are a smart woman. You will know what to do when the time is right. And whatever that decision is will be the right one for you."

"For me, yes. But what about my family?"

"You will make the right decision. I guarantee it. And I'll be here to help."

"Thank you, Tom," Anna said, wiping the final tears from her face. "All right. We've got a crafts fair to put on. Let's get back to work," Anna said.

"Let's," agreed Tom.

They left the rectory and went back into the church.

Anna spent the rest of the morning, happily sorting clothing and household items at the church with other ladies donating their time. At noontime, Anna went to Aunt Lil's. She was to have lunch with Lil and then they would work on the crafts they were fashioning for the fair. The cry in Tom's rectory was just what the doctor ordered for Anna. She was extremely relieved and happy. Not only did she have two wonderful friends, Ausable was back in her life and she decided to let that take her wherever it did.

Aunt Lil greeted Anna at the door.

"Hello, dear," said Aunt Lil.

"Hello, Lil," Anna said. Then, excitedly, "I've just come from the church and there are so many donations of clothes and household items. This is going to be the best fair we've ever had."

"That's wonderful news," Aunt Lil said. "Come, let's sit down to lunch."

As they sat down at the dining table, Aunt Lil said, "Anna, you seem considerably happier than I've seen you in quite a while. To what do you attribute this good humor?"

Anna replied, happily, "Oh, everything is going so well. Paul is excelling at playing Romeo in the summer play. I'm so proud of him. My ribs are much improved. Idlenook is restored, even better than it ever was. Will and the workers did a brilliant job. The whole town is pretty much back to normal. All is well with the world." Anna smiled and starting eating.

"I'm so glad to hear all this. And I'm looking forward to seeing Paul in the play," said Aunt Lil.

"He and Sam have been rehearsing together. It's very sweet to see," Anna said.

"How lovely," Aunt Lil agreed. "So am I to assume things between you and Will went well while he was here?"

"Oh, yes," said Anna. "We worked well together getting the house back in order."

"I see," Aunt Lil said. "Is that all? You worked well together?"

"Lil, you know how things are. It was a step in the right direction," Anna said. "I can only hope things keep moving that way."

"Well, good," Aunt Lil said. "I'm glad to hear it."

They ate and talked of the crafts they were making. Anna had an idea for a potholder in remembrance of "The Great Cloudburst of 1897." She wanted to do one side of the potholder with a sewn-on cutout of Giant Mountain as it was before the storm, and on the other side, a cutout of Giant with the large wash of granite on it now. Aunt Lil thought it was a brilliant idea. And a potholder was perfect because it had two sides to it. It would be easy to fashion so they could easily make a lot of them in time for the fair. Anna told Lil it was her guidance and tutelage over the years that inspired her always. Aunt Lil was very accepting of the compliment. They spent the afternoon finishing up crafts in progress and making a pattern for "The Great Cloudburst of 1897" potholder.

That evening, Anna and the boys had finished an early dinner at Anna's behest. She had prearranged a story with Margaret that they were meeting at her house to work on more items for the fair. So Anna had to leave early, as there was so much to do. She'd try to be home before dark, but if it got too dark, she would stay the night. Anna packed an overnight bag, just in case. Millie agreed to keep an eye on the boys and make sure they went to bed on time. Anna left, saying Margaret was sending her horse and buggy to pick her up.

Anna walked up the drive carrying her bag, until she was out of sight of the house. She ventured off the drive into the adjacent meadow in order to sneak back to the river and meet Ausable on the beach. As she walked, she was almost giddy with excitement. She couldn't believe she was doing this, sneaking out of her house and lying to her family. But somehow, she thought, she didn't care. Anna happily swung her bag around her at the tall grasses, almost dancing along. She couldn't believe this feeling. It was something she had never known before. As much as she had loved Will, she never felt like this. She couldn't explain, even to herself. But she was going to enjoy it and keep this feeling alive for as long as she could.

When she got to the river, she walked along its banks toward the beach. She cheerfully kicked a few rocks into the running water, enjoying the splashes.

She reached the beach, but Ausable wasn't there yet. At least she couldn't see him. He was good at appearing out of nowhere, so he could be right there any second, she thought, and giggled to herself, girlishly. She called, "Ausable?"

Well, he hasn't popped out, she thought. So she sat on the bench and looked at her pendant watch. She was a bit early. Anna looked through the trees, up at the scenic Adirondacks high above her. They soared in their beauty and her heart soared right along with them. The Adirondacks had always brought her joy and happiness. Now they brought her this unexplainable feeling. How stunning they are.

Anna looked at her watch again. He should have been here by now. She stood up and peered across the river to where she thought they had gone into the woods yesterday. She tried to see through the trees to the path they had come down. She didn't see him.

"Ausable?" Anna called. "Are you there?"

No answer. Anna sat back down on the bench and waited.

She waited for over an hour. She was beginning to worry. After what happened between them yesterday, she was confident he would have done anything to see her. Perhaps something had happened to him. He could be hurt. After all, he was alone and no one knew he was here. Except her.

Anna decided she had to try to find his camp. She knew it would be like finding a needle in a haystack, but she had to try. She had hiked these mountains all her life and wasn't afraid of getting lost. She just wasn't really dressed for hiking. So she lifted up her dress, picked up her bag, and, not worrying that her boots would get soaked, she crossed the river to the other side.

Anna got up on the bank and as she stepped, water spurted out of her boots. Oh well, she had more boots. Just not with her in her bag. She went into the woods where they had gone in the last time. She looked around. She remembered taking a fairly straight path to his camp. She didn't remember many twists and turns. So she headed straight into the woods. She looked for any sign of broken branches or tamped-down leaves. As she continued, she saw a broken fern, which gave her some hope. She kept walking in as straight a path as she could. She saw a very large pine with a broken branch from the cloudburst, which she thought she remembered seeing before. But there had been so many trees with broken branches since the storm.

Anna checked her watch. She remembered it had only taken them twenty minutes to get to the camp. She had five more minutes to go. She kept going, hoping that she would find Ausable and his camp. Or some sign of where he might be.

After another five minutes, she looked around for any sort of small clearing where his camp could be. She might be walking slower than she had with him, so she continued further. She called, "Ausable? Are you here? It's Anna." No answer.

She walked a bit further and decided she was perhaps now past where his camp was. So she thought she should walk back and forth across the path she came up and search the area for the camp.

Anna walked from one side to the other, slowly working her way down the mountain. She made six passes, and saw nothing. She kept calling for Ausable and got no response. The camp had to be nearby. There had to be some sign of it. How could he be gone? she thought. If she couldn't find the camp, then perhaps he wasn't hurt, but had to leave in a hurry for some reason. And he was good at leaving no trace. But why wouldn't he tell her? He could leave her a note or some kind of sign that he had to go.

Anna made a few more passes, looking for any sign of Ausable. Nothing. She was back at the tree with the broken branch. So his camp was gone. She would have found it by now. What happened? Where would he go? And why?

"Ausable! Where are you?" she cried.

Anna was crushed. She thought the worst. Was he afraid because they had said they loved each other? She couldn't know. All she did know was that he was gone. So she headed back down the mountain. She was crying. Tears were streaming down her face. She stopped and dropped her bag and sat on the ground, crying again. She had been so happy. Ecstatic from all the extraordinary feelings. Now, she was feeling so much worse than before she had met Ausable. He had given her love and hope. And that was now drifting away.

She looked around and noticed that night was drawing on Giant. She needed to pull herself together and get down the mountain. As she stood up, she looked at her dress and saw she had pine needles and twigs stuck to her. How was she going to explain this? Well, first things first. She had to get back down. Anna picked up her bag and started heading down, in as straight a path as she could. She thought she was finding trod-upon leaves that she might have caused on the way up. Yes, there was the broken fern. Soon she could hear the river. She breathed a sigh of relief.

When she emerged from the woods, she was exactly where she had entered. In some measure, she was proud of herself for that. It was the only good news she could think of. Anna hiked up her dress and crossed the river. She sat down on the bench. At least she had made it home. She looked at her watch. She had been gone less than three hours. Was it too soon to go home? She looked herself over and tidied herself up, pulling off the pine needles, leaves, and twigs entangled in her dress. She also had needles in her hair. Luckily she had a hairbrush in her bag. She looked at the dress in her bag and considered changing. But that would be silly. She'd have to explain one way or another. Also, her boots were soaked.

As Anna thought more about Ausable and the situation she was now in, she began to again wonder if this was a big mistake she was making. She had been swept up in all the romance, and now she was crashing back down to earth. Her life seemed empty before Ausable. She had only known him for such a short time. But in that short time, he had changed her life. As ridiculous as it might seem to the rest of the world, and even to Anna, she couldn't let go of that. She couldn't. And he couldn't just disappear from her life. She had to find him. She didn't know how, but she was going to make a plan. Tom and Margaret would help her. She would get Ausable back into her life.

CHAPTER TWENTY-FOUR

Early the next morning, Anna sent Colleen to tell Tom that she needed to speak him. She also sent word to Margaret to meet her at the church at noon. The boys were asleep when Anna had gotten home the night before. Anna gave no explanation for her wet boots and disheveled appearance, but she could see Colleen and Millie giving each other questioning glances. Anna simply asked them to clean her dress, and do the best they could with her boots. She didn't care. She had only one goal now. To find Ausable.

Just before noon, Anna took the carriage and headed to the church. Passing Aunt Lil's house, she saw Lil on the porch sewing, so Anna stopped to talk.

Look," Aunt Lil said, holding up a potholder with Anna's design on it.

"Oh that looks wonderful, Lil!" Anna exclaimed.

"I've made almost a dozen of them so far," Aunt Lil said proudly. "And I've kept them a secret from everyone. It will be a great surprise at the fair."

"That's such fun," Anna said. "I'll be by later on to help you. I've a few more things to help out with at the church first."

"All right, dear," Aunt Lil said. "I'll see you in a while."

"Good bye," Anna said and rode off.

When she got to the church, she saw Margaret's carriage. Anna tied her horse to the rail and went into the rectory. Tom and Margaret were there, talking.

180

"I can't imagine what's going on," Margaret said to Tom as Anna entered.

"Neither can I," said Tom, not seeing Anna.

"Ausable has disappeared!" Anna said, startling them.

"Oh, Anna, I didn't see you," Tom said. "You said he disappeared?"

"Yes. I went to meet him last evening, and I waited for over an hour," Anna said.

"Oh, no, Anna," Margaret said. "No sign of him at all?"

"No, so I hiked up my dress and crossed the river and scoured the woods where I thought his camp had been."

"I thought you said there was no clear path to his camp," Margaret said.

"There wasn't. But I wasn't going to let that stop me. I climbed to where I thought his camp should be and found nothing. Then I walked back and forth across the mountain to see if I could find it. There was no sign anyone had ever been up there."

"Oh, Anna. Where do you think he went?" asked Tom.

"The only thing I can think is that he got cold feet because we told each other we loved one another," Anna said.

"From what you told me, he doesn't seem like that type of fellow," Margaret said. "Perhaps there was an emergency back home and he had to leave."

"I can't believe he would leave without some kind of note or something, saying where he was going and why," Anna said emphatically.

"True," said Tom.

"So here's why I asked you to meet me here," Anna said. "I need to find him. I have to see him."

"Anna, are you sure?" Tom asked.

"I can't let him slip away this fast. I need to be sure," said Anna.

"I see," Tom said.

"So now we need to figure out how to find him," Anna said. "And I need your help."

"What can we do?" Margaret asked.

"Well, he did tell me he lives on Louisburg Square in Boston."

"My, he is quite fancy, isn't he?" said Margaret.

"I could send a note to him via Brown and plead with him to come back and discuss things," Anna said.

"You don't know that's why he left, Anna." Tom said. "But sending a note is a good idea."

"I could send a wire to my brother in Boston," Margaret offered. "He could try to find his house and see if he's there. It might be faster."

"That's wonderful," Anna exclaimed. "Do you think your brother will do that?"

"Of course. I'll say it's for a dear friend of mine," Margaret said.

"That's very sweet of you, Margaret. Okay, then, as far as people here in the valley, the only people who know him are Brown and Uncle Bull-Bull, so I can let them know again that I am looking for him," Anna said.

"You know, I'm thinking about your trek in the woods last night," Tom said. "Perhaps you were off by a bit and his camp is still there. Why not hire a skilled guide to see if you can find the camp? Or any traces of it."

"That's a wonderful idea, Tom," Anna said.

"Who do you suggest, Tom?" asked Margaret.

"The best there is. Old Mountain Phelps," Tom said.

"Of course," Anna agreed. "Will and I have met him several times. He lives up on Prospect Hill."

"That's right," Tom said. "He's a funny old guy. But if anyone can find the camp, it's him. We can ride up there right now if you'd like."

"That would be wonderful," Anna said excitedly. "Do you want to come, Margaret?"

"Of course," Margaret said. "This is the most fun I've had in the valley in years."

"Great. Let's go on a treasure hunt," Tom said enthusiastically.

"I can't thank the two of you enough," Anna said, putting her hands on their backs and hugging them.

They took Margaret's carriage, which was larger. They had to pass Aunt Lil's house to get to Phelps's cabin and, of course, she would wonder where they were going.

"Well, why don't we just tell her," Margaret said.

"Are you serious, Margaret?" asked Anna, shocked.

"Look, she knows about the Indian who saved you. We tell her that we heard he is camping in the mountains, and we want Old Mountain Phelps's help to find him. You want to give Mr. Hancock a proper 'thank you' since he left so quickly," Margaret explained. "This way, we can also tell the same story to Old Phelps, and you'll be in the clear. You don't want it getting out what you're really doing, do you?"

"Margaret, you're amazing," Tom said.

"Thanks. Who ever would have ever thought honesty would be my first intention?" Margaret said lightheartedly.

"Margaret, it's so much better to have you on my side," Anna said, teasing.

They all had a good laugh and rode on. When they passed Aunt Lil's they told her their story and, though Aunt Lil was somewhat skeptical, she reluctantly gave her blessing. She did agree that if anyone could find the Indian's camp, it would be Phelps.

When they arrived at Phelps's ramshackle cabin, his wife came out to greet them. She knew Tom from church.

"Hello, Mrs. Phelps," Tom said.

"Well, hello there, Pastor," she said.

"I believe you know Mrs. Tattersall," Tom said. "And this is Mrs. Bancroft.

They all greeted each other.

"What brings you up here?" asked Mrs. Phelps.

"I need your husband's help, Mrs. Phelps," Anna said. "Is he about?"

"He should be," Mrs. Phelps said. "Orson?" she called loudly.

They heard a squeaky-voiced reply from up the hill. "Yes dear?"

"Some people here to see you," she called.

Around some bushes came Old Mountain Phelps. He was a small man with bushy hair under a brown felt hat and a long white beard. A small pipe was clamped between his teeth. His legs were bowed and he looked like he had been in the same clothes for much too long. And when he got close, it smelled like it too. It was said he had no use for soap. As he approached, he recognized Pastor Tom.

"Pastor Baker. Greetings," Old Phelps said in his high-pitched voice, shaking Tom's hand.

"Hello, Mr. Phelps," Tom said. "You're looking well."

"Cain't complain 'bout nothin', Pastor," Old Phelps said. "As long as I'm in these here mountains, I'm a' home." He looked up at Anna.

"I remember you," Old Phelps said to Anna, twisting his pipe quizzically.

"Hello, Mr. Phelps," Anna said. "I'm Anna Tattersall. My husband Will and I have met you several times."

"Oh course, Mrs. Tattersall. Good to see ya. And I know your husband's Aunt Lil as well. Wonderful woman. I like her strong spirit."

"That she has, Mr. Phelps," Anna agreed. "That she has indeed."

"And this is Mrs. Bancroft," Tom said, indicating Margaret.

"Nice to meet such a breath o' loveliness, Mrs. Bancroft," Old Phelps said, bowing slightly to her.

"Well, how kind of you, Mr. Phelps," Margaret said, blushing a bit.

"Why don't we all have a sit down?" Old Phelps offered. He indicated two large logs set up as benches in front of his cabin. They all sat on the logs and were surprisingly comfortable.

"My, this is a spectacular view of the Adirondacks," Anna said.

"Yes, I can see why you chose this spot," Margaret added. "It takes your breath away."

Old Mountain Phelps removed his pipe and smiled with his small mouth, hardly visible under his scraggly beard. He rated people on his own personal scale of understanding the beauty before them. They had passed his test.

"So what can Old Mountain Phelps do for ye today?" he asked.

"I'm the one who needs your help, Mr. Phelps," Anna said. "I don't know if you heard but I was up on Giant when the cloudburst hit."

"Darn tootin', was that you?" Old Phelps asked. "I heared tell of a woman hurt up there."

"Yes, that was me," Anna said.

"Well, y'n don't look none worse fer wear, I'd a' say," said Old Phelps.

"Thank you," said Anna. "A few broken ribs, but they are healing very nicely. I was saved by an Indian man named Ausable Hancock."

"Ausable Hancock? He saved you?" asked Old Phelps. "I know Ausable. He'n I been hikin' these mountains together over the years. N'fact, t'be honest, he's a better tracker'n I."

"Oh, I doubt that, Mr. Phelps," said Anna. "You know these mountains better than any person on this earth."

"Well, anyhoo," Old Phelps said, "so people say."

"You haven't seen Mr. Hancock in the past few days, have you, Mr. Phelps?" Anna asked hopefully.

"Cain't say that I have, Mrs. Tattersall."

"You see, I've heard that Mr. Hancock is back in the valley and has a camp up on Giant somewhere very remote. Off all the usual trails," Anna told Old Phelps.

"That sounds like Ausable," Old Phelps said.

"I really want to find him to thank him properly for saving my life," Anna said.

Old Mountain Phelps puffed on his pipe for a bit, and looked up over at Giant, thinking. "Giant's a pretty big mountain. And ye say he be off the trails, eh?"

"Yes, but I have heard of the general area he's in," Anna said prudently.

"Well, that's a start," Old Phelps said.

"Do you know where my house, Idlenook, is? Where the river bends around our land?" Anna asked.

"I do," said Old Phelps.

"I've heard his camp is up behind there, not too far up," Anna told him, carefully choosing her words. "I tried a search myself. But I'm not an expert guide like you are. I had no luck."

"Since you narrowed it down a sum, I think I might'n be able to help ye," Old Phelps said.

"Oh, that's wonderful, Mr. Phelps," Anna said, eagerly. "I can't thank you enough. And of course I'll pay you."

"No need for that. I enjoy a random scoot in the woods," said Old Phelps. "A random scoot" were his words for going off the beaten track.

"I'd like to go with you, if that's all right," Anna said. "I've been climbing these mountains most of my life."

"And I'd be happy to have ye along on this rigmarole," Old Phelps said.

"When can we go?" Anna asked.

"Is tomorry too soon for ye?" Old Phelps asked.

"Tomorrow it is," Anna said happily. "Mr. Phelps, I really can't thank you enough."

"Think nothing of it. I'm happiest when I'm up in these mountains. Any of ye others jernin' in?"

"This is Anna's quest," said Margaret.

"Yes," agreed Tom. "And she'll be in expert hands. Plus I have too much to do for the fair."

"Well then, it's you and me, Anna," said Old Phelps.

Anna was a bit taken aback by his familiarity. Only close friends and family used first names. Old Mountain Phelps noticed Anna's reaction.

"I'm sorry. I see yer a some put off by me callin' ye Anna," said Old Phelps. "But let me tell ye sumpin'. I only call thems I reelly like by their given names. So I hope that be all right."

Anna smiled, heartily. "I'm very honored, Mr. Phelps."

"How 'bout Orson?" he said.

"Orson it is," Anna said warmly.

They agreed to meet the next morning at Idlenook and hike off from there. Anna was filled with a fragment of hope again.

CHAPTER TWENTY-FIVE

Millie and the boys were helping Anna with her hiking gear. The boys were anxious to meet Old Mountain Phelps. They had heard all sorts of stories about him and his adventures, most of which were folderol, but the boys didn't care. Mr. Phelps was a legend and they would get to meet him. They were most disappointed that they couldn't go on the hike with him, but Anna was insistent. They would be going through rough terrain and she didn't want to have to worry about them getting hurt.

There was a knock at the front door and the boys bounded to the front of the house to answer it. Paul pulled the door open and there stood Old Mountain Phelps. The boys stared at him, confused. This was the legend guide they had heard of?

"Hello," Old Phelps said in his high, squeaky voice.

And he sounded like that, they thought?

"I'm Mr. Phelps. Is Anna Tattersall t' home?" Old Phelps asked.

Anna came to the door. "Hello, Orson. Paul, please invite Mr. Phelps in."

"Oh, sure," Paul said, letting Mr. Phelps in.

"Thank you," Old Phelps said.

As he passed Sam, Sam made a face and whispered to Anna, "Mother, he stinks."

"Shhhh," Anna admonished, hoping Old Mountain Phelps didn't hear him.

"Orson, these are my boys, Paul and Sam. Boys, say hello to Mr. Phelps."

"Hello," Sam said.

"Nice to meet you," said Paul.

"Well, you two look like two rough and ready hikers," Old Phelps said. "Are you coming with us today?"

"No. Mother won't let us," said Sam.

"She says it's too rough where you're going," Paul added.

Old Mountain Phelps looked up at Anna who shook her head and mouthed "No."

"Well, your mother be a wise woman, ya know," Old Phelps said. "We won't be on no trails today and we wouldn't want ye young 'uns to get lost and eaten by no bears er nuthin'."

"Bears!" Sam exclaimed.

"I doubt we'll see any bears," Anna said, giving an eye to Old Phelps. "But it will be unsafe territory today."

"Not ta worry," said Old Phelps. "I know most of them bears up here parsonally. Why, they walk right up to me and shake ma hand."

"Really?!" said Sam, impressed. "I want to shake a bear's hand."

"One day, when ya's older, I'll take ye out to meet one, Sam," said Old Phelps.

"Oh boy! That would be great," said Sam.

"I think we should be going, Orson," Anna said.

"Right-o," said Old Phelps. "After you, Anna."

Millie helped Anna on with her pack basket. Colleen came out from the kitchen carrying a cloth bag.

"Missus, I made some lunch for the two of you. Do you have room for it?" asked Colleen.

"I think I might," Anna said.

"I do," said Old Phelps, taking the bag. "That's right nice of ye. I heerd about yer cookin' from Bull. I'll be lookin' ferward to this."

"Thank you, Mr. Phelps," said Colleen.

"All right, boys. You be good," said Anna. "We'll be home before dark." A pause, then, "Won't we, Orson?"

"Maybe yes, maybe no," Old Phelps said, teasing. "Deepends on what we's findin' out der. You don't mind asleepin' under them stars, do ye?"

Anna just smiled and shook her head, "Ha, not at all."

They went out the front door and across the meadow.

Sam looked after them. "You know, he may smell funny. And he sure doesn't look like a legend. But if he has bears for friends, he's okay in my book."

Colleen, Millie, and Paul laughed and closed the door.

Old Phelps led Anna to a spot in the river where two large trees had fallen and it was very easy to cross.

"Oh, I wish I had known about this when I went looking for the camp," Anna said. "I slogged through the river."

As they crossed, Anna looked at the trees. They had just recently fallen.

"Orson, this must have just happened in the storm. How do you know about it already?" Anna asked.

"It's ma callin', Anna," said Old Phelps. "I knows this here area better'n I know meself."

They headed into the woods and Old Mountain Phelps walked straight ahead.

Anna said, "I was told his camp is only about a twenty-minute walk up in this direction somewhere."

"And who be it that told you this?" asked Old Phelps.

"Well… it was actually a person I know who was told by another person. So I'm not exactly sure where the information came from," Anna said.

"I see," Old Phelps said.

They hiked a bit further, Anna following in Old Phelps's footsteps. The guide seemed to be walking determinedly in one direction.

Old Phelps asked, "When you'n came alookin' on yer own, do ye remember where ye went?"

"I hiked up from behind our house," Anna said. "I crossed the river from our beach and went pretty much straight up. When I didn't find anything, I walked back and forth on my way down."

"Mighty smart of ye," Old Phelps said. "That be a clever technique to use."

"Thank you, Orson," said Anna.

As they hiked, Old Phelps pointed out rocks and other hazards for Anna to watch out for. He just kept going, as if he knew right where he was going.

After a while, Anna asked, "Orson, if you don't mind my asking, we seem to be hiking straight ahead in one direction. Are we headed somewhere?"

"Yes'm. Up this here trail," Old Phelps said, pointing.

"Trail?" Anna asked, looking around at a bed of leaves and pine needles between a lot of trees and brush. "What trail?"

Old Mountain Phelps stopped and squatted down.

"Come 'ere an' look, Anna," Old Phelps said. "Let me show ye suptin'."

Anna squatted down next to Old Phelps.

"Now look vera careful dere," Old Phelps said pointing. "Ye see how these here piney needles are pressed into the soil? And only in small spots like this? Thems are footstep markin's."

"Really?" Anna said. "How did you ever see them? They are barely visible."

"Oh, they be very visible to me," said Old Phelps.

"I was looking for broken branches or cracked twigs," Anna said.

"Oh, dey help too," Old Phelps said. "I been seein' sum o' dem. But dees markin's be much betta. More regaler."

"Are you sure these aren't from some animal?" Anna asked.

"No'm. These be from Ausable."

"They are?!" Anna said surprised. "How can you tell?"

"'Cause I know me how he tries to hide his tracks," Old Phelps said. "As I say befer, he taught me a lot. So I figered, if his camp be up behind yer house as ye say, then the most logical way up der is over them trees we crossed te river on. I'm sure he'd a found dem, too. From der, I didn't spot his tracks right away. He hid de best he could down there near de

190

river. But in no time, I spotted his trail. And we been follerin' it ever since."

"Really? So you think he's up here?" Anna asked excitedly.

"Hard to tell, Anna," said Old Phelps. "Them tracks was made a couple days ago. But we'll see when we get der. By the by, I been seein' yer tracks crossing back and fort across dis trail. You come preety dang close."

As they walked on, Anna tried to look carefully at the "trail" they were following. She was having quite a hard time seeing what Old Mountain Phelps saw. She would have to walk much more slowly and keep stopping and looking much more closely to see what Old Phelps was following.

They came to a small clearing and Old Phelps stopped. He slowly began to look around.

"His camp was here," Old Phelps said.

Anna looked around. "You're right," she said. Then disappointed, "This was it. There's the log."

Old Mountain Phelps was a clever fellow. And not only about the Adirondacks. He thought there was more to this search than met the eye. And now he was sure. Anna Tattersall had been here before. And she had most likely been here with Ausable Hancock. When Ausable left, he speculated that Anna tried, but couldn't find her way back up here alone. Old Phelps was also a gentleman who wouldn't dare embarrass a woman. Plus he didn't know the details and had no right to intrude. So he continued on as if she hadn't said that.

"See here," Old Phelps said, "You can see where t'ings have been tamped down a bit."

He picked up a stick and scraped away some leaves.

"And he covered this well." Old Phelps showed Anna. "There was a fire here."

"I see," Anna said, sadly.

"Sorry you missed him, Anna," Old Phelps said. "I'm sure ye'll catch up to him sometime."

"Yes. Thank you, Orson," Anna said. "I really appreciate your taking the time to help me."

"It were a lovely hike with a lovely lady," Old Phelps said.

"Thank you. Well, we found what we came for. I suppose we should head back," Anna said.

As she turned she saw, hanging by twine on a tree, a painting on bark. Anna had to catch her breath. It was one of Ausable's paintings. It was of the mountains, and in silhouette, a man and a woman walking, holding hands. Anna went to the tree and took down the painting.

"Look, Orson, he was here. And he left this," Anna said showing it to Orson.

"He's quite the arteest," Old Phelps said.

As she turned the painting for Orson to see, Anna saw there was something written on the back.

> A.T
> I'm sorry to leave so suddenly.
> My mother is ill.
> I will be back as soon as I can.
> A.H.

Anna's heart stood still as she stared at the words he wrote. He hadn't had a change of heart. There was an emergency. All her silly thoughts were just that. Silly. He did leave word for her, in the safest way he could. He knew she would be able to find the camp again. Anna was beside herself with joy. She held the painting to her chest.

Old Phelps could tell there was something more going on. He said, "Anna, yer Colleen made us a deelicious lunch. Mayhaps we should stay here a spell and eat," Old Phelps suggested.

"That's a wonderful idea, Orson," Anna said, in very high spirits. "I'd love that."

So they sat and had a lovely lunch together, enjoying the day and each other's company.

CHAPTER TWENTY-SIX

Anna had been euphoric since finding Ausable's painting. And for the past week and a half, she put all her exuberance into the annual crafts fair. It was the end of the day for the fair, which had been a great success. The grounds around the Country Club were festooned with ribbons and bunting. Tables were set up all over and each of the ladies had shown off her craft specialties and had done well selling almost everything.

Anna and Aunt Lil had made several dozen cloudburst potholders, as well as many other crafts to sell for charity. The potholders were a sensation and no one was surprised that they sold every last one. Colleen and Millie had pooled their pennies, enough to contribute and buy one of the potholders. Aunt Lil was very grateful. A lot of household items and clothing had been collected and distributed to people who lost things in the storm, most of whom were year-round residents of the valley and all of whom were very grateful.

Margaret had to make a trip to visit her sister and handle some family business, so she wasn't able to attend the crafts fair. Before Margaret left, Anna had told her and Tom the result of her climb with Old Mountain Phelps, and they had called off the search. Margaret hadn't been able to reach her brother in Boston by the time she heard the news from Anna, so no one was the wiser. Anna hid her new painting along with the other one Ausable had given her. The one she had gotten as a child still hung on the dining porch wall. Anna and Martina were making the rounds of the tables to see if there were any unsold items that they might want.

"Oh, I want to stop by Joan's table again," Martina said to Anna. "She had some very creative table napkins. The more I thought about them, I realized they would match a tablecloth I have back home."

"I hope she still has them," Anna said.

They stopped at Joan's table. She earlier had beautiful embroidered napkins, tablecloths, and tea cozies.

"Joan, do you still have those darling napkins?" Martina asked. "The ones with the little yellow flowers?"

"Oh, Martina, I'm sorry, I don't," Joan said. "I've sold almost everything."

"Oh, that's too bad," Martina said. "I think they would have gone nicely with a tablecloth I have."

"All your things were so lovely, Joan," Anna said. "I can see why they sold."

"That's so kind of you to say, Anna," Joan said. "Martina, I'd be happy to make some more napkins for you."

"That's very sweet, Joan," said Martina. "I couldn't impose on you like that."

"Not at all," Joan said. "I'd be happy to. How many do you need?"

Anna spotted Tom across the fair. "You two talk this over," Anna said. "I want to speak to Tom."

Anna went across to the other side where Tom was speaking with the Wardwells.

Philip Wardwell was saying, "Pastor, I'm so glad we were all able to pitch in and help the people hit by the storm. You really did a bang-up job organizing all this."

"My pleasure, Mr. Wardwell," Tom said. Then noticing Anna coming up to them, he added, "And with people like Anna here to help, we couldn't lose."

"Oh Tom. Such a flatterer," Anna said.

Elizabeth Wardwell reached into her bag. "And I've got my wonderful potholder to prove it," Elizabeth said, holding up her cloudburst potholder. "They are inspired, my dear."

"Thank you, Elizabeth," Anna said. "I'm glad they were such a success."

"Well, we should be going," Philip said. "Nice to see you both again."

They all said their goodbyes.

"It's been a great event, Tom," Anna said. "Aunt Lil is over there counting the proceeds."

"I'm sure we beat last year's amount," Tom said. "There was so much enthusiasm from everyone this year."

"Yes. I think the storm shook people out of their usual complacency," Anna said. "And not only for the fair. In general, everyone seems to be a lot kinder. Less manipulating and disapproving."

"I agree. And one main reason, I think, for that, "Tom said, "is that you and Margaret have become friends."

"Really?" Anna said. "How do you mean?"

"Margaret was one of the main instigators of all the mean gossip and infighting among the summer valley folk," Tom said. "You gave her the chance to show the real woman underneath all the bluster. And that's all it was. She was a woman who was afraid to be herself. It wasn't just that you had something to hold over her either. She wanted the chance to show who she could be, and I give you a lot of credit for bringing that out in her."

"My goodness, Tom," Anna said. "You've really thought a lot about this."

"I have," Tom said. "I've noticed the change in a lot of people. But especially in the women Margaret was friendly with. They are all nicer for it."

"I think you're right," Anna agreed. "They are all still friends, but the nastiness is no longer there." Then, thinking, "Of course, it was some fun, too."

"Oh, no doubt about that," said Tom. "But as pastor, I must express, it's much better to have everyone be kinder to each other."

"Yes, Pastor Tom," Anna said playfully. "We're such good friends, I sometimes forget you're still a pastor who needs to set a good example for his congregation."

"Yes," Tom said. "But a little gossip now and then never hurt."

They both laughed.

"Oh, Anna," Aunt Lil called from her table, waving Anna over.

"Aunt Lil must have her count," Anna said.

Anna and Tom went over to Aunt Lil's table.

"How much did we take in, Lil?" Anna asked.

"It's more than we ever made before!" Aunt Lil exclaimed. "Let's call everybody around."

Tom called out and everyone gathered around Aunt Lil's table.

"Everyone," Aunt Lil said. "We should be very proud of ourselves this year. Not only did we make it through that terrible storm, but with this year's crafts fair, we have topped ourselves."

Everyone excitedly asked "How much?" "Yes, tell us."

"One hundred and forty-seven dollars and twelve cents!" Aunt Lil exclaimed.

Everyone gathered clapped enthusiastically.

"Oh my, that's wonderful, Mrs. Tattersall," Tom said.

"This is really going to help the local charities," Anna said. "Especially this year."

"I think the storm caused people to be more generous this year," Aunt Lil said to Anna.

"Tom and I were just talking about that," Anna said.

Aunt Lil called out to the crowd, "Thank you all for all your generosity and imaginative crafting!"

Everyone applauded, and headed back to their tables.

"Let me help you gather everything up, Lil," said Anna.

"I'm glad that Margaret wasn't here today. You know I never liked that girl," Aunt Lil said to Anna. "She always rubbed me the wrong way."

"She's changed, Lil," Anna said. "She has been a wonderful friend to me in the last few weeks."

"I'm not so sure," said Lil. "Be careful. A leopard cannot change her spots that easily."

"I think she can if the spots were just a camouflage for what was really underneath," Anna said.

"I hope you're right, dear," said Aunt Lil.

The workers from the Country Club were starting to move the tables back inside as Holmes appeared. He put their things in Aunt Lil's carriage. Anna had her carriage there and would drive herself home. It had been a very long day and everyone was happily exhausted. Anna told Tom that, after all the work they had put in for the fair, she needed a day of fun and shopping. So tomorrow she was going to Lake Placid. She had heard the town now had a textile store and she wanted to find new fabric to make curtains for Idlenook. She would overnight at the luxurious Grand View Hotel. Tom wished her well, and Anna said goodbye and headed home.

As Anna turned into the drive to Idlenook, she was reminded of Ausable's surprise appearance at the head of the drive. Every time she turned into the drive, Anna looked into the bushes hoping he would emerge. But once again he wasn't there. It had been two weeks since she had seen him and her heart was aching for him more with each passing day. Especially now, knowing how he felt about her. She hoped his mother would be getting well soon so he would come back to her. If he didn't return soon, she might have to make plans for a visit to Boston.

Anna stopped the carriage next to the stable and secured the horse. She would ask the boys to stable the horse for her. She was quite weary from the day at the crafts fair. As she turned to go toward the house, something near the path to the beach caught her eye. It was shady there, but next to the boys' playhouse, on the tree she could see something hanging. Anna's heart leapt. Was it what she thought it was? Anna hurried across the meadow to the tree. It was one of Ausable's paintings. He was back!

All of Anna's weariness disappeared. She pulled the painting down. It showed Ausable's clearing up in the woods. She turned it over and looked at the back.

197

A.T.
I am here.
Waiting for you.
A.H.

Anna hugged the painting and ran to the house. She told Millie she was going to take a walk in the woods and hurried upstairs to change into walking clothes. She was ecstatically happy. She couldn't wait to be in Ausable's arms again. She carefully hid the painting with the others and ran downstairs. She told Colleen not to wait dinner. She'd had plenty to eat at the fair. Then Anna dashed out the door.

Taking Old Mountain Phelps's route, she went through the meadow next door and used the logs to cross over the river. She now easily recognized the markings on the ground that Old Phelps had shown her and quickly followed them up the mountain. Ausable had come back. She was overjoyed. It felt like an eternity, but she finally reached his camp. It was all set up similar to before. But he wasn't there.

"Ausable?" she called.

Ausable came out from behind some brush.

"It's you!" he said. "I heard someone coming and didn't want to be found. I'm so glad it was you."

"Me too," she said.

He swept her up in his arms and they kissed, so passionately, as if they had never kissed before.

"Oh, Ausable," Anna said. "When you didn't meet me on the beach, I was devastated."

"I'm so sorry, Anna. I didn't know how to tell you where I was going," he said. "But I hoped you would find a way up to the camp and find my note for you. I assume you did."

"Not at first," she said. "I waited over an hour, and when you didn't come, I thought something might be wrong. So I crossed the river and tried to find the camp. I looked all over up here, but I couldn't find a trace of it."

"Oh, my poor dear Anna," he said, kissing her again.

"I had almost given up hope. I thought you had gotten cold feet and didn't want to see me anymore."

"Oh no, of course I want to see you."

"I told Tom and Margaret about your disappearance and they were helping me find you. Margaret was going to wire her brother in Boston to try and find your home on Louisburg Square."

"I wouldn't have been there. I was with my mother at her house."

"How is your mother?" asked Anna. "Well now, I hope."

"Yes. She had developed pneumonia and was in a dangerous state for a while. But happily she is much improved and well on her way to recovery," Ausable told Anna.

"I'm very happy to hear that, Ausable," Anna said.

"I am, too," Ausable said. "But wait. If you didn't find the camp, how did you get my painting?"

"Tom had the idea of hiring Old Mountain Phelps to help me search for your camp," Anna said.

"Ah, Orson. If anyone could track me, it's him," Ausable said laughing.

"He was wonderful," Anna said. "He taught me how to find your barely noticeable tracks in the woods. I followed them again just now."

"I guess they aren't as hidden as I thought," Ausable said. "How did you get him to help you? Did you tell him about us?"

"Well, partially," Anna said. "I told him you had saved me during the cloudburst, and I wanted to find you to properly thank you."

"Good thinking," Ausable said.

"Yes, it even worked when my Aunt Lil saw us heading to Orson's cabin," Anna said.

"So am I to assume you want me to come down and show myself?" asked Ausable.

"In time," Anna said. "When Orson and I located your camp, but you weren't here, I told everyone you had left. So there is no rush. I want you all to myself as long as I can."

They kissed.

"That sounds fine to me," Ausable said, holding her close.

"And I had a wonderful idea as I was climbing up here," Anna said.

"What is it?" Ausable asked.

"I am planning to go to Lake Placid tomorrow for some shopping. I'm going to spend the night there. So I thought…"

"Oh. That is a wonderful idea," Ausable exclaimed.

"It would be so nice to finally share a real bed with you," Anna said.

"Where are you staying?" Ausable asked.

"The Grand View," said Anna. "Have you ever been?"

"Uh, no," Ausable said haltingly. "You see, hotels like that aren't particularly welcoming to Indians."

"Oh dear," Anna said. "I hadn't thought about that. I was only thinking we'd be away from Keene Valley where everyone knows me and in Lake Placid where I don't know a soul."

"Let's give it a try," Ausable said. "You never know. They may let me stay there."

"Right," Anna agreed. "And if you're made to feel unwelcome, well, I'll sneak you in the back or something."

"That sounds like fun," Ausable said. "When do we leave?"

"I'm taking the eleven o'clock stage from Bailey's," Anna said. "And if you just happen to be there, well, you can ride the stage with me."

"Just to be on the safe side, why don't I meet the stagecoach in Keene at the Graves Hotel?" Ausable asked. "So there won't be any awkwardness."

"I understand what you mean. Good idea. Thank you. But when we return, I think it will be time for the proper 'thank you' you deserve," Anna told him. "I'll say we met in Lake Placid and I brought 'my savior' home to meet everybody. We'll have a big party."

"I would love that," Ausable said happily.

"I'm glad. Me too," Anna said contentedly.

"Oh, Anna, I'm so happy to see you again," Ausable said. "I missed you so."

They held each other close, caressing one another.

"I'm overjoyed to be in your arms again," Anna said. "I never want this feeling to end."

They made tender love and both felt as though it was the first time all over again.

Hating to part, Ausable walked Anna down the mountain toward her home. She would meet him at the Graves Hotel in Keene when he'd join her on the stage to Lake Placid. Both were overjoyed.

CHAPTER TWENTY-SEVEN

In the morning, Millie drove Anna to Bailey's to meet the stagecoach.

"Ma'am, you must have quite a night planned. I saw you packed that lovely yellow gown of yours," Millie said.

"Oh, I do, Millie," said Anna. "I am in need of pampering after all the work on the crafts fair. I'm dining in style in the Grand View's Banquet Room. It has a magnificent view of Mirror Lake from up on the hill."

"Oh, my, that should be wonderful fun," said Millie.

She couldn't tell Millie the real reason it would be wonderful. They passed Aunt Lil's house and Lil came out to wish Anna an enjoyable time in Lake Placid.

When they arrived at Bailey's, the stagecoach was already there. Millie spoke to the driver about Anna's valise. The driver came over and offered his hand to Anna. He spoke with a thick Italian accent.

"Scusi. Nice-a to meet-a you, Mrs. Tattersall. Everyone calls-a me Antony."

"I'm happy to meet you, Antony," Anna said. "May I ask your last name?"

"You may-a," said Antony. "But-a the reason everybody call me Antony is because-a my last-a name is-a so long-a Italiano name, no one can-a say it." He chuckled, as did Anna.

"Very well," said Anna. "Antony it shall be."

"Is there anyone else going to Lake Placid, Antony?" asked Anna.

"Thera ar-a three gentlamen joining us in Keene-a, Mrs-a Tatterasall."

"Thank you, Antony," said Anna.

Antony opened the stagecoach door, "Please-a?"

Anna walked to the stagecoach. She got in and settled herself into the back seat. It was a slightly different coach than the one from Westport. Perhaps a bit smaller, but it seemed to be better appointed. Anna was anxious to get to Keene and see Ausable again.

As she rode along, watching the beautiful Adirondack Mountains pass by, she couldn't believe how happy she was. It had been so long since she felt this way, if she ever had. And at the same time, still feeling conflicted. How could she be doing this? She knew she was being selfish, but, as was expected of her, she had always thought of others first. It was time that she thought of herself and did what felt good to her. And this felt right.

As they pulled up in front of the Graves Hotel, Anna leaned her head out the stagecoach window. Ausable stood there on the road, watching the stage arrive. He was dressed in the finest cutaway suit, a silk puff tie, and wearing a very stylish top hat and red vest. And this was not premade clothing. These garments were hand-tailored. Anna had only seen him in his hiking gear. This man was a gentleman.

The stagecoach pulled up to the hotel and Ausable tipped his hat to Anna. She exited the stagecoach and Ausable helped her down.

"Well then, how was the ride?" Ausable asked.

"Too long. I couldn't wait to get here to see you," Anna said, then, a little nervously. "I think I'm having a bit of a moment here. This is the first time I've seen you out in public and dressed so exquisitely. I'm taken aback."

"It is strange for me, too. We've really only been alone together in the woods," he said.

As the two of them were talking, the other two men taking the stagecoach went over to speak with Antony. They then got into the coach. Antony came over to them and extended his hand to Anna.

"We are-a ready to-a go," Antony said. "May I help-a you in, Madam-a?"

"I'd be happy to do that," Ausable said.

"Uh. Maya I-a speak to you, Sir?" Antony asked Ausable.

"Of course," Ausable said.

They went a few steps away from the stagecoach as Anna looked on, questioning. Ausable nodded his head and patted Antony on the back. He came back to Anna.

"Apparently the gentlemen in the stagecoach are not very keen on riding with an Indian," Ausable told them.

"Oh, Ausable," Anna said, annoyed. "That's ridiculous."

"Now, now. It will be fine," Ausable said. "I'll ride up here with Antony."

"Well, I'm appalled," Anna said. "I'm so sorry, Ausable."

"Please, please. You have to realize, this is the way things are," Ausable explained. "I'm used to it."

"I don't know if I can ride in this coach with those men," Anna said.

"Please, Anna," said Ausable. "We'll have a wonderful time together in Lake Placid. Let's just get there. All right?"

"Well, all right. Let's go," Anna said.

Ausable helped her into the coach. As she got in, the two men were sitting where she had been sitting before.

"I'm sorry, I was sitting in that seat," Anna said, coldly.

"Oh, of course," one of the men said. "Our apologies." They moved to the other side of the coach as Anna took her seat.

"Allow me to introduce myself. I'm Mr. Taylor and this is Mr. Cole."

"How do you do?" Mr. Cole said.

Anna just nodded at them and didn't speak. Mr. Taylor and Mr. Cole gave each other a look.

"If I may ask, are you acquainted with the Indian man?" Mr. Taylor asked.

"Yes, as a matter of fact, I am," Anna said.

"We heard you outside," Mr. Cole said. "You see, it's just not done, riding with an Indian. I wouldn't feel safe."

"Oh, you wouldn't, would you?" Anna bellowed at them. "Well, let me tell you something. You know nothing about him. That man saved me from certain death in that cloudburst we had. He took care of my broken bones and carried me down Giant Mountain by himself. He saved my life! And you wouldn't feel safe with a man like that?! How dare you?!"

The men reacted, a bit frightened. Antony called from up on the stagecoach seat, "Is-a everything-a all right down-a there?"

Anna called up to him, "We're fine, Antony. Thank you." Anna sat back and glared at Mr. Taylor and Mr. Cole. It was a very quiet ride to Lake Placid.

CHAPTER TWENTY-EIGHT

They arrived at Lake Placid in the late afternoon. The Old Mountain Road had been repaired and much improved since the storm so it didn't feel as treacherous as usual. Antony deposited the two men off at his usual stop, The Stagecoach Inn. Antony said that since the two men were so rude to Mr. Hancock, he would drive the lady and the gentleman up to The Grand View Hotel. He explained that, being a recent immigrant, he understood how it felt to be separated out. He held the door for Ausable so he could ride the rest of the way inside with Anna. Ausable sat down and put his arm around Anna, holding her comfortably close.

"I really want to commend you, Anna, for speaking on my behalf," Ausable said.

"I really scared them," Anna said. "I thought they might jump out of the stagecoach."

"Hah. I wish they had," Ausable said, and they had a good laugh.

"You know, I was thinking that both you and Margaret live in Boston. She's on Commonwealth Avenue. But I'm sure you have had entirely different experiences."

"I'm sure we have," Ausable said.

"How did you end up living in Louisburg Square?" Anna asked.

"Actually, when I bought the house, my parents were against it," Ausable said. "They thought it was too ostentatious for me to live there. They also had been through a lot of difficult experiences. Of course, I went to Harvard and associated with a wider variety of people than my parents. I've had good and not so good experiences, but I felt I had earned the right to live where I wanted if I could afford it. So I did."

"And you didn't have any issues with the person selling you the house? Or your neighbors?" Anna asked.

"The man who sold me the house was an old business acquaintance I had known for a long time," Ausable told them. "He was happy to sell me the house. He did warn me about some of the neighbors. And the ones who gave me difficulty were the same ones he had trouble with. If people want to be bothersome, they are going to be, no matter who you are. And believe me, I've had enough occurrences to know the best ways to deal with such people."

"It's quite fascinating, really," Anna said. "I grew up with such privilege and so little association with anyone other than those in similar circumstances to me. But then again, I am much more welcoming with our hired help. My parents and Aunt Lil are not happy with the relationships I have with Colleen and Millie. But I don't really understand the issue. And, after meeting you, well, you are really widening my perspective. Aunt Lil will certainly be disapproving, I'm afraid."

"Speaking of that, let me warn you," Ausable said. "I'm quite certain this hotel may have just run out of rooms if I go in and ask for one. I think to be safe, why don't I come in the back unnoticed and join you?"

"I suppose that would be best, to keep our wits about us," Anna said.

Antony pulled the stagecoach in front of the Grand View. The hotel doorman opened the stagecoach door and assisted Anna out of the coach. When Ausable descended, the doorman was taken a bit aback. Anna noticed and realized Ausable was right. He might not be able to get a room at this hotel. This was all very new and somewhat discomforting for Anna. Her life had been so traditional and staid. She knew her place in the world and how to perform appropriately. No one had told her what would happen if she and her husband became distant. She knew women and men who had taken lovers, but it was extremely frowned upon. Although it happened, it was "not done" and never spoken of. At least not in good company. She was entering uncharted territory, with no skills but her own acumen and common sense, which was being sorely tested now. And to make matters worse, she had fallen in love with an Indian. This wasn't going to be easy. But she had to see where life would take her and if she was able to handle it.

The Grand View was a magnificent hotel, high on Grandview Hill overlooking Mirror Lake and the Adirondack mountains behind. The hotel was decorated in the latest luxurious fashion. It had all of the current amenities including running water, and the most modern sanitary appointments.

The bellhop showed Anna to her room. This hotel had a steam-driven elevator which they rode to the second floor. The room looked out the front of the hotel with a magnificent view over Mirror Lake.

She had made a reservation for dinner at eight o'clock and hopefully the darkness of the dining room would keep people from noticing Ausable too closely. After she unpacked, Anna found the back stairway of the hotel, probably used by hotel staff. She went down and luckily there was a door going outside to the back of the hotel. As soon as she opened the door, Ausable saw her and quickly hurried inside. Anna was feeling a bit childish, but it was also quite fun.

They hurried up the back stairway and Ausable and Anna went into her room. Anna and Ausable were alone in the room, finally. And Anna was a bit nervous.

"I left two drawers in the dresser for you," Anna said to Ausable. "And there is room in the wardrobe if you want to hang anything up."

Ausable didn't say anything. He just dropped his valise on the floor. He walked to Anna, put his arms around her and kissed her passionately. They both shuddered with excitement. Alone in a beautiful hotel room with a welcoming bed.

Ausable lifted Anna and laid her gently on the bed. He stood above her and took off his jacket and unbuttoned his vest.

Anna watched, getting more and more blissful as Ausable removed his belt and unbuttoned his pants. He removed his tie and then unbuttoned his shirt, which he threw on the floor. His hard muscles shimmered in the electric light. Anna reached up for him and he put his hands on either side of her, holding himself up over her. She reached up and caressed his powerful arms, feeling them up and down. She moved her hands to his brawny chest and felt his solid build. He lowered himself down on top of her and they kissed.

He helped Anna unbutton her dress. She wore a silk combination undergarment. Ausable unbuttoned the camisole bodice, down to just above the attached knickers, and pulled it open. With her breasts exposed, Ausable began to sensuously nuzzle them. Anna arched her back to meet him. With his tongue, he moved down her stomach and teased her below the top of her knickers. Anna giggled with delight. Ausable continued to unbutton her undergarment as far as he could and then slowly, sensually, pulled them down her legs.

He undid his trousers, pushed them off, and removed his drawers. He stood before her, totally naked. Anna lay there, gazing at him, taking in his entire masculine splendor. He smiled sweetly down at this beautiful naked woman before him, getting more and more excited.

Anna raised herself up and caressed his penis. She teased him with her tongue, tickling the tip. She had never taken a man's penis in her mouth before. And she really wanted to now. So Anna moved slowly in, letting her tongue swirl around. She pushed her mouth a little and Ausable gasped with pleasure. He was breathing heavy. It felt so right to Anna as they got in rhythm with each other. Ausable moaned low. She was enjoying this so much and she could hear he was as well. She moved faster and faster, then stopping for a few seconds, then starting again, making Ausable pant with desire. Ausable reached down between Anna's legs and began massaging her. She started moving even faster, feeling the moment was right for him. He pressed his fingers in deeper. At the exact moment he climaxed, Anna did as well. She shuddered in pure pleasure as he throbbed above her and grabbed her shoulders to steady himself.

Ausable fell exhausted and exhilarated on the bed next to Anna. They both lay there breathing heavily. He reached for her hand and grasped it. They both turned and looked at each other and smiled. They just lay there for quite a while, so joyful to be together.

CHAPTER TWENTY-NINE

Anna and Ausable were dressed exquisitely as they cautiously exited the room, looking up and down the hall. They had agreed that she would take the elevator and Ausable would take the stairs and meet in the lobby. It was silly, but Anna didn't want anyone to get any hint of impropriety.

She exited the elevator and Ausable met her at the door as planned. They walked through the lobby toward the dining room, and passed the ballroom where an orchestra played and people danced. Anna hoped Ausable knew how to dance and they would go in there later. They walked up to the maître d's station and looked at the dining room. It rivaled New York restaurants for its fine food and lavish décor.

The maître d' came to the door and reacted, seeing Ausable. Keeping his composure, he greeted the guests.

"May I help you?" the maître d' asked.

Ausable spoke, eloquently, "I believe you have a reservation for Mrs. Tattersall," indicating Anna.

Anna nodded and smiled at the maître d'. The maître d' looked impressed by Ausable, not only his voice but also his obviously hand-tailored attire. He looked in his reservation book. Anna didn't see Ausable slip the maître d' a five-dollar bill.

"Ah yes, Mrs. Tattersall. I see you are staying with us. I have a lovely table for you overlooking the veranda. Will that do?" the maître d' asked.

"Quite well. Thank you," Anna said.

"Right this way, please," indicated the maître d' as he led them to their table, which was glittering with stemmed glassware and stunning silverware and china. There were glances at Ausable from several of the other diners.

"Why don't you sit where you can see this beautiful room best," Ausable said. The maître d' helped Anna with her chair. Ausable sat with his back to the room.

"Your waiter will be over right away," said the maître d' before he left.

"I saw a few uncomfortable stares as we crossed the room," Ausable said. "I felt it best to face away from them."

"I understand. Isn't this dining room glorious?" Anna asked. "And I hear the food is first rate."

The waiter came to the table with a bill of fare for each of them.

"Good evening, lady and gentleman," said the waiter. "Welcome to the Grand View Banquet Room."

He handed them their bills of fare and they thanked him. He walked around the table, removing the napkins and placing them in each of their laps.

"May I suggest you begin with a bottle of one of our local New York wines?" the waiter asked.'

"Anna, would you enjoy some wine," asked Ausable.

"That would be lovely," Anna said.

The waiter handed the wine card to Ausable.

"May I suggest starting with a light white wine, such as a Cassian Brothers Chablis?" asked the waiter.

Ausable studied the wine card.

"I think a claret would be better," Ausable said. "And you have the Chateau de Rose." The waiter reacted. "That is a particularly fine wine. Is that all right with you, Anna?"

"Sounds wonderful," Anna said.

"We'll have the Chateau de Rose, 1886," Ausable said.

The waiter hesitated, and then said, "Sir, I just want to be sure you know, that is one of our most expensive wines."

"I appreciate your concern," Ausable said. "Please bring that wine."

"Very good, sir," said the waiter as he hurried off.

"At least when you are a pariah, it's good to have money," Ausable said.

Anna laughed and started looking over the bill of fare.

"Everything sounds so wonderful," Anna said. "Oh, look. They have steamed lobster. We can get that in Fairfield, fresh from the Sound. But I haven't had any this summer up here. I think I'll have that. Mmm."

"The rack of lamb is prepared well. It should do nicely," Ausable said.

Anna reached over and held Ausable's hand. They beamed at each other. The waiter returned with the wine. He reacted to Anna holding hands with an Indian. But being the good waiter he was, he didn't let on that he found it unsettling. He presented the wine to Ausable to confirm it was the requested vintage.

Ausable looked at the label on the bottle. "Very good," he said.

The waiter removed the cork and placed it on the table in front of Ausable. Ausable picked up the cork, squeezed it, inspected it, and smelled it. He nodded and put the cork back on the table. The waiter poured a small amount of wine into Ausable's glass. Ausable picked up the glass, swirled the wine, looked at the glass to see how the wine coated it, and smelled its bouquet. Anna watched, fascinated with Ausable's aplomb. Ausable tasted the wine, swilling it in his mouth before swallowing. He placed the glass on the table.

"Perfect," said Ausable to the waiter. "You may serve it."

"Very good," said the waiter as he poured wine for Anna and then filled Ausable's glass.

Ausable lifted his glass. "A toast. To a magical time in Lake Placid."

"To magic," said Anna.

They clinked glasses and had a sip.

"Oh, that's marvelous wine," said Anna.

"I'm glad you like it," said Ausable.

"The orchestra in the ballroom sounds delightful," Anna said. "Do you dance, Mr. Hancock?"

"Why, of course, Mrs. Tattersall," he responded in kind. "Shall we take a twirl after dinner?"

"Oh, I'd love that," Anna said happily.

A man came up to the table and introduced himself. "Hello, I'm the hotel manager, Mr. Allen," he said.

They both stiffened a bit. This could be bothersome to Ausable.

"I believe you are Mrs. Tattersall," Mr. Allen continued.

"Yes, I am," Anna said. "It's nice to meet you, Mr. Allen. This is Mr. Hancock."

"Nice to meet you both. I hope everything is satisfactory so far," Mr. Allen said.

"It's a magnificent dining room, Mr. Allen," said Anna. "I'm looking forward to tasting the food I've heard so much about."

"I'm sure you'll enjoy it. We have master chefs from New York cooking for us," said Mr. Allen. "Mr. Hancock, you are not staying with us?"

"Why, no, Mr. Allen," said Ausable. "I'm here dining with this lovely lady."

"I want you to know that, as manager of this hotel, I'm happy to have you stay here if you ever require lodgings," said Mr. Allen.

"That's very kind of you, Mr. Allen," said Ausable.

"I know there might be people who wouldn't be amenable. We here at the Grand View welcome everyone," Mr. Allen said. "If anyone causes you any trouble, please inform me of it. I won't stand for any of that nonsense."

They both breathed a sigh of relief.

"I'm very grateful, Mr. Allen," Ausable said.

"I bid you both a wonderful evening," said Mr. Allen. "And I hope you'll enjoy some dancing in our ballroom after dinner. I've hired a summer orchestra for the season."

"We've been listening," Anna said. "They sound wonderful."

"Mrs. Tattersall, Mr. Hancock," Mr. Allen said, nodding to each.

Ausable stood and shook Mr. Allen's hand. "Again, thank you."

"My pleasure." Mr. Allen left the table.

"Isn't he kind?" said Anna.

"Very," said Ausable, feeling quite comfortable.

"There will be no more sneaking you in the back door now," said Anna. "You're going up with me in the elevator. Together."

They both laughed.

They ordered and enjoyed their delicious meals, drinking wine and clinking glasses. While they were having coffee, Mr. Allen even sent over complimentary desserts of harlequin ice cream and petit fours, which were mouthwatering.

"That was one of the best meals I think I've ever had," said Anna. "Who needs to go to New York City for fine cuisine?"

"It was a delectable dinner," Ausable said. "Though I think the wine and the company certainly helped make this such a memorable meal."

Anna grasped Ausable's hand across the table. "I agree," she said, beaming at him.

The waiter came to the table. "Will there be anything else?" he asked.

"I believe we're quite content," said Ausable.

"I could eat this whole meal all over again," Anna said. "But I won't." They laughed.

"Then if there is nothing else, shall I bill this to your room?" the waiter asked.

"No, I'll take it, if I may," Ausable said.

"Oh no, Ausable," Anna said. "This is my treat."

"Thank you, Anna," Ausable said. "But please, let me be the one to treat you."

"As you will," Anna acquiesced with a smile.

Ausable looked at the check and pulled out his wallet, which contained a large number of bills. He took some out and handed them to the waiter.

"That's all set. Thank you," said Ausable.

"Thank you, sir," said the waiter very graciously and he retreated.

"Shall we work off this meal with a bit of dancing?" asked Anna.

"I've been looking forward to it," Ausable said.

They stood up and Ausable took Anna on his arm and they exited the room, already moving to the beat of the orchestra in the other room. As they walked through the restaurant, they received many disapproving looks. They were in such good moods, they didn't notice. On leaving the restaurant, Mr. Allen came up to them.

"I hope everything met with your satisfaction," he said.

"Thank you for one of the best meals I've had," said Anna. "I'll tell all my friends."

"Thank you very much," Mr. Allen said. "I've arranged a table in the ballroom for you. It's under Mr. Hancock's name."

Ausable was touched. "That's very kind of you, Mr. Allen."

"No bother," he said. "Please enjoy yourselves."

"We will," Anna said.

They crossed the lobby and entered the beautiful ballroom. It was lit with flickering candles in its crystal chandelier and in sparkling lamps all around the walls. The orchestra was playing a beautiful waltz and couples were gliding on the dance floor together. A maître d' approached them.

"Mr. Hancock," he said. "May I show you to your table?"

"Thank you," Ausable said.

He led them to a table on the edge of the dance floor. The maître d' helped Anna with her chair.

"Would anyone care for a cocktail?" he asked. "We have quite an array here at the Grand View Ballroom."

"Ooo, a cocktail," Anna said cheerfully. "That sounds like fun."

"Have you ever had a Tom Collins, Anna?" Ausable asked.

"I don't think so," Anna asked. "What is it?"

"It's a sweet, fizzy drink," Ausable said. "I think you'll like it."

"Sounds perfect," Anna said.

"All right," Ausable said. "One Tom Collins for the lady. And I'll have a gin and bitters martini, please."

"Very good, sir," said the maître d' and left to place their order.

All the tables were covered with white linen tablecloths and on each was a small bouquet of local flowers and pinecones. Each table also had a candle in a crystal lamp matching those on the walls. The orchestra finished the waltz and the gathered people applauded.

"This really is such an outstanding room," Anna said looking about.

The orchestra started to play a livelier tune.

"Anna, may I have this dance?" said Ausable.

"Absolutely," Anna said enthusiastically.

Ausable offered his hand to Anna and led her to the dance floor. He put his arms in the correct dance position, grinning at her. Anna took his hand and they began to dance. It was a two-step, popular for the time, and they were in perfect rhythm with each other. It was as though they had been dancing together all their lives. They swirled and wheeled, staring into each other's eyes. There was magic happening on the dance floor. Everyone observing could feel it and many couples stopped their own dancing to watch. As the music reached a crescendo and ended, the pair made a final twirl and those watching applauded. They embraced and Anna gazed up into Ausable's eyes. They stood there, lost in each other. And then they kissed. Public shows of affection were looked down upon, especially with an Indian, but after the flawless performance they put on, no one seemed to really mind. The orchestra started to play another song. Anna and Ausable walked back to their table, arm in arm.

The drinks were at the table. As Anna was about to take her seat, she looked across the room and saw two familiar faces staring at her in disbelief. What? she thought. Eric and Joan Montgomery from Keene Valley were here! She thought for moment, then pulled herself together and gave them a small wave. She sat down.

"Oh no!" she said, desperately. "Eric and Joan Montgomery are here!"

"Who are they, Anna?" asked Ausable.

"People I know from Keene Valley," Anna told him. "What am I going to do? They saw us dancing." Then a deeper thought, "And we kissed! They are going to tell everyone I kissed you!"

"Oh dear," Ausable said. "I'm so sorry, Anna. I should have known better than to have made such a spectacle in public. I just couldn't help myself with you."

"What am I going to do?" Anna asked, anxiously.

"Why don't you ask them over, as if nothing is wrong. Tell them what you were planning to say to everyone. You ran into me here in Lake Placid and are bringing me back to meet everybody."

"Really?" Anna asked

"We can nip this in the bud right now by confronting them head-on."

Anna was clearly shaken and confused. "I don't know," she said. "I was so caught up in romance, I was hoping to put off reality for at least another day." She took a sip of her Tom Collins, then looked over at the Montgomerys again.

"Joan, Eric. Hello," Anna called. "Won't you come join us for a cocktail?"

Eric and Joan had taken their seats at their table. They looked at each other and exchanged a few words.

"We'll be right there," Eric called.

Eric and Joan came over to them and as they stepped up to the table, Ausable rose.

"Hello," Anna said, trying to sound cheery. "I didn't know you were in Lake Placid."

"We arrived on the late stage," said Joan.

"Eric, Joan, this is Mr. Hancock," Anna said. "He's the man who rescued me on Giant during the cloudburst. Ausable, this is Mr. and Mrs. Montgomery."

"How do you do?" Ausable said, shaking Eric's hand, although Eric initially was bit reluctant to extend his hand, then finally did.

"I ran into Mr. Hancock here in Lake Placid today," Anna began. "I've been looking for him since he helped me off the mountain. Will and I really wanted to thank him properly.

218

Happily, he has agreed to come back to Keene Valley with me tomorrow so I can do just that. I'll be having a large party and I hope you can come."

"Oh, well, we'd love that, wouldn't we, Eric?" Joan said, hesitantly.

"Oh yes, we would," Eric agreed.

"Wonderful," said Anna.

"Anna is a delightful dancer," Ausable said. "So practiced, wouldn't you say?" Holding up his martini, "Cheers to you, madam." Anna picked up her drink and they toasted.

"Yes, the music, and this magnificent room," Anna said. "And the excitement of finding the one who saved my life. I think it all really added up to quite an emotional happenstance."

"Oh yes," Joan said. "Very emotional."

"Will you sit with us?" Ausable offered.

"No, thank you," Eric said. "We should be going."

"Yes, we have a big day of shopping to do tomorrow," Joan added.

"I will be shopping, too," said Anna. "I'm interested in seeing that new fabric shop. Perhaps we'll see you on Main Street."

"Oh, I do hope so," said Joan.

"Are you staying here at the Grand View?" Anna asked.

"No, we're over at the Allen House," Joan said. "Good evening." They left the ballroom.

Anna let out a frustrated breath and hung her head.

"Anna, don't," Ausable said. "Everything will be all right. We'll work this out, I'm sure."

"Oh, Ausable," she said. "Did you hear what she said? She saw us dancing. She saw what we did. I've no doubt she's going to tell everyone. I don't know what I'm going to do." Anna put her head in her hands, and then looked up at Ausable. "Ausable, I'm so sorry," Anna said. "I'm so in love with you, but explaining this to my family and friends is going to be very difficult. It's going to take time to get them to even start to understand. I was hoping to take this a lot slower."

"I understand, my love," Ausable said. "You can take all the time you want. I'm never going anywhere again. Without you."

"Oh my dear, sweet Ausable," she said. "Would you mind if we left? Suddenly this music isn't so magical anymore."

Anna quickly drank the rest of her drink. Ausable placed a few bills on the table and they left the ballroom.

CHAPTER THIRTY

They awoke in the morning after a fitful sleep for Anna. Ausable tried to gently hold her in his arms and console her. Anna was downhearted.

"Ausable, I feel so wonderful being with you," Anna said. "If only the rest of the world could feel as wonderful about this as I do."

"What happened last night may have been a blessing in disguise," Ausable said.

"How do you mean?" Anna asked.

"Those people last night gave you a good indication of what you are going to face back home," said Ausable. "There will be gossip and innuendo. And not everyone will be kind."

"I can see that," Anna said.

"And don't forget your family. They will be the harshest critics," Ausable said. "It's going to be very difficult handling all of this. I've had to go about my life as an outcast. I have to outperform everyone else to prove that I am even a bit close to being equal with them. And even so, most people will not accept me."

"But you saved my life," Anna exclaimed. "Doesn't that mean something?"

"Yes, I'm the hero. And I'm wealthy and educated. None of that matters when all people see is red skin," Ausable explained. "We'll go back to Keene Valley and everyone will 'act' kind to me and 'congratulate' me for my bravery. But

221

there will be very little sincerity, I can assure you. People just have a very hard time trusting that I am anything but a savage."

"Oh, Ausable," Anna said. "I can't believe that. Not everyone is that way."

"No, there are a few exceptions," he said sweetly, pointing at her and touching her nose.

"Well then, it will be our mission to change their minds," Anna said boldly.

Ausable shook his head, smiling. "We'll try," he said, knowing this was not going to be easy.

Anna got out of bed. "Do you want to shop with me, today?" Anna asked.

"If you don't mind, I'm not much for fabric shopping. I think I'll hike a bit around the lake. I'll meet you at the Stage Coach Inn in time for the afternoon stage, if that's all right," Ausable said.

"That's fine with me," Anna said. "But I'll miss you." She kissed him quickly. "Now let's get dressed for breakfast."

They decided to have breakfast on the front veranda since it was becoming a warm day. The waiter told them the hotel was serving Eggs Benedict, which had, just recently, begun to be served at the Waldorf Astoria in New York City. He explained it was a dish with a toasted, buttered English muffin topped with poached eggs, ham, and a hooker of hollandaise sauce to pour over. They thoroughly enjoyed the new breakfast fad.

After breakfast, Anna went up to her room to freshen up and Ausable went out on his hike. Anna was given a ride in the hotel carriage down to the Main Street and the shops. She arranged with the driver to pick her up at two o'clock at the Lake Placid House where she would be having lunch.

She first stopped in at the Lake Placid Trading Post, which usually had a good assortment of locally made arts and crafts. Anna chatted with the owner, Mr. Gordon, and browsed through the store. She saw many well-made woodcarvings and found a vase made entirely of polished pine that she wanted to purchase. There were quite a few paintings of the area, which she admired greatly. Then Anna spotted something. There,

222

hanging on the wall, were two of Anna's cloudburst potholders.

"Mr. Gordon?" Anna said. "Where did you get these lovely potholders?"

"Oh, those are from the arts and crafts fair in Keene Valley," Mr. Gordon said. "I go there to see what people have made and always pick up a few things to sell. I think that design is particularly clever. It shows the before and after of what happened to Giant Mountain during the great cloudburst they had earlier this summer."

"Yes, I can see that," Anna said.

"Are you interested in them?" Mr. Gordon asked.

"Very," said Anna.

"Well, just to let you know, these were made for charity, so any money I make from them will be given back to their charity," Mr. Gordon told them.

"Oh, that's very honorable of you, Mr. Gordon," Anna said. "You know, now that I think about it, I have enough potholders. But the design is very smart. I'm sure you'll have no trouble selling them."

"I've already sold three of them today. Just these two left," Mr. Gordon said.

"I'm glad to hear that," Anna said.

Anna purchased the vase she liked and went on with her shopping. She found Lamoy's Textile Shoppe and perused all the new items from New York, Paris, and the Far East. Mr. Lamoy, the draper, showed her a broad selection of rather bold colors and patterns with wide stripes, which he said were the latest fashion. Anna particularly liked a heavy lace consisting of embroidered motifs and considered it for the new curtains she wanted to make for Idlenook. There was also an extensive array of decorative trimmings. New sheer fabrics that were like fine chiffon also drew her eye. She decided on an ivory lace fabric for the curtains. And since bold colors were all the rage, she also opted for red tassels, braid, and fringe. It would really brighten up the parlor at Idlenook. Mr. Lamoy would have all of her items packed and put on the stagecoach for delivery tomorrow. Anna was looking forward to sprucing up her house just as her life had been spruced up lately. Even with all the turmoil and uncertainty, she was still happier than she had been in years.

She walked further down Main Street and stopped in to see the new Lake Placid Library. It had opened just last summer and she wanted to compare it to theirs in Keene Valley. Because of the generous donations of the Dunhams in Keene Valley, their library had far more books. Anna left with a feeling of pride.

She stopped at a few more shops and ended up at the Lake Placid House for a bite to eat. The hotel overlooked the lake and she had a nice table with a spectacular view of Mirror Lake. Inexplicably, the main street of the town of Lake Placid was on Mirror Lake, not Lake Placid itself, which was just a bit north of the village proper.

It seemed all the best dining rooms were using the cookbook by "Oscar of the Waldorf." The Lake Placid House's dining room was no exception. Anna decided to continue along with her breakfast choice and ordered a Waldorf salad. As she enjoyed the view and the salad, it gave her time to ponder the reality of arriving in Keene Valley with Ausable. She wondered if this was all just a fantasy. She knew she was following her heart. She couldn't deny how she felt. She also knew, deep down, that this could never work and that thought made her despondent. Then again, she didn't really know that it couldn't work. Will hadn't been a loving husband for many years. And she was still young and vital. She had to make choices that were best for her, yet also best for her children. Then she asked herself, could she have made a more difficult choice than falling in love with an Indian? She wished he weren't so remarkable.

She finished her lunch and the carriage from the hotel was there to meet her at the appointed time. It brought her back to the Grand View and she had time to freshen up. Her luggage was brought down to the carriage, which took her to the Stage Coach Inn to meet the stagecoach back to Keene Valley. Ausable was there, waiting for her.

"Hello, Anna," Ausable said. "How was your shopping?"

"Oh, I found some lovely fabrics for my curtains," Anna told him. "They will really dress up Idlenook."

"That's good to hear," Ausable said.

The driver told them it was time to go. Anna asked, "Is anyone else riding with us today?"

"Not here," said the driver. "But we will pick up a lady in North Elba."

"Very good," Anna said. "Thank you."

They both climbed into the stagecoach and Anna sat next to Ausable.

"I hope the woman getting on in North Elba doesn't have a problem riding with you," Anna said to Ausable.

"It's not an issue," Ausable said. "I can ride with the driver."

"It's just not fair," said Anna. Then she cuddled up to him. "You feel so comfortable. It's as if I've known you forever."

"We have in a way," Ausable said.

"Well, yes, we did meet when we were children," Anna said. "It really is astounding," Anna said. "And I kept your painting all these years. And still have it hanging here in Idlenook. Everyone knows the story of that painting. What would they say if we tell them you are the very same boy I met way back when?"

"My painting style hasn't changed much since then," Ausable said. "If anyone sees my new paintings, they may put two and two together."

"Aunt Lil loves the Adirondack painters," Anna said. "We'll have to use that to our advantage to ease her over to tolerating you. She will be the toughest egg to crack."

"Whatever will help, I'll do," he said.

"You're such a dear one, Ausable," Anna said. "We can only do our best and hope."

She cradled her head on his shoulder and in no time was asleep. The lack of sleep the night before had caught up with her. Ausable smiled down at her and held her as they bumped along on the rough road.

Anna awoke when they stopped in North Elba. There was happily no issue with the woman boarding the stagecoach there. She wasn't particularly friendly to Ausable, but she took to knitting to keep herself occupied. Anna fell asleep again, this time leaning away from Ausable. She was so tired that she didn't even wake up when the woman exited the stagecoach in Keene.

CHAPTER THIRTY-ONE

The driver called down that they would be at Bailey's in a few minutes. Anna woke up rather confused as to where she was, blinking her eyes and shaking her head to orient herself.

"Oh my goodness," Anna said. "I was really out. I usually can't sleep on a bumpy ride like this."

"You got little sleep last night," Ausable added.

"Yes, I really needed that nap," Anna said.

She picked up her handbag and retrieved her small hand mirror. Looking at herself, she exclaimed, "Oh, I'm a fright." She pinched her cheeks to try to restore life to her pale face.

"You always are a vision of loveliness to me," Ausable said.

"You're sweet," she said. "But I need to get myself looking my best and ready for whatever lies ahead in Keene Valley. There will be no way of getting past Aunt Lil's without stopping and introducing you. I need to be prepared."

"Just be calm and strong-willed, Anna," Ausable said. "You'll do fine."

The stagecoach stopped at Bailey's and Ausable opened the door and got out to help Anna. As he did, he looked around a bit confused at what seemed like quite a gathering of the townspeople, all staring at him. They couldn't all be taking the stagecoach, he thought. He leaned into the coach.

"Anna, we seem to have some sort of welcoming committee," he said.

"What do you mean, Ausable?" she asked as he helped her down from the stagecoach.

In bewilderment, Anna surveyed the crowd. There must have been at least twenty people. Then she saw them. In the middle of everybody was Joan Montgomery standing right next to Aunt Lil. Anna's stomach flip-flopped. Anna said quietly, "Well, just act like everything is fine." Anna, with her head held high, smiled and walked right toward Aunt Lil. Ausable followed her lead.

"Lil!" called Anna. "How nice of you to come down to meet me. Hello all." Then a bit strained, "Hello, Joan."

"Anna, we need to speak," Aunt Lil said sternly.

"Of course, Lil," Anna said. "But first, I have great news. I want you to meet the man who saved my life. Aunt Lil, this is Ausable Hancock. Ausable, this is my Aunt Lil Tattersall."

Ausable stepped forward, with his hand out, and speaking in his strong, assuring voice, "So very nice to finally meet you Mrs. Tattersall. Anna has told me so many wonderful things about you."

Aunt Lil was taken aback, but still kept her composure. She didn't take his hand, but nodded to him, "Mr. Hancock." Ausable nodded back.

"Oh Lil, isn't it wonderful," said Anna excitedly. "I was in Lake Placid and who do I run into but Ausable. I've wanted so to properly thank him for all he did for me. And now I can. I talked him into coming to Keene Valley for a visit and I'm going to plan a wonderful party. And you're all invited," she said, gesturing to the crowd.

The uncomfortable throng looked at each other, not knowing what to say. They had all obviously had heard Joan's story and weren't sure what to make of this.

"It will be such fun," said Anna.

"Well, we'll see about that," said Aunt Lil. "I think right now we should get you home, Anna."

"Oh, don't trouble yourself, Lil," Anna said, trying to keep her composure. "I see Millie is here to take us to Idlenook."

"Us?" Aunt Lil said, crossly.

"Yes, Ausable and me," said Anna. "I've asked him to stay with us while he's here in Keene Valley."

Aunt Lil was completely astonished. "Anna. Do you think that's proper?" she said.

"Lil, this man saved my life," Anna said, trying to appear confident. "It's the least I can do. And we have plenty of room."

"Anna, I don't want to impose," said Ausable.

"Nonsense," said Anna, looking at Aunt Lil. "My mind is made up."

"Well, I never," said Aunt Lil, aghast.

Anna said, "Shall we, Ausable?"

He nodded and started toward the carriage. Anna turned to Aunt Lil. "We'll talk tomorrow, Lil," she said, giving her a kiss on the cheek.

"Yes. We will," said Aunt Lil sternly.

"Let's go, Millie," Anna said.

They got into the carriage and rode away, leaving an astounded group of people.

Anna scrunched down in the carriage to hide. "I just embarrassed Aunt Lil in front of the whole town," Anna said. "I'm in such trouble. That woman will never forgive me!"

"Anna, I believe you were perfectly respectful to her," said Ausable. "You explained everything and said you would talk tomorrow. I don't think she was embarrassed."

"Oh, you don't know Lil," said Anna. "Any slight she takes as an act of defiance. I know that look she had. She is incensed."

"Anna, I don't want to cause you consternation with your Aunt," said Ausable. "I am happy to go stay up at my camp to keep the peace."

"Thank you, Ausable," she said. "But that won't be necessary. I already made a fuss about this. I want her to see that everything with you is aboveboard. That you are a well-bred person who deserves her endorsement. It will take time, but if we give in right from the start, we will only put the power back in her hands. I won't do that."

"Well then, on to Idlenook," he said. "I can't wait to meet your boys. And see the painting that I did when I was a child."

"Oh, Millie, with all the brouhaha, I didn't introduce you to Mr. Hancock," Anna said. "He's the one who rescued me."

"So pleased to meet you, Mr. Hancock," said Millie. "You did a wonderful thing."

"Thank you, Millie," said Ausable.

They arrived at Idlenook and Colleen came out to greet them.

"Welcome home, Missus," said Colleen.

"Oh, Colleen, look who I found in Lake Placid," Anna said. "This is Mr. Hancock. My savior."

"Howdy do, Mr. Hancock," Colleen said. "Mrs. Tattersall told us how she was rescued by an Indian gentleman. That was a mighty fine thing to do."

"Thank you, Colleen. It's nice to meet you," said Ausable.

"Let me get your valise, Missus," Colleen said.

"Thank you, Colleen," Anna said. "Mr. Hancock will be staying with us. Will you please get the guest room ready?"

"Right away," said Colleen. "I'll take your bag as well, Mr. Hancock."

"Are the boys home, Colleen?" Anna asked.

"Not yet, Missus," she said. "They should be home soon for dinner."

"Fine," Anna said. "Come in, Ausable," said Anna. "Let me show you Idlenook."

They went up the steps into the screened porch. Anna said, "Ausable, come over here."

She led him into the dining area of the screened porch and pointed to his painting on the wall.

"Look," she said. "It's been hanging here since we bought Idlenook."

"Well, look at that," he said. "My technique has changed some over the years. I've learned a lot since I did that one. But I kind of like the primitive quality it has."

"I've always loved that painting," Anna said. "I've kept it all these years to remind me of that wonderful moment we met. It has really meant a lot to me to have it. There was always

230

something about it that enchanted me. And now meeting you again, I know why."

Ausable smiled at her and took her hand, briefly. She smiled back, so happy and so loving.

"Let me show you the rest of the house," Anna said.

She took him through the kitchen and the parlor and out onto the front porch to see the view of Porter and the Twins. The sun was just setting behind the mountains and the exquisiteness of it all took their breath away. As they stood there admiring the beauty, Sam and Paul came walking into view up the drive. At the site of Ausable lit by the setting sun, they stopped dead in their tracks.

"Who's that with Mother?" Sam asked Paul.

"I don't know," Paul answered. "That's an Indian! Hey, that must be Mother's Indian!"

"Oh boy!" said Sam. "Let's go!"

The boys ran up to the porch, stopping before the steps and staring up at Ausable.

Anna and Ausable looked down at them.

"Boys, aren't you going to say something?" said Anna.

"Uh huh," said Paul. They looked up in awe.

"Sam, Paul. This is Mr. Hancock," Anna said. "He's the man who saved me during the storm. Stop staring and give him a proper greeting."

"Oh. Hello, Mr. Hancock," Paul said, reaching out to shake his hand.

"How do you do, Mr. Hancock?" said Sam, giving a bow.

"Hello, Paul. Hello, Sam," said Ausable. "I am very happy to make your acquaintance. Paul, I hear you are playing Romeo this summer."

"Yes, sir," said Paul. "The play is in a few weeks. I think I'll know my lines by then."

"I've been helping him practice," said Sam. Then showing off, "He's doing quite well, if I say so myself."

"I'm sure he is," said Ausable. "And I'm sure you're a big help to him. I hope I can come see you in it."

"You have to tell us all about saving Mother on the mountain, Mr. Hancock," said Sam.

231

"I'd be happy to, Sam," Ausable said.

"Let's do that at dinner, boys," Anna said. "Mr. Hancock will be staying with us for a few days, so you'll have lots of time to talk."

"Oh boy!" exclaimed Sam.

"You two go clean up for dinner," Anna told them. "We need to get settled."

"Yes, Mother," said Paul. "Come on, Sam."

They ran inside.

"Wow. We are going to have a real Indian living with us!" Sam said as they ran up the stairs. "I can't wait to tell the fellows at the club. They'll be so jealous."

Anna looked to Ausable and they both laughed.

Anna said, shaking her head, "I'm sorry about that."

"Not to worry, Anna. They are pure joy. They remind me a lot of my brothers and me when we were that age."

"I'm glad you are staying here," Anna said. "I think it will be wonderful for all of us. Let me show you to your room."

"I'm looking forward to staying here, too," Ausable said as they went inside.

Anna took Ausable upstairs and showed him the guest room. He looked in and his valise was already there. He looked at the next room down the hall.

"Is that a sleeping porch?" Ausable asked.

"Yes, it is," Anna said. "It sleeps four. We all sleep out there on hot summer nights."

"Do you mind?" said Ausable, indicating the room.

"Of course not," Anna said.

They went onto the sleeping porch.

"I love that you can hear the river from this room," Ausable said. "Do you mind if I sleep in here?"

"Be my guest," said Anna. "After all, it is the Ausable River you'll be listening to," she said, smiling happily.

"Yes it is," he said. He looked around carefully, and then gave her a quick kiss. "Let me get my bag."

"I'll have Millie bring up a wash basin for you," Anna said.

Anna went downstairs and Ausable got his bag out of the guest room. As he came out of the guest room, he noticed a

232

door cracked open just down the hall and an eye peeking out. He pretended not to notice, but slowly moved past the door and hid on the other side of it. Sam, who was peeking out, slowly opened the door to see where Ausable had gone. When he looked around the door, he came face to face with Ausable.

"Hello, Sam," he said.

Sam squawked, "Mr. Hancock!"

Ausable smiled and said, "Are you spying on me, Sam?"

"No. No. Um, I just… ," Sam stammered.

"It's all right, Sam," Ausable said. "I know it's unusual to have a real live Adirondack Indian staying in your home. I'm sure you're curious. But trust me, we are just like you. I don't have a headdress. And we don't run around with tomahawks and scalp people anymore."

"No?" Sam said, sounding disappointed.

"No," Ausable said. "I'm sure you are disheartened to hear that. But I'm really just a businessman now."

"Really? A businessman? Like Father?" Sam asked.

"I'm afraid so," Ausable said. "But I still like hiking and camping in the woods. In fact, I have a camp hidden up on the mountain near here that no one knows about. Only me. I'll take you and Paul and your mother up there if you'd like."

"Yes!" Sam exclaimed. "That would be wonderful fun."

"All right, but you have to promise me something," Ausable said.

"Anything," Sam said.

"You can't tell anyone where my camp is," Ausable said. "It will be our secret."

"Oh boy," Sam said eagerly. "Our own secret Indian camp! Can I tell Paul?"

"Yes, but only if he promises first not to tell anyone else," Ausable warned. "It's our secret."

"Got it," Sam said. "Our secret."

And he dashed into his room, slamming the door. Anna poked her head around from the stairway.

"That was very sweet of you, Ausable," Anna said.

"Did you hear all that?" Ausable asked, chuckling.

They walked into the sleeping porch.

233

"Well, when I hear one of my children cry out, I usually come running," Anna said. "I think your invitation is very generous. My only regret is that 'our' secret hiding place will no longer be secret."

"Don't worry," Ausable said. "I'm sure we can find another." He smiled.

"You are going to have to," Anna said. "If you think my boys can keep a secret camp a secret, they won't."

"All right. When we go up there with them, they can help me bring down my personal things and then they'll have the 'secret' camp all to themselves. And their friends."

"You are a very nice man," Anna said. "You'll make a wonderful father one day."

"I hope to," Ausable said.

They looked at each other knowing that they both wanted to make passionate love at that very moment and couldn't. The energy passing between them was palpable. They both just stared into the other's eyes. Such wanting. Such lust. Such love. Soon, Anna thought. Soon.

"You unpack and rest, Ausable," she said. "I'll call you for dinner."

Ausable smiled and nodded. Anna smiled, left the room and closed the door. She couldn't believe how time after time, he just got more and more perfect. Perfect for her. She had to find a way to make this work.

She went down the stairs and into the parlor.

"Hello, Anna."

There sat Aunt Lil, back straight and stiff as a board and loaded for bear.

CHAPTER THIRTY-TWO

Anna knew this was trouble. Aunt Lil was the highest mountain she would need to get over if this was ever going to work. If she couldn't get Aunt Lil on her side, she would be stuck in her unhappiness for the rest of her life. She had to find some way to make Aunt Lil understand. Lil knew there was difficultly between Will and her already. Couples didn't part company. Everyone heard stories of affairs, but it was never discussed in good company. Couples simply kept on in unhappy marriages. It was so sad for Anna to think about. She didn't understand how people could go on like that. And she was sure she wouldn't be able to go on much longer. Especially now, having Ausable come into her life.

But first things first. She had to explain to Aunt Lil why she had kissed an Adirondack Indian while dancing. One hurdle at a time. Or so she thought.

"Lil," said Anna calmly. "No one told me you were here."

"Anna, the walls are very thin in this house," said Aunt Lil.

"What are you trying to say, Lil?" Anna asked.

"We need to have a discussion," Aunt Lil said sternly. "But I want it to be in private."

"We can go out to the summerhouse," Anna suggested.

"Very good," Aunt Lil said stridently, standing. "Let's go."

Anna led Aunt Lil through the house and outside. They walked in silence to the summerhouse and sat down.

Trying to remain calm, Anna asked, "Lil, what is this all about?"

Lil collected herself. Then spoke. "Anna, I've known for some time now that the relationship between you and Will has been deteriorating. You've taken solace with Pastor Tom and you've become friends with that questionable Margaret Bancroft."

"Lil," Anna interrupted.

"Let me finish," Aunt Lil said. "I know Will would rather live the big city life and you like it here in Keene Valley and at home in Fairfield. I've seen you two grow apart and it breaks my heart. I don't think it is anyone's fault. These things happen and we all try to keep up appearances and keep things going along as they should."

"Lil, I've tried," Anna said. "Will works very hard for us and loves what he's doing. I can't fault him that. And he knows that I am not one to enjoy the things he does, even though I've made an effort. It's all very painful and sad."

"I'm so sorry, my dear, Anna," said Aunt Lil. "I wish I could make it better. But I'm afraid that it's getting worse."

"Now, Lil," Anna said. "I'm a grown woman. I can take care of my own life and handle what is happening. I really need your support in this because if you can understand, then you can help me convince everyone else."

"Anna, you know I will do what I think is right," said Aunt Lil. "But I have something very distressing to discuss."

"Now, Lil," Anna said.

"Anna," Aunt Lil said, stopping her. "Let me speak."

"Very well," said Anna.

Aunt Lil seemed not to know where to start. This wasn't like her. Anna was ready for the axe to drop.

"Anna. Jim Stoddard was in New York last week."

"Jim Stoddard?" asked Anna. What was this about?

"Yes," said Aunt Lil. "Jim was at a business dinner at Delmonico's and Will was at the same restaurant."

Anna was perplexed. This wasn't about Ausable kissing her in Lake Placid? Had Joan Montgomery not said anything?

"Will was not alone," Aunt Lil continued, then stopped, seeming not wanting to say any more.

Anna was getting anxious now.

"Lil?" said Anna. "Who was Will with?"

Aunt Lil hesitated, then, "He was with a woman. And they were apparently quite affectionate with each other."

Anna was in shock. She said nothing. She didn't know whether to be happy or angry. She couldn't believe that she actually felt hurt over this. She felt a huge emptiness in the pit of her stomach. Here she was having an affair with Ausable, and the thought of Will seeing another woman made her feel ill. She was so confused. She started shaking.

"Anna," Aunt Lil said. "I'm so sorry to be the one to tell you this, but better coming from me than hearing it as gossip. Of course, everyone knows. Jim Stoddard arrived here yesterday evening. And by this morning, that Patricia Stoddard had told everyone but me. It took awhile to get to me. I only know because Holmes overheard it at Bailey's. I confronted Jim Stoddard and he confirmed it."

Anna just sat there. She looked like a stricken bird.

"I know you are hurt and angry, Anna," said Aunt Lil. "You have every right to be. He may be my nephew, but I think of you as my family too. He is in the wrong. Even if you are having marital problems, he has no right go out in public and humiliate you like this. I'm very upset and disappointed in him. I wrote him and told him so. But now, you need consoling."

Anna pulled herself together. She had to get her feelings straight about this.

"Lil, I can't thank you enough for telling me this," Anna said. "I know it was very difficult for you and I sincerely appreciate hearing this from you. And thank you for all your love and support. You are a rock."

"Thank you, Anna," Aunt Lil said. "Give yourself time. We can talk about this more after you've had time to think about it."

"I will, Lil," Anna said.

Aunt Lil took Anna's hands in hers and squeezed them. It felt good to Anna and she realized this might be the first time that Lil had ever shown her comfort like this. Her rarely seen soft side was showing through. They sat in silence for a while.

"Thank you, Lil," Anna said. "You have been very kind, but now, I better return to the house. I have a houseguest to entertain."

"About that, Anna," said Aunt Lil. "I know you've just been through this difficulty, but do you really think it's appropriate to have a man staying with you? An Indian man, at that? Anna, it's just not done."

"Lil, you need to get to know him," Anna said. "He is the most wonderful man. He was so kind and caring to me up on the mountain after the storm. Promise me you'll try to have an open mind and get to know him. I guarantee he will win you over."

"Well, I don't know," said Aunt Lil.

"Lil, if he weren't an Indian, you'd want to thank him for saving me. And you'd find him as charming as I do. Correct?"

"I suppose you are right," Aunt Lil conceded.

"Why not have dinner with us tonight?" Anna asked. "I'm going to need your help to keep myself together after this news about Will. I could really use your support."

"You really know how to hit a tough old lady's soft spot," said Aunt Lil.

Anna got up and gave Aunt Lil a hug and kissed her on both cheeks.

"Now you are really buttering me up," said Aunt Lil. "All right, I'd love to come to dinner and get to know your Indian."

"Ausable," Anna said.

"Mr. Hancock will do," said Aunt Lil.

"All right, Lil," said Anna.

"Can you send Millie to my house to tell Rose I won't be home for dinner?" Aunt Lil asked.

"Of course," said Anna. "Let go inside."

They walked toward the house.

"Now let's try to get your mind off things," said Aunt Lil. "How was Lake Placid?"

"Oh, I found some wonderful fabric in Lake Placid for the parlor curtains," said Anna. "They are lace. And I purchased red tassels and fringe to go on them."

"Red?" said Aunt Lil. "Oh, I don't know about red."

"It's the latest style from New York," Anna told her. "I think it will really brighten up the room. I'm going to need a bit of brightening up in my life now."

"You're right," Aunt Lil said. "Red is a wonderful idea."

They walked into the house, arm in arm.

CHAPTER THIRTY-THREE

Dinner had gone well. Anna held her head high and didn't let the conflict going on inside her show. Ausable regaled the boys with the tale of the cloudburst on Giant, adding a few exaggerations to spice it up. They also made plans to hike up to his camp tomorrow. The boys were beside themselves. They would be the most envied boys in the valley!

Ausable charmed Aunt Lil and even made her laugh, a rare occurrence. Especially with strangers. When she challenged him on his knowledge, he surprised her with his wide comprehension. They discovered they even had acquaintances in common. Aunt Lil was surprised to hear that some of them actually did business with an Indian-owned company. But it helped her begrudgingly move toward accepting Ausable.

She still wasn't happy that Anna had a single man staying in her house without Will there and she took Anna aside to tell her. But Anna reminded her that Colleen and Millie and the boys were there. Nothing untoward would happen. Still not convinced, Aunt Lil took her leave. It was dark so Ausable offered to accompany Aunt Lil home since she had driven her buckboard over on her own. Aunt Lil shuddered at the suggestion. She took pride in her independence and a short ride home was well within her capacity. Ausable acquiesced to her. But she did say she appreciated his courtesy. They all said their goodbyes and Aunt Lil went on her way.

"She is everything you said. And more, Anna," said Ausable.

"Oh, she certainly is," Anna agreed. "She has a good heart and means well. But she is very sure about things and it takes a lot to move her even a millimeter."

"I like her," Ausable said. "She reminds me of my grandmother."

"Really?" Anna asked.

"Yes, my Tota," Ausable said. "She was very firm and strong in her opinions. I think Aunt Lil would have liked her a lot."

"Tota," Anna repeated. "I like that."

"I adored her," Ausable said. "She was wonderful to me. Taught me so much. She's the one who gave me my first paintbrush and paints." He looked wistful. "I do miss her enormously."

Anna put her hand on his. "I'm sure she is still watching down on you and is very proud."

Ausable smiled, a sad smile.

"Ausable," said Anna. "There is something that Aunt Lil told me earlier that I need to tell you."

"What is it, Anna?" he asked.

"Well, it seems that one of our friends up here was in New York City. And he saw my husband, Will...." She stopped, getting that sinking feeling in her stomach again.

"What about Will?" Ausable asked, gently. "Is he all right?"

"Oh yes," Anna said. "More than all right." She paused again, not being able to say the words. Ausable squeezed her hand.

"I'm here for you, Anna," he said. "Take your time."

Anna summoned up the courage to say it aloud. "Will was seen at Delmonico's in New York being very affectionate with a woman." She took a deep breath. "Ausable. My husband is having an affair. And at the very restaurant where he took me and the boys - as a family!" Then she started to cry.

Ausable put his arm around her and comforted her. She put her head on his shoulder and sobbed. Ausable just held her and let her get it out. Colleen came in from the kitchen, hearing Anna. Ausable gestured that she should step away and she did.

He hoped the boys upstairs were deep in sleep and not hearing her.

"Anna. Shhh. Shhh," he whispered. "I don't think you want your boys to hear you."

Through her tears, she softly said, "Oh, Ausable. I'm acting so inane."

"No you're not, Anna," he said.

Then she blurted, "But I'm doing the same thing! I don't have any right to be upset. It's absolutely unconscionable. Oh, why does it hurt so much?"

"Anna, you feel shocked and betrayed by this. And it is very natural to react the way you are," he said.

"I don't know," she said. "I'm just baffled by how I feel. I should be happy. Relieved. Will and I haven't been close in so long. Of course he would look for love with someone else. Maybe I just wanted to be the one to hurt him first."

"I don't think so, Anna," Ausable said. "You aren't like that. You didn't go looking for me."

"No, I just fell into your arms and blacked out," Anna said.

"Ha," he chuckled. "You found me when you needed me. And I'll bet you the same goes for Will. You are both good people. Neither of you wants to hurt the other. And when other people come along, it's because both of you need that to happen. And I must admit, I am very glad I happened upon you."

Anna smiled, wiping away the last of her tears, "And so am I."

She kissed him. She didn't care if anyone saw. She was kissing the man she loved and soon everyone would know it.

"I guess Joan Montgomery didn't say anything about seeing us in Lake Placid. At least not to Aunt Lil," Anna said. "She probably considered that the news of Will was enough gossip about me for one day."

"I'd say it was," Ausable agreed. "You are quite the talk of the town."

"Yes," Anna said. "And now that this is known to everyone, I don't know that it's proper for me to give a party celebrating you."

"I really don't need a party," said Ausable.

"I think you do," Anna said. "It's the next step of easing you into our little valley society. The more they get to know you, the easier life will be for us."

"I understand, Anna," he said. "But as I've told you, I will never be accepted as much as you think I should be."

"Well, look at Aunt Lil," Anna said. "You've already begun to win her over. And if you can do that, the rest will follow, whether they like it or not. She is the matriarch of our family and she is pretty much the matriarch of the entire valley. Everyone cowers to her."

"Except you," said Ausable.

Anna chuckled. "She and I have a good relationship. I think she respects me. And, now that I think of it, I'm not really afraid of her. I'll do what she says because I want to. Not because she tells me to. And I think she understands that."

"Good for you," he said.

"Now I have to figure this out," Anna said. "Do I play the grieving woman whose husband wronged her? Or do I take the bull by the horns and say, 'Will, be damned!' I want a party to celebrate the man who saved my life."

"I don't think you are the grieving woman type," Ausable said.

"No, I'm not," Anna said firmly. "So that's what I should do. I can be strong and show everyone I'm not a poor little wife whose husband cheated on her. I have my own life and I'd like to live it. I know some will be appalled. I don't care. Let them get their noses out of joint. They are doing the same things or worse. They just keep it all hidden. The people I care about will be behind me."

"Sounds like that's settled," Ausable said.

"Good," said Anna. "I'm very tired. It's been quite a day. Let's go to bed."

"Good idea," Ausable agreed.

They went up the stairs and stopped on the top landing. They looked into each other's eyes and kissed. A tiny, silent kiss. They parted and went into their own bedrooms.

CHAPTER THIRTY-FOUR

The next morning, Colleen served a hearty breakfast and the boys were very excited about the hike up to Ausable's camp. They peppered him with questions about being an Indian throughout breakfast. Anna tried to intervene, but Ausable was obviously enjoying the boys, so she let them prattle on. Ausable promised to teach them Indian tracking skills so they could learn to orient themselves if they were ever lost in the woods. The boys were thrilled at the prospect. They ran upstairs to get into their hiking gear.

Anna said she'd like to go into the village and see Tom and discuss what was happening and asked Ausable if he would take the boys up to his camp alone. Ausable understood and said he'd be very happy to hike with the boys on his own. Anna took the carriage and was soon at Pastor Tom's church. She found him in the church putting hymnals in the pews.

"Hello, Tom," Anna said.

"Anna, I'm so glad you're here," Tom said. He walked over to her and gave her a hug. She needed a hug from Tom.

"You've, of course, heard the news of Will?" Anna asked.

"Yes, I have," he said. "I'm glad you brought it up, because I wasn't sure if you had."

"Aunt Lil paid me a visit last evening to tell me," said Anna. "She was very thoughtful about it all. I'm glad she was the one who told me."

"Yes, it has been all over the valley," Tom said. "Spread very quickly too."

"Margaret is due back today," Anna said. "I wonder if she's heard."

"Oh, you can bet I have," said Margaret, entering the church.

"Margaret!" Anna exclaimed.

"I heard this morning and was on my way to your house when I saw your carriage outside," Margaret said. "Poor Anna." She gave Anna a hug. "And I heard Ausable is back."

"Yes. We went to Lake Placid together," Anna said, blushing.

"Really?" asked Margaret and Tom, in unison.

"It was quite enchanting, actually," Anna said. "Until I was dancing with him at the Grand View and we got caught up in the moment and kissed each other."

"That's perfectly normal, my dear," Margaret said. "I'm sure no one even noticed."

"Oh, but someone did," Anna said. "Tom and Joan Montgomery were there and they saw it happen."

"Oh my," Tom said.

"I saw Joan this morning," Margaret said. "We chatted about Will but she didn't say anything about you and Ausable."

"Really?" said Anna. "I'm amazed. That's very kind of her."

"It's good to know that not everyone gossips if it might hurt someone," Tom said.

"Who told you about Will, Anna?" Margaret asked.

"Aunt Lil," Anna said. "She was very sweet to me about it. And she's furious at Will."

"I wouldn't want to be in his shoes," said Tom.

"Do they know who the woman was?" Margaret asked.

"Not that I know," Anna said. "And I don't really care."

"You seem quite calm about all this, Anna," Tom said.

"I'm having very contrary feelings," Anna confessed. "When Aunt Lil told me, I felt ill. Picturing Will with another woman really hit me hard."

"Of course it did," said Margaret. "Being cheated on is an awful feeling."

"But even when I'm cheating as well?" Anna asked.

"It's natural to have this kind of reaction, Anna," Tom said. "It's still betrayal. And it can still cause pain."

"I'm beginning to understand that," Anna said. "But it does make things a tiny bit easier for Ausable and me. One less barrier to knock down. Ausable was even able to charm Aunt Lil last night. I think she actually might learn to like him."

"I'm looking forward to meeting him," said Tom.

"So am I," said Margaret.

"Why don't you two come to dinner tonight?" Anna said.

"I'd love that," said Tom.

"Me, too," said Margaret.

"He's taken the boys hiking up to his camp this morning. They are very captivated by him," Anna said. "Now, I need your advice. After hearing this news of Will, is it wrong of me to still have a party in Ausable's honor? To introduce him as my rescuer to the valley. Is it too soon?"

"I suppose, under the circumstances, things like this usually aren't done," Tom said. "But I don't think these are usual circumstances."

"No, they aren't," said Margaret. "And Anna, you are not a 'usual' girl."

"No, I am not," Anna stated. "Why should I hide? I desperately want everyone to get to know Ausable and maybe put a dent in their prejudices toward Indians."

"That's my girl," Margaret said. "You've found this wonderful man. You really don't need Will anymore so that shouldn't stop you."

"Anna, I know this incident with Will is very upsetting," said Tom. "Are you sure you want to do this right now?"

"I do. And the sooner the better. I don't think anything is occurring this weekend," Anna said. "Why don't we go over to the Club and see if I can host a party there."

"You two go ahead," said Tom. "I've things to do here. What time do you want me for dinner?"

"Why don't you come by at six?" said Anna.

246

"I'll see you then," said Tom.

Anna and Margaret rode over to the Country Club and found John Norman, the manager, sweeping the front veranda.

"Hello, John," said Anna.

"Oh, Mrs. Tattersall. Mrs. Bancroft," said John. "I'm surprised to see you out and about, Mrs. Tattersall."

"I'm not dead, John," Anna said. "I'm surviving all this bothersome mess."

"I'm very sorry to hear of your troubles," John said.

"That's very kind of you, John," Anna said. "Is the club room free this Saturday evening?"

"I believe it is," John said. "Let me get the ledger." He stepped inside and came out with a journal. "Yes, it's free."

"Wonderful," Anna said. "Please reserve it for me. I'm having a party to thank Ausable Hancock for rescuing me during the storm."

"Oh. You mean that Indian?" John asked.

"Yes, that Indian," Margaret stepped in and said strongly.

"Oh dear. You know, Mrs. Tattersall, I just recalled that the room is going to be closed this Saturday," said John. "We have a terrible mouse problem and we are going to be fumigating. We are told we can't let anyone use the building for several days."

"Are you sure that's the reason, John?" Anna accused.

"Oh, yes," John said. "Usually the building is booked weeks in advance. That's why I was surprised it showed it was free. I hadn't written down that the room would be closed. I'm so sorry, Mrs. Tattersall."

"I see," said Anna. "Very well. Thank you, John. Let's go, Margaret."

They went off in their carriage.

"They are fumigating, are they?" asked Margaret.

"I am sure they are not," stated Anna. "He's just afraid of what having an Indian at the club would mean to the members and he doesn't want to cause any stir. I'm so angry!"

"We should cancel our memberships," Margaret said.

"Maybe so," said Anna. "But working from within is probably the best way to make change."

"I suppose you are right," said Margaret. "Now where are you going to have your party?"

"I'll do it at Idlenook," Anna said. "The meadow near the summerhouse is cleared of debris from the storm. It will be a fine spot to celebrate. And easier."

"John's attitude at the club has me thinking," said Anna.

"About what, Anna?" asked Margaret.

"We can put together the grandest party ever, but if no one comes because of mindsets like John's, there will be no party," Anna said.

"Don't you think they will come out of curiosity alone?" Margaret asked.

"Perhaps," Anna said. "But we need a secret weapon to get them to come."

"What secret weapon?" Margaret asked.

"What if we have the invitations come from Aunt Lil?" said Anna. "No one will turn down an invite from Aunt Lil. We'll be guaranteed a full house."

"Do you think she will do it? Margaret asked.

"Let's stop by now and ask," Anna said. "She was quite taken with Ausable last night. I might be able to talk her into it."

"Let's go," said Margaret, and they drove their carriage over to Aunt Lil's house. She was sitting in a rocker out on her front veranda, crocheting a scarf.

"Hello, Lil," Anna called as they arrived.

"Anna, dear, how are you feeling?" asked Aunt Lil.

"I'm doing as well as can be expected, Lil," said Anna.

"Hello, Mrs. Tattersall," said Margaret.

"Margaret," said Aunt Lil coldly.

"In fact, I'm doing well enough to still have a party for Mr. Hancock," Anna said.

"Oh, Anna, is that wise?" asked Aunt Lil. "What will people think?"

"I don't really care," said Anna. "And if I know you, I would wager that you wouldn't care what people thought either."

"Well, I suppose you are right," Aunt Lil admitted. "But decorum requires a proper amount of time."

"Oh balderdash!" said Anna, to which Aunt Lil reacted, taken aback. "I'm the one wronged here. Why should I be the one not having any fun?"

"Well, I cannot fault your thinking," said Aunt Lil.

"Besides, Mr. Hancock deserves a proper party for what he did, don't you think, Mrs. Tattersall?" said Margaret.

"Yes, he does," said Aunt Lil, cautiously agreeing. "And I was a proponent of you thanking him after the storm."

"You were very kind about that, Lil," said Anna. "And you met him. He is a very nice man."

"Yes. I found him quite amiable," said Aunt Lil.

"To be honest, Lil," said Anna. "I'm afraid people will not come to a party for an Indian. I asked about having the party at the club. But when they found out it was for him, the room suddenly was unavailable."

"Oh, dear," said Aunt Lil.

"So I decided to have the party at Idlenook. But if no one came, Lil, it would hurt Ausable's feelings very much."

"Not to mention that it would be rude," said Margaret.

"Yes, well, people are very set in their ways," said Aunt Lil.

"So that's my conundrum, Lil," said Anna. "How do I get everyone to come and not snub me? Especially in my fragile state of mind. I need a party like this to cheer me up."

"It would be unkind for people not to attend," said Aunt Lil. Anna had gotten her point across.

"You know, Lil," said Anna, acting like she just got an idea. "The invitation could come from you."

"Me?" said Aunt Lil.

"That's a wonderful idea, Anna," said Margaret. "No one would turn down an invitation from you, Mrs. Tattersall."

"No. I suppose not," said Aunt Lil, contemplating.

"Oh, Lil, would you do that for me?" asked Anna. "It would be a great help."

"Of course, Anna," said Aunt Lil. "Anything for you."

She hugged Aunt Lil. "Oh, thank you so much. Margaret and I can write out the invitations this afternoon. I am thinking of having the party this Saturday evening."

"Very well," said Aunt Lil. "And please say on the invitation, 'at the request of Lilian Tattersall.' That should do it."

"Oh, Lil, you're a gem," said Anna.

They said their goodbyes and headed over to Idlenook to attend to the invitations. Besides, Margaret was looking forward to finally meeting Ausable.

CHAPTER THIRTY-FIVE

The night of the party in Ausable's honor turned out to be a warm summer evening. Anna used the summerhouse to serve all sorts of delicious food. She and Colleen had outdone themselves preparing everything. They had roasted duck, trout almondine, deviled eggs, and Anna came up with her version of the Waldorf salad she had had in Lake Placid. She added wild turkey to the recipe to make it more of a main dish. Since Ausable was not a secret anymore, Anna had his paintings placed around the summerhouse for all to see. Everyone, especially Aunt Lil, was impressed.

It appeared that no one who was invited had turned down "Aunt Lil's" invitation. As they arrived, they dutifully greeted Aunt Lil and were properly cordial to Ausable. Many of the women were very taken with his handsome looks and gentility. Especially the single ladies. And many were impressed with his business acumen and the ease with which he could fit into any conversation. Paul and Sam proudly told everyone their story of how Ausable taught them to track in the woods.

Margaret and Tom were talking off to the side.

"She really pulled this off," Tom said. "It's a beautiful party."

"I'm very proud of her," said Margaret. "She got everyone to come."

"Most everyone seems to be quite friendly to Ausable," said Tom. "It's nice to see."

A few guests were standoffish and just couldn't bring themselves to do more than give Ausable a polite greeting. Aunt Lil took notice of this and decided to attend to one unsuspecting violator. She came up next to Charles Robinson standing with a plate of food in his hand.

"Hello, Mr. Robinson," said Aunt Lil. "So kind of you to attend."

"Thank you, Mrs. Tattersall," said Charles. "I'm honored to be here."

"Frankly, I wasn't sure whether it was proper to have a party such as this," said Aunt Lil, baiting Charles.

"Oh really?" asked Charles. "Why is that?"

"Well, he may have saved my niece's life," said Aunt Lil. "But he is, well, you know what I'm trying to say."

"Oh I do," said Charles. "And I'm so glad you are bringing it up. I didn't want to say anything because you are a patroness of this party."

'Oh, really," said Aunt Lil, egging him on.

"Oh yes. And I understand, he does deserve some recognition for what he did. But we can't go too far letting Indians have their way in the world. They can't be trusted. I read stories from out west in the newspaper. They are still savages."

"Ah, savages," Aunt Lil said. "You've had a lot of savage encounters with Indians, Mr. Robinson?"

"Well, no, I haven't, thank goodness," he said. "Just the drunk ones we run into around here."

"So you haven't had any contact with someone like Mr. Hancock?" asked Aunt Lil.

"What do you mean, Mrs. Tattersall?" asked Charles.

"Don't you do business with Johnson Ironworks?"

"Yes. They are one of my largest suppliers," said Charles.

"I thought so," said Aunt Lil. "And did you know that Mr. Hancock sits on the board of Johnson Ironworks?"

"That Mr. Hancock?" said Charles, stunned.

"Yes, Mr. Robinson," said Aunt Lil. "In fact, he does business with many people whom I'm sure you know."

"You don't say?" said Charles. "Well, I'll be."

252

He thought for a moment.

"Perhaps I had him wrong," said Charles, seeing an opportunity. "I think I'll go over and introduce myself to Mr. Hancock."

"Good idea," said Aunt Lil. "Why don't you do that."

Charles hightailed it across the meadow to where Ausable was regaling several people with a story about painting with Winslow Homer up on Mount Marcy.

"You are a wily one, Lil," said Anna, coming up behind her.

"Almost as wily as you, Anna," said Aunt Lil.

"What do you mean?" asked Anna.

"You think I didn't see through your tricks to get me to help you have this party?" said Aunt Lil.

"Why, what do you mean?" asked Anna.

"Oh, come now," said Aunt Lil. "I was happy to go along with the charade just to make you happy."

"That's very sweet of you, Lil," said Anna and she kissed her on the cheek.

"Oh now, none of that," said Aunt Lil, brushing her off, embarrassed. Anna looked around.

"It's a very nice party, isn't it?" said Anna.

"You did a marvelous job putting it all together," said Aunt Lil.

"And look how well Ausable is fitting in," Anna said. "I'm happy for him."

"It's a very kind thing to do, Anna," said Aunt Lil.

"I've made a special cake for Ausable as a way of saying thanks so everyone can join in," said Anna. "I think it's time for the presentation."

Anna made an indication to Colleen who went inside to get the cake. She and Millie brought it out to the summerhouse, trying to keep it hidden from view. Anna stood up on the top step of the summerhouse to make an announcement.

"Everyone," she called. "May I have your attention?"

They all came over and gathered around her.

"Ausable, would you join me up here?" said Anna.

Ausable came up and stood beside her.

"My friends, during the great cloudburst this summer, I almost lost my life. If it weren't for this man, I would not be here enjoying this lovely evening with you."

Everyone nodded in agreement.

"I am so happy that I was able to reconnect with Mr. Hancock so I could thank him appropriately."

Ausable indicated that it wasn't necessary.

"Now, now," said Anna. "I am eternally grateful. Not only for rescuing me, but for becoming a wonderful friend to my boys and me. And to say thanks one more time, I have this for you."

Anna stepped aside just as Colleen lit a sparkler on top of the cake. Everyone applauded, oohed and aahed, and Ausable looked quite touched. He then stepped forward.

"Mrs. Tattersall, this is very lovely of you to do, but very unnecessary," said Ausable. "Anyone would have done what I did on that mountain. I am just glad I was there when I was. Thank you for this party and this beautiful cake."

All applauded.

Then to everyone, "I also want to thank all of you for being so kind to me tonight and making me feel at home. It has been a joy to meet you all."

"I haven't met you yet," said a friendly, familiar voice in the crowd.

Everyone turned to look and Will stepped forward. The company was hushed. The boys ran up to him.

"Father," they yelled, and hugged him.

"Hello, boys, I'm so glad to see you," Will said.

"Will?" said Anna, a bit uncomfortably. "We didn't know you were coming."

"I'm sorry. It was a sudden decision," said Will.

"Hello, William," said Aunt Lil.

"Lil, so good to see you," said Will who kissed her on the cheek. She stood still and hard.

"And you must be Mr. Hancock," Will said to Ausable. "I owe you for saving my wife's life."

"Not at all, Mr. Tattersall," said Ausable. "Good to meet you." And they shook hands. All were still quiet.

"This looks like a lovely party," said Will to everyone. "Please, continue having a good time. Don't stop on my account."

Everyone went back to mingling and chatting.

Margaret was standing next to Anna as Will went up to her.

"Margaret. I didn't expect to see you here," Will said.

"The same could be said for you," said Margaret.

"Hello, Anna. I think we need to talk."

"Oh, Will," said Anna, starting to break down. She looked at him, then turned and hurried to the house. Of course everyone noticed and they all stole looks at Will.

"Father, what's wrong with Mother?" asked Sam.

"I'll go see," said Will as he walked to the house.

"Come on, boys," said Ausable. "Let's have some of that cake!"

"Oh boy," said Sam and he and Paul went up into the summerhouse.

Inside, Will found Anna in her room, sitting on her bed. She was facing the open door.

"Can I come in?" he asked.

"Close the door," she said.

He came in and closed the door. He pulled up a chair and sat facing Anna. They sat in silence, neither quite knowing what to say.

"Anna, I know you've heard things. And I want to assure you that what you heard is not true," Will said.

"Oh really?" said Anna, not believing him. "Jim Stoddard saw you in New York. Why would he make that up?"

"He misunderstood what he saw," Will said.

"He saw you kissing, Will. Kissing for a long time. How does someone misunderstand that?"

"I... I don't know," said Will, unconvincingly. "Anna, it's been so long since we've been together. I had too much to drink and you know how Margaret can be."

Anna sat up straight. She was in shock. "Did you say Margaret!?"

"Yes," Will said.

Anna started to shake.

255

"Didn't you know it was Margaret?"

"How could you? With Margaret?" Anna said, disgusted.

"We ran into each other at the restaurant," Will explained.

"Come now, you aren't that easily fooled. She went to New York with a plan to find you and seduce you," Anna said.

"Why would she do that?" Will asked.

"Because she knew that you and I were drifting apart. And she saw an opportunity."

"You told her about us?" asked Will. "But you despise one another."

"She and I mended our differences. At least I thought we had." Anna growled. "How could she?"

"You and Margaret? Friends?" Will asked, astonished.

"Yes. But I see now she was just playing me. To get to you!" Anna said, furious.

"Well, that explains why she is here."

"She won't be here for long when I get back down there."

"You're going back to the party?" Will asked.

She stood up. "I have a garden full of people out there who all know what you did. And I can't look at you anymore."

Anna opened the door and went out. Then she came back into the doorway.

"By the way, Mr. Hancock is staying here as my guest, on the sleeping porch," she said. "I just thought you should know." She went downstairs leaving Will there. Will hung his head.

Downstairs, Anna looked at herself in the hallway mirror. She patted her hair and pulled herself together. Everyone outside knew what was going on. She had to act strong and she headed out to the party.

Tom met her halfway.

"How did that go, Anna?" asked Tom.

"Where's Margaret?" Anna snarled.

"She had to go. Why?" Tom asked.

"You are not going to believe this, Tom," Anna said. "The woman Will was kissing in New York… it was Margaret."

"Margaret?" said Tom, shocked. "What a crafty fox."

"Aunt Lil was right about her," Anna said. "A leopard doesn't change its spots. She's wanted Will since we were kids. She was always jealous of me for marrying him. And now she's found a way to get back at me. How could I have been so stupid?"

"Anna, she's always been very conniving," said Tom. "She's had a lot of practice manipulating people."

"Well, I'm not going to take this lying down," Anna declared. "If Margaret wants a fight, she's going to get it."

"Now, Anna, let's talk this through before you do anything rash, please," Tom said.

"You're right," Anna said. "But for now, I need to get back to the party."

Aunt Lil came toward them.

"Anna, is Will in the house?" she asked.

"Yes, Lil," Anna said. "But this really isn't the time, do you think?"

"I'll be the judge of that," said Aunt Lil and she strode past them toward the house.

"Oh, I don't envy Will right now," said Tom.

They watched Aunt Lil as she went into the house, calling for Will.

The party started to wind down quickly after Will arrived. People politely said their goodbyes to Anna and thanked her for a delightful time. And many said, quite sincerely, how nice it had been to get to know Ausable. Millie had taken the boys in and put them to bed.

Ausable, Tom, and Anna had been talking, sitting in wicker chairs in the summerhouse. Anna was exhausted.

"What am I going to do about Margaret?" Anna asked. "I'm so furious with her. And how could Will be so dumb to fall for that?"

"I'm so sorry you're hurt, Anna," said Ausable. "What Margaret did was unconscionable."

"It's obvious she took advantage of our friendship only to get to Will," Anna said.

"I've known her a long time," said Tom. "She carries a lot of extra baggage."

"That's no excuse," Anna said.

Colleen came out to bring in the rest of the cake.

"Colleen, have you seen Aunt Lil and my husband?" Anna asked.

"Yes, Missus.," Colleen said. "They left. I saw Mrs. Tattersall's buckboard leaving."

Colleen went inside with the cake.

"I have a feeling Lil will make Will stay in her house," Anna said.

"It's probably better under the circumstances," said Tom.

"Anna, maybe I better go stay up at my camp," Ausable said. "I don't want to be in the way."

"That's thoughtful of you, Ausable. But it's late," Anna said. "Let's see how things work themselves out. I'd like you to stay here tonight."

"Maybe I'll stop by tomorrow and see if Will would like to talk with me," Tom said.

"That's nice of you, Tom," Anna said. "You are a very good man."

"That's my job," said Tom, smiling. He got up to leave.

"Ausable, you really gave those people something to think about," said Tom. "You might have changed a few minds."

"I hope so," said Ausable. "Thank you, Tom."

"Goodnight," said Tom.

Tom walked down to his carriage.

Anna scooted her chair closer to Ausable and rubbed her foot up his leg.

"Tom is right," Anna said. "You were impressive tonight."

"Thank you. I'm always happy to expand the horizons of others," said Ausable. "And, thank you for a marvelous party. I actually had a good time."

"I'm so glad," said Anna.

"I thought I'd be ostracized, but I didn't feel that way at all. Most were very cordial. Some, even friendly," Ausable said.

"You can thank Aunt Lil for that," Anna said. "She was able to manipulate the worst offenders of the bunch into getting to know you."

"I'll have to thank her for that," he said.

Anna took Ausable's hand. "Oh, Ausable. I don't know how to handle this with Will," she said. "I hadn't expected to see him just yet."

He kissed her hand. "Right now, the two of you have a lot of talking to do. You need to work things out, one way or another. You have two boys to think about."

"They are my first concern," Anna said. "I'm so glad they've taken such a liking to you."

"They are delightful boys. You've reared them well," he said.

"They are, aren't they?" she agreed, and smiled. "All right, I'm very tired. This has been quite a day."

"Yes, it has," he said. "I'm ready for bed."

He stood up and offered his hand to Anna and helped her up, and into his arms.

"I'm glad it's dark out here," he said. And he kissed her unreservedly.

When they broke, Anna said, "Oh, I've been waiting all night for that." And they kissed again.

They took a step back from each other, turned and walked, apart, toward the house. As they walked, an unseen figure appeared from behind the playhouse. Will stepped into the dim moonlight.

CHAPTER THIRTY-SIX

Anna was usually the first one up in the morning. But she slept late, being very tired from the party and the events the night before. When she came down the stairway, she heard talking and laughing from the dining porch. She found Ausable, the boys, and Will, all sitting at the table, having already finished breakfast. Anna didn't quite know what to make of this scene.

"Hello, sleepyhead," said Will.

"Good morning," Anna said sleepily. "I guess that party really did me in."

"Mother, we're going to take Father up to Mr. Hancock's camp later," Paul said.

"Yes, we're going to show him the secret tracking we learned, too!" said Sam.

"Oh, that will be fun, boys," Anna said. "Are you up for that, Will?"

"Of course," said Will. Then emphasizing, "The boys are our first concern, aren't they, Anna?"

Anna and Ausable reacted to this. "Of course, they are, Will," Anna said.

"Ausable here's been telling me all about his business," Will said. "I might be able to do some legal work for his family."

"Oh. Well, isn't that wonderful," Anna said, unsure of what was going on here.

"Yes. In my business, I am always in need of legal assistance," said Ausable, a bit uncomfortably.

Colleen came into the breakfast room with a cup of coffee for Anna.

"Hotcakes, Missus?".

"Uh, no. Thank you, Colleen. Just coffee for now," Anna said. She sat down at the table with her coffee. Colleen looked at the clock.

"Paul, don't forget you have rehearsal this morning," said Colleen.

"Oh yes," Paul said. "I was so excited to see Father, I forgot." He got up from the table.

"I'll go with you," said Sam. Then to his father, "I've been coaching him. I want to see how he's coming along."

"Good for you, Sam," said Will.

"Can we go up to the camp after lunch, Father?" said Paul.

"I don't see why not," said Will.

"Great. We'll see you then, Father," said Paul, and they left the house.

"I've never seen Paul excited about doing a play," said Will.

"He has eyes for his Juliet," said Anna.

"Ah," Will said.

Then there was an uncomfortable silence. Ausable stood.

"Why don't I leave you two alone," said Ausable.

Will grabbed Ausable by the arm, pulling him back into his chair. "No, Ausable. Please sit," Will said firmly. "I think the three of us need to talk."

"As you wish," Ausable said.

"Will, I don't think we need to involve Ausable in our affairs," said Anna.

"Oh, I think he's already involved, isn't he Anna?" said Will. "And 'affair' is the right word, isn't it?"

Anna and Ausable were taken aback.

Will continued, "I saw you two last night in the summerhouse. Anna, suppose one of the boys had seen you. What then?"

"You're right, Will. That was careless of me," Anna admitted. "And I'm sorry you had to find out this way."

"I don't really think you are," Will barked.

"Well, I must say, you're one to talk. At least we were alone in the dark. You were seen at Delmonico's! With Margaret Bancroft!"

"All right, Anna, I regret that," Will said. "It was unkind of me to embarrass you like that. Aunt Lil made it all too clear to me last night. She obviously doesn't know about you and Ausable, though."

"No. She doesn't," Anna said. "And I'd like to tell her when we think the time is right."

"The time is right?" said Will, incensed. "Anna, its one thing for a man to see another woman. It's a very different thing for a married woman to see another man."

"Oh come now, Will," Anna said, irritated.

"Ausable, you're a man," Will said. "You must understand that this just isn't done."

"I'm sorry, Will," said Ausable. "I've lived my life fighting double standards because I'm an Indian. This is just one more social convention utilized to hold different classes apart. My people believe that we are all part of one spirit. Man. Woman. Both the same. I'm sure that sounds quaint to you, but, believe me, it helps me get through life."

"Well, in our world, this can't happen," said Will. "A man's wife doesn't cheat on him."

"Oh, Will, just stop it," demanded Anna, angrily. "You and I haven't been husband and wife for a very long time. This was bound to happen. And I've got news for you. There are a lot of women out there who have needs too. And they are getting those needs filled. So don't fool yourself into thinking it just isn't done!"

"But Anna, it's made all the worse that this man is an Indian, goddammit!"

Anna turned beet red with anger. "How dare you, Will!"

"Now, Anna," said Ausable. "It's all right. I understand his feelings."

"No. No. I won't let you say that. Neither of you. Ausable, don't demean yourself. And Will, how dare you say that to Ausable? He's a man, just like you. And he's sitting right here, at our breakfast table, no less a gentleman than you. Plus he saved my life! Don't forget that!"

Will was taken aback by Anna's anger.

"Will, I know you probably hate me right now," Ausable said. "And you have every right to. I'm sure you think what's happening here is wrong in every way. And you don't want to hear this, but Anna has opened up a place in my heart that I didn't even know I had. She's an amazing woman, full of life with a lot of love to give. And she needs to do that. And frankly, it doesn't sound like you have let her."

"How dare you?" Will said indignantly.

"He's right, Will," Anna said. "What are we fighting about? Our marriage has been over for years. We don't give each other what the other one needs. And that hurts, so we get angry at one another about that. I haven't been happy for so long. And I don't think you have either. We have grown apart. We want different things now. You love life in New York. And I love a simpler life. Neither of us is in the wrong here."

Will shook his head, feeling defeated. "Oh, I don't know what to think anymore."

"If it's any consolation, Will, I still love you. And I'm very sorry," Anna said.

"I'm sorry too, Anna," Will said.

They all sat in silence for a few moments.

"I don't know what we should do now," Will said, overwhelmed.

"We don't have to do anything right away," Anna said. "We need to let all this sink in and then we'll figure out the right thing to do."

"But what about the boys?" Will asked.

"That won't be easy. But we'll figure that out, too," Anna said sadly.

She got up and went around to Will and put her arms around his shoulders. Will started to cry.

• • •

That afternoon, Ausable thought it best to go up to his camp at the Upper Lake. Anna agreed. And she had her mind set on only one thing. Margaret Bancroft. She had to figure out how to confront her on what she had done. Anna thought the best approach should be to hit her when she wouldn't know what was coming, so she decided to go up to Margaret's house, acting as if nothing was wrong. Then set her up for the fall.

As she turned into Margaret's drive, she encountered her husband, John, walking down.

"Good afternoon, John," Anna said.

"Hello, Anna," John said grumpily.

"Is Margaret at home?" Anna asked.

"Yes, she's up there somewhere," John responded.

"John, I suppose you have heard about my husband, Will, and what happened in New York," Anna said.

"Well, I don't like all that gossip like you hens do, but, yes, I did hear," John said. "And I'm sorry to hear that."

"Thank you," said Anna. "That's very kind of you." Then, as if just having a thought, "You know, your wife has had quite a crush on Will ever since they were children. And she still likes to flirt with him."

"Why do you say that, Anna?" John asked.

"Oh, I was just thinking out loud. Don't mind me." Anna said. "Well, I'll go find Margaret now. Goodbye, John."

John looked after Anna, pondering. Anna rode up the hill with a self-satisfied smile.

As Anna's carriage approached Margaret's house, she came out on the veranda.

"Hello, Margaret," Anna called, as she waved.

Margaret was hesitant as Anna stopped her carriage next to the house. "Hello Anna," she said.

Anna got out of the carriage. "You left the party without saying goodbye."

"Oh, I apologize, Anna," said Margaret. "I suddenly had a sick headache and had to leave."

"I'm sorry to hear that," Anna said. "What do you think brought it on?"

"I'm not sure. Maybe too much cake," Margaret said. "It was delicious, though."

"I'm glad you liked it," Anna said. "Are you feeling better?"

"I think it's going away," Margaret said.

"Oh, good," said Anna.

"Um, so, how is it going with Will?" Margaret asked. "I left before I was able to hear."

"We talked. He tried to deny it," Anna said. "But when I told about Jim seeing him, he didn't know what to say."

"So he didn't tell you more of what occurred?" asked Margaret.

"What more is there to tell?" Anna asked. "Besides, I wouldn't want to hear it anyway."

"That's probably smart. So how are you feeling about all this?" Margaret asked.

"Well, considering he's not the only one having an affair, it's hard to really be angry."

"True," said Margaret, a bit relieved. "What's your next step?"

"I'm going to move on as if nothing has changed," Anna said. "Why should I let this put a damper on things?"

"Good for you," said Margaret.

"Yes. And I want to have some fun," Anna declared. "What can we do that's fun?"

"Why don't we get all dressed up and go down to the Club and stir up some trouble?" said Margaret. "That's always fun."

"Sounds good to me. I'm in the mood to stir up trouble," Anna said. "I'll go home and change and pick you up in a couple of hours."

"Great," said Margaret. "See you then."

Anna got into her carriage, smiled and waved goodbye. This would work perfectly. In front of all the women at the Club, she would expose Margaret Bancroft for the man-stealing witch that she is.

After changing into an especially attractive tea dress, Anna headed back to pick up Margaret. She left a little early so she could stop and see Tom. She needed to tell him that Will knew about her and Ausable. And she wanted to tell him of her plan against Margaret. She went into the rectory and found him at his desk.

"Hello, Tom," Anna said.

"Oh, Anna," he said, getting up and hugging her. "Tell me how you are doing after last night."

Anna flopped down in one of Tom's big armchairs. "Well, Tom, Will heard Ausable and me talking last night after you left. And he knows what's going on with us."

"Oh my," said Tom. "I suppose it was bound to happen."

"Yes. So he confronted both of us this morning about it. It got pretty ugly."

"Anna, that's too bad," Tom said. "I'm sure it's hard for both of you."

"It is," she said. "It's all so confusing. Who knew we would both end up like this? I didn't think we were the kind of people to do something like this."

"Anna, there is no certain 'kind of people' this happens to," Tom said. "Not that I condone any of what either of you are doing, but I have to admit, I understand. When two people go in different directions, these things happen. Believe me, I hear it more than you would imagine."

"Really? Who?" asked Anna.

"Anna, you know I wouldn't tell you," Tom scolded

"I know," she said. "But it is sort of comforting to know we're not the only ones."

"Where did you leave things with Will?" Tom asked.

"We have a lot more talking to do," Anna said. "I still don't know how things will end up, yet."

"If you would both like to come to me as a couple, I'd be happy to do that," said Tom.

"That probably wouldn't work," Anna said. "Will would think you were on my side because we're so close. But I'll mention it to him."

"Good. So where are you going all dressed up?" Tom asked.

"That's the other reason I came by," Anna said. "I went to see Margaret today."

"You did? How did that go?" he asked.

"Just fine," Anna said. "I was as friendly as friendly can be to her."

"I don't understand," Tom said.

"It wouldn't have been enough to tell her off at her house," Anna said. "I need to do it in front of as many of her friends as possible. So I'm on my way to pick her up and we're going to the Club where I can call her out in front of everybody."

"Oh, Anna, are you sure that's the right thing to do?" Tom asked.

"I don't really care, Tom," Anna said. "She deliberately went to New York to seduce Will. I can't let her get away with that."

"I understand you are angry," Tom said. "But are you sure you want to stoop to her level?"

"Unfortunately, I think it's the only way to get through to a woman like her," Anna said. "Besides, she deserves it."

"Anna, no one ever deserves revenge."

"Thank you, Pastor," Anna said, a bit annoyed. "I get what you are saying. But I have to handle this my way."

"I understand. Just think about it," Tom said.

"I will. Thank you, Tom," Anna said.

Anna left and went to pick up Margaret. She was waiting at the end of her drive.

"I couldn't stand another minute up there with John today," Margaret said as she was getting in. "He's acting surlier than ever for some reason."

"Whatever could be bothering him?" asked Anna, as they started off.

"I haven't a clue," Margaret said. "He's always got a bee in his bonnet about something. Let's not talk about him. We're off to have some fun."

"Indeed we are," Anna said as they rode off to the Club.

They arrived and the piazza was filled with ladies having tea. Anna and Margaret made their entrance and joined them to a lot of hellos. They all complimented Anna on the wonderful party the night before and how nice it was to get to know Ausable.

"Anna, I'm surprised to see you here," said Sally Merrick. "Will hasn't left again, has he?"

"No, Sally, he's still here," Anna said. "He may have done this atrocious thing, but he's still my husband and we have a lot of talking to do. In fact, while I have your attention, ladies, I'd like to talk about something right now, if you all don't mind."

They all agreed. "Not at all." "What do you have to tell us?"

"You all know the story," Anna began. "My husband was seen with a woman in New York. Jim Stoddard saw her, but he never said who Will was with," Anna continued.

Margaret started to get uncomfortable. "I don't think he saw her face," Margaret said. "Did he?"

"No, 'he' didn't see who it was, Margaret," Anna said. "But..." Then Anna stopped. The words Tom had said earlier came back to her. "Don't stoop to her level." "No one ever deserves revenge." Damn that Tom, she thought. She heaved a sigh and realized she couldn't go through with it.

"But I don't know who that woman is. And I don't care. And I just want to tell you all that if you do hear who it is, please keep it to yourselves because I don't want to know."

Everyone nodded and whispered amongst themselves. They went back to enjoying their tea. But Margaret felt very uneasy now.

CHAPTER THIRTY-SEVEN

August brought with it hot, steamy weather. Will had returned to New York a few weeks earlier. Nothing had changed between Anna and him, nor had they resolved anything. There was no hurry. This was all new to them. They had never expected anything like this to happen. They discussed it over and over but weren't ready to take any next steps. It was all very painful. Yet they both felt they were trapped in the cage of a loveless marriage.

Anna was all right with this since she wanted to be sure about her relationship with Ausable and had an uphill climb getting people to accept him. Ausable stayed at his camp until Will left. He came back to stay at Idlenook, much to the irritation of Aunt Lil, especially with the whole valley knowing the ins and outs of the family's business between Anna and Will. Aunt Lil was beside herself trying to portray respectability and propriety.

Anna and Ausable were able to spend more quiet time getting to know each other since Will left, intimately and otherwise, being very careful to not let on to the family at home or the valley citizens. So far no one, except Margaret and Tom, and Will, knew about them. They were getting closer and closer and the knowledge that this might be a reality was sinking in. And it wasn't scaring either of them. They were both extremely happy. Margaret continued her fling with young Peter Brown and would emerge, from wherever they could secret themselves, glowing and contented. Anna tried to avoid Margaret whenever possible. She knew this confused Margaret so perhaps this was punishment enough.

Aunt Lil became more and more suspicious as to why Ausable was staying on, especially at Idlenook, and made it clear on several occasions that she had her eye on them. To ease things, Ausable suggested he return to Boston to handle some business affairs and check on his mother, whose health continued to improve. Anna agreed that this was a good idea but was sad to see him go. She spent the time making the curtains for the parlor. Millie helped with the tassels and trim and when they were done, she thought the room looked very smart.

Along with the August heat came the Gypsy Circus. The boys were beside themselves with excitement. When the circus arrived in town, the company paraded themselves down the main street. Anna, the boys, and Aunt Lil, along with Colleen and Millie, went down to Bailey's to watch the procession. First came fanciful dancing horses with feathers in their manes leading a caravan of coaches, some with open cages. They had a lion, two tigers, a slew of monkeys, and one cage full of what seemed to be hundreds of white doves. Two happy clowns and one sad one danced along with the coaches, handing out candy and balloons to the children. On one colorful wagon, acrobats leaped about, doing somersaults and balancing acts. Then came a wagon bouncing with gypsy women dancers, scantily clad, twirling and clapping castanets. The men applauded this loudly while the women averted their gazes and tried to hide their children's eyes. The parade wound up with the elephants, draped in colorful, glittering cloths and tassels. Millie thought they looked like Anna's new curtains, which Anna found quite amusing, especially coming from Millie. A circus barker rode the last elephant.

"Come one, come all, to see the magnifico Gypsy Circus!" the barker cried with a Slavic accent. "Two nights starting tomorrow at dusk! We will be just near the Elizabethtown road, past that Bradley Farm from your beee-utiful little hamlet here. We have magical dancing, incredible flying men, remarkable music, a mysterious fortune-teller from the East, and fascinating games where you will win bountiful prizes!"

"Oh, goody! Bountiful prizes!" Sam yelped with delight.

"We will see you all under the big top!" the barker concluded with a flourish as he rode off atop his elephant.

"Well, that was quite stirring," said Aunt Lil.

"It should be a fun time for all of us," Anna said.

"At least it will be something to take our minds off this dreadful heat," Aunt Lil said, fanning herself.

"I'm so looking forward to it, Mother," said Paul.

"Me too," said Sam. "Do you think we can ride the elephants?"

Anna chuckled. "You never know, Sam."

Anna saw Tom and went over to speak to him. "Will you be going to the circus, Tom?" she asked.

"Of course," he said, happily. "I look forward to when they come. It's a wonderful distraction."

"Good. Why don't you come with us?" Anna asked.

"I'd love to, Anna," he said. "Are you going tomorrow?"

"Yes. The boys wouldn't wait one more day to go," she said. "There are quite a few of us going. Perhaps we can double up in your carriage as well."

"Of course. Glad to," he said. "Will Aunt Lil be joining us?"

"Oh, yes. But don't worry. I won't make you ride with her," Anna said, teasing.

"Ha," he chuckled. "That's sweet of you."

"Wonderful. We'll see you tomorrow evening," Anna said, and then calling, "Come on, boys. Let's get home and ready for dinner."

The next evening, the household was getting ready to depart for the circus. At least, the adults were getting ready. The boys had been ready to go since breakfast.

"Mother, when are we leaving?" Sam yelled from the carriage they had parked, ready to go, in the drive.

Anna looked out her bedroom window. "How long have you had that poor horse standing there?" she asked.

"Um. Oh, not too long, Mother," said Paul.

271

"Uh huh. Well, please give him some water. It's extremely humid. We'll be out soon," Anna said. She got her things together and went downstairs where Colleen and Millie were coming out of the kitchen.

"We better hurry or those boys will go off without us," Colleen said. Anna and Millie laughed.

They went outside and found Paul watering the horse.

"Thank you, Paul," Anna said.

They all got into the carriage. Colleen and Millie sat up front and they headed down the drive.

"We're picking up Aunt Lil first..."

Sam interrupted, "Really, Mother? She won't be any fun at the circus."

"Now, Sam," Anna said. "That's not very nice. The circus is her treat, remember?"

"Oh, yes. I forgot," Sam said.

"So you also need to remember to thank her properly," Anna said.

"Do we have to kiss her?" asked Paul.

"That would be nice, Paul," Anna said.

Both boys groaned.

"Boys," Anna warned.

"Yes, Mother," said Paul.

"All right," said Sam.

"But, to make things a little better, we're also meeting Pastor Tom at the church," Anna said. "So we'll ride with Aunt Lil. And you two can ride with the pastor."

"Yay," said Sam and Paul.

"I thought you'd like that," said Anna.

"I like Pastor Tom," said Sam to Paul. "He's way more fun than Aunt Lil."

Anna just shook her head and smiled.

As they pulled up to Aunt Lil's house, she came out the door.

"Seems we have quite a full house in the carriage," Aunt Lil said. "Are you sure you want to ride all that way crammed in together like this?"

"No worries, Lil," Anna said. "Pastor Tom has offered to go with us so we'll stop at the church and the boys will go with him."

"Oh, good. Very well," said Aunt Lil as she came down the steps to the carriage. Paul and Sam got out..

Paul started, "Aunt Lil, Sam and I want to thank you so much for taking us to the circus."

"Yes, we really are very grateful," Sam said as he walked up to her and gave her a peck on the cheek.

Paul followed suit.

"Well, thank you both very much," Aunt Lil said. "I'm glad to do it."

Aunt Lil got into the carriage and sat next to Anna.

"You coached them very well," Aunt Lil said to Anna.

Anna smiled. "They'll do anything to get to go to the circus."

Sam and Paul scrambled back into the carriage, rocking it to Aunt Lil's dismay.

"Careful, boys," Anna said. "Let's go to the church, Colleen."

"Boys, I've arranged to get us seats right up front inside the big top," Aunt Lil told them. "You'll be able to see everything up close."

"Oh boy," Sam said excitedly. "But I just hope that sad clown leaves us alone. I didn't like him in the parade."

"Why not, Sam?" Anna asked.

"Oh I don't know. He reminded me of the way Father looked when he left," Sam said.

Anna and Aunt Lil gave each other a look.

"Oh, Sam, don't worry," said Anna. "Your father was just sad to leave Keene Valley and not be able to see you boys. He'll be back as soon as he can and he'll be happy again."

"I hope so," Sam said. "He looked like he was a different kind of sad."

Aunt Lil whispered to Anna, "Little ones are very perceptive."

Anna worriedly said, "I'm afraid so." Then loudly to Sam, "Now, don't you worry about that sad clown, Sam. If he comes near us, we'll do everything we can to make him happy. Right everyone!"

They all yelled in agreement and Sam seemed satisfied.

They arrived at the church and Tom was ready with his carriage.

"Hello all," Tom said. "Mrs. Tattersall," he said to Aunt Lil, tipping his hat.

"Evening, Pastor," Aunt Lil replied. "It's very nice of you to join us."

"I appreciate the invitation," Tom said. "I love the circus. Come on, boys, you can ride with me."

The boys clambered out and jumped into Tom's carriage. Tom got in to join them, as Aunt Lil and Anna got more comfortable.

"Shall we race, Colleen?" Tom asked.

"You're on, Pastor Tom," Colleen said.

"Oh no, you're not," Aunt Lil announced. "I won't be part of any race."

"I'm just joshing, Mrs. Tattersall," Colleen said. "I'm sorry about that."

"That's all right, Colleen," Aunt Lil said. "You know what? Today should be all about fun. Let's race."

"Really, Mrs. Tattersall?" Colleen exclaimed.

"Why not? It's the women against the men," Aunt Lil said, with a rare joy in her voice.

"Giddyap!" Colleen yelled as she gently slapped the reins. The horses jolted and got into a fast trot. Millie grasped the seat and closed her eyes.

"Come on, Pastor Tom!" Paul cried. "We can't let Colleen beat us!"

"No, we can't," Tom said as he whacked the horse with his hand and got him moving into a quick canter.

Both carriages jostled and bounced down the dirt road. Tom was gaining on Colleen as the boys cheered him on. Colleen yelled ahead for people in the road to clear out of her way. As people ran for safety, Aunt Lil apologized as they quickly dashed past. They saw Brown driving the stagecoach into town and both swerved to avoid him. Brown yelled out to them angrily to be careful. The road narrowed ahead as they got out of the village center. It was now or never for Tom to overtake Colleen's carriage. Tom slapped the reins and yelled to his horse. The horse obeyed and picked up the pace. The two carriages were now next to each other. Luckily, no one was coming toward them as Tom tried to get his horse moving a bit faster. But Colleen had a trick up her sleeve. This particular horse seemed to understand Colleen's voice commands better than anyone else's voice. So in a soft, calm voice, Colleen said, "Gallop." And that horse took off like a rocket, with the carriage bounding behind as Anna and Aunt Lil held on for dear life. Colleen was able to pull ahead of Tom and block him. She did it just in time, as the road narrowed and she was able to slow back down to a comfortable trot.

"Don't let the curls fool you, Pastor Tom," Colleen called. "I'm quite a horsewoman!"

"I concede defeat," Tom called.

The women cheered and clapped and waved to Tom and the boys. The boys booed, then slumped back down in their seats. "We'll win on the way home," Sam said.

Aunt Lil was quite pleased by the whole escapade. "My compliments, Colleen. I am very impressed with the gentle command you have with the horse."

"Thank you, Mrs. Tattersall," Colleen relied. "That was the most fun I've had in a while."

"I'm exhilarated," Anna said. "On to the real circus!"

CHAPTER THIRTY-EIGHT

As they neared the circus grounds, there was a crush of carriages and horses. Colleen, Millie, and Tom said they'd take care of the horses and the rest should go off and enjoy the circus grounds. They would catch up in a few minutes. Aunt Lil gave Colleen and Millie their tickets and the boys bounded out and ran toward the entrance.

"Wait, boys," Anna yelled. "You can't get in without your tickets."

The circus grounds were festooned with colorful flags and banners extolling the sideshow acts of Sergei the Sword Swallower, the Real Gypsy Queen Fortune Teller, and Prince Constantin, the Smallest Man in the World! Carnival game stalls were set up all around the grounds. And behind it all, the huge big top in all its red and yellow striped glory. Anna and Aunt Lil went up to the boys standing, mouths agape, at the entrance, where a barker was enticing "one and all to come on in and enjoy the magnifico circus!"

Anna put her arms around the boys. "Come on. Let's go in."

Aunt Lil gave the barker their tickets and into the magic land they went.

"You boys stay with us," Anna told them. "I don't want you getting into any trouble in here."

"Oh we won't, Mother," Paul said.

"Can we play ring toss?" Sam asked.

"Yes, let's see if you can win something!" Anna said excitedly as she handed Sam a nickel.

"Here, Mister," said Sam as he gave his nickel to the game operator. "Can I play?"

"Sure thing, young man," he said and handed Sam five red wooden rings. "Now all you have to do is get one of these five rings over those stakes back there and you win a fantastic prize."

"Here goes," said Sam. He threw the first ring and it bounced off the wall.

"A little easier toss, Sam," Anna suggested.

Sam threw the second ring and it missed. So did the third and the fourth, but they were close. Sam wasn't deterred. "This one is it," Sam said as he tossed the last ring. But his throw was so fast that the ring bounced off the wall and flew back over their heads, just missing Aunt Lil.

"Oh, gracious," Aunt Lil cried and she ducked out of the way.

"I'm sorry, Sam," Anna said. "You tried."

"Let me give it a go," said a voice behind them as the ring glided in over their heads and landed right on one of the stakes. They all reacted in shock and clapped, then turned to see Ausable standing behind them.

"Ausable," Anna exclaimed. "Where did you come from?"

"I'm back in the valley and I figured you all would be at the circus," Ausable said.

"Mother! Mr. Hancock won!" Sam cried.

"Yes, he did," said the game operator. "And since it was with your ring, young man, you get to pick which prize you want."

"Oh, boy!" yelled Sam as he looked over the array of stuffed animals and toys. "How about that truck?"

"It's yours," said the game operator as he gave Sam the wooden truck.

"Wow, this is great!" Sam exclaimed. "Thanks, Mr. Hancock!"

"My pleasure, Sam," Ausable said. He turned to Aunt Lil. "And it's wonderful to see you again, Mrs. Tattersall."

"That was very nice of you, Mr. Hancock," Aunt Lil said. "You have good aim."

"Thank you, Mrs. Tattersall," he said. "It's quite humid up here, isn't it?"

"Dreadful heat," said Aunt Lil. "The circus is a pleasant diversion, though."

"When did you get here, Ausable?" Anna asked.

"Just now," Ausable said. "In fact, I think I passed you all racing up the road."

"Oh, you were in the stagecoach," Anna said. "Poor Brown. He was quite disgusted with us."

"Who won the race?" Ausable asked.

"I did," said Colleen as she, Millie, and Tom approached them.

"Well done, Colleen!" said Ausable.

"I didn't know you were in town, Ausable," said Tom, shaking Ausable's hand.

"Just arrived, Pastor," said Ausable. "Good to see you."

"Welcome back," said Tom.

"You must sit with us in the big top," Anna said.

"I'd love to, Anna," said Ausable.

"Mr. Hancock, let's see what else we can win," Sam said.

"Now, Sam, Mr. Hancock already helped you win something," Anna cautioned.

"I'm glad to, Anna," Ausable said. "Come on, Sam, what's next?"

"Let's see," Sam said, looking around at the game stalls. "Oh, there's a fishing one. I'm a great fisherman!"

"Then the fishing game it is," Ausable said.

They all started over to the fishing game as Anna held Tom back. "I can't believe he's back," Anna said. "I'm overjoyed!"

"I'm happy for you, Anna," Tom said, giving her a little hug.

They joined the others. Sam and Paul were each holding fishing poles with large wooden hooks on them over a large tub of water. In it floated wooden fish with stringed loops that they could catch with the hooks. The game operator turned over a large hourglass. "Time starts now!" he yelled. "You have one minute to hook a fish."

Sam and Paul maneuvered their poles around, trying desperately to hook a fish as the rest of the group cheered them on. Sam got close to hooking a fish and pulled up on his pole a bit too quickly and lost it. At one point their fishing hooks tangled together and the operator had to undo them.

"The sand is almost running out," the game operator yelled. "Time to hook a fish!"

Paul got his hook very close to a fish and, with slow precision, he eased the hook into the loop and pulled out a fish. Everyone cheered.

"That's my boy, Paul!" Anna said.

"Great job, son," said the game operator. "What will be your prize?"

"Um, let's see," Paul said, looking over the prizes. "How about one of those kewpie dolls?"

Everyone reacted. A kewpie doll?

"It's yours," said the game operator. "Do you have a pretty girl to give this to?"

Paul blushed. "Uh, actually, I do," he said, shyly, taking the doll.

"Is that for Clara?" Anna asked, smiling.

Paul looked down, embarrassed. "Yes."

"Paul, that's very sweet of you," Anna said.

"She's supposed to be here tonight." Paul said, trying to hide his excitement.

"I saw the Robinsons as we were entering," said Aunt Lil. "I'm sure we'll run into them."

They had time before the show in the big top started, so they wandered around, trying to win more prizes. No one won anything else, but they had a great time. They stopped to see the sword swallower. Aunt Lil was repulsed and the boys were amazed. They passed the animal cages and saw the tigers pacing back and forth. There was the large monkey cage with ropes and swings and they enjoyed watching the mischievous primates play about. The boys relished the wares from several of the candy stands, enticed by the booming voices of the

279

candy barkers. They passed the fortune teller and had a long discussion over whether any of them should have their fortune told. Aunt Lil, of course, thought the whole thing was silly. Finally they decided Anna should do it. Millie was afraid of fortune tellers so she didn't want to go in. Colleen offered to stay outside with her.

They went into the small tent and met Violeta, the Gypsy Queen. She sat at a table with a glass ball in the center, candles burning all around, and the smell of incense.

"Hello," Violeta said, bowing her head. "I am Violeta, the Gypsy Queen Fortune Teller. I see there are quite a lot of you. Let me see," she said, looking the group over, then landing her gaze on Anna. "You are the one who would like a reading."

"I am," said Anna, amazed.

"Please, be seated," said Violeta, indicating the chair across from her. "I must ask the rest of you to please be silent so I can concentrate on this woman." She stopped and stared into the ball. "This woman whose name begins with A."

Everyone was taken aback.

"It does," said Anna, startled.

"Don't tell me," Violeta said. "It starts with an A… and… I think it ends with A."

"My goodness," said Anna. "It does!"

She held her hand up, "I'm sorry. I see more important things here in the crystal ball," said Violeta, trying to move on. "Your name is?"

"Anna."

"Anna. Very good," said Violeta. "Now, I need total silence. Let's see what we have here," as she gazed into the ball. "Give me your hand," she commanded, taking Anna's hand in hers. "And please don't speak unless I ask you to." Anna nodded in agreement. "Hmm, this is confusing to me. I see great sorrow, but I also see great joy." Anna reacted, but didn't speak. "It involves a man. No. Two men." Anna was starting to get worried at what Violeta might say. "One has hurt you deeply and the other… what do I see here? He's a darker man. This one saved you somehow."

"My goodness," said Anna. "You are quite good. Yes, this man here," indicating Ausable, "He saved my life. How could you know that?"

"Violeta sees all," she said. "And I can tell you, your life will turn in a new direction. I see great happiness in your future."

"That's wonderful," Anna said enthusiastically. "I can't thank you enough." Then, to everyone, "I think it's time to get to the big top."

She stood and everyone started to file out. Violeta held Anna back. When everyone else was gone she whispered to Anna, "And that man there is the one who will make you happy. There will be much difficulty to overcome, but much more happiness over all." Anna reacted. "I thought maybe you would not want the others to hear that."

"Thank you, Violeta," Anna said. "Thank you very much." Anna exited the tent.

"Well, that was quite enlightening," Aunt Lil said. "I don't know how she did it."

"Neither do I," said Anna. "But she certainly has a gift."

"Mother?" Sam asked, "What man hurt you?"

"Oh, oh, Sam, she had that part wrong," Anna said. "I haven't been hurt by anyone. But she got the part about Mr. Hancock right. That was what was so amazing."

"Yes, Mother," said Paul. "How did she know that?"

"The Gypsy Queen sees all," said Anna dramatically. "Come on. Let's go see the circus."

They all joined the crowed walking over to the big top. Anna pulled Tom aside. "She spoke to me after everyone left."

"What did she say," Tom asked.

"She said that Ausable is the one who will make me happy. She knew so much."

"God works in mysterious ways," Tom said, smiling.

Anna laughed. "Yes, he does, Pastor."

They joined the others and entered the big top. It was large and colorful with the smell of hay and animals. Two large posts held up the tent, with wires strung between them and long swings at either end. A band was playing a happy march.

Everyone seemed to be walking in to the beat of the band to get to their seats, which circled the tent. One could hear the creaking of the grandstands as people sought their places. Aunt Lil, Anna, and the boys sat in the front row. Colleen, Millie, Tom, and Ausable sat behind them. The boys were talking excitedly and pointing at all the fascinating apparatuses.

Aunt Lil leaned over to Anna, "That was quick thinking with Sam back there."

"Thank you," Anna said. "I didn't think we'd find a fortune teller who was actually able to see things, or I wouldn't have gone in there with the boys."

"At least she was discreet enough to not say more, if she indeed did know any more," Aunt Lil said.

"She might have," Anna said. "She knew a dark man saved me. That's quite a detail to know."

"I agree," said Aunt Lil with a little shiver. "Makes me sort of uncomfortable."

"I know what you mean," Anna said.

The music stopped and the ringmaster, the same circus barker from the town parade and the front gate, entered the ring, carrying a megaphone. "Ladies and gentlemen, boys and girls! Welcome to the magnifico Gypsy Circus!"

Everyone applauded enthusiastically as the music began again. This time the band marched in playing, followed by the grand parade. One after another, each more colorful than the next, all the performers, all the horses and elephants, entered and circled the arena to thunderous applause, the likes of which the boys had never heard. They were ecstatic. The performers all filled the arena and bowed simultaneously to the crowd. Then, as if by magic, the grand pageant disappeared rapidly in every direction, leaving only the band that marched, still playing, to their seats in the bandstand. The crowd applauded appreciatively.

"That's not all, is it, Aunt Lil?" Sam asked.

"Oh no, Sam. That's just the overture," Aunt Lil said.

The ringmaster reentered and stepped to the center of the big top. "If you will permit me, it is now my great pleasure to introduce the magnifico Romanescu Tumblers of the Gypsy

Circus!" And out they came, leaping and rolling, two men and two women, dressed in brightly colored leotards. One man walked out, rolling on a large white and red barrel. They spent the next few minutes enthralling the audience with leaps and somersaults over the barrel and banners that they held. Then a white horse ran out, as if it escaped from backstage, and ran around the arena as the acrobats vaulted over, and on and off, the beast. It was a marvel.

It was the clowns' turn next to entertain the crowd, which they did to great laughter and applause. The elephants lumbered out right in the middle of the clowns' ending act. Acting like it was a mistake, the clowns proceeded to have fun with the elephants that stood on their hind legs, lifted two of the clowns up with their trunks, and even danced to the music with them.

Next, the white Arabian dancing horses came out and enthralled the audience with their precise steps around the arena.

Capping off the night were the trapeze artists. They entered and climbed up both posts to the very top of the gigantic tent. They grabbed the bars and swung into the arena, sailing from one swing to another and performing a thrilling double trapeze stunt. Then one of the performers, carrying a small bag over his shoulder, swung down on his trapeze. He stopped its motion in the center of the ring and stood on his head on the bar. He balanced perfectly and proceeded to change his clothes, have a cup of tea, and then twirled amazingly fast while firing guns in a blaze of glory. The crowd were on their feet applauding.

"But it's not over yet, folks!" called the ringmaster. "It is now time for the magnifico, breathtaking, Slide for Life. Please look to the uppermost point of the big top."

Everyone looked up and saw one of the trapeze artists sitting on a wire strung between the two posts. And coming from the top of the tent to the floor near the bandstand was a thin, taut rope. The band started a drumroll. Millie closed her eyes and couldn't look, but everyone else was mesmerized. The trapeze artist stood up and placed one of his feet carefully on the downward-sloping rope. The audience held their collective breath as he placed his other foot on the rope. He then let go of the top wire and started to slide, his speed increasing in an awe-inspiring slide to the floor of the circus tent. He landed perfectly on the ground, and then leaped in the air doing a triple-flip just as what seemed like a hundred white doves flew out from where he landed. They circled the big top, around and round, exiting en masse. It was a masterful ending to a fantastic night. The crowd roared their appreciation as all the performers came out to take their bows.

Everyone was breathless and excited as they walked out of the big top and toward their carriages. And Sam said, "I think that was truly a 'magnifico' circus!" Everybody laughed at his clever little joke.

CHAPTER THIRTY-NINE

Anna invited Ausable to stay with them at Idlenook, even though it exasperated Aunt Lil. Anna had to keep at it, hoping one day Aunt Lil would get used to the idea. As the Gypsy Queen said, Ausable was going to make her very happy. Anna knew that was already happening, but it was nice to have her otherworldly affirmation.

The boys had such a great time at the circus that all the excitement exhausted them and they were quickly fast asleep. Anna and Ausable took a walk down to the beach in the moonlight. It was a warm, still night as the humidity hung in the air. They held hands as they walked down the path. At the beach, Anna took off her shoes, lifted up the hem of her skirt, and walked into the refreshing river water in a shallow spot. She splashed water on her face and arms to cool herself.

"You are so beautiful," Ausable said, gazing lovingly at her.

"Come cool off with me," she said.

Ausable rolled up his trousers and walked into the river to her.

"Ahh, that feels nice," he said as he put his hands in and splashed water on his face and head, running the cool water through his thick, black hair.

"Here, let me help you," said Anna, and she splashed some water at him.

"Oh. So you want to play, do you?" Ausable said as he started splashing her.

They splashed more and more water on each other, laughing and having a wonderful time. Then Ausable slipped on a rock and fell into the water, laughing. Anna went to him.

"Let me give you a hand," she said, offering her hand to pull him up. Instead, he pulled her into the water on top of him. They both splashed around, laughing joyfully, happy to be together, in love, and soaking wet. They lay next to each other in the cool water, holding one another, smiling. They began to kiss, so willingly reunited. In no time, they began to make love, with the Ausable River babbling around them.

They dragged themselves up to the beach, still wearing their heavy, damp clothes. It felt good to be sopping wet on this humid night. They lay down on the beach and looked up at the moon.

"Ausable, I want to leave Will," Anna stated firmly out of the blue.

"This is quite sudden," he said.

"Not really. I've been thinking about it for years," she said. "But now, I have good reason to leave."

"You mean because Will cheated?" asked Ausable.

"No. I mean you," Anna said. "If you'll have me?"

"If I'll have you? I've never been happier in my life," Ausable said. "Do you think Will will grant you a divorce?"

"I'm not sure. He cheated on me. Perhaps he will. It would be the best for all. Especially the boys. I don't want them living in a loveless home. What kind of example would that set? It will be confusing for the boys at first, but I'm sure it will be better in the long run for them. I need to talk with Will and see how he feels."

"Is he due back up here anytime soon?" asked Ausable.

"I haven't heard anything from him since he left. I've written as usual to tell him what the boys are doing, but no letters from him," Anna said. "I reminded him that Paul's play is this weekend. He wouldn't dare miss that. In the meantime, you and I will have some time together."

"Anna, we have the rest of our lives together, I hope," said Ausable.

"Oh, Ausable, we will!" Anna said elatedly and she kissed him. "Let's get back to the house and out of these wet clothes."

"Good idea," Ausable agreed.

They went back to the house and had a good night's sleep.

The dawn came with a wonderful thunderstorm that woke up the entire household and cleared out all of the humidity, leaving the valley cleansed and revitalized. All the townsfolk felt the relief and the village was bustling with activity. Anna as well, and she was even stronger in her conviction to leave Will. She could write him a letter and tell him how she was feeling. But she thought again how that would be too cold. After all, they had been intimate and loving for a long time, and she owed him more.

She reminisced about the fun they had had when they were young and first met. She so enjoyed teasing him then, and he was an easy target because he always let her. They both knew even then that they were in love. Anna thought how sad it was that their common interests had changed and slowly pushed them apart. She hoped that Will felt the same way about her and could remember the good times.

Ausable went to check out his camp. While he was gone, Anna went into the village for groceries and to pick up on the gossip going on. She had been the latest big story, but hopefully something else had taken her place. And wouldn't you know it, she ran into Mary Brown, who had quite a story to tell. Anna couldn't wait to get to the Club now. She ran into Tom as she was leaving the market.

"That was a fun time at the circus," Tom said. "Amazing feats."

"It certainly was," said Anna. "The boys were overjoyed."

"Where's Ausable?" asked Tom.

"He wanted to check on his camp since he's been away for a few weeks," Anna said. "I'm on my way to the Country Club to stir up a little trouble. Would you like to join me?"

"I'm not sure," Tom said. "What are you up to?"

"Oh, you'll see," said Anna.

Tom smiled and said, "Well, I do need to speak to John at the Club about the church choir singing on Performance Night. So I'll come along. How's Paul doing with his performance?"

"From what I've heard coming from his room, I think he'll do Shakespeare proud," Anna told him.

"I'm looking forward to seeing it," Tom said.

They left in Anna's carriage. Anna seemed quiet.

"Is everything all right, Anna?" Tom asked.

"Tom, I need your advice," Anna said.

"Of course," Tom said.

"I'm thinking of leaving Will."

"Oh my goodness, Anna. I'm sorry to hear that," Tom said. "I do understand, but are you sure?"

"Yes, being with Ausable has given me the strength to come to my senses and do something about this loveless marriage I'm in. There's no point to staying with him. But I'm just not sure how to approach him."

"Do you feel confident enough that you two can sit down and have a civil conversation about this?" Tom asked.

"We sort of did that when Will was here," Anna said. "Will ended up crying."

"Well, that shows he still has some feeling for you, I would think," Tom said.

"Yes, and I for him," Anna said. "I don't want to hurt him, but at the same time, I know Ausable is the right one for me. Will and I once had a wonderful life together. But that's been over for a long time."

"It's too bad," Tom said. "On the surface, you and Will seem so good together. A perfect match, yet, on closer inspection, there's just emptiness. No rancor, but no connection anymore. Anna, I'm sure he feels the same way."

"I know. I'm just afraid he might not want to divorce me because of the boys. But I think staying together would be worse for them," Anna said.

"It's true," Tom said. "I've never told you this, but my parents didn't get along. It's probably why I never married. I had to watch them argue or not speak for years. Now that I'm older, I realize it was worse for me because they stayed together. It took me a long time to come to terms with it. Luckily I had a lot of guidance from God and prayer. I'd be happy to share my experience with Will if he would like to listen."

"I'd really appreciate that, Tom," Anna said. "I think you are right. I'm sure he and I can have a civilized talk about this and come to an amenable conclusion."

"I hope so, Anna," said Tom.

They turned into the Country Club drive and saw many ladies gathered on the piazza. They got down from the carriage and went up to greet them. Aunt Lil was sitting next to Martina. Joan, who had seen Anna and Ausable in Lake Placid, and Margaret were whispering to each other.

"Hello there," called Aunt Lil. "Pastor Tom."

"Afternoon, Mrs. Tattersall. Ladies," said Tom, tipping his hat.

"Hello, Lil," said Anna. "I stopped by your house and Mary told me you were here."

Anna gave Martina a kiss on the cheek. "We haven't played whist in too long, Martina. We must play again soon," Anna said.

"There's a game here tomorrow," said Martina. "I'd love to play with you."

"Wonderful," said Anna. "It's a date."

Anna went over to Joan and Margaret. "And what are you two whispering about?" she shamelessly asked.

"Oh, nothing important," said Margaret.

"Yes, we were just talking about going to the circus tonight," said Joan.

"Oh, it's great fun. We all had a wonderful time," said Tom.

"Yes, and don't miss the fortune teller," Anna said.

"Even I was impressed with her," said Aunt Lil. "She told Anna things she never could have known."

"Anna, she did a reading for you?" asked Margaret. "And what did she uncover?"

Anna smiled, wryly. "She knew that I had been rescued by a darker man. There's no way she could have known that Ausable rescued me. It was eerie."

"Well, that is impressive," said Margaret.

"I hear he's back in the valley," said Joan.

"Yes, he is. He's staying at Idlenook," said Anna, brazenly. Aunt Lil reacted, rolling her eyes and shaking her head.

"How very kind of you, Anna," said Joan, with a knowing smile.

"Let's not get into that. So listen, I have a juicy piece of gossip."

"You do?" asked Margaret. "What is it?"

"It concerns Peter Brown," Anna said.

Margaret reacted. "What about Peter Brown?"

Anna looked around, and then softly said, "Mary found rubbers in his pants pocket. And I don't mean the kind you wear in the rain."

"Oh dear," Aunt Lil said.

"Mary thinks he's seeing some girl here in the valley. But he won't disclose who it is," said Anna, as she smiled at Margaret.

"Phew," said Margaret, unintentionally. Then quickly, "Oh, well, it's probably one of the locals. And that would be well below his station."

"I don't think we'll be seeing him playing tennis anymore, though," said Anna. "Mary has him chopping wood and such to keep his mind off things."

"Darn," said Margaret. "I mean, I should think tennis would also be a good way for him to get out his 'anxieties,' wouldn't you?"

"Yes, I agree," said Anna. "It is very good exercise, but I think she wants him close to home to keep an eye on him."

"I suppose that's probably best," said Tom. "I'll have to speak to his father and see if he thinks Peter would like someone to talk to,"

"That's very good of you, Pastor," said Margaret.

"Thank you, Margaret." Then to Anna, "I'm going to speak with John," and went inside the clubhouse.

"Anna, have you had any word from Will?" asked Aunt Lil.

"No. I sent him a letter reminding him about Paul's performance this weekend, but he hasn't written."

Anna noticed some of the ladies whispering about this.

"But I'm sure he will be here for Paul," said Anna.

"Yes, I'm sure he will," said Aunt Lil.

"Well, I need to pick up a few things at the general store," said Anna. "Lil, would you mind telling Tom where I went?"

"Of course, dear," said Aunt Lil.

Anna got into the carriage. Margaret came up to her.

"Well, doesn't that just take the cake?" said Margaret.

"I'm so sorry, Margaret," Anna consoled her.

"Isn't it always the way? Just when I'm having a good time up here," Margaret said.

"It's probably for the best," Anna said.

"Quite a way to let me know," said Margaret.

"Oh, it was just too good not to share with everyone," Anna said.

"Anna, are you sure we're still friends?" asked Margaret.

"Why, of course we are," Anna said. "Why would you even think something like that? Well, I'm off to the store."

She slapped the reins and went off, smiling to herself.

CHAPTER FORTY

It was Saturday and tonight would be the great performances by the Keene Valley Players. Paul was a bit nervous, but still ready to perform his scene from "Romeo and Juliet." He was more upset than nervous, since Will had not shown up. He and Sam had gone down to Bailey's the previous afternoon hoping Will would arrive on the stagecoach. He didn't. But there was at least a letter from him to Paul apologizing that he had a big law case in New York and couldn't get away. Paul was sad and Anna was angry.

"How can he do this to Paul?" she asked Ausable. "He really isn't the man he used to be. He never would have done this in the past. He's a different man and my mind is made up. I'm going to ask him for a divorce."

"Oh Anna, I'm so sorry. And I'm sorry for Paul," Ausable said. "The poor boy looked quite sad."

"It breaks my heart," said Anna. "He's so excited to show off for his father, and Will does this. We have to do something extra special for Paul after the show tonight, to cheer him up."

"I know how to make chocolate ice cream," Ausable said. "Do you think he'd like that?"

"Oh, Ausable, would you?" Anna asked.

"Of course," he said.

"That would be very special. Let's make sure there is plenty of ice in the icehouse. We want it to stay nice and cold."

They went into the icehouse and it indeed was filled with lots of ice.

"There must have been a delivery yesterday," said Anna, rubbing her arms, shivering a little.

"Here, let me warm you up," Ausable said as he took her into his arms.

"Ooo, you are nice and warm," said Anna. "And you are so sweet to offer to make Paul ice cream." She kissed him.

"I should go into the village right now and get some rock salt and the rest of what I need," Ausable said. "I'm sure Alexander's has some."

"Oh, thank you," Anna said as they exited the icehouse and closed the door. "Is there anything I can get ready for you here?"

"If you can find two mixing bowls of different sizes, that would be great," Ausable said.

"I'm sure we have some," said Anna.

"I'll be back soon," he said as he went out the door.

Anna watched as he sprinted up the drive. He didn't take the drive all the way to the road. He cut through the meadow before the thicket and Anna watched him for a bit. She just stood there, smiling broadly as he disappeared around some trees. She couldn't believe her luck. To have found such an unlikely man who answered all her prayers. She thought about how the path ahead would be rocky. A woman wasn't allowed to petition for a divorce. Would Will grant her one? He obviously was too busy for the children so they would stay with her. And Ausable was wonderful with them. They would have a great life and guidance from him. It would be a difficult transition for them. She didn't want to put them through it. But there was no other choice. He couldn't even make time for one weekend for Paul. That was unconscionable. And, in the future, if he could make time, she would of course let them see their father whenever he or they wanted. She didn't want their parting to be ugly. She was very angry with Will, but she could never hate him. There was no reason to make this any more unpleasant than it already was. The next time Will came up here, if indeed he did, she would confront him. This had to be resolved so she could move on and enjoy her new and, hopefully, happy life.

That evening, the ice cream had been made and was chilling in the icehouse. Colleen was impressed with Ausable's expertise in the kitchen. Anna thought, "Is there anything this man can't do?" Paul was already at the clubhouse, preparing for the show. Everyone was dressed up for the occasion. Even Sam had put on a tie.

"You look very handsome, Sam," Ausable said.

"Thank you, Mr. Hancock," Sam replied. "I put in a lot of hard work to get my brother in shape to be Romeo. So I should look good for doing that."

"You did help Paul a lot," said Anna.

"Thanks, Mother," said Sam. Then, with annoyance in his voice, "I suppose we have to pick up Aunt Lil on the way?"

"Now, Sam, that's not nice," said Anna sternly. "You should have more respect for your Aunt Lil."

"I'm sorry, Mother. She's just so scary sometimes," Sam said.

Anna tried to hide a smile. "Well, don't be afraid of her, Sam. Aunt Lil's bark is worse than her bite."

"She bites?" Sam said, frightened.

"It's just a saying, Sam. Aunt Lil doesn't bite," Anna assured him. Then aside to Ausable, "At least I don't think she does." They chuckled.

Anna, calling, "Colleen, Millie, are you ready?"

"Be right there, Missus." Colleen said. She came into the room. "I was just making sure the surprise was staying nice and cold."

"Surprise?" said Sam. "What surprise?"

"It's a surprise for Paul," Anna said. "Something Mr. Hancock made for him."

"You made a surprise, Mr. Hancock?" asked Sam excitedly.

"I did indeed," said Ausable. "And I'm sure you are going to like it, too."

"Oh boy. Hmm... what could you have made?" Sam said, thinking. "Is it a canoe?"

"A canoe?" asked Ausable. "No, I don't know how to make a canoe." Sam looked disappointed. "I did make something really delicious to eat."

"Oh. Something to eat," Sam said. "And it's staying nice and cold." They could see he was thinking very hard about this. "Ahh. Ice cream! You made ice cream?"

"All right. I confess," said Ausable. "I made ice cream. But please we want to keep it a secret from your brother. It's a surprise for him."

"Can you do that, Sam?" asked Anna

"Of course, I will, Mother," said Sam. "I'd keep any secret to get homemade ice cream! What kind is it?"

"Let's let that be your surprise, all right?" said Ausable.

"All right, Mr. Hancock," Sam said.

"I think we ought to be going," Anna said.

They all started out the door and to the carriage. Sam couldn't stand it, "Is it chocolate?"

Ausable laughed. "I'm not telling. You'll just have to wait and see."

"Awww. Not fair," said Sam as he trudged to the carriage.

Colleen and Millie rode up front and drove over to Aunt Lil's. She was waiting on the veranda. She had a wrapped present with her.

"Hello, Lil," Anna called as they stopped.

"Hello, all, "Aunt Lil said, standing. "Don't you all look nice? Especially you, Sam. Very snappy."

"Thank you, Aunt Lil," Sam said, quite pleased with himself. Then, quietly to Anna, "You're right, Mother. She isn't always so scary." Anna shushed him, but smiled.

Ausable helped Aunt Lil into the carriage and they headed off to the Country Club.

"I have a gift for our 'Romeo,'" Aunt Lil said.

"That's so sweet of you, Lil," Anna said.

"I hope it will make him feel better. I'm so sorry that Will isn't here to see Paul," Aunt Lil said. "I'm actually quite shocked that he couldn't get away."

"I'm very peeved," Anna said. "Especially now."

"I agree," Aunt Lil said. "It really doesn't look good for Will not to be here."

"No, it doesn't," Anna agreed.

"But we'll put on a good face and no one will be the wiser," said Aunt Lil.

They arrived at the Country Club and everyone was dressed to the nines. It was an occasion that everyone proudly attended, as the valley's best showed off their talent. The nets on the tennis courts had been taken down and chairs were set up on the courts. A makeshift stage had been constructed at the end of the courts.

Anna and Sam went inside the clubhouse to give Paul a pep talk.

"Now, Sam, remember, don't spoil the surprise," Anna reminded him.

"Don't worry, Mother. I won't," Sam said.

They found Paul, dressed as Romeo, sitting on a chair next to Clara, his Juliet. They were going over their lines.

"Hello, Paul. Hello, Clara," Anna said.

"Hello, Mother," Paul said.

"Hello, Mrs. Tattersall," Clara said.

"You both look wonderful in your costumes," Anna said.

Paul looked at Sam who was standing there with his mouth clenched. "What's the matter with you, Sam?" Paul asked.

Sam just clenched his jaw tighter and shook his head.

"He's trying not to tell you something," said Anna. "We have a surprise for you back at the house after the show."

"Really?" asked Paul. "That's so nice. I guess Sam knows what it is."

Sam nodded and clenched.

"We better get going before Sam bursts at the seams," Anna said. "Have a great show."

"Thanks, Mother," said Paul.

Anna led Sam out of the clubhouse. Sam unclenched his jaw and let out a huge sigh of relief. "Oh boy, that was hard."

"Well, I'm very proud of you, Sam. Good job," said Anna.

"Believe me, it wasn't easy," Sam said.

Anna saw Tom chatting with Margaret.

"Sam, you go save me a seat next to Aunt Lil. I'm going to speak to Pastor Tom. Sam ran off and Anna went to Tom and Margaret.

"Anna, what a beautiful dress," said Margaret.

"I'm happy to see that we aren't wearing the same one this time," Anna said.

Margaret wasn't sure how to take this.

"I heard Will won't be here for the show," Tom said.

"I can't tell you how furious I am at him," Anna said. "He really hurt Paul's feelings and I can't abide that."

"He's being irresponsible under the circumstances, don't you think?" said Margaret.

Anna steeled herself to keep from throttling Margaret. "Yes," Anna agreed. Then to Tom, trying to ignore Margaret, "He may be mad at me. Or himself. But he shouldn't take it out on the boys. They are the ones who will be hurt most by all this. And he's just making it worse."

"How are they taking it?" Tom asked.

"Paul is very disappointed," Anna said.

"I'm so sorry. Listen, I'd better make sure everyone in the choir is ready," Tom said. "We're starting off the show tonight."

"Have a good show, Tom," said Anna.

"I'll give Paul a little pep talk, too," said Tom.

"Thank you, Tom," Anna said.

Tom went into the clubhouse.

"Is John here, Margaret?" Anna asked.

Margaret laughed, "Are you kidding? He wouldn't like culture if it came with bread and butter. I'm on my own."

"I'm sorry to hear that. Well, enjoy the show," Anna said as she left a stunned Margaret standing alone.

Sam saved a seat for Anna between himself and Aunt Lil. Sam was next to Ausable and Colleen and Millie were behind them. There were programs on the seats. Paul would be on after the intermission. A piano and drums were set up next to the stage and the musicians now entered and sat down. The drummer began a drum roll. Glen McCann came out and introduced the church choir, who filed onto the stage as the audience applauded. The piano player began to play the "Star Spangled Banner" as the choir sang with gusto. There had been talk of making this song the national anthem, and these patriots in attendance from the northeast pretty much had already done so. The whole crowd joined in for the rousing song and there was a huge round of applause at the end.

The choir stayed onstage to sing. Tom stepped out to announce that, even though they were a church choir, tonight they weren't in church and were going to sing popular songs. So they sang "The Sidewalks of New York" and "Sweet Rosie O'Grady," then ended with an oldie but a goodie, "Yankee Doodle." They were very good and the audience loved it and gave them a standing ovation.

As the choir shuffled off the stage, four chairs were set up and four musicians came out: two women with violins, one with a viola, and the last with a cello. Glen introduced them as the Adirondack String Quartet. These women were summer visitors to the area. The only one any of them knew was Constance Robinson, the mother of Clara, who was performing with Paul. She was one of the violinists. The others were visitors to other towns. They were a surprise to everyone. No one knew these four had been practicing together. And when they began to play, everyone was even more delighted because they were very good. They played a Bach serenade and a Mendelssohn minuet. The sound of the strings on this lovely evening in the Adirondacks was mesmerizing and the audience was enthralled. There was a thunderous standing ovation for them as they took their bows.

It was intermission time and most remained standing or went off to find refreshments. A set piece resembling a castle balcony was brought out on stage and some plants were placed around.

"Paul is on next. I'm so nervous for him," Anna said.

"I'm sure he'll do well," Ausable said. "After all, he had a very good teacher, right, Sam?"

"I taught him everything he knows," Sam said, very satisfied with himself.

"He'll be the highlight of the show," Aunt Lil said. "At least to us. Would you like some apple cider, Sam?"

"Yes, thank you, I would," said Sam.

"Would anyone else like any?" Aunt Lil asked.

"Thanks, Lil, yes," said Anna.

"Come with me, Sam. Let's go get some cider," Aunt Lil ordered.

"Yes, Aunt Lil," Sam said, looking at Anna, pained.

They went over to the refreshment table.

"Well, look who's been let out for the night," Anna said to Ausable, pointing to Peter Brown. "That's Peter Brown."

"Oh. The one Margaret was seeing?" asked Ausable.

"Yes. And look who's seen him, too," Anna said, indicating Margaret.

They watched as Margaret walked over near to where Peter was and he saw her. He smiled and Margaret indicated with her head to follow her. He got up, telling his parents he needed to use the facilities. Anna and Ausable watched them disappear behind the clubhouse, unseen by his parents.

"That Margaret is quite something," said Ausable.

"She certainly is," Anna agreed. "I can't believe I trusted that woman. After all these years, I should have known better."

"She hasn't told anyone about us," said Ausable.

"That's true," Anna said. "Of course, I know about her and Peter and haven't told anybody."

"You are a good person, Anna," Ausable said, smiling.

"Thank you," Anna said, chuckling. Then, "I just thought of something. When I came here to the Club to inquire about having a party for you, the people at the club were put off by that. And since our party, people have gotten to know you. Now you are here, and not a soul has treated you differently than anyone else."

"I don't mean to burst your bubble, Anna," Ausable said, "But that's not quite true."

"What do you mean?" she asked.

"I agree. No one has acted badly toward me tonight," he said. "But if you notice, no one has acted at all. Not a person has come by to say hello to you or me."

"Hmmm, I didn't see it that way," Anna said.

"All around, people are mingling and greeting each other, but we are quite removed from the rest," he said.

Anna now noticed the very obvious gap between them and the rest of the crowd. "Very interesting," Anna contemplated. "I'm not accustomed to noticing things like this yet. I suppose I will be in time. But as long as we have our friends who know better, we should be all right."

"I love your spirit," Ausable said. "And I love you," he whispered.

"At least we can talk freely with no one nearby," Anna said, laughingly.

Aunt Lil and Sam returned with mugs of cider for everyone.

"We went in to tell Paul good luck, and I gave him his gift," said Aunt Lil. "He looks so handsome in his costume."

"I'm on pins and needles," said Anna. "The first lines are all Paul's."

The piano player came out and started playing, indicating the show was resuming. When everyone was back in their seats, Glen introduced Act 2, Scene 2, of Shakespeare's "Romeo and Juliet," played by Clara Robinson and Paul Tattersall. The audience gave a warm round of applause as Paul entered alone and stood center stage and looked up toward the balcony. Clara had climbed up behind and now appeared on the balcony.

Paul (as Romeo)
But soft, what light through yonder window breaks?
It is the east and Juliet is the sun!
Arise, fair sun, and kill the envious moon,
Who is already sick and pale with grief
That thou her maid art far more fair than she.
Be not her maid, since she is envious;
Her vestal livery is but sick and green,
And none but fools do wear it. Cast it off.
It is my lady, O, it is my love!
O that she knew she were!

He stopped, thinking. Anna could see a look of panic on his face. He had forgotten his next line. Paul repeated, "O that she knew she were!" Another pause. Paul looked around, not knowing what to do.

Sam couldn't take it and yelled out, "She speaks, yet she says nothing!" Then he clamped his hand over his mouth in embarrassment as the audience chuckled.

Relief appeared on Paul's face.

"Yes!" he said.

Paul (as Romeo)

She speaks, yet she says nothing; what of that?
Her eye discourses, I will answer it.

The audience applauded and Paul continued, not missing another beat. He and Clara were wonderful together. They made a perfect Romeo and Juliet. They neared the end of the scene.

Clara (as Juliet)

'Tis almost morning; I would have thee gone:
And yet no further than a wanton's bird;
Who lets it hop a little from her hand,
Like a poor prisoner in his twisted gyves,
And with a silk thread plucks it back again,
So loving-jealous of his liberty.

Paul (as Romeo)

I would I were thy bird.

Clara (as Juliet)

Sweet, so would I:
Yet I should kill thee with much cherishing.
Good night, good night! Parting is such
sweet sorrow,
That I shall say good night till it be morrow.

Clara came down from the balcony and joined Paul onstage for their bows as the audience applauded heartily. Anna and Sam were clapping wildly. Sam even whistled, at which Aunt Lil bopped him on his head with her knuckle. Paul and Clara exited the stage as the choir came out again. They sang

"Turkey in the Straw" and ended with "My Country, 'Tis of Thee" which everyone joined in on. It was a wonderful show and Anna was so proud of her son.

The family, including Aunt Lil and Ausable, plus Clara and her parents, all gathered back at Idlenook for Paul's surprise treat. He was very proud of his accomplishment and was also very happy to have chocolate ice cream to celebrate with and to top it all off. He did confess it would only be better if his father had been able to be there.

CHAPTER FORTY-ONE

It was almost Labor Day, a new holiday created just a few years before, but which was already becoming the new sign of the end of the season. Most of the summer people in Keene Valley would be returning home during September. The dance at Eggerfields' Hotel was the final social gathering. All the women saved one special gown they hadn't worn for this night. It was another grand affair, although not as grand as the Wardwells' ball several months earlier in Keene Valley. This dance served only after-dinner cocktails. Anna had written Will several times, and once asked if he would be back up for the dance or to help close up the house for the season. But she had no response. She wrote to Will's mother, Kathleen, in Fairfield and had heard from her, but she was unable to give Anna any information on Will's plans. She said they rarely saw him, only when he would stop on his way from Boston to New York.

Ausable had been back and forth to Boston a couple of times, but was unable to stay away from Anna. He told her he missed her so much when he was away that he got his brother to take care of much of the family business for him for the time being. Anna was flattered beyond belief. They had to figure out a way to be together. Ausable had been a kind of fill-in father for the boys and they took very easily to him. It made Anna happy to see. And since she had no word from Will, she was planning on asking Ausable to take her to the dance.

"Ausable?" Anna asked, "What would you think about being my date for the Eggerfield's dance this weekend?"

"You know I'd love to, Anna," Ausable said. "Are you sure I'll be welcome there? Not all hotels are like the Grand View."

"You're never been to Tahawus House?" Anna asked.

"Actually no," Ausable said. "Even though it's right here in the valley, I've never had occasion to."

"Well, I can't imagine the Eggerfields will have any issue with you being there," Anna stated firmly. "I've seen all sorts of, shall I say, seedy customers coming in and out of there. You are much higher class than that."

"But this is a big society affair," Ausable said. "That's different."

"You already know all these people who will be there," Anna said.

"I just don't want you to be embarrassed if something unkind happens," Ausable said, sweetly.

"Embarrassed? Me? Ha!" Anna said. "If anything happens, I'll give them a piece of my mind."

"Oh Anna," Ausable chuckled. "I wouldn't want a scene either."

"All right, you know what I'll do?" Anna said. "I'll stop by there and make sure there's no problem, if it would make you feel better. Then we'll know what we will be in for."

"That would be very kind of you," Ausable said.

"Aren't you taking the boys and their friends fishing today?" Anna asked.

"Yes, we're going this afternoon," Ausable confirmed.

"Great. I'll get Tom and stop by Tahawus House and we'll chat with the Eggerfields."

"Sounds good to me," Ausable said. "And thank you," he said, kissing her.

"Be careful," she said, pulling back and looking around. "Everyone is out, but you never know when they might come back. I need to move slowly with the boys."

"All right," Ausable said. "But I will be able to dance with you?"

"Oh yes," said Anna. "We'll be in public and it will all be on the up and up."

"You have a funny way of reasoning," Ausable said. "But I love it." He looked around, furtively, and not seeing anyone, gave her a big kiss, then stopped and walked away, leaving Anna breathless.

That afternoon, she stopped at the church and explained the situation to Tom. Tom was happy to join her, but was sure there wouldn't be a problem.

Eggerfield's Tahawus Hotel was in a large meadow near the main road. From its two-story piazza there was a magnificent view of the Adirondack range, from Noonmark to Spread Eagle Mountain. It was another great place to watch night drawing on Giant. There were quite a few carriages at the hotel, as it was a popular place for climbers to stay.

"Looks like the end-of-season travellers are getting in their last hikes," Tom noted.

They pulled the carriage up to the side of the hotel and a stableman took care of the horses for them. The hotel was serving tea on the piazza.

"We might as well take tea while we're here," Anna said.

They were led to a table where they sat looking at the glorious view.

"I hate to think of going back home soon," Anna said. "I always miss the beauty up here."

"That's why you keep coming back," Tom said.

"I'm afraid my circumstances are really going to complicate that for me, now," Anna said.

A waiter came to the table with a tray of pastries, teacups, and a pot of tea, which he poured.

"Thank you," Anna said to the waiter. "Do you know if George or Peg Eggerfield is about?"

"Yes, madam, they are," said the waiter.

"Could you please ask them to stop by?" Anna asked. "I'd like to speak to them about the dance."

"Very good, madam," said the waiter, and he left.

"I hope George comes over," said Anna. "I'm not too keen on that Peggy. She's a bit of a mousy little woman." Anna made a mousy face, as if chewing little bites. "I bet she just gnaws at cheese all day."

Tom laughed. "Anna, you are a pip." Anna made the face again and they both laughed just as Peg Eggerfield walked up to them.

"Hello, Pastor," said Peg. "Hello, Mrs. Tattersall."

Anna and Tom looked up at her and burst into more laughter.

Trying to stifle his laugh, Tom said, "Oh, Mrs. Eggerfield. How nice to see you?"

Anna had to turn away to compose herself.

"I'm sorry," said Tom. "Mrs. Tattersall just told me a very funny story."

"Oh, I'd love to hear it," said Peg.

"Um, oh, I don't think you would appreciate it," said Anna, finally holding back her laughter. "It's about someone you don't know."

"I understand," Peg said. "I was told you wanted to see me?"

"Yes, Peg, thank you," Anna said. "I wanted to ask you something about the dance this weekend."

"Of course," said Peg. "It's going to be a grand affair. We've hired a wonderful new band from Rochester. Seventeen pieces. Wait until you hear them."

"I'm looking forward to it," Anna said. "My question is, you invited my husband and me, but I'm not sure if Will can make it up here. We have Mr. Hancock staying with us and I am wondering if it would be all right to have him accompany me."

"I'm sure that would be fine," said Peg. "Have I met this Mr. Hancock?"

"I'm sure you have. He's the man who rescued me during the storm," Anna told her.

"Oh. The Indian gentleman," said Peg, thinking. "I remember seeing him at events in town. Don't think I met him though." She stopped, thinking some more. "Everyone seemed to be getting along fine with him, even though he is an Indian."

"Yes, they are," said Tom, trying to help. "He's quite a well-spoken man of letters and wealth."

"Really? I didn't know," said Peg.

"He's a very kind gentleman, Peg. He's been staying with us most of the summer," Anna told her.

"We've had Indians stay here at the hotel with no problem." Peg said. "Why not? If someone at the dance doesn't want to be around an Indian, they can just leave."

"Oh Peg, that's so kind of you," Anna said. "I very much appreciate it."

"It's almost the turn of the century," Peg said. "Times are changing and we need to keep up."

"Good for you, Peg," Tom said.

"Now I need to get back to the kitchen. We're making cheese balls for the party."

She left and Anna and Tom looked at each other for just a moment, then burst out laughing. Everyone on the piazza stopped what they were doing and looked over at them.

"You are going to get me in big trouble one day," Tom said to Anna.

"Oh, I hope so," Anna said, teasing.

CHAPTER FORTY-TWO

Tonight was the Eggerfields' dance. Anna hadn't heard a word from Will and Ausable was happy to take Anna to the dance and to be able to appear properly in public together. Aunt Lil said she was suffering with neuralgia and probably wouldn't be attending. Anna wasn't sure, but thought that Aunt Lil didn't want to witness Anna dancing with Ausable, so her neuralgia was just a story. Still, it was a relief to Anna. There would be enough unkind stares from the summer people, she was sure. Aunt Lil's looks would have been darts that Anna would feel. Lil would still take a lot more persuasion to really accept Ausable.

But at this moment, Anna didn't care about any of it. She was going to the dance with the man she was in love with and expected to have a grand old time.

Millie helped Anna into her stylish midnight blue gown for the dance. The sleeves were puffy from the shoulder to the elbow. The bodice trim continued down the swooping tulip-form skirt, smooth over the hips that flared dramatically to a wide hem with scallops of braid and lace sewn diagonally. Anna knew it was the height of fashion and she would be the envy of every woman there. And she would be on the arm of the handsomest man there. Life couldn't be better.

Ausable was waiting in the parlor, dapper in his black tailcoat, a small, white, tidy bow tie, a black low-cut vest with shawl lapels, black trousers, and a heavily starched white shirt. Millie had helped with the starching.

Anna made a dramatic entrance down the stairs with the rustle of her dress introducing her. Ausable held his breath. He was captivated.

"Anna, every time I see you, you are more beautiful than the last," said Ausable.

Anna smiled. "And you are quite the handsomest man. We are going to stun everyone at the dance. I can't wait."

"Then let us proceed," said Ausable, offering his elbow to Anna.

"Hold on for a minute, Missus," Colleen said, coming in from the kitchen with Millie. "You both look so wonderful, we need to take a Kodak of this." She brought out the camera on a tripod. "Let's go out on the front veranda where the sun is best."

"What a wonderful idea, Colleen," said Anna.

They all went out to the front of the house. Colleen set up the camera on the grass as Anna and Ausable posed, arm in arm, smiling on the front porch, the sun shining on them.

"Wonderful. Now hold still," Colleen said as she snapped the photo.

"That will be a good one!" said Millie.

"I hope so," said Anna. "Thank you."

They left in their carriage as Colleen and Millie waved goodbye.

"I'm a little nervous, Ausable," Anna said.

"I can understand that, Anna," he said. "This is rather a big step for us."

"It is. We've never been on view like this before. We might cause a commotion," she said.

"I thought you liked that," Ausable pointed out.

Anna chuckled, impishly, "I do. Anyway, all I have to do is look into your eyes and the rest of world will disappear from view."

Ausable put his arm around her, "I'm really the luckiest fellow, aren't I?"

"You certainly are," Anna affirmed, cuddling up to him. They rode for a bit, but when Anna saw another carriage coming toward them, she moved slightly away from his grasp. Ausable understood and he gave her a supportive nod.

As they neared the Tahawus Hotel, they could hear the band playing a bouncy song. Peg was right. It was a marvelous band. They left the carriage with a stableman and went up onto the veranda where drinks and refreshments were set out. Anna noticed the aforementioned cheese balls and gave a little smirk.

Sally Merrick came over to them. "Anna, that dress is a sensation!" She was joined by several other women who listened in.

"Thank you very much, Sally," Anna said. "You look very stylish, too."

"Thank you. And hello, Mr. Hancock," Sally said. "Wonderful to see you here. Anna, where's Will?"

"Oh, he's at home in Fairfield. Work, you know. I don't even know if he'll get back here to close up the house this year," Anna told her. "So I persuaded Mr. Hancock to accompany me."

"Well, aren't you the lucky one," Sally said, looking Ausable up and down.

"I am the lucky one," said Ausable.

"Let's go inside," Anna said to Ausable.

They went into the main room of the hotel where the band was playing and people were dancing. As they entered, many heads turned and noticed them. Margaret was standing across the room with her husband.

"I really want to expose that Margaret for the shrew that she is," Anna said.

"Anna, you know Tom was right," Ausable said. "Besides, it would only make Will look worse."

"I know, but it's so hard to keep being 'nice' to her," Anna said.

"You are a better person for it," said Ausable.

"Oh, no. I think she's coming over here," Anna said.

And, indeed, Margaret came over to them.

"Oh my goodness. You two look like models from Harper's Bazaar!" Margaret said. "Anna, that dress is dazzling."

"Isn't it, though?" she said, trying to be convivial.

"When you two walked in, the whole room gasped," Margaret said.

"Oh, you're exaggerating, Margaret," said Ausable.

"Well, maybe a little," Margaret confessed. "Anna, where's Will?"

Anna took a deep breath, then said, "Oh, he had too much work to come up just now."

"Oh, I'm sorry to hear that," Margaret said.

"I'm sure you are," Anna said, to herself. Luckily, with the band playing, Margaret hadn't heard her.

"Are you two going to dance?" Margaret asked.

"Let's have a cocktail first," said Anna.

"I'll get you something, Anna," said Ausable.

"I'll go with you," Anna said.

They went outside, leaving Margaret standing there.

Outside, Pastor Tom came up to them. "Anna, you are breathtaking," he said.

"Oh Tom, you really think so?" she asked.

"Absolutely," Tom said. "You've outdone yourself and everyone here."

"Hello, Ausable," Tom said.

They shook hands. "Good to see you, Tom," Ausable said. "I'll get you that drink, Anna. Anything for you, Tom?"

"I'm good, thanks," Tom said.

Ausable headed over to the refreshment table.

"You know, Tom, this is all a bit disquieting. I really need something to calm my nerves," Anna said.

"Anna, there's nothing to worry about," said Tom. "You're just going to dance and have an enjoyable time."

"You're right," Anna said. "I am just here to have fun."

Ausable came back with a cocktail for Anna. "Here you are, Anna," he said.

"And this will help me have fun," Anna said, and she downed the drink. She was winded for a moment and shook her head, letting out a big breath. "I think I'm ready to dance." She took Ausable by the arm and led him inside and out to the middle of the dance floor. The band was playing a sprightly waltz. Anna and Ausable took a dance position and started to waltz around the room. They twirled as one, in perfect step with each other, staring into each other's eyes, magically avoiding everyone else dancing. It was hypnotic. Tom looked on amazed. Margaret was watching, too, still not sure where things stood. Soon, the rest of the people in the room began watching, as well. Others came in from outside to witness. It wasn't long before the other couples stopped dancing and everyone watched with fascination. Anna and Ausable moved to the beat in perfect synchronicity. Gliding. Whirling. It was thrilling to watch. Around and around they went. Then, as if they'd been dancing to this song forever, they ended with a flourish, Ausable dipping Anna as she bent backwards over his extended arm, just as the last beat of music played. Ausable held her there. The room was silent, but only for a moment. Then everyone erupted in applause. Even the band. Anna straightened up, shaking her head, as if coming out of a trance. She looked around at all the happy, applauding people and couldn't believe her eyes. They were accepted. It was going to be all right. Everything was going to be all right.

Anna and Ausable nodded to the crowd and the band, smiling broadly, very grateful for the acknowledgment. As the applause diminished, they started back over to Tom. But one person behind them was still clapping, loudly and slowly. The room went silent. Anna and Ausable turned. And from the back of the room, Will stepped out from the crowd, the lone clapper. He kept it up. Standing there, weaving a bit, clapping.

"Will, stop it, please," Anna pleaded.

"Why, Anna? You deserve it," Will said, with callousness in his voice. He stopped clapping. "The two of you were remarkable out there. I could never compete with that."

"Will, this isn't a competition," Anna said.

"Oh no, Anna? I know it is. And I lost!" Will swung around, looking at everyone staring back at him. "You all know why I lost? I lost because he won," he said, twirling around and pointing right at Ausable. "Him. That Indian. He came along and he not only saved my wife's life, he stole my wife. From me!"

The crowd let out a collective hushed gasp.

312

"Will, this is not the place for this," Ausable said.

"Why not, Indian?" Will asked. "Everybody is going to know soon enough. My wife is in love with you!" Will yelled.

Anna couldn't take it anymore. "Oh Will," she said, with tears in her voice, and she ran through the crowd. Margaret was standing near the door. As Anna passed her, she said, with her voice shaking, "See what you did!"

Margaret reacted in shock. Other people nearby heard this and looked at Margaret as Anna left the room. Tom followed Anna out. Ausable stayed, staring at Will. Will slumped as he stood there. He had said his piece, but now he was embarrassed.

"Aw damn, you can have her," he said, defeated. He stumbled through the people at the back of the room and left. Ausable stood for a moment as everyone stared at him.

"I'm very sorry to have ruined your evening, everyone. Please go back to having a good time. Mister bandleader, please," Ausable said, gesturing to the band.

The bandleader took the hint and started to play. As the room filled with music again, people began to lose the tension that had built up. They whispered to each other, glancing at Ausable, as he turned and left the room, passing Margaret. Margaret grabbed his arm.

"Ausable. Does Anna know about Will and me?"

Ausable hesitated.

"She does, doesn't she?" said Margaret.

"She does, Margaret," Ausable said. "Will told her. Now I have to find her."

He left the room as Margaret glanced about guiltily to those nearby. Ausable looked around off the veranda and spotted Anna with Tom down in the meadow. He sprinted over to them. Anna was crying.

"Oh, Anna, I'm so sorry that happened," Ausable said as he comforted her, holding her in his arms.

"Will was just horrid," Anna said. "It's not like him at all. He must be so hurt to have acted like that."

"Maybe so, Anna," said Ausable. "But it still doesn't excuse such bad behavior."

313

"I agree. Actions like that should be done in private," said Tom.

"Well, he didn't. And now everyone knows about us, Ausable," Anna said. "It's all out in the open."

"I know it's not how you wanted it to happen, Anna," Ausable said.

"No, it isn't," Anna agreed. "But now that it has, I suppose I'm happy. Now we can move on with our lives. There is no way Will won't let me go now. We should get home. I don't want Will seeing the boys in the state he's in."

"I'll get your carriage for you," Tom offered and ran off to retrieve it.

"I'm not sure I should come with you," Ausable said. "It might only anger Will more."

"It might, but I'd like you to be with me," Anna said. "I would feel safer. Will's in a bad way."

Tom came up with the carriage and got out. He wished them well and Ausable and Anna headed up the road toward home. They passed Aunt Lil's house. Her bedroom was dark so she must be sleeping. Anna hoped Will didn't bother her because of the pain she was in.

They continued on to Idlenook and Ausable stabled the horses as Anna went inside. "Hello?" she called.

Colleen came out of the kitchen, "Home so soon, Missus?" she asked.

"Mr. Tattersall isn't here, is he?" Anna asked.

"No, Missus. I thought he wasn't going to be here," said Colleen.

"He wasn't supposed to be," Anna said. "But he showed up at the dance. He had been drinking and was very unpleasant. Are the boys asleep?"

"Yes, Missus," Colleen said. "All is quiet."

Ausable came into the house and Colleen left the room.

"He hasn't been here," Anna said.

"That's good," Ausable said. "You know, I don't think there's really anything to worry about. Just after you left the room, he pretty much gave up."

"He did? What do you mean?" Anna asked.

314

"He said, in front of everyone, that I could have you," Ausable told her.

"Really?" Anna said, astonished.

"He looked totally defeated," Ausable said. "I think he finally realized he's lost you."

"My goodness. Maybe he's done fighting," Anna said. "Hopefully, he'll spend the night at Aunt Lil's or somewhere else and stay away from here. He said such nasty things to you. I'm so sorry, Ausable."

"Not to worry. I've heard much worse, believe me," Ausable said. "Oh, and Margaret asked me if you knew about her and Will."

"I told her it was her fault as I passed her on the way out," Anna said. "If Will said you can have me, well, he can have Margaret. He deserves that witch."

"Now come on, you wouldn't really wish her on Will, would you?" asked Ausable.

"I suppose not. He's been through enough. And so have I. I think the best thing to do would be to leave Keene Valley immediately," Anna declared.

"Anna, let's discuss this. Are you sure that's what you want to do?" Ausable asked. "You've just been through a terrible scene. Maybe you should wait and see what transpires."

"Ausable, I know what I want and nothing is going to change my mind," Anna said. "It's time I took control of my life."

"I understand how you feel," Ausable said. "And I'll be there right beside you, whatever you decide to do."

"Thank you, my love," Anna said, giving Ausable a kiss. "Can we go to your home in Boston?"

"Of course," Ausable said.

"And I will want to bring the boys with us," Anna said.

"No question," Ausable assured her. "I adore those fellows."

"You're so sweet. All right, in the morning, we'll tell the boys we're taking them on a surprise trip to Boston," Anna said. "In time, when we know better what is happening, we'll tell them what is really going on."

"You are a caring mother, Anna," he said.

"Thank you," she said, putting her arms around him. "Now, we have a lot to do."

CHAPTER FORTY-THREE

Anna and Ausable stayed up all night, quietly packing. Ausable was in the stable putting things into the carriage when Colleen and Millie awoke and came into the parlor and saw all the packed luggage.

"Missus, are you going somewhere?" asked Colleen.

"Colleen, Millie, please sit down," Anna said. "I need to discuss something with you." They sat on the divan in the parlor.

"I am sure you have realized that something is amiss lately, what with Mr. Tattersall not being here and all," Anna began to explain. "He and I have been drifting apart for quite a while now. And I have sad news. I have decided to leave him."

Colleen and Millie reacted, a bit shocked. "Oh Missus, I'm so sorry to hear this."

"Yes, Ma'am, it is very sad news," agreed Millie, who started to cry a little.

"I'm going to go to Boston for now," Anna told them.

"What about the boys, Missus?" Colleen asked.

"I'll be taking them with me," Anna said. "I haven't told them anything yet and they know nothing of this. I'm just going to tell them we are going to Boston for a visit right now."

"I think that's best," said Millie.

"I would like the two of you to come with me, but the decision is up to you. We will be staying at Mr. Hancock's home in Boston," Anna said.

"Of course we will come, Missus," said Colleen.

"I'd be happy to, Ma'am," said Millie. "You'll need a lot of help when you get there."

"Thank you both," Anna said, appreciatively. "Now, you'll need to get yourselves packed. We'll be taking the stagecoach this afternoon."

"What about closing up the house?" asked Colleen.

"We'll worry about that later," Anna said. "I'm going upstairs to wake up the boys."

"I'll get breakfast ready," Colleen said.

"While you're doing that, I'll get us packed," said Millie.

Anna went upstairs and into the boys' room to find them both sound asleep. Anna stood between their beds and gave them each a little shake.

"Good morning, boys. Time to wake up," Anna said.

They both stirred and sleepily opened their eyes.

"Good morning, Mother," they both said.

"I've got a surprise for both of you," Anna said.

"A surprise?" asked Paul.

"I love surprises," said Sam, suddenly very awake.

"We're going on a trip a Boston," Anna said, excitedly.

"Boston? I've never been there," said Sam

"Father works in Boston sometimes. Is Father going to be there," Paul asked.

"Not right now, Paul," Anna said. "We're going to stay with Mr. Hancock. He has a great house right in the center of Boston."

"Oh boy, that should be fun, Mother," said Sam. "When are we going?"

"Today," Anna told them.

"Today?" asked Paul

"Yes, today. So I need you two to get packed. We are taking the stagecoach this afternoon," Anna said.

"This will be such fun," Paul said.

"We'll start packing right now," Sam said.

"Why don't you get dressed and go downstairs to breakfast first," Anna said. "Then you can do your packing."

"All right, Mother," said Paul.

The boys jumped out of bed to dress as Anna left the room. She met Ausable coming up the stairs.

"I've got everything we've already packed in the carriage," Ausable said.

"Thank you," Anna said. "I've told the boys and they are very excited to be going."

"Wonderful. We'll show them a good time there," said Ausable.

"And Colleen and Millie will be coming with us," Anna told him.

"I'm glad. That will make things easier for you and the boys," Ausable said. "I've plenty of room for everyone."

"I'm looking forward to seeing your house," Anna said. "I remember as a child, we were on a tour of Boston and we went through Louisburg Square, with all its brick houses. It was very impressive."

"It's a lovely part of Boston," said Ausable. "And the Public Garden is just nearby. The boys will enjoy a ride in the swan boats there."

"Oh, I'm so looking forward to all this," Anna exclaimed.

The rest of the morning, everyone was busy packing and getting ready for their big trip. Anna knew she owed it to Aunt Lil to go and tell her what was going on. She took a horse and rode over to Aunt Lil's house. She also expected she might run into Will there. She was ready for bear as she tied up her horse in front of Aunt Lil's veranda.

She opened the screened door and went inside.

"Hello," she called. "Is anyone here?"

Rose came out from the kitchen. "Hello, Mrs. Tattersall. Nice to see you."

"Hello, Rose," Anna said. "I came to see Mrs. Tattersall. How is she feeling?"

"Much better," Rose said. "She's still in bed resting though. Just waiting for her lunch."

"Is she seeing visitors?" Anna asked.

"She'll always see you, Mrs. Tattersall," said Rose, smiling.

"Thank you, Rose," Anna said, knowing that was all about to change. "I'll go up and say hello."

Anna went up the stairs. Aunt Lil's door was open. Anna peeked in. Aunt Lil was sitting up in bed, doing some crocheting. "Hello Lil," she said.

On hearing Anna's voice, Aunt Lil stopped what she was doing, but didn't look toward the door. She just stared at her crocheting. She took in a breath, then turned and looked at Anna. "Come in, Anna," she said, coldly.

Anna steeled herself and entered the room. "I hear you are feeling better. I'm so glad."

"Thank you. Yes, I am," Aunt Lil said. "What can I do for you, Anna?"

"Lil, I wanted to come say goodbye," Anna said.

"Goodbye? I thought you weren't leaving for a few weeks," said Aunt Lil.

"My plans have changed," Anna said. "I'm going to stay in Boston for a while."

"Boston? Ah, I see what's happening," Aunt Lil said, angrily. "Oh, Anna, you are such a bright girl. Do you really think you can have a life with that Mr. Hancock?"

"As a matter of fact, I do," Anna declared, strongly. "I'm leaving Will. We have nothing together anymore. And last night, he proved it."

"I heard what happened last night," Aunt Lil said. "From Will."

"Will was here?" Anna gasped.

"Yes. This morning. He was in a terrible state," Aunt Lil said. "Anna, he was feeling so bad for what he had done. The way he had done it. He knows he was wrong."

"Well, that's a blessing," Anna said. "Lil, he was cruel last night. He is not the man I knew anymore."

"I know what he did wasn't right, but you gave him reason to act that way, you know," said Aunt Lil.

"That's hogwash," Anna snapped. "He cheated on me. You know it is over between us. Life has a way of taking the right course. And right now, mine is to Boston."

320

"Anna, I think you are making a big mistake," Aunt Lil said.

"Maybe," said Anna. "But I'll be making my own mistake. I have to try to find a good life for myself and my boys."

"You are taking the boys?" Aunt Lil asked, aghast.

"Of course," Anna asserted. "Will is never home. He can't care for two boys the way they should be cared for. I'll speak to him when things calm down and work out arrangements. I don't want him to not see them. He's their father. And believe it or not, Lil, I still love Will very much. I miss him. I'll try as hard as I can not to hurt him."

"Oh Anna, this is all too terrible," Aunt Lil said.

"I know," Anna said.

"When do you leave?" asked Aunt Lil.

"Today," Anna said.

"Oh my. So soon? Will you bring the boys over to say goodbye, please?" asked Aunt Lil.

"I'd be happy to," said Anna. "And Lil, once we get settled, I'd love it if you came to see us in Boston."

"That's very nice of you. I'll have to think hard about it," Aunt Lil said.

"I wrote Will a letter explaining everything," Anna said. "It will be at the house for him."

"I can have my people help Will close up Idlenook, if he likes," Aunt Lil offered.

"That's very kind of you," Anna said. "This may have been the last summer I spend at Idlenook. It does belong to Will. I'll miss it so."

"Perhaps Will can work something out," Aunt Lil said. "He hardly uses it."

"That's true," Anna said, realizing Lil was softening. "We'll stop by on the way to the afternoon stage, Lil." She gave Aunt Lil a kiss, a tear coming to her eye.

Aunt Lil, also close to tears, "You take care now."

Anna took her leave.

At Idlenook, everyone was bustling about, excited to go to Boston. The carriage was packed and ready to go to Bailey's to meet the stagecoach. Anna had one more thing to do. She went into a cupboard and took out all of Ausable's paintings, wrapped in cloth. She brought them downstairs and went to the one that hung on the wall for so many years. She took it down and wrapped it up with the others. She held them tightly to herself as she looked around. She breathed in one last wonderful breath of balsam, smiled contentedly, for the first time in oh so long. She walked outside and stepped into the waiting carriage.

"Onward, Ausable," she cheered. "Next stop, Louisburg Square!"

THE END

ABOUT THE AUTHOR

A. Dudley Johnson, Jr. spent several weeks every summer, when he was a child, at his grandmother's house in Keene Valley with his family. Later in life, he attended Emerson College in Boston. He became a television writer and producer for "Diff'rent Strokes" and "Webster." Dudley is a member of the Writers Guild of America. He went on to produce computer and video games for Disney for many years. Dudley lives in Altadena, California, with his husband, Barry. This is his first novel.

www.ingramcontent.com/pod-product-compliance
Lightning Source LLC
Chambersburg PA
CBHW020334180626
46812CB00001B/204